Julia Schlesinger

Workers in the Vineyard

Julia Schlesinger

Workers in the Vineyard

ISBN/EAN: 9783337334826

Printed in Europe, USA, Canada, Australia, Japan

Cover: Foto ©Andreas Hilbeck / pixelio.de

More available books at **www.hansebooks.com**

WORKERS ɪɴ ᴛʜᴇ VINEYARD

A Review of the Progress of Spiritualism,

Biographical Sketches, Lectures,

Essays and Poems.

BY

JULIA SCHLESINGER

EDITOR FOR TEN YEARS OF THE "CARRIER DOVE," ALSO OF THE "GLEANER,"
AND "PACIFIC COAST SPIRITUALIST."

*"Come and labor in my vineyard, for lo, the harvest now is ripe but the laborers
are few."*

SAN FRANCISCO, CALIFORNIA,
1896.

DEDICATION.

TO THE MEMORY OF THE BRAVE PIONEERS
WHO HAVE TOILED IN THE VINEYARD OF TRUTH, AND MADE
POSSIBLE THE BENEFICENT RESULTS OF THE PRESENT ERA
OF MENTAL AND SPIRITUAL LIBERTY THIS VOLUME IS
LOVINGLY DEDICATED BY THE

AUTHOR.

PREFACE.

The author has endeavored in this volume to present a brief historical sketch of the progress of Modern Spiritualism since the raps at Hydesville announced the ushering in of a new dispensation bringing light, truth, and proof of immortal life to humanity. Nearly half a century has passed since that memorable day, and many of the pioneers who went forth proclaiming the new revelation to the world have passed to spirit life leaving no record of their labors save that which lingers in the hearts and memories of those who were blest through their ministrations. This lack of authentic records of much that should have been preserved and formed the history of so great a movement, is an irreparable loss to Spiritualism, and an injustice to those who so grandly proclaimed the truth when it required almost the heroism of a martyr to brave the taunts and ridicule, the ignorance and intolerance of friends and foes, and the vituperations of pulpit and press. Such persecution is not the lot of the present-day worker, save from narrow minds whose avenues of information and enlightenment are limited, or whose eyes are so blinded by superstition that the truth can not be seen when presented to them.

The value of the lessons to be learned from the experiences, the struggles, defeats, and conquests of other lives, cannot be over-estimated. They serve as beacon lights along a stormy, rock-bound shore, warning others of the dangers, reefs, and shoals, and pointing the way to a safe harbor. In the brief histories of individual effort and labor in the field of reform as depicted in these pages, such lessons can be gleaned by coming generations long after the workers in the vineyard of to-day have gone to their eternal homes. They will bear fruit in the heroic lives, devotion to truth, and grand humanitarianism of those who are to follow.

During the past twelve years' experience as editor, for ten years of *The Carrier Dove*, also for a time of *The Gleaner*, and lastly of *The Pacific Coast Spiritualist*, I have been prepared for this work, and a vast amount of material—sufficient for several volumes—has been collected. If my humble efforts in this line meet the approval of Spiritualists, and there is a demand for another volume, it will be forthcoming.

During all these years of struggle and trials consequent upon rearing a family, and incessant toil with hands and brain, I have ever been conscious of the loving guardianship of angel friends. They have comforted me in seasons of sorrow, encouraged and strengthened me when almost doubting and despairing, rejoiced in my success, and sympathized with me when failure seemed written on everything. They have ever taught the highest and purest principles as the rules of daily life and conduct. They have ever stimulated noble impulses and the highest aims; they have taught lessons of charity, patience, forbearance and justice. When the hasty word of criticism and censure has been uttered, their gentle reproaches have brought remorse and repentance. They have been a daily inspiration to a life of generous deeds, kindly words and tender compassion for all humanity. To them— my dear angel benefactors in spirit life, and the dear angels still in mortal form, who have given me strength in times of weakness, hope in days of dark despair, faith in the ultimate good, and aid spiritual and material to do that which was given me to do—to them am I indebted for whatever merit or success my labors deserve.

JULIA SCHLESINGER.

INTRODUCTION.

One of the most important epochs in the history of the world dates from March 31, 1848; for upon that day dawned the recognition of a new world of being,—nay, of a new universe, of which previously men had had faint glimmerings and fitful gleams, but of which demonstrative evidence of actuality had never before been systematically presented. From the little beginning at that time, at Hydesville, New York, there has arisen the grand and mighty movement called Modern Spiritualism,—a movement whose beneficent sway has been extended into all parts of the civilized world, even into the remote regions of Japan and China, Australia and New Zealand, India and Africa.

The crowning glory of this new evangel of life and light is its demonstration of the existence of the spiritual universe and of a future life for man; and concomitant therewith, and almost of equal value, is its demonstration of the true character of that universe and of man's estate therein. Not alone is Spiritualism probative of a future life for all mankind, but it reveals to us a natural, rational, progressive spiritual existence, in full accord with the highest, best aspirations and hopes of the human heart. It dispels forever the darksome dogmas and superstitious myths regarding the nature of the life after physical death that have for ages been regnant in the world, and imparts to mankind here on earth a joy and happiness beyond compare. To the enlightened Spiritualist the universe assumes a new aspect; all being is responsive to the felicity and serenity of his enraptured mind. The heavens wear a gladdening smile ne'er seen before and earth seems robed in silvery sheen.

Spiritualism now encircles the earth, and embraces millions of earnest adherents. To what agencies is this wondrous progress due? To the combined action of the inhabitants of the Morning Land, the spiritual spheres above, and of the "workers in the vineyard here below. Little could have been accomplished, in disseminating the truths of the philosophy and religion of Spiritualism, by our spiritual friends alone, without the co-operation of the faithful workers still encased in flesh and blood. Spiritualism stands where it does to-day because of the untiring zeal, the unselfish, philanthropic labors of a host of true-hearted men and women. These "workers in the vineyard" have toiled on, and struggled on, regardless of the obloquy and ridicule, the persecutions and misrepresentations, so freely showered upon them by an unthinking, unbelieving world. Little recked they of the abuse and slander meeting them at every turn. They knew that they were right, they knew what their duty was; that duty they fearlessly performed, and they are still in steady performance thereof. To-day, all over the world, the sturdy "workers in the vineyard" are at their posts, aglow with enthusiasm, inspired with devotion to the holy cause enshrining their life-work. It is fitting that record be made of the good work that has been done and is being done by these laborers for the good and true. One of the important centers of action, in furtherance of the Spiritualistic gospel, has been the Pacific Coast of America. In addition to many noble workers native to it or resident therein, this coast has been enriched by the presence and labors of a number of the leading "workers in the vineyard" from all parts of America, and from England and other countries. In this initial volume of a projected series, it is purposed to present a faithful summary of the life-work of some of the men and women who have been active in the sustentation and presentation of the phenomena and philosophy of Spiritualism on the Pacific Coast,—the mediums, the lecturers, the writers, the workers in the societies and the lyceums, the sustainers and promoters of the good work by their means, their time, their influence, etc.,—the active "workers" in the cause, whether with voice, pen, money, or otherwise. In succeeding volumes, perhaps, similar record may be made of the "workers", in other parts of America and of the world.

Among the host of unselfish, devoted "workers" on the Coast stands the compiler and publisher of this volume, Mrs. Julia Schlesinger. For a dozen years past she has stood in the forefront of the struggle for the advancement of Spiritualistic truth here. In the ten years of the publication by her, in Oakland and San Francisco, of the CARRIER DOVE, she became possessed of a vast amount of historical and biographical information anent the progress of Spiritualism and the life-lines of its advocates and champions on the Coast. The cream of this, amplified and improved, is embodied in this volume. I know of no one on the Coast better equipped or better qualified for the preparation of this work than its present author.

To relieve the monotony and to add variety to the work, there will be scattered through the volume selections from the many writings of Mrs. Schlesinger while editor of the CARRIER DOVE, upon subjects of interest to Spiritualists and reformers; also a choice selection of original poems upon matters of contemporaneous interest.

WM. EMMETTE COLEMAN.

San Francisco, Cal., Jan. 1896.

A REVIEW OF THE PROGRESS OF SPIRITUALISM.

In casting a retrospective glance over the history of one of the greatest movements the world has ever known—one fraught with so much of interest to the human race, revealing to mankind secrets which have hitherto puzzled the most eminent scholars, theologians and scientists, concerning the fact of continued life after the change called death, and of the state or condition of those who have experienced the change, we are struck with the magnitude of the movement which in less than half a century has attained such gigantic proportions. Born in humility and obscurity, persecuted and maligned in its infancy and youth, doubted, ridiculed and derided on every hand, it has, nevertheless, steadily grown into public favor and acceptance, until, at the end of this brief period, it has many millions of adherents. It has crept silently into the pages of popular books, magazines and newspapers throughout the land, and unconsciously has the public mind been educated and moulded into conformity therewith. True, it has not yet entirely overcome all bigotry and superstition, the outgrowth of an ignorant past; but that it has had a decidedly counteracting and liberalizing effect cannot be denied. The pulpits everywhere, under the magical influence of the inspiration of the present, are voicing its truths, and either silently ignoring the errors of the past, or boldly proclaiming their worthlessness to meet the demands of the growing intelligence of mankind. Much remains to be done in this direction before the complete breaking of the shackles of ignorance, which have for centuries enslaved and degraded humanity. But the prognostications of seers indicate a new era of development for the race—an era which had its beginning with the tiny raps at Hydesville, and will culminate only in the distant cycles of the future, far beyond the reach of mortal vision or conception. A brief outline of the origin and growth of the light of the nineteenth century—Modern Spiritualism, cannot be amiss in this introductory chapter.

In a book entitled "The Missing Link," written by A. Leah Underhill, one of the "Fox sisters," it is stated that the raps which had been heard for some time in the house at Hydesville, grew to be so annoying, that at last the neighbors were called in to witness the manifestations, and decide upon their origin and meaning. Upon the eventful night of March 31st, 1848, the family, consisting of John Fox, his wife Margaret Fox, and their two daughters, Margaretta and Catherine, or "Cathie," as her mother called her, had retired early in the evening, hoping to have a good night's rest, free from the disturbing noises which had so annoyed them for several weeks previous. They had no sooner retired, however, than the rapping began, and the children (who slept in the same room with their parents, having been brought in on account of their fear when occupying a room alone) imitated the sounds by snapping their fingers and clapping their hands. Cathie, the youngest, said: "Mr. Splitfoot, do as I do," clapping her hands. The sound instantly followed her, with the same number of raps. Then Margaretta said: "Now do just as I do; count one, two, three, four," striking one hand against the other, which was immediately imitated, as before, by the raps. Mrs. Fox then began to ask questions, and obtained answers by the raps. She asked the spirits to rap out her children's ages, which was done correctly each time. Mr. Fox was so much astonished at this that he went out and invited a neighbor to come in, who, in turn, went out after others, until a large company had assembled. By asking questions which could be answered by yes and no (two raps signifying no, and three raps yes) it was ascertained that a peddler had been murdered in that house some years before, and his body buried in the cellar, and the name of the murderer given. This created a great excitement, and the next day hundreds of people visited the house. The excitement increased, and it was found impossible for the family to remain there longer. They went to the residence of a married son, David Fox, living about two miles distant, until their own house, which was not yet completed, should be ready for occupancy. The raps followed them, and it was soon discovered that the two little girls were the mediums. The eldest sister, A. Leah Underhill (then Mrs. Fish,) was residing in Rochester, and hearing of the strange occurrences at Hydesville, determined to visit her parents and ascertain what it all meant. Arriving at Hydesville, she found the "haunted house" deserted, and learned that the family were living with her brother David. She found her mother almost ill from the effects of the trying scenes through which they had been called to pass. After remaining two weeks, during which time remarkable manifestations occurred, Mrs. Fish returned home, taking the younger sister, Katie, with her, as the mother thought that by separating the family the disturbance would cease. In this they were disappointed, as the raps followed them on their journey home, and on arriving there they found it impossible to sleep nights the disturbance was so great. Articles of furniture were moved, doors opened and shut, the sound of persons walking about was distinctly heard, the beds upon which they were sleeping would be raised from the floor and dropped down again, until they were obliged to take the bedding and lay it on the floor. Many other wonderful and startling things occurred, until it was thought best to send for Mrs. Fox, as the little daughter was almost ill through fright. She immedi-

ately left for Rochester, taking the other daughter, Margaretta, with her. Upon their arrival a family council was held, but nothing could be decided upon but to await events and pray for protection. The manifestations increased in power until, feeling that they could no longer bear it alone, they consulted with Isaac and Amy Post, who were much amused at what was told them, and believed the family were "suffering under some psychological delusion." But when they witnessed some things in their own home they became interested, and invited some friends to witness the manifestations also. Though the family begged that everything should be kept a profound secret, they soon found that it was not so kept. The spirits were determined that the truth should be given to the world, and these were the instruments through whom it was to be given. They directed that private circles should be held at different houses, and they would manifest for promiscuous companies. The first meeting was held at the residence of Isaac and Amy Post, the spirits directing whom to invite. They were all prominent persons—lawyers, doctors and editors. Among the number was Frederick Douglas, editor of the "North Star." After several very satisfactory meetings, at which the spirits demonstrated their ability to rap sufficiently loud to be heard in a large hall, they instructed the mediums to give public seances in a large hall. Corinthian Hall, then the largest in Rochester, was designated. It was engaged, and the meeting was advertised for the evening of November 14, 1848. At the meeting an investigating committee of five prominent skeptical gentlemen was appointed, to make a report at the next meeting. Contrary to the expectations and wishes of the audience assembled, the report of the committee was in favor of the mediums, and another committee was appointed to make the next report. The report of this committee was also favorable, as no solution could be given of the method by which the raps were produced. The excitement

LEAH FOX UNDERHILL.

was at this time intense, and there was talk of mobbing both mediums and committee. At the third meeting, those who expressed most dissatisfaction with the previous investigations were appointed, and formed what was called the "Infidel Committee." They met at the rooms of Dr. Gates, in the Rochester House. Three ladies were appointed, who took the mediums into a private room and had them disrobe and put on garments that had been selected for the purpose. They were then conducted into the presence of the committee, composed of five gentlemen who were determined to "fathom the fraud." After waiting some time and no manifestations of importance occurring, the girls were told they could "go home and get their dinners," and perhaps then the "ghosts" would be more sociable. Then Leah said: "No, we shall not stir from this room until the time for this investigation shall expire, which will be at 6 o'clock P. M. The following is what occurred, as related by Mrs. Underhill:

"Some of the Committee exclaimed 'Good for the Rappers! That looks like business. Ladies and gentlemen, let us have dinner in this room. We will give the girls fair play.' A sumptuous dinner was prepared and brought in to us, and all took seats at the table. They taunted us in every way. Sometimes we felt ourselves forsaken, and disposed to give up in despair. Our friends were locked out, and not permitted to come into the room; but we could hear their faithful footsteps outside the door, in the hall of the hotel, Isaac and Amy Post, Mr. and Mrs. Pierpont, George Willets and others. My young sister Maggie was by my side, bathed in tears. Dr. Gates was carving, I was struggling with a choking emotion, and could not taste food. The party were joking and funning at our expense, when, suddenly, the great table began to tremble, and raised first one end and then the other, with loud creaking sounds, like a ship struggling in a heavy gale, until it was finally suspended above our heads. For a moment all were silent and

looked at each other with astonishment. The waiters fled in every direction. Instantly the scene was changed. The ladies threw their arms around us, one after another, and it was their turn to cry. They said to us: 'Oh, you poor girls, how you have been abused! Oh, how sorry we are for you; after all *it is true!* The gentlemen, with one accord said, 'Girls, you have gained a victory. We will stand by you to the last.' Let it be understood that this Committee of ladies and gentlemen took us to the parlors of the Rochester House, which could be divided into two rooms by closing the folding doors. After dinner the gentlemen of the Committee insulated the table by putting glass under the legs, procured two sacks of feathers, and advised the ladies how to conduct the investigation. They then closed the doors and retired, leaving us and the lady members of the Committee alone. By this time the Committee had become kindly disposed towards us. They suggested to us that we should stand upon the sacks of feathers on the table, with our dresses tied tight above our ankles. We complied with all their suggestions cheerfully. Immediately the sounds were heard on the table, floor and walls: The ladies instantly opened the doors, and the gentlemen came in and witnessed the manifestations themselves."

At the conclusion of this investigation, the Committee received a note warning them that if they went to the hall that evening with a report in favor of the girls, they would be mobbed. The friends of the mediums also urged them to remain at home, but the spirits said, "Go, you will not be harmed." Accordingly, at the appointed hour, they went and found a rowdy element in the audience, who would have stopped at nothing short of violence had not the police been notified of the anticipated trouble, and been present in sufficient numbers to quell the disturbance which was commenced by the explosion of torpedoes in every part of the hall. The mob was quickly dispersed and the mediums publicly vindicated.

Thus was inaugurated the public work of these chosen ones, and conducted at the risk of their lives many times, before the ignorant, bigoted masses could be convinced that they were not in league with his Satanic Majesty, and that they would be doing God's service by killing them. In a brief sketch like this, it is impossible to give but few of the interesting events in the lives of these world renowned mediums. The pioneers in the ranks of Spiritualism are, many of them, personally acquainted with the subjects of this article, and have, like them, suffered persecution for doing the bidding of the angels; therefore, it is not for them that this record is given, but for those who are at present investigating this great truth, and for those recently convinced who are unfamiliar with the origin of the movement.

After the successful termination of the Rochester meeting, the mediums were informed that they must go forth and give the truth to the world. Accordingly arrangements were made for a series of public meetings in Albany. The "Fox Family," as they were called, consisted of Mrs. Fox and the three daughters— Leah (Mrs. Fish), Margaretta and Katie. They were accompanied by Calvin Brown, an adopted son of Mrs. Fox, who was the ladies' escort. Their success, both in public and private seances, was remarkable. Their rooms were thronged with the more intelligent portion of the community, among whom were lawyers, actors, college professors, ministers, editors and honest infidels, judges, etc. They were deluged with letters of invitation to visit other places by those who wished to investigate; but having made arrangements to go from Albany direct to New York, they could not deviate from the course marked out for them. At the urgent solicitations of friends they were induced to spend a few days in Troy before visiting New York. Their success here, as elsewhere, was highly gratifying. The first appearance of the "Fox Family" in New York was in June, 1850. Horace Greely was their first caller. He announced their arrival in the *Tribune* and published their rules of order. Their seance-room at the hotel was a large parlor, containing a long table with thirty seats. The public parlors served as ante-rooms, in which visitors waited their turns to be admitted to the seance-room. Three public seances were given daily, from 10 to 12 A. M., 3 to 5 P. M., and 8 to 10 P. M. These meetings would lengthen out until there was scarcely time given the mediums for eating and sleeping, the evening sessions frequently extending until midnight, and private sittings often being given before breakfast. Many times were these mediums compelled to submit to the most crucial test conditions in order to satisfy the extremely skeptical that the manifestations were not the result of trickery. It is gratifying to note that in all such instances mediumship triumphed. During their first visit of three months at the great metropolis, thousands of people visited them and received their first demonstrated proofs of a future life. "A special investigation by a large committee of the first men of New York, in scientific and literary, as well as social distinction," took place at the residence of Rev. Rufus W. Griswold. Among the company present were: J. Fenimore Cooper, the novelist; Mr. George Bancroft, the historian; Rev. Dr. Hawks, Dr. J. W. Francis, Dr. Marcy, Mr. N. P. Willis, Mr. Wm. Cullen Bryant, the poet, and Mr. Bigelow of the *Evening Post,* Mr. Richard B. Kimball, Mr. H. Tuckerman, and General Lyman. Mr. Ripley, one of the editors of the *Tribune,* made a report of the proceedings, which any one can read by looking over the files of that paper for 1850, the sum of which was that the seance proved a very interesting and satisfactory one to the committee and friends. Mr. Cooper, upon his death bed, a little over a year afterward, sent them the following message: "Tell the Fox family I bless them. I have been made happy through them. They have prepared me for this hour."

In September it was decided to return to Rochester for rest and recreation after

MARGARETTA FOX KANE.

the months of unceasing labor in New York. Before doing so they were invited by their warm friends, Mr. and Mrs. Greeley, to spend a fortnight at their hospitable home on Nineteenth street. After the return of the family to Rochester, Horace Greeley published a lengthy statement in the *Tribune* of the result of their visit to New York, vouching for the perfect integrity and honesty of the mediums, but making no attempt to explain the nature of their manifestations.

We can but briefly sketch the busy lives of the sisters, after entering into the work appointed them by their invisible guardians. Their visits to various cities, while many times marked with great trials and difficulties, of which the mediums of the present time have little conception, were usually successions of triumphs over the bigotry and ignorance of their enemies, who attempted to explain the manifestations in many improbable and impossible ways, such as the "*toe and knee-joint theory,*" "electrical vibrations," etc. Among the number who most successfully distinguished themselves as consummate ignoramuses were three learned professors of the University of Buffalo. These gentlemen—Austin Flint, M. D., Charles A. Lee, M. D., and C. B. Coventry, M. D.—published an article in *The Commercial Advertiser*, of February 18, 1851, in which they explained in a most elaborate and scientific manner (which must have been extremely gratifying to the public), the process by which the three Fox girls had been so successfully humbugging the people for three years. Their scientific explanation was something really wonderful, and reflects great credit upon the trio of astute M. D's. It consisted in advancing the theory that the "raps" were produced by a partial dislocation of the knee-joints which produced a loud noise and the return of the bone to its place occasioned another sound which, being continued, were the rappings which had so deceived thousands of people who, not being as learned as they, had failed to discover the source of the mysterious sounds. This startling an-

nouncement was reproduced in the *Buffalo Medical Journal* and led to a thorough investigation in which the utter absurdity and impossibility of the theory was fully demonstrated and the honesty of the mediums proven beyond all cavil or doubt. In 1852, at the urgent solicitations of friends, the mediums located permanently in New York. Here they met many of the most brilliant minds of that great city and formed strong and lasting friendships. Alice and Phœbe Cary, Horace Greeley and Mrs. Greeley, Judge Edmunds, Rev. John Pierpont, and Prof. Mapes were among their many warm friends.

The actors in this great drama which ushered in a new era of spiritual enlightenment, have all passed to spirit life; but the memory of the little "Fox Sisters" will ever be enshrined as a priceless treasure in the hearts of grateful millions all over the earth.

The work begun in so humble a manner has met with unprecedented success. It has its teachers and adherents in every portion of the civilized world, among all peoples and nations. Its literature comprises many thousand volumes from the pens of the most learned and scientific, the most brilliant authors, poets, journalists and professional men. Newspapers and magazines devoted to the exposition and propagation of its teachings are published in many different languages and countries. Russia, Germany, France, Italy, Spain, England, Holland, Brazil, Guatemala, Australia, India, and the United States, all have their Spiritualistic journals.

The knowledge of, and belief in Spiritualism is quite general upon the Pacific Coast. As far back as the year 1857 Spiritualism was openly advocated by some advanced thinkers in California. Most prominent among these was Colonel Ransom, publisher of the *Marysville Herald*, who was an avowed Spiritualist, and one of his sons, Elijah, was a medium. When the *Banner of Light* first made its appearance in that year, Colonel Ransom, its agent, scattered the new paper among the people in the city of Marysville.

In the city of San Francisco seances were held at the house of Russel Ellis on Sansome street, at the International Hotel, and also at the residence of J. P. Manrow, on Russian Hill, where the most remarkable manifestations occurred.

The first lectures on Spiritualism delivered in San Francisco were given by Mrs. Eliza W. Farnham, in 1859. Mrs. Farnham also lectured in Santa Cruz, and with her intellectual and energetic friend, Mrs. Georgiana B. Kirby, did much to aid the spread of liberal thought in that part of the State. Nelson J. Underwood. W. H. Rhodes, G. W. Baker, a young man named Beauharnais, and others lectured occasionally, but no regular course of lectures was established until 1864, when Emma Hardinge came to this State. Mrs. Hardinge lectured, and organized The Friends of Progress, and the meetings were free to the public.

In 1864 Mrs. C. M. Stowe and Mary Beach, mediums, arrived overland. Mrs. Stowe lectured in Pickwick Hall, Congress Hall, and other places. From that time until the present, California has been favored with visits from some of the best mediums and finest orators in the world. Mrs. Cora L. V. Tappan has visited the State three times—the last time as Mrs. Richmond. She did much to advance Spiritualism on this Coast.

Mrs. Laura Cuppy (who became Mrs. Smith, and afterward Mrs. Kendricks) labored constantly on the platform for ten years. Benjamin Todd arrived in September 1866 and lectured throughout the State for several years, during a part of the time editing a spiritual paper here. Mrs Laura De Force Gordon came to the State in 1867, and lectured in San Jose, Sacramento and this city. Selden J. Finney, a brilliant orator, a man of great culture and intellect, spent the closing years of his life here, and did much to advance the cause of Spiritualism. The speakers who have occupied the spiritual rostrum during the last twenty-five years make a long list.

Among prominent ones from abroad are the following: J. M. Peebles, Warren Chase, Benjamin Todd, Dean Clarke, J. S Loveland, Gerald Massey, P. B. Randolph, Wm. Denton, Thomas Gales Forster, Chauncey Barnes, Bishop Beals, Geo. Chaney, Lois Waisbrooker, Fanny Allyn, Jenny Leys, H. F. M. Brown, Belle Chamberlain, Miss Augusta Whiting, G. P. Colby, W. J. Colville, J. J. Morse, Charles Dawbarn, Moses Hull, Mrs. R. S. Lillie, Mattie Hull, Prof. Lockwood, Cora L. V, Richmond, Dr. J. R. Buchanan, Prof. A J. Swarts, Mrs. Longley, Walter Howell.

One of the first mediums who gave her services to the public was Mrs. Deiterlee, residing on Capp street. Ada Hoyt Foye advertised to give sittings at 131 Montgomery street in 1866. Mrs. M. J. Hendee, who had for several years served the cause as a healer in Sacramento and Petaluma, opened an office in San Francisco in 1869. Charles H. Foster, Henry Slade and Jesse Shephard have visited the State and given the public evidence of spirit return through their wonderful mediumship. Among the early mediums we find the names of Mrs. Sproule (now Mrs. Robinson), Mrs. Breed, Lou. M. Kerns, Mrs. E. Beman, Mme. Clara Antonia, Mrs. C. M. Stowe, Mary Beach, Wella and Pet Anderson, Amanda Wiggin, Mrs. Babbitt. Of those of later years there are a great many.

The first California State Convention was held in San Jose, in May, 1866. It elected a State Central Committee, consisting of J. H. Atkinson, J. D. Pierson, P. W. Randle, J. C. Mitchell, H. J. Payne, J. H. Josselyn, C. C. Coolidge and C. C. Knowles of San Francisco; A. C. Stowe, J. J. Owen and W. N. Slocum of Santa Clara; Henry Miller, W. F. Lyon, H. H. Bowman and C. W. Hoit of Sacramento; E. Gibbs, San Joaquin; A. B. Paul, Inyo; Lena Hutchinson, Mona; Thos. Loyd, Nevada; A. Shellenberger, Yuba; B. A. Allen, Butte; Dr. Hungerford, Napa; Mrs. Thomas Eager, Alameda; J. Glass, Tuolumne; C. P. Hatch, Sonoma; L. A. Gitchell, Del Norte; James Christian, Plumas; J. J. Fisk, Yolo. This committee issued an address to Spiritualists, asking co-operation in efforts to advance the cause, sustain local societies and annual conventions. The result of this effort was productive of good for a time; but gradually the work languished, and finally ceased.

In the year 1874 a secret society of Spiritualists was originated by A. C. Stowe, and "circles," as they were called, were instituted in San Francisco, San Jose and Sacramento. Mrs. Laverna Matthews was President of the San Francisco branch, serving two terms. This society was also a failure. Other local societies were formed, and after serving their purpose passed away, leaving little record of their work.

The first Children's Progressive Lyceum organized in the State was in Sacramento, early in 1865, by Mr. R. Moore, of New York. Mr. Moore then came to San Francisco, and organized the first Lyceum in this city, July 16th, 1865, at a hall on the corner of Fourth and Jessie streets. Mr. Moore was chosen Conductor, and J. C. Mitchell Assistant, with a full corps of Leaders of Groups, among whom were Mrs. E. P. Thorndyke, Mrs. S. B. Whitehead, Dr. J. R. Payne and J. W. Mackie. The Lyceum did good work for two years, and then suspended. Several attempts were made to revive it, but they were short-lived efforts, and not until June 14th, 1872, was a permanent Lyceum established. Mr. Wm. M. Ryder was the first Conductor, and Mr. J. M. Mathews Secretary and Treasurer. Mrs. Laverna Mathews was next elected Conductor, and served for many years. That Lyceum is still alive, and is ably conducted by Mr. and Mrs. Wadsworth, Mr. Gilman and Mrs. Richardson.

The first Oakland Lyceum was started in 1776, with Father Mabry as Conductor, assisted by Mrs. Mabry, Marshall Curtis and others. It also was discontinued. The second Oakland Lyceum was organized in 1882, with Mrs. M. A. Gunn as Conductor. It was in the interests of this Lyceum, in which Mrs. Julia Schlesinger was an active worker, that the

CARRIER DOVE was started in September, 1883. The first number was issued as a little Lyceum paper, edited by Mrs. Schlesinger and Mrs. Jennie Mason. That Lyceum has continued until the present time, and is now ably conducted by Mrs. Chas. Gunn.

The first society incorporated under the incorporation laws of the State of California was "The First Spiritual Union of San Francisco," of which Mrs. Laverna Mathews was the able President. This society suspended its meetings when "The Golden Gate Religious and Philosophical Society" was organized and incorporated in the year 1885. The former society still exists, and its Trustees hold regular business meetings, while the latter society has become entirely a thing of the past, although at the beginning it seemed to promise great results. Its meetings were held at Metropolitan Temple, under the business management of M. B. Dodge, with Mrs. Elizabeth L. Watson as speaker.

The Society of Progressive Spiritualists was incorporated in 1883, with H. C. Wilson as President. This society owns property to the value of about forty thousand dollars, the donation of Mrs. Eunice Sleeper, and hopes sometime to build a temple worthy of the cause in this city. It also owns the largest spiritual library on the Pacific Coast, and supports the leading meetings in the State, always employing the best speakers and mediums to occupy the platform.

Another incorporated society that did grand work during the four years of its existence was "The Spiritualists' State Campmeeting Association," organized in October, 1884. This movement was first inaugurated by Mrs. Julia Schlesinger and Mrs. Frances A. Logan. These two ladies outlined the plan of a State Campmeeting, which they presented to Mr. H. C. Wilson, who was then President of the Society of Progressive Spiritualists. He at once entered into the spirit of the movement, and gave them encouragement and assistance, inviting them to present their views upon the platform.

Mrs. M. Miller, then one of the Directors in the same society also entered heartily into the work, and the result was a call for a convention to be held at the Neptune Gardens, Alameda, where Mrs. Logan and her brother, Walter Hyde, then resided. At that convention the State Campmeeting Association was organized and incorporated. Mr. H. C. Wilson was elected president. The following year the meeting under its auspices was held at San Jose, and considerable interest was awakened. The two following years the conventions were held in Oakland, and the very best talent obtainable employed. Mr. J. J. Morse, of England, was first brought to this coast under its auspices, W. J. Colville, Mrs. R. S. Lillie and Edgar Emerson, the celebrated platform test medium, also came here under engagement of the Campmeeting Association During the two years of its great success, its tents were pitched upon the beautiful banks of Lake Merritt, in the city of Oakland. The last year it was held there, Dr. and Mrs. Schlesinger published a little paper called *The Daily Dove*, in which was reported the full proceedings each day. This was continued during the entire month of the campmeeting, with the exception of the last five days, when the regular monthly *Carrier Dove*, containing a full report of the meeting was issued.

The failure of the State Campmeeting was the result of a change of the officers who had worked it up from the beginning to the height of prosperity and influence. The following year a tent meeting was held in San Francisco under the new management which was a decided failure, and ended the work and usefulness of what was once a strong organization, that wielded great influence for good and for the advancement of the cause.

The press notices of the Convention during the two years it was held in Oakland were fair and liberal, and many were brought to a knowledge of the truth thereby. The failure of the State Association had a disheartening effect upon the old workers and leaders in the movement, and Spiritualism received a blow from which it has not recovered.

Since the suspension of the State Association, other Campmeetings of a local character have been held in Oakland, Summerland and San Bernardino. In Oregon, the New Era Camp has attracted some attention; also the meeting held in Washington. In Portland, Or., are several flourishing societies. In Seattle and Tacoma, Wash., and as far north as Victoria, British Columbia, are societies where local talent is employed, and where much good work is being done.

Spiritual societies exist in many towns and cities throughout the State of California. The most prominent outside of San Francisco are in Los Angeles, San Diego, San Bernardino, Riverside, Summerland, Santa Cruz, San Jose, Oakland, Stockton, Sacramento, Pasadena and National City. In San Francisco there are eight incorporated societies, holding meetings and employing speakers and mediums.

Of spiritual papers there have been quite a number published at intervals during the past thirty-five years. The first Spiritual paper published on this coast was *The Family Circle*, issued in in San Francisco in 1859. It was short-lived, and so little impression did it make on the Spiritualists of that day that very few even recall its existence.

Then followed *The Golden Gate*, started by Fanny Green McDougal, in Sacramento. It was a well written sheet, as might be expected under the control of a woman of such ability and experience, but it was impecunious from the start, and starved to death before it had time to make its merits known.

That failure served as a warning against further attempts until 1867, when Benjamin Todd, lecturer, and W. H. Manning, practical printer, issued the *Banner of Progress*, headquarters in San Francisco. This was a large, well-conducted paper, and continued nearly two years, when it suspended. The next was *Common Sense*, started in 1874 by W. N. and Amanda M.

KATIE FOX JENCKEN.

Slocum, which managed to live through the first year and a few weeks into the second, when it suspended. In May, 1875, *The Philomathean*, a pamphlet-shaped weekly, was started by Prof. W. H. Chaney, which also passed away after a brief existence.

A number of years elapsed before the next venture in Spiritualistic journalism, which was made by Mr. and Mrs. Winchester, publishers of *Light for All*. This paper did a good work during the two years of its existence, but it finally suspended publication. During a portion of the brief career of *Light for All*, the paper had a rival in *The Reasoner*, published by Dr. J. D. MacLennan of San Francisco. The reason for publishing *The Reasoner* was never apparent, unless the paper was intended to serve as an advertising medium for its owner. This method of advertising, however, was too expensive, and the effort was abandoned.

In September, 1883, *The Carrier Dove* was started in Oakland, by Mrs. J. Schlesinger, as a Lyceum paper. It soon outgrew its juvenile character, and assumed the proportions and nature of a first-class illustrated monthly magazine. It was the first spiritual magazine in the world that made a specialty of publishing portraits and biographical sketches of prominent Spiritualists. After being issued three years and a half as a monthly, it was changed into a weekly, but still retained its magazine form and illustrations. The *Dove* continued until the latter part of 1893—just ten years from its first appearance—when the name was changed to the *Pacific Coast Spiritualist*, and to the form of a large eight-page weekly newspaper. This publication was not as successful as the *Carrier Dove*, and after months of hard work on the part of the proprietors—Dr. and Mrs. Schlesinger—the latter's health failed completely owing to the long continued and constant taxation of body and brain and the *Pacific Coast Spiritualist* ceased to exist when its editor could no longer wield her pen.

During the existence of the *Carrier Dove*, another paper, called the *Golden Gate*, was started, which was ably edited by Mr. and Mrs. J. J. Owen. It was a fine eight-page paper, and did good work during the six and a half years of its publication.

The *Pacific Leader* was started in Alameda, but it only lived three months.

The *World's Advance Thought* is an excellent publication, conducted by Mrs. Lucy Mallory of Portland, Oregon.

A paper called *The Reconstructor* was published by Prof. J. S. Loveland, in Summerland, Cal., for some time; but it changed hands, and was called *The Summerland* by the new management. It suspended in 1893.

During the last year three small Spiritual papers have made their appearance in California: *The Medium*, of Los Angeles, the *Herald of Light*, of San Diego, and *Progress*, of San Francisco.

In July, 1895, the Spiritualists of Southern California organized a Camp-meeting Association, and the first meeting was held in Santa Monica. Mr. S. D. Dye was the president. It continued three weeks and much good was accomplished. Many able speakers and excellent mediums occupied the platform. At the conclusion of the camp-meeting some of the most prominent mediums and speakers visited Los Angeles and held a Spiritualists Congress continuing six days with three sessions daily. A great interest was awakened in the cause.

When the congress was ended, Dr. Schlesinger of San Francisco, Mrs. Cowell of Oakland, and Mrs. Frietag of National City, assisted by Mr. S. D. Dye, secured the Los Angeles Theatre and began a series of meetings which were remarkably successful. Immense audiences packed the theatre every Sunday night to hear the wonderful tests given by Dr. Schlesinger and Mrs. Cowell and the beautiful inspired addresses of the young trance medium—Mrs. Maud Freitag. The result of their labors was the organization of a new Society called

The "Harmonial Spiritualists Association." The theatre was secured for a year and the good work inaugurated under most favorable auspices. Dr. N. F. Ravlin was engaged as their speaker and the best mediums are employed to co-operate with him. There are three other societies in that city holding regular meetings. A new society has recently been incorporated in San Francisco called the "California Psychical Society" which promises good work. Under its auspices Mr. J. J. Morse of England was engaged and a spirit of investigation awakened, far reaching and beneficial in its results.

It is impossible in a brief review of the work and workers of Spiritualism during the past forty-eight years to give more than a cursory glance at each. The work is so great, and the workers so many that it would take many volumes like this to do justice to all. It is a heaven inspired movement and the angels are its directors and evangels. Its mission is to break the fetters and chains which were forged in an ignorant and superstitious past and set humanity free, turn their faces sun-ward, and give them glimpses of glory unspeakable.

Many of our noble pioneers have passed on leaving no written record of noble deeds and unselfish lives. Such are remembered only by the influence they exerted for good upon the lives of others which, however, is permanent, and lasting at the stars.

All have done good in their own way and awakened an interest in the grand truths of Spiritualism that will some day bear fruit and bless humanity, even though the pioneers who sowed the seed amid persecution and misrepresentation may have passed away, and their names be forgotten among men. In the land of souls they will live and be loved for their unselfish deeds, their devotion to truth, and fidelity to an unpopular cause, which the present generation cannot understnd.

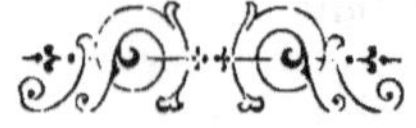

Sincerely Yours
Julia Schlesinger.

JULIA SCHLESINGER.

Inspirational Medium, Writer, and Editor.

It has been said that the history of a man's life and labor in any public capacity is best written by his friends, and the same may be said of a woman's work. Taking this view of the subject, in response to the oft-repeated request for a "sketch" of myself, I have gleaned a few words from the published writings of those whom I am proud and happy to number among my choicest, dearest friends, for such they have been to me through storm and sunshine, ever the same steadfast, unwavering friends. First among these, I quote William Emmette Coleman's tribute on the tenth anniversary of the CARRIER DOVE, which was celebrated Sept. 20, 1893, at the opening of the new home, No. 1 Polk Street. Mr. Coleman said:

"Some ten years ago a little woman living in Oakland issued the first number of a little paper devoted to the children in the Spiritual Lyceum, called the CARRIER DOVE. The publisher and editor were without experience in journalistic ventures or in writing for the public. It was the tentative effort of an active mind and an earnest heart throbbing and pulsing with humanitarian impulse to do a little something for the advancement of truth and reform in the world. The little paper struggled along under difficulties, but it was issued regularly, and before a great while it grew to larger proportions, and its field of endeavor was expanded. Now, not alone were the little ones in the Lyceum included in its purview; children of a larger growth (and we are all children in Nature's primary school on this planet) were taken into its fold, and the gospel of Modern Spiritualism—the evangel of "glad tidings of great joy,"—was preached in its pages "for the healing of the nations."

Year by year the CARRIER DOVE grew and thrived, increasing in size and circulation. A removal from Oakland to San Francisco accelerated its progress and development, until from the tiny sheet of its initial number it became the large quarto magazine, richly freighted with choice viands of intellectual and spiritual food, with which you are all doubtless so familiar. Year after year has continued this constant evolution, until now, by a segregation of material and endeavor, the whilom monthly has been succeeded by the PACIFIC COAST SPIRITUALIST, a popular weekly filled with current events and matters of interest to the Spiritualists of all shades of opinion and in all fields of action. Phenomena, philosophy, science, literature, all find a place in its pages.

All this has been the work of the indomitable little woman whom we have met this evening to honor. She may well be proud of the record of her ten years' arduous labor in the field of Spiritual journalism. Never has she faltered, never turned back from the work devolving upon her. With her face ever to the front, with soul afire with enthusiasm for the task she had so bravely undertaken, she has pressed on and on and on. The culmination of her good work we have gathered to-night to accentuate, by our presence and sympathy, and it may be, in some cases, by some more substantial evidence of our appreciation of her noble labors faithfully executed. She well merits all the encouragement, all the kindly aid, that may be bestowed upon her.

Nor should the zealous labors of her faithful co-worker be overlooked. According to the law of nature, the two sexes are requisite to make the perfect whole. Neither is complete without the other. S , *pari passu* with the activity in the domain of mind, ofttimes of body, also, of the woman projector and carrier forward of the DOVE, has been the active work of the male coadjutor in the realms of the material and financial. A heavy debt of gratitude is due to the latter for his unswerving devotion to the interests of his better half's literary venture, his self-sacrificing toil and tireless efforts in behalf of the success of the DOVE in all its vicissitudes, from first to last.

To both of them, then, the editor and the publisher, we extend our hearty congratulations upon the success so far attending their joint labors, with the sincere wish that what has already been attained may be only a slight foretaste of the much richer and grander results with which their future endeavors may be crowned."

Another well-known writer and speaker, also editor and publisher of the *Lyceum Banner* of London, England, Mr. J. J. Morse, recently published a portrait and brief sketch, from which we take the following extracts:

"In publishing the portrait of Mrs. Julia Schlesinger, the editor of '*The Carrier Dove*, published in San Francisco, in the LYCEUM BANNER, the editors desire to pay a graceful compliment to an earnest Spiritualist, a faithful and devoted worker, a warm friend of the children, and one deeply interested in all that pertains to Lyceum methods.

Mrs. Schlesinger is one of the women that have come to the front in the ranks of American Spiritualism, and as editor, writer, and speaker has rendered invaluable service to our work in San Francisco.

The writer of this short sketch and his family are indebted to her for many kindly actions, and from their present home send warm greetings to their esteemed and far-away friend.

As a devoted wife and mother, Mrs. Schlesinger bears an honored name, while her husband, Dr. Louis Schlesinger, is one of the most notable mediums of the United States, whose fame is wide-spread, and whose work has converted hundreds to our cause.

Mrs. Schlesinger wields a facile pen, writes ably on all women's questions, and takes a broad and liberal view of human duties in the state and in the home."

The following is partly composed of extracts from a brief sketch published in the CARRIER DOVE some years ago with additional items concerning later work , from the pen of that grand pioneer medium, Mrs Hendee-Rogers.

In the DOVE's pages the reader discovers the true index to the character of its editor. She stamps it with her individuality in its general appearance, style and make-up ; and the nature of its contents reflects her broad, liberal views not only through the editorial department but in the judicious selections which form an important feature of its contents. Born and reared in the West, Mrs. Schleslinger partakes of the spirit of freedom and liberality characteristic of its broad and rolling prairies, its towering mountains and majestic rivers. The restraints and conventionalities of "society" are irksome to such a nature, and its shams and artificialities have no place or part in her life. Her home and children are more precious to her than all the fashionable world outside and in it she finds the time and conditions that enable her to do an amount of literary work that is quite astonishing.

From bitter personal experience she learned that only through individual freedom can women be lifted above the power of men of low moral character to crush and enslave. She saw that in order to be free women must be financially independent, that justice must be accorded to them, not only in the payment of equal wages for equal service, but in the means of acquiring a knowledge of practical affairs. The educational facilities of woman should be on on equality with those of the other sex, and no limit should be placed to the sphere of her action in life. The deep convictions and sympathetic feelings of Mrs. Schlesinger in relation to this and kindred branches of reform led her to extend her field of labors beyond the columns of the *Dove*, and in January, 1890 she began the publication of an illustrated magazine of 62 pages called *The Gleaner* devoted to the interests of women, socially, industrially and financially. This work was continued six months, at the end of which time Mrs. Schlesinger was obliged to suspend its publication owing to ill health through over-taxation in doing all the editorial work on both publications. The publi cation of the *Dove* continued until the PACIFIC COAST SPIRITUALIST was established in Aug. st, 1893.

In addition to her household and journalistic work Mrs. Schlesingor has been for several years collecting and arranging material for a work of great value as a historical record of Spiritualism on the Pacific Coast, embodying portraits and biographical sketches of not only the early pioneers in the cause but also the present-day workers.

During the past year she has been, and still is, a regular contributor to *Light of Truth*, published in Cincinnati, Ohio, the largest weekly paper devoted to Spiritualism in the world. She has also written,

under a *nom de plume*, articles upon the social and industrial problems of the day which have been published in various prominent secular papers.

Unobtrusive and silent as to public speaking, yet powerful in deed and written expression for the truths she holds dear. What wonderful inspiration has been given her to start and carry out the publishing of the *Carrier Dove* for ten years under the most trying conditions, and surrounded by family cares; and now, by the inspiration of her guides and in the face of great difficulties she has gone bravely on, relying on the good angels to sustain her, and has at last opened the dove cote for another fledgling, born of truth, love and earnestness, to come forth in the cause of Spiritualism. Her heart is ever open to befriend and assist others. Surely her mediumship is of a very high order when she silently obeys the influence of her angel guides to go forth and do their bidding, and has been so wonderfully prospered in sustaining her work, when others who have started with aid and friends to sustain them have fallen by the wayside, and the sound of their voices are heard no more. May the Pacific Coast Spiritualists and liberals, and all good-minded people stand by this brave woman and assist her in her present noble undertaking to rescue from obscurity and forgetfulness the memories of our pioneer workers in the Vineyard of Truth.

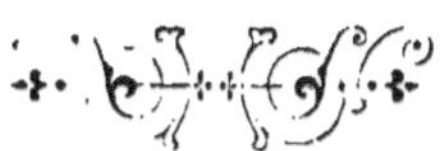

DR. LOUIS SCHLESINGER.

Dr. Schlesinger was born in Liverpool, England, April 17, 1832. Ho was reared in the Jewish faith, to which he adhered until middle life when he became a Spiritualist.

When about 16 years of age he came to America, and at once engaged in business in which he proved very successful, traveling throughout the United States and Mexico wherever his commercial interests led him. He amassed wealth and spent it freely among the poor and needy.

He became convinced of the truth of spiritualism through the mediumship of the celebrated Charles H. Foster of New York.

During his investigations Dr. Schlesinger's own medial powers were developed, and he at once entered into the work with the earnestness and zeal which characterized all his undertakings. His whole time was devoted to giving sittings and healing, in each of which he was remarkable successful. His tests were astonishing, and convinced many stubborn skeptics of the truth of spirit communion, and his cures embraced many obstinate cases that had resisted all other medical treatment.

There is probably not another medium living who has done more for the cause of spiritualism than Dr. Schlesinger. His time and talents were for many years given freely to the public. In fact, he never charged for sittings until the *Carrier Dove* was started in 1883 and then the guides told him that he could ask those who came to him for sittings to subscribe for the *Dove*, which was one dollar a year, as it was for the spread of the truth and they would become agents of the spirit world in disseminating light and knowledge. As the *Dove* grew in size, and expenses increased, the price was raised and Dr. Schlesinger gave sittings free to all subscribers, but was obliged to charge others for his services in order to sustain the paper. For ten years he gave his entire time to this work, and the result of his labors was the support of the *Dove*. None but those came into the privacy of his home life know the sacrifices he made to sustain that work. He has traveled extensively, being absent from home and loved ones for many months at a time, in order, as he said, "to keep the *Dove* on the wing." When it was decided to start a weekly paper *The Pacific Coast Spiritualist* he entered heartily into the work with the enthusiasm of a much younger man, bending all his energies to the task of supplying the funds with which to sustain the new enterprise, and every dollar he earned, aside from the absolute necessities of his family, was devoted to this one object until the overtaxed editor-Mrs. Schlesinger was obliged to give up her literary work for a time on account of failing health, and the paper was discontinued.

Dr. Schlesinger's special work is the conversion of skeptics. In this line he is unsurpassed, as the thousands of testimonials from the press all over the country verifies. During his travels he received hundreds of press indorsements from the leading newspaper men of many States. These are not "paid for puffs," but the voluntary reports of those who have tested his wonderful mediumship and who became converts to Spiritualism through the positive evidence given them. He possesses the remarkable power of curing tobacco and morphine habits. In

Cordially Yours
Dr Louis Schlesinger

rare cases he has failed; the failures being when the person was morally weak and incapable of realizing the dreadful results following such unnatural indulgences upon the spirit when disrobed of the earthly body. As a healer he has been remarkable successful. Hundreds of testimonials from grateful people all over the country whom he has treated during his travels, and who have visited him at his own home, bear witness to the virtue of his treatments and their efficacy in curing obstinate and difficult cases, such as rheumatism, sciatica, partial paralysis, and many ills that afflict humanity. Hundreds have been cured of chewing and smoking tobacco. This (like converting skeptics) is one of the doctor's special phases of mediumship, and one in which he takes great pleasure in exercising, and in which he is almost invariably successful.

Dr. Schlesinger was at one time a prosperous tea-merchant, worth many thousands of dollars, but when he became converted to Spiritualism he at once set about doing good with his wealth relieving the distress of the poor and destitute until his fortune was gone, and he had nothing more to give. Even then he trusted implicitly to the guidance of his spirit friends, confident that they would sustain him in his efforts to bless and comfort the needy and comfortless. In this he has not been mistaken; for, although unable to accumulate wealth again, he has been enabled to do a blessed work for humanity that shall endure long after he has been "gathered to his fathers."

Looking back over the years that have elapsed since Dr. Schlesinger became converted to spiritualism, and renounced "The faith of his fathers," we see them crowned with good deeds, made blessed with sweet charities and hallowed with spiritual treasures which have been freely dispensed to the spiritually poor and blind. An indefatigable worker, he wearies not in well doing, but early and late is found at his post of duty, laboring to build up a cause to which he is devoted heart and soul. His public services are always freely bestowed, and to the thousands to whom he has given the first evidences of a future life, he will ever be held in greatful remembrance.

During his early experiences as a medium he suffered many persecutions from those who, like Saul of Tarsus, felt that they were doing God's service by persecuting one who dared dissent from the faith in which he had been reared; but ever true to the voices of the dear guides whom he could hear (being clairaudient), he wavered not but remained true to the new light which had dawned upon him knowing that though earthly friends had failed him, he had a band of grand, true souls on the other side who would guide his feet aright and place them firmly at last on the everlasting mountains of rest and peace.

N. F. RAVLIN'S ACCOUNT OF HIS CONVERSION TO SPIRITUALISM THROUGH THE MEDIUMSHIP OF DR. SCHLESINGER.

I was hostile to Spiritualism, and believed its basic claims to be founded in falsehood and deception. Of all subjects it interested me the least. It comprehended all that was immoral and vile. To know that one was a spiritualist was enough. There was no necessity of any further acquaintance. As I valued my soul's eternal salvation, I would steer clear of them. It is in this way people generally reason about spiritualism. I was no exception to the rule. I verily thought I knew a great deal, while, in fact, my knowledge was exceedingly limited. I did not believe in spirit return, and I knew my kindred would never come to me through a third person.

But my unbelief did not change facts, and my knowledge of what my loved ones would or would not do was proven to be mere ignorant assumption. The memorable sitting with Dr. Schlesinger was what would be termed an accident; that is, there was no design in it on my part. He was a stranger to me. I never saw him before, and did not know that he was either a spiritualist or medium. Hence, I did not go to him for a sitting. Why should I when I did not believe in spirit return, or that mediums were anything but fakirs and charlatans. I was accidentally or providentially in his office upon a literary errand. Then he told me frankly who he was and what he was. I was caught. But it was decidely against my principles to run, even for Satan himself. So I resolved to stand my ground and have a litile fun at the old gentleman's expense. But the expense was on the other side. My false premise was inundated by a cyclonic flood from the spirit world, and all my conclusions were overwhelmed thereby. My loved ones did come to me through a third person. They proved their identity beyond all question. In each case their full names were given, the diseases with which they died and the towns where they died, together with a characteristic message from each; my son gave a lengthy quotation from his own funeral sermon which I preached ten years previous in the city of Chicago, not a word of which was ever written or printed.

My father had been a Baptist preacher for nearly fifty years, and in addition to giving his name, he gave an epitome of my life for thirty years more minutely than I could possibly have written it out.

My kindred that I mourned as dead were all communicating with me alive and happy. The power that demonstrated the conscious existence of my loved ones who had died dug the grave of my orthodox religion. The same ceremony that interred the one enthroned the other. I saw the errors of my old theology. From the pulpit I publicly repudiated every tenet of the religion in which I had been raised, laid down my credentials and gave up my salary. I openly avowed myself a Spiritualist, and suffered all the ostracism and reproach meted out to such as swerve from the old faith. But I do not regret it. What was loss to me I count gain for the Truth's sake. Hence I have made no sacrifice. I owe not only my present knowledge, but my life to Dr. Schlesinger. Not only was he the open gateway through whom my kindred manifested themselves, but an intemperate smoking habit of twenty years was effectually broken up. Before this I should have been a mental wreck had it not been for him. He was made the instrument of saving me from this deplorable fate. It is impossible in this brief tribute to do him justice. His mediumship is pronounced, and his tests are clear cut and convincing. The charge of fraud has never stained his mediumship, nor has he in a single instance been exposed as seeking to impose upon a credulous public.

Honest skeptics will find in him an honest and most reliable medium. His tests are simply wonderful, affording proof positive that our loved ones live beyond the grave. Any atheistic materialist or agnostic, who may truly desire to know the facts as to man's future, will find the truth, if honestly sought, through Dr. Schlesinger's supernormal gifts. Every effort may be made to account for the phenomena upon some other hypothesis than that claimed, but at last the most rational conclusion will be accepted, viz., that man lives after so-called death, and that, as a conscious intelligent being, he can return under certain conditions and communicate with those he has left behind him in the mortal form.

I find the profoundest satisfaction in the knowledge of this fact. Spiritualism demonstrated to be true embraces within itself all there is of truth in all the religious philosophies and sciences of earth, besides embodying the stupendous idea of eternal progression as the heritage of every one of earth's children.

MRS. M. T. LONGLEY.

MRS. M. T. LONGLEY.

The subject of this sketch was born in South Boston Mass. May 6, 1853. Her parents were John B. Shelhamer—a native of Wuttemberg, Germany, who came to this country when a young man of about twenty and Mary O. Pratt—Shelhmer, a native of Boston, Mass. One of a large family of children, four of whom are still in the mortal, each endowed with rare mediumistic qualities. Mary Theresa at the age of twelve, was taken from her studies in the public school, that she might assist the busy mother in caring for the younger children of the household; and never from that day, has this lady, whose eloquence and rhetoric while under the inspiration of her guides, have astonished large audiences received any instruction of a scholarly character. We mention this fact, because many who have listened to the public utterances of Mrs. Longley insist that she must be a highly educated lady; but it is strictly true that all the schooling this medium ever acquired from teacher and classes, was derived from the public schools alone, when she was between the ages of six and twelve years.

In 1862, the father of the family enlisted as a volunteer in the Union army for a term of three years, and valiantly marched to the front, leaving his heroic and patriotic wife to care for her five little ones, which she faithfully did, contributing largely to their support by plying her needle, sometimes late into the night, upon the azure garments which were to be worn by soldier boys upon the tented field.

It was during the three years absence of her husband upon the battle field, that Mrs. Shelhamer became a spiritualist, and never was there a more devoted advocate of our glorious Cause than this brave woman who faced the deacons and the prominent members of the Calvinistic Baptist Church of which she had been a member, stating to them her conviction of the truth of spiritualism her inability to longer subscribe to the creed of the church, and requesting a letter of withdrawal from the same, which after much dissent, argument, and denunciation on the part of the deacons, was granted. About this time, Fred the youngest boy of the family, then a child of six years, became developed as a rapping and tipping medium, and many messages were received by the mother and friends through the agency of a heavy mahogany dining table, with only the tiny hands of the child resting upon it.

It was in 1868 however, February 10, that the daughter, whose name has become world wide from her connection as a medium with the *Banner of Light* became entranced for the first time by a spirit. This occurred in the public circle of M. E. Beals, a well known test medium of Boston at that time. The child thus influenced by a spirit was made to personate the characteristics, and to give others identification of the intelligence operating upon her, which was recognized fully by the relative to whom the spirit came.

From that date onward for a number of years, the child continued to be controlled by various individual spirits who came from the other life to give evidence of immortality to mourning friends of earth.

Anxious that others should gain the same comfort and truth from the angel word that had come to her, Mrs. Shelhamer opened her house free to the public and on Sunday, Tuesday and Thursday evenings of each week for a period of *three* years, held circles of investigation for all who chose to come.

At these tri weekly seances the house was filled with the curious, and the earnest seekers, and it was not till the failing health of the medium, and the state of her furniture and carpets which had been worn out in the service de· manded a change, that the good lady suspended these free meetings and began to charge a small fee for those who desired to gain audience with the spirit world, through the mediumship of her child.

In the meanwhile, the husband and father had returned to his home, a confirmed and broken invalid, one of the many wounded soldiers, who bore the marks of the fearful battle of Gettysburg and other fields of conflict to their graves. Mr. Shelhamer was not a spiritualist; for many years he had been a confirmed materialist, believing that the death of the body is the end of all consciousness for man. For some time after his return, he opposed his wife's efforts to spread the truth as she understood it and refused to enter the circles where his daughter, entranced, gave messages of cheer and consolation to bereaved hearts, but when at length he did consent to investigate, the trusty soldier became convinced of spiritualism and held it as a cherished blessing to his last day on earth.

In January 1878, one of the spirit band of the medium privately told her that she was developing for the work of giving spirit messages for publication and that he wished her to write to the publisher of the *Voice of Angels*, a semi monthly spiritual paper then printed in Boston, by D. C. Densmore, asking him if he would print any spirit messages that her guides might furnish him. At first, the young lady demurred, but finally consented to write Mr. Densmore whose paper she had never seen, and who himself was un· known to her. The result was, that Mr. Densmore replied he had been told a week earlier by his guide, L. Judd Pardee, that the spirits had prepared a message medi· um for the *Voice of Angels* from whom a letter would be received in a few days, and this was just the work the little paper was established to perform.

From that time on through a course of years, Miss Shelhamer held a weekly seance at which messages were spoken by individualized spirits through her lips reported for the *Voice of Angels* and printed in the regular issues of that paper from which Mr. Densmore received corroborative evidence of their correctness, sent to him by strangers from all over the country. During her connection with the *Voice of Angels*, Miss S. was inspired to write hundreds of choice poems, sketches, essays, editorial and other matter all of which were printed in that paper; and for three years—before and after the transition of Mr. Densmore this lady performed all the editorial work upon that paper which continued until her withdrawal, owing to other duties and labors from that office, six months previous to the suspension of that valuable journal that had many hundreds of readers throughout the United States.

Meanwhile, the *Banner of Light* was in need of a medium in its Message Depart· ment and in obedience to spirit prompting its honored Editor, Luther Colby sought Miss Shelhamer, whom he had never before met, at her home to hold an audience with her guides.

It may here he mentioned, that, under the intelligent and skillful practice of spirit Dr. John Warren, Miss Shelhamer was at this time giving successful medical examination and prescriptions by letter and by personal sittings, and that for a period of three years this public work went on, until, owing to other labors it was discontinued until the season of '92 and '93, when it was in a measure taken up, and in connection with psychometric delineative work, again made a most of successful part of this medium's field labor.

As we have said, Editor Colby visited Miss S., to interview her guides, she supposing he wished to consult her spirit physician upon some medical case. The result of that sitting however proved most important, for it was the begining of a work for the *Banner of Light* by Miss Shelhamer and her spirit band which has extended to a period of fourteen years.

In October of 1879, this lady was engaged to give her first public circle at the *Banner of Light* establishment, and through every season since that date, she has presided as medium upon its platform mostly, at two weekly circles—save, when, for three years owing to the state of her health, she shared her labors one day in the week with Mrs. B. Smith, a fine test medium. During this time, under the able management of her beloved guide, who answers the questions propounded at these circles, which queries are not seen or known by the medium before they are read by the chairman, John Pierpont, many thousands of personal messages have been voiced from returning spirits to individual friends, words of instruction and truth spoken to the public generally, by such able minds from beyond as S. B. Brittan, A. E. Newton and others, and philosophical and scientific subjects discussed, all of which have been printed in the columns of the *Banner of Light.* It has always been the custom of the proprietors of the *Banner of Light* to hold a weekly seance with their spirit friends for the purpose of discussing with them matters of interest and importance pertaining to the welfare of the Cause, of their paper, and to subjects of personal moment. These seances are private; for the fourteen years of his medium's service spirit Pierpont has been their presiding intelligence and has become a valued friend to all connected with those weekly sittings.

As is well known, the medium under consideration has written and published a large number of stories, serials of a most instructive and entertaining character, the merits of which, those of our readers who have read such stories from her pen as "Crowded Out" "Crooked Paths" "Toilers for Bread" and others that have been printed in the CARRIER DOVE, have judged for themselves. She has also printed two large and important books which are handsomely gotten up, " Life and Labor in the Spirit World, " a work of over four hundred pages, and, "Outside the Gates" a volume of five

hundred and fifteen pages which the author considers her finest work. We have not mentioned the many useful spirits belonging to her band, nor will space permit our designating each one separately; yet we cannot forbear stating that the Indian spirits are largely represented and that they are honored by their medium for their fidelity and their service. *Lolela*, the sprightly Indian medium who had been only in spirit life a few months, and was but seven years old, when she was brought to her medium to be trained as a messenger, has been with Mrs. Longley fifteen years, and she is well known by the readers of the spiritualistic press, for her name and work have often been mentioned in its columns.

So completely engaged with her mediumistic work had Miss Shelhamer always seemed to be, her friends did not think it possible that she could have any matrimonial intentions, and it was therefore a matter of great surprise, as well as of congratulation, to a host of well wishers, when Mr. C. P. Longley, the well known composer of spiritual songs and music, and Miss M. T. Shelhamer were united in the—in *their* case—"holy bonds of wedlock." This happy event occurred at the home of the bride's sister, Mrs. F. B. Hatch, Jr., on the evening of November 22, 1888.

This union has proved a most happy and harmonious one. Each is a companion to the other, and mutually helpful in the spiritual work the Angels prompt them to do, and it surely seems that this was a marriage planned by pure and good spirits before it was consummated on earth.

Mrs. Longley has been associated in mediumship and press work for two years with "*Light of Truth*, a prominent spiritual paper published in Cincinnati, Ohio, and at present serves that paper as associate editor, correspondent and message medium. *Light of Truth* has recently published a spiritual novel, in book form, entitled, "When the Morning Comes," from her pen, and other similar works will soon follow.

Although a veteran in mediumship she is still young enough to accomplish much more for the spiritual Cause, and it is her desire to be so fitted for the work that her angel guides design for her, as to prove their useful and trusted instrument.

Mr. and Mrs. Longley spent the winter of 1893 and 94 in California, making their home with Dr. and Mrs. Schlesinger, in San Francisco, during which time Mrs. Longley conducted a department in the *Pacific Coast Spiritualist*, edited by Mrs. Schlesinger. The Society of Progressive Spiritualists secured her as their speaker during her entire stay of seven months; and many were the grand lessons of spiritual truth and wisdom given by the intelligences on the other side through the mediumship of this noble little woman. Mr. and Mrs. Longley were so delighted with the beautiful climate of California that they returned in October, 1895, and located in Pasadena, in the Southern part of the State, where they intend to remain for some time.

C. PAYSON LONGLEY.

C. P. LONGLEY.

The well-known musical composer and song writer, Chalmers Payson Longley, is a native of Hawley, Mass., where among the beautiful hills and genial breezes he passed the first ten years of his life, breathing in the sweet inspirations and beautiful influences which free contact with mother nature ever gives to such poetic and sensitive souls as his. The subject of this sketch was the seventh child of Col. Joshua and Elizabeth Hawkes-Longley, and one of a family of ten children, each of whom displayed in some particular a remarkable and especial line of talent and ability.

Only one of this gifted family, however, remains on earth besides the musician of whom we write—an elder brother, Mayor H. A Longley, who for over thirty years served as Sheriff of Hampshire County, Mass., with honor and distinction, and who might be filling that post at the present time had he desired to do so.

One of the six brothers, Roswell, who passed away at the early age of thirty three, was a remarkably brilliant orator and poet, whose powers of composition and eloquence commanded the attention of cultivated minds of his day; and another, Augustus, was the author of many fine poems and other productions that live below, while he who produced them is journeying on toward higher attainments in the heavenly world.

Chalmers P. Longley was born with the spirit of song within him. His worthy father, who was known for many miles as a man of active business qualities and integrity, led a choir of trained voices for many years, and an atmosphere of music pervaded the entire household. Therefore, it was not strange that this, the seventh born, should inherit the gift, although it was a subject of remark and wonder that the little fellow could not only sing, but could carry his part correctly while still a nursing child at his mother's breast; and when but three and four years old, would stand in the open air, singing for the passing neighbors, receiving many a penny and love pat of approval for his efforts in this direction.

When about ten years of age, Chalmers removed with his parents to Belchertown, Mass., where in the more advanced mental atmosphere of a town larger than the one he had left, the training and moral poise of a sterling character and liberal mind were found for the growing youth.

Let it here be noticed that Mrs. Longley, the mother, was a woman of rare depth of thought and breadth of judgment, and although one of a family from which ministers, deacons and exhortors of the ecclesiastical school had sprung the progressive tendency of her nature would not allow her to remain fastened to old creeds, and by reasoning upon many passages of scripture, this worthy lady found a spiritual meaning within them, with which she confounded the ministers and deacons who sought to trammel and retard the growth of her mind and spirit by the utterance of dogmatic opinion and conservative declarations of faith.

At the time the Rochester knockings were first heard, and Spiritualism began to appear as a herald of immortality, Mrs. Longley read and pondered upon them as announced through the public prints, and said emphatically to her family and friends, "There's a truth," recognizing the importance and reliability of this great movement that had dawned upon the world.

Becoming a pronounced Spiritualist soon after, this heroic woman met the objections of the world with a brave spirit, and lived the knowledge and truth within her while she remained on earth. Two of her sons, Augustus and Chalmers, also accepted the truth and teachings of Spiritualism with their mother, the former having married a lady who proved to be a powerful medium for the production of physical phenomena, through whose agency many startling manifestations of spirit power and wonderful evidences of spirit identity were given to the world.

During his residence in Belchertown, and while a young man, Chalmers P. Longley became acquainted with Dr. S. B. Brittan, that noble and fearless advocate of Spiritualism, than whom no more eloquent and thoughtful speaker ever graced the public rostrum—an acquaintance which soon ripened into a warm friendship in both hearts, that lasted not only while Dr. Brittan remained on earth, but has extended beyond the grave, and is now bearing fruit in many delightful tokens of love which the arisen one displays for and to his earthly friend. So ardent was his attachment for the spiritual cause, that although Spiritualism was as unpopular as it well could be in a conservative New England town of that period, and although a young man dependent upon the patronage and custom of his neighbors for his living, he having learned the tailoring trade, and set up in that line of business for himself, the subject of this narrative, when Dr. Brittan was engaged by a few earnest workers to lecture on Spiritualism in the town hall, took his little melodeon upon a wheel barrow and manfully marched to the meeting, where he contributed to the service and to the inspirations of the speaker by his fine singing of the choice compositions which already had begun to write and sing themselves through his gifted soul. And it may be added that on such occasions the eloquence of Dr. Brittan and the fervor and music of young Longley were sufficient to crowd the hall to its utmost capacity.

About this time the young man began to express in outword form the music which had been singing in his soul during his whole life. That beautiful and immortal poem, "Over the River," which has appeared in collections of standard poetry, books for school lessons, works on elocution, magazines, newspapers and publications without number, and which was written by Nancy Priest, a young mill girl, upon a piece of brown paper one day at the noon hour, was then going the rounds of the press for the first time, and as it caught his eye, the soul of the young musician was filled with melody, and seating himself at his little instrument, he at once composed beautiful music to these words, and produced a song, the first two thousand copies of which were sold immediately upon their issue from the press, and which has had a phenomenal success as a standard song during all the succeeding years, winning the finest encomiums from the public press. This song, "Over the River," lay in manuscript twelve years before it was published, although the composer had secured the consent of Nancy Priest to set her poem to music and give it to the world at the time when its melody first inspired him.

"We Are Coming Sister Mary," another beautiful song, was also composed by the young man at that time, which was followed by the production of a large number of sweet melodies, any one of which might have won for its author fame and distinction, among which may be mentioned "Love's Golden Chain," "In Heaven We'll Know Our Own," "Open the Gates," and that never to be forgotten and exquisite composition, "Only a Thin Veil Between Us," until at the present time, we believe Mr. Longley stands as the most accomplished and prolific composer of tender and spiritual melodies that the world has known.

The trade of tailoring had not been congenial to the inspired musician, and when a new opening appeared to him he hailed it with satisfaction. This came when the elder brother, Mayor H. A. Longley, was Sheriff of Hampshire County, and who had in consequence removed with his family to Northampton to take charge of the public jail. Being in want of an assistant in his arduous duties of caring for the prisoners, Mayor Longley secured the services of Chalmers, his brother, who for sixteen years acted in that capacity, having charge over the prisoners, and coming in contact with various phases of human nature, some of which were extremely heart-rending, but all of which no doubt served to deepen the inspirations and still further develop the musical genius of the sensitive man, for some of his finest productions were expressed while he was an officer and inmate of the county jail. During that time, the prisoners, one and all, manifested the sincerest regard and affection for their keeper, and the utmost solicitude and kindly thought for his wife, Mrs. Harriet Maria Longley, who was an invalid for four years.

Just here it will be proper to state that while a young man, C. P. Longley wedded an extremely beautiful and cultivated young lady, Miss H. M. Shaw of Belchertown, who through all the years of her married life proved the best of counsellors and a sustaining spiritual force to her husband. Mrs. Longley, after an illness of years, passed to spirit life from the home of her faithful physician and friend, Dr. S. B. Brittan in Newark, N. J. Dr. Brittan admired this lady so much for the bright, energetic qualities of mind and spirit, that he paid her a most extended eulogy, and never failed to attest to her ability and worth as a woman and a thinker during his remaining days on earth.

Chalmers Longley, like all minds of genius, seemed to possess that trusting nature which reposed confidence in his fellows, and was the cause of losing for him the savings of a life time. By placing large sums in the hands of other men, in some instances for personal investment, in others to aid his friends out of pecuniary difficulties, he has hopelessly lost a sum that is estimated light at forty thousand dollars; and there have been hours when he hardly knew where to procure the means for another week's living, while others were fattening upon the fruits of his toil; and yet he has been heard to say that these very experiences have helped to draw out the richer part of his nature, and to unfold the melodious gift of song, perhaps more fully than any other discipline could have done.

C. P. Longley had remained a widower some twelve years when he led to the altar the well-known *Baner of Light* medium, Miss M. T. Shelhamer, a lady whose poetic compositions had often furnished themes for the musical settings of the composer. This marriage, which occured November 22, 1888, although conceded by all to be singularly appropriate and pleasing, was yet a matter of surprise to the host of friends of both parties, as it was supposed that, in their chosen field of work, neither had any thought of wedlock; but the result has produced a most happy and harmonious union, which has brought an increase of usefulness in the spiritual work of the happy pair.

Shortly after his second marriage, Mr. Longley published a large number of his songs in sheet music, also a collection in book form entitled, "Echoes From an Angel's Lyre," a title given to him by Dr. Brittan years before. Thousands of copies of these songs have been sold, and their popularity is still unabated. The notices from the press and from gifted pens in favor of these and preceding publications have been flattering.

He has recently issued a new volume containing fifty eight of his delightful songs. The work is handsomely gotten up, the title page bearing fine portraits of the composer and his medium wife. It is sheet music size, printed on fine white paper, elegantly bound in cloth. "Echoes from the World of Song" cannot fail to command an extensive sale.

In closing we will state that Mr. Longley has never received a musical training nor has he taken a lesson in playing or in composition in his life. All that he posseses in talent and execution is nature's gift, supplemented by the quickening power of spiritual attendants; and yet the gentleman has comforted and inspired thousands by his singing, and by the delicacy of those inspiring melodies that he has given to humanity.

GATES OF GOLD.

GEO. W. MORSE.

O, gates of gold! how fair, how bright,
  On heaven's great verge you stand;
There's naught so pleasant to my sight
  In all that upper land!
Once near the silent, azure sea,
   Entranced I stood, and gazed on thee!

And there upon that restful shore
  Self confident I grew—
So near the glory of the door
  I ventured to look through,
And breathing then one word of prayer,
  "Forgive," I said, and entered there:

And loving arms were round me thrown,
  And lips were pressed to mine—
The softest I have ever known,
  And fragrant as new wine ;
And then I knew the joy, the bliss
  Of angel's love—of spirit's kiss.

And when I waked my little room
  Was full of living beams,
And all my garments were in bloom,
  As though they, too, had dreams ;
And soul and sense within me stirred
  At what I saw, and what I heard.

MRS. P. W. STEPHENS.

MRS. P. W. STEPHENS.

The subject of this sketch was born in the city of Schenectady, State of New York, in October, 1822. When she was two years of age her parents, Samuel and Charlotte Wilson, removed to Oneida County, near the lake, where she was raised.

Her father, though having a good education, was tinctured with ideas common to those early days regarding the education of women, considering the only desirable accomplishments being a knowledge of housework and the care of children. Consequently his daughter was never sent to school. Although possessed of a strong desire to study, books were scarce and work plenty, therefore little opportunity was offered for mental development, and she grew to womanhood a machine for labor and a child of Nature.

From early childhood she was clairvoyant and clairaudient, but supposed the voices she heard was God speaking to her, and thought everybody heard them. Her mother was also clairvoyant, often seeing her "dead people" as she termed them. When a child, she was frequently visited by a spirit who would say: "*I am Granny Hadlock, don't be afeard, I like little gals.*" Mrs. S. said in after years she asked her mother if she ever knew any one by that name, and her mother answered, "Yes, Granny Hadlock was my great grandmother, and raised my mother, who was left an orphan, but I never saw her myself."

One day her twin brother was missing, and as there was a stream of water near the house, it was feared he had fallen in and was drowned. Diligent search was being made when suddenly Mrs. S heard a voice say: "He is in the huckleberry lot, " which was half a mile distant. She ran to her mother, saying, "Jacob is picking huckleberries." "How do you know?" said her mother. In a whisper she answered: "Because God says so." Her brother was found at the place designated.

In the year 1844 her father passed to spirit life. The following year the family removed to Illinois. In 1846, she was married to William Kinsey, a Quaker, (or Friend). While conversing with Mrs. S. not long since, when speaking of this portion of her life, with much emotion she said: "All the years of my neglected childhood, all the toil, trials, and disappointments of maidenhood, stand out to-day in shining radiance, beside those six weary years of wifehood. Perhaps they were needed to teach me the lesson of humility, and cause the flame of sympathy to ever quickly kindle in behalf of the suffering and down-trodden of earth, especially of my own sex."

During these six years of marriage Mrs. Stephens became the mother of six children, three of whom passed to spirit life. At the age of thirty she was left a widow. Six weeks after the death of her husband her mother passed away. They both soon gave remarkable evidences of their ability to communicate with her. In 1850, her brother E. V. Wilson, whose name is a house-hold word wherever Spiritualism is known, visited her, and through his mediumship she received her first knowledge of the truths of Spiritual ism. She was soon controlled to speak in a remarkable manner, and would write essays upon subjects of which she was entirely ignorant. Spiritual literature was not abundant in those days, but she read the *The Spiritual Telegraph*, as long as it was published; then followed *The Banner of Light*, which she called her loving friend.

In 1857 she married Philander Stephens, who proved a kind loving husband, and father to her children. In 1862 they joined a train composed of one hundred and fifty persons and came overland to California. During this perilous journey they met with many exciting adventures, being several times attacked by Indians. On one of the-e occasions Mrs. S. and another lady volunteered to mould bullets while the men were fighting the Indians. They also stood guard the whole night, exposed to the enemy's bullets. During these trying hours she was constantly encouraged by the "voices" which were always more clear and distinct in times of greatest distress. After many tribulations they arrived in California and settled in Calaveras County.

In the summer of '65, Mrs. S. was prostrated with a severe illness. Her attending physician thought her recovery doubtful. She was visited by her spirit daughter who gave her a prescription that restored her in one hour. Upon his next visit the physician expressed much surprise at the change. When informed of what had occurred he pronounced the prescription an excellent one, but said he had not thought of it, and laughing, said it was a lucky *dream* for Mrs. S. The next day her babe, which was then two weeks old, was placed in her arms for the first time. She immediately heard Mr. Stephens' spirit wife say: "The baby will die." Mrs. S. said. "No; this strong healthy baby will not die." The voice again said: "The babe will die." "When?" exclaimed Mrs. S. "To-morrow," was the reply. Her husband, who was absent had been telegraphed for, as it had not been thought she would live, and the family were expecting his return. She then asked the spirit if Mr. S. would get home before it died, and the reply was: "No; but I will take your darling and care for him." The child was taken suddenly ill that night and expired at four o'clock the afternoon of the next day. Mr. S. arrived at six.

In January, 1867, the family moved to Sacramento City, after having resided for a short time in El Dorado County. Up to this date Mrs. S. had never heard a spiritual lecture, or witnessed any of the phenomena of Spiritualism, except what had occurred through her own mediumship, or that of some member of her family. Mrs. Laura Cuppy was lecturing in Sacramento at that time.

Mrs. S's mediumship developed so rapidly under these new and favorable conditions that in six weeks after settling in Sacramento her house was daily crowded with people seeking evidence that their loved ones were not lost to them. She soon became a trance speaker, giving in glowing language the philosophical evidence of a continued life. Her first public lectures were delivered in Sacramento in the autumn of '69. She also visited adjacent towns and cities, spreading the truth by lecturing and giving tests. In the spring of '72, she visited Utah, attracting much attention during the few months of her sojourn in that section. After her return she visited many places in California and Nevada, doing much pioneer work for the cause. In April, 1874, obeying the instructions of her guides, she started for the East, stopping in Nevada, Utah, Wyoming, Colorado, Nebraska, and Iowa, visiting all the principal cities on the way, lecturing and exercising her mediumistic gifts. In September, while attending the Spiritualists' Convention in Chicago, Mrs. S. was informed by her guides that her son in Sacramento would pass into spirit-life in November. She hastened home and the statement was verified by the death of her son by accident on the 19th of November.

In the Spring of '76, she again visited the East. Stopping at the home of her brother, E. V. Wilson, in Illinois, she attended the meeting held in Rockford in June, where her usefulness was fully appreciated by her brother and the vast numbers who attended, as the records of the convention and favorable comments of the press demonstrate. In October, at the request of her brother, she accompanied him eastward, assisting him at the meeting in Binghampton. At its close she visited many places in the East, spending the winter in Northern New York. Her ministrations attracted much attention and gave great satisfaction, receiving very favorable notices from the local papers in every city she visited.

The following spring she returned to her field of labor in the West. During the next few years she resided a portion of the time in Reno, Nevada; also in Oregon, which State she canvassed quite extensively, carrying "glad tidings" of immortality to many doubting ones by her superior ability to *demonstrate* its truth.

In 1883, Mrs. S. was directed to go East as far as Cheyenne, Wy. visiting Colorado and Arizona during her absence. *The Denver Times*, speaking of her presence in that city, says: "Mrs P. W. Stephens, of Sacramento, California, again interested the people of this city with a lecture in Warren's Hall. She is an elderly woman, a graceful speaker, and impresses her hearers with the truth of her convictions almost irresistibly. She spoke last night upon subjects chosen by the audience, of which was "The Higher Life," which was well handled. "Then Chinese Immigration" was treated, and if the ideas of the spirit are correct there are dark days before the people of the West from this *evil*, as they are

termed. Altogether her work here is of a fine order; but then we had rather think Mrs. S. is a smart, educated woman than to attribute it all to spirits."

While in Arizona the *Prescott Miner*, speaking of her, says: "Mrs. Stephens gave her second lecture last evening to a large audience. The subject, which was chosen by a committee from the audience, was "The Aztec." To say it was marvelous and instructive would fall short of the letter. We heard learned men say they would give the ablest man in the territory one month in which to prepare a lecture on this subject and defy them to outdo this. It was highly reasonable and in accordance with the views of the most learned of the day. We care not how the lady received her knowledge it was a grand effort, and every man and woman in this land so full of the relics of an unknown and extinct race, ought to have heard it."

After her return home from this trip she lectured in Sacramento until August, 1884, when she was attacked with a severe illness which disabled her from public work for some time, but she finally recovered and resumed her public work. Mrs. Stephens was a prominent speaker and medium at the Campmeetings held in Oakland during the years of 1887 and 1888. Many who were present will remember the inspired addresses of this veteran medium and her beautiful inspirational poems.

Mrs. Stephens passed to spirit life on the 18th of January 1889 from her home in Sacramento, California. She was ill but a short time, having contracted a severe cold which resulted in pneumonia. Dr. Cook conducted the funeral services and many friends followed the mortal form to its last resting place.

She died beloved by all; and her memory remains a fragrant blossom in the desert of many lives, made brighter and happier by her tender ministrations.

E. D. LUNT.

EDITOR "THE MEDIUM," LOS ANGELES.

The subject of this sketch was born in Jamestown, New York, July 11, 1844. His parents were members of the M. E. Church, but soon after the advent of Modern Spiritualism became firm believers in, and consistent advocates of that philosophy. In 1859 Mr. Lunt entered the office of the "Hancock Jeffersonian," at Findlay, Ohio, as an apprentice to the printer's trade, and in 1861 removed to Des Moines, Iowa, where at the age of seventeen he enlisted as a private in the Fifteenth Iowa infantry regiment, and served with honor until the close of the war. He took part in several of the great battles, and was finally captured by the Confederates and confined several months in Andersonville and Florence prison pens. During his term of service he had many narrow escapes from death and capture, several of which he has since been able to trace to the direct intervention of spirit power. During the years since the close of the war he has been, most of the time, engaged in the newspaper business in Iowa and Nebraska, with varying success.

Mr. Lunt came to California in February, 1893, and located in Los Angeles. In January, 1895, seeing the need of a Spiritualist paper on this Coast, he established *The Medium*, which, although but a small paper, has had a wonderful growth, and has extended its circulation into every State in the Union. The tone of this paper has a genuine ring and is clear and outspoken in the cause of right and justice. While it aims to present a fair and impartial record of the work of all mediums, it draws the line at notorious frauds and fakirs, and gives them the benefit of being ignored. *The Medium* has been self-sustaining from the start, as the proprietors steadily refuse any and all assistance except as it comes through advertisements and subscriptions. They hope to enlarge it very soon and add several new and attractive departments.

Mr. Lunt has strong mediumistic powers, and one peculiarity of his newspaper work is that he seldom writes out any of his editorial articles. He sets the type himself without notes, and often in a semi-trance condition, frequently producing in this way a long article without having the least idea what it is about until he sees the proofs of it. He is ably assisted in his work by his wife and helpmeet, who is a fine clairvoyant and musical medium.

E. D LUNT.

HON. JOHN A. COLLINS.

HON. JOHN A. COLLINS.

The following sketch, with closing editorial notice of the death of Mr. Collins is reproduced from *The Carrier Dove* of April, 1890.

Hon. John A. Collins, of this city, is well known as one of the earliest and oldest believers in the science of Spiritualism now living. He was born in October, 1810, in the State of Vermont, and being left in infancy an orphan, without resources, grew up to manhood with very limited assistance from relatives, acquiring a liberal education and support by his own exertions. An injury received when a babe having permanently affected his constitution, his health has never been good, but his indomitable will power has carried his infirm body through a longer life than most men are privileged to enjoy.

At the age of twelve he began his apprenticeship as a printer, and was, for more than two years, associated with Horace Greeley, who was learning the same trade. They became very warm and intimate friends, a relation which existed until the death of Greeley. Young Greeley's character and views, quaintly and logically fortified and enforced in his peculiar manner, had a good influence upon his youthful companion, lasting through his whole life.

Having prepared himself by patient and persevering study and energetic exertions, he entered Andover Theological Seminary to prepare himself for the ministry as his future profession. While pursuing his studies here his attention was first called to the philosophy of Spiritualism as exemplified by clairvoyant, magnetic, and other spiritual phenomena, which were then attracting some attention a dozen years prior to the advent of the Fox girls. He investigated the subjected, and receiving some remarkable private tests, became a believer in and advocate of the doctrine of Modern (so called) Spiritualism, though it was then, as now, forbidden subject for investigation among Collegiate authorities. With his usual persistence in the pursuit of truth and knowledge, he has continued his investigation of the phenomena and philosophy of Spiritualism, for more than fifty years, and is as well prepared as any man living, to give his reasons for the faith within him, and has done much to teach its truths and principles to others. Knowing the firmness of its foundation, in reason as well as in facts, he has the will and courage to proclaim his faith to all the world and defend its principles against every assault. "With malice toward none, but with charity or all," who differ from him, he dares in the language of the immortal Lincoln "maintain the right, as God gives him to see the right."

Before finishing his course at Andover he was called away to engage in the anti-slavery movement which was then well under way. Though licensed to preach, and sometimes occupying the pulpit temporarily he was never ordained or settled in the ministry, preferring the more active field of the Abolition agitation.

Mr. Collins was a born reformer, no doubt, for during his whole life his name has been prominent as an earnest and active worker in the Temperance, Anti-Slavery, Woman Suffrage, Spiritualistic and Industrial Co-operation Reforms.

Prior to and during the Washington Temperance agitation, he was an earnest and effective advocate of temperance and did much to reform the custom, then prevalent among all classes of the constant and daily use of distilled liquors as a beverage.

HIS CAREER AS AN ABOLITIONIST.

Long prior thereto he appeared before the public as one of the most energetic and effective workers, both as a speaker and an organizer in the great anti-slavery movement, in connection with Wm. Lloyd Garrison, Wendell Phillips, Authur Tappan, Isaac T. Hooper, C. C. Burleigh, Gerrit Smith, and others. In this field Mr. Collin's superior executive ability, and his earnest and convincing arguments and cogent reasoning upon the rostrum gave him great prominence as one of the most efficient leaders in the great anti-slavery agitation of fifty years ago.

Oliver Johnson, the Secretary of the old anti-slavery society, in his sketch of "William Lloyd Garrison and His Times," thus refers to his work in behalf of the cause. "Mr. John A. Collins came to us from Andover Theological Seminary at the time of the division in Massachusetts, taking the place of general agent, left vacant by the resignation of Rev. Amos A. Phelps. His executive power was remarkable. He did much to infuse courage into our broken ranks, to overcome opposition, to collect funds, and devise and execute large plans of anti-slavery labor. He traveled much at home, and once went to England on a mission in behalf of the cause. A man of tremendous energy, nothing could stagnate in his presence. He could set a score of agents at work in the field, and plan an executive campaign on the largest scale. At one time a series of one hundred Conventions, extending over several States, East and West, was held by an organized corps of lecturers under his super intendence. He came to us in a critical hour and his services were exceedingly valuable."

His experience in addressing excited and turbulent audiences at a period when abolitionists were so very unpopular, even in the Northern States, was, on some occasions, of a very unpleasant character, and would have proven dangerous, but for his wonderful personal magnetism, presence of mind and unruffled temper. While patiently and good-naturedly enduring their derisive epithets, rotten eggs and stale vegetables, he would often in the end, secure their respectful attention, and frequently at the close of his address, rousing cheers would be giving for the speaker.

A Quaker poet in Philadelphia, who had attended a number of Mr. Collins' meetings, selected a dozen prominent abolitionists and wrote a verse concerning each. Among the number was Mr. Collins, whom he served up as follows :

> John Collins, I wonder
> If thou woulds't krock under,
> If Satan himself should appear;
> I question his bluster
> Thy temper could fluster,
> Or cause thee to feel any fear,
> John Collins;
> Or cause thee to feel any fear.

GOES TO ENGLAND.

His mission to England was very successful, in correcting public opinion there, in regard to the real object and scope of the anti-slavery movement in America, and the course of its leader, Mr. Garrison, towards the Colonization Society, which was fostered by the churches and had raised a strong opposition to his agitation in favor of the abolition of slavery. He was also successful in raising funds in aid of the cause. During his visit he took an active part upon the rostrum, in the famous Anti-Corn-Law agitation of that period, as a repealer. Upon his return to America after an absence of nearly a year, he brought back an address with over ten thousand names attached, all Irish, headed by Daniel O'Connel, urging their countrymen here to vindicate the

Irish love of liberty by supporting Mr. Garrison and his party in his efforts to destroy slavery, which had good effect in favor of the cause.

HE BRINGS OUT FRED DOUGLASS.

While engaged in his duties as general agent, at a meeting of colored people in New Bedford, Mass., he listened for the first time, to an eloquent five-minute speech by the now famous Fred Douglass, who had recently escaped from slavery, and of course possessed very little education. Mr. Collins was so favorably impressed with the native ability manifested by the young colored orator, that he took him into service to travel with him and assist at public meetings as one of the attractions. Possessing a good memory, Douglass soon gained a knowlege of the subject by listening to Mr. Collins' speeches, and was soon, under the latter's tuition, able to deliver an interesting and eloquent speech of an hour, and thereafter became popular as an anti slavery orator and acquired a world-wide reputation for his eloquence and ability. Recognizing the black orator as entitled to equal rights with himself, insults and indignities were often bestowed upon both, while traveling to lecture in all parts of the country, on account of the popular prejudice against the negro. It did much, however, to educate people upon the equal natural rights of all men, without regard to color or previous condition of servitude.

WOMAN SUFFRAGE.

In the Women's Right's movement, he took an active part, both as a speaker and a writer in the public journals, in its early history at the East, and later on this Coast, doing good service with his eloquent pen. Though to act as a teacher and leader of men in effecting great social reforms, is generally a thankless task, involving great labor, much self-denial, grievous disappointments, and weary waiting for fruition, yet Mr. Collin's sympathy for his fellow men, suffering from the wrongs and evils of the present state of society is so great, especially when he sees the weaker portion oppressed or overcome by the strong, that his philanthropic soul is at once enlisted in their defense, and his whole energy both mental and physical, exerted in their behalf. And, if he may not live to see women enfranchised, he knows that the cause he has so long advocated has been greatly advanced by his efforts, and firmly belives that it will surely triumph in the near future.

EMIGRATES TO CALIFORNIA.

Arriving in California early in June, 1849, Mr. Collin's became one of the poineer merchants of San Francisco.

After about two years' experience, during which time he was burned out five times, losing a large amount of valuable property thereby, including a monthly income from rents of seven or eight thousand dollars, he turned his attention to mining as a speedier and surer way to make a fortune, with which to return East and carry out his plans to inaugurate a system of co-operative industry similar, though less comprehensive, to that described later in this article. His attention was attracted to the rich quartz veins of Grass Valley, in Nevada County, where he built and successfully operated the second quartz mill erected in California. He foresaw the great wealth hidden in the quartz ledges of California, and was one of the first to practically demonstrate their value, as the original source from whence the Placer gold was derived, and which, by reason of their number and richness, insured the permanence and prosperity of the mining industry of the Pacific Coast.

A NATIONAL CO-OPERATIVE SOCIETY.

It was Judge Collins' purpose to agitate for the abolition of modern slavery, until public opinion is aroused to the necessity of the reform in our industrial system which he proposed, as the true and only peaceful and practical solution of the problem, before it assumes the form and force of a destructive and bloody conflict between classes. For this purpose a National Co-operative Homestead Society has been formed in this city, by himself and a number of others entertaining similar views, and issued numerous pamphlets and circulars to popularize the same by means of the press and platform, and prepare the way for the necessary legislation by Congress

This Society sent a petition to Senator Stanford, asking the passage of a law establishing the new system of National Co-operation. This petition including the form of the proposed law was presented in the Senate by him in February last. Senators Stanford and Stewart have each introduced bills embodying their own views, for goverment encouragement to Co-operative, enterprises on a limited scale, but not embracing a complete National system of Co-operation, providing means, and directing the formation and magement of Corporate Associations, under uniform laws, comprising all branches of industry, both productive and distributive. These several bills were referred to a committee and will naturally be considered together at some future time.

This reform Mr. Collin's regarded as the most important of all that he has engaged in, and hoped to live to see it inaugurated by appropriate Congressional legislation.

DEATH OF MR. COLLINS.

Hon. John A. Collins of this city passed to spirit life on the morning of April 3d. He had been ill for a long time and only his superior will power kept him at his post of duty when laboring under physical disabilities that would have prostrated many a less determined man. In the latter part of February he had recovered his strength somewhat and took a trip to Los Angeles to attend to some business. He returned from there on the 15th of March very ill with pneumonia, since which time he has not left his bed until the spirit, weary of its struggle to overcome the infirmities of the worn out body took its flight to broader fields of usefulness, and larger opportunity. Mr. Collins was the beloved president of the Society of Pro-

gressive Spiritualism of this city, and a most earnest worker in the cause. His great love of justice, his deep sympathy for the weak and helpless, his contempt for the shams and wickedness of those in high places, made him the firm friend and able advocate of the poor and oppressed everywhere. In him the mediums found a noble champion and defender; and if he erred it was through his great goodness of heart, his deep, earnest devotion to truth, his fine sense of honor and integrity; his great charity for the weaknesses and failings of humanity. Judging others by his own high standard of excellence he always found more good than evil, more truth than falsehood, more love than hate, more honor than dishonor; and therefore he had more pity than condemnation for those who were unfortunate victims of circumstances and conditions over which they had no control. It is useless at this moment to endeavor to pay a fitting tribute to the memory of this great, good man. Words are inadequate to express all that could or should be said of him. His life was one continual labor of love, and unselfish devotion to humanity. Volumes could be written of what he has accomplished in his almost four score years. No one day was lost; every hour bore the fruit of noble deeds, generous sympathy and helpfulness. Standing by his bedside as the life forces were slowly ebbing away we could still discern the great, grand soul of the man, the lion-hearted hero, as in moments of consciousness it would flash forth from the eyes, and in clear tones voice the deep interest it still retained in humanitarian work.

As president of the Society of Progressive Spiritualists his interest in all that pertained to its welfare was unabated to the last; and his solicitude for its future prosperity was the one theme he dwelt most upon in those last hours. May his mantle fall upon his successor and the place be filled by one as deeply earnest and conscientious as himself.

EDWARD FAIR.

EDWARD FAIR.

The subject of this brief sketch was born in Baltimore, Md., in the year 1826. When quite a youth he became a member of the Methodist church, and served as chorister for the famous revivalist—Inskipt—at Dayton, Ohio, for many years. As but little data is available at this time concerning the earlier life experiences of this brave exponent of Spiritualism we will make a few extracts from a valedictory address delivered by Mr. Fair in Kansas City, Mo., in the year 1874, and published in the *Religio-Philosophical Journal.* In this address, which was delivered on the occasion of his retirement from the position of President of the Spiritual Society of that city, he gives an account of his experience in the investigation of Spiritualism and also some of his early impressions concerning a future life. We will quote his own words which were as follows: "From the time of my sixth year until four years ago the eight day of last March, I had not a tangible proof, nor one faint glimmer of immortality, although for years I had sought such evidence in tears. The first circle which I had the privilege of attending met in Mr. Pond's house in this city. While attending that circle I first entered the great soul temple through the pearly portal of trance; and that which I then saw and heard, language fails me in describing. From that time until now, I can positively say to you that not a shadow of doubt has ever crossed my mind as to the realities of our eternal state; nor has there a month passed during those four years that I have not had additional evidence from the other side of life's bright abode. Such evidence often comes to me in the holy hush of night, or during my business hours, or when I am in church or when listening to lectures. The witnesses I present you are three of my senses; seeing, hearing and feeling; and therefore I know that the dark night of death has never penetrated a grave so deep, but instantaneously the sleeper's brow is bathed in the roseate sunlight of a resurrection morning.

My first impression of death, although a preverted one, I shall never forget. Grasping the hand of a sister with whom I then stood in front of our old country home, I witnessed emerging therefrom a funeral procession following the form of an elder sister, as I then supposed, to "that bourne whence no traveller returns." Although a mere child this was my first impression of death, an oh, what a terrible one it was! There I stood, feeling with my right hand for evidence of my heart throbs, my left grasping more firmly that of my sister, my eyes turned in the direction of the mourners as they moved slowly away from our dear old home, made desolate and dreary by this mysterious and relentless visitor, *death*; and from that day and through many changing years death has been to me a singular paradox to all the principles in nature, a principle which takes from us, giving nothing in return, leaving the heart bereaved and desolate.

If such thoughts were not formerly mine, I can now associate them with my first impression of death; but an evidence of immortality was the great boon for which I continually aspired; and all through my after life, having early associated with the church, I have heard again and again from the pulpit, of a speculative heaven and a prospective immortality. Singular as it may appear, in my gleanings from all the pulpit oratory to which I have listened, I have yet to hear the first intelligent idea of heaven or of hell.

In my earlier years I was a devoted church member. Having had charge of a choir for fifteen years, and being frequently called upon to sing at funerals during such solemn ceremonies I often ventured beyond the beaten boundaries of thought and wondered why heaven was so indifferently described and immortality so incomplete. No perfect heaven no perfect immortality, until after the resurrection of an old, worn out body, and the resurrection is to occur—God only knows when or where, and then not until Gabriel has blown a great blast upon his wonderful trumpet; and such blast is to be heard—*not by the spirit*, for that has long since been confined to heaven or hell; but it is an old *defunt body which is to hear*.

I have stood by many graves and at such times when the stricken hearts of bereaved friends were lacerated with inconsolable grief my prayers have gone out to God for a tangible evidence of immortality; and believing that Deity was his own interpreter through his written or revealed word, my chief desire was to eliminate therefrom that evidence for which my soul had hungered and thirsted from early boyhood. Language fails me in describing my utter helplessness. After dilligently searching the scriptures from Genesis to Revelations I could not find a simple promise given by God to man of immortality. The word is mentioned but twice within the lids of the entire book. Paul says, "God *only* hath immortality." Adam was driven from the garden to prevent his acquiring a knowledge of immortality as it reads: "And now, lest he put forth his hand and take also ot the tree of life and eat and live forever, therefore, the Lord God drove him from the garden."–Gen iii, 22.

"Man lieth down and riseth not till the heavens be no more. They shall not wake nor be raised out of their sleep." 'For that which befalleth the sons of men befalleth the beasts; as the one dieth, so dieth the other; yea they have all one breath; so that man hath no pre-emi-eminence over a beast."Eccl. iii, 18–22. After having carefully perused the book, I forever closed it, knowing, that therein cannot be found a single promise given by God to man of immortality. I can never forget the terrible travail of soul through which I then passed. In trying to free myself from the thraldom of such miserable vagaries as are taught the world over, I found myself in darkness impenetrable and bleak as death. What could I do? Go to my spiritual adviser? No! Should I thus try to roll the stone from my orthodox sepulchre, and frankly tell him of my failure to find in the Bible a tangible way to the other side of Jordan, my name would have been marked upon the orthodox slate as heterodox; hence my lips were sealed, and the church to me a forlorn hope.

My earnest desire is to grow beyond those ideas my earlier years venerated. My purpose shall be to deal justly with all ideas, all isms. If through the stormy past I only gathered from the church the thought of an ideal heaven and prospective immortality, for such hope I am thankful."

From the above it will be seen that the path of our arisen brother from the orthodox track to that of Spiritualism was not strewn with flowers. It required courage and manhood to throw off the bondage of creeds and come out among the world's workers for truth and right. During the many years of his ministrations upon the spiritual rostrum his trust in the ultimate triumph of truth never wavered, and his denunciation of wrong and injustice was ever clear, ringing, and certain. The last four years of his life was a season of continual pain. Throughout all he was brave, courageous, hopeful and unflinching, looking calmly and trustingly to the end when the release should come. Through the long, trying ordeal of sickness and pain his devoted wife was his constant attendant, nurse, and patient watcher.

She was his best friend, adviser and trusted helpmate, his loving companion, comforter and staff; the one who, alone shared his weary days and nights of pain and followed his footsteps down to the brink of the river of death; and her love, deathless as the stars, shown like a beacon light across the dark waters until his feet had pressed the other shore. In her loneliness and grief he now ministers unto her, even as she so tenderly, lovingly ministered unto him. In his love she will find her tower of strength and be enabled to meet life's battles as calmly and bravely as before this shadow came between them. She will hear his voice above the din of life's conflict, in un-f utterable tenderness speaking words o comfort, hope and cheer. Human sympathy and love is hers from the hearts of many true friends.

Mr. Fair passed to spirit life on the 30th of April, 1890. The funeral services were conducted by Moses Hull and Mr. Battersby, on May 4th, at Metropolitan Temple, San Francisco.

LIDA B. BROWNE.

Among the younger "workers in the vineyard" is Lida B. Browne, editor of *Progress*, a weekly magazine devoted to Spiritualism and general progressive topics, published in San Francisco. She is a native of Herkimer Co., N. Y. and appeared upon the mundane sphere in February 1862. Her parents were both spiritualists, being among the first to realize the truth of this divine philosophy, her mother Mrs. Scott Briggs, being well known both on the Pacific Coast and in the East as an ardent worker in the cause. In 1881 Mrs. Browne graduated with honors from the Normal College of New York City and immediately thereafter was married to Frank L. Browne, at that time employed upon the New York "Truth Seeker" and since connected with various reform journals in different parts of the country. In 1885 Mrs. Browne held the position of teacher in the Freethought University of Liberal, Mo., her husband being at that time in charge of the "The Liberal," a local progressive weekly, well know among Spiritualists. Afterwards returning to the Eastern states, they were not content with the more conservative elements of the older section, and in 1888 started for San Francisco, which they have made their home since. Although a firm believer in Spiritualism, it is only within a few years that Mrs. Browne has had evidence, through her own organism, of the positive truth of the philosophy.

In February 1895, being continually at the public meetings as musician, she saw the need of a spiritual paper in San Francisco, there being none published in the city at that time, and *Progress* was the result. The venture met with approval and success from the start, and its editor feels that her life's work has really commenced, and hopes to be the means of bringing many into the light; eliminating the fear of death, and heralding far and near the truth that our loved ones who have passed onward can and do return and communicate with us.

LIDA B. BROWNE.

MOSES HULL.

MOSES HULL.

Like old Mother Partington, Moses Hull was born at a very early period of his career. In fact he came within one of not being born at all, and he has been heard to say, it would have been money in his pocket if he had not been. There were two of them, and he was born as No. 2, of a pair of twins that came to the residence of Dr. James and Mary Hull, near the village of Waldo, in Marion Co., Ohio, on Jan. 16, 1835. He is now, therefore well started in the sixties.

As children both of the twins were weakly; and Aaron the eldest of the two only lived a little over two years; Moses halted between life and death during the whole period of his childhood. With manhood came vigor; and now, he is stouter, heartier and able to do more work than at any period of his younger days.

Mr. Hull is everywhere recognized as a natural born preacher. He says, people should not blame him for it. He cannot help it; it is a birth mark, and he has tried earnestly and faithfully to overcome it, but cannot. He is doomed to preach. He says with Paul, "Woe abides me if I preach not the gospel." It is as natural for him to preach as it is for a bird to sing.

He commenced exhorting and preaching before he was sixteen years old; and at the age of seventeen was an ordained minister. As a "boy preacher" he had a wonderful reputation. As a revivalist he had few equals. Between the time he was seventeen and twenty-nine he immersed over 3,000 people.

He now recognizes that during the whole of that period he was a medium working under an irresistable psychic force. A peculiar trembling came on him always before the delivery of his more powerful sermons. On one occasion particularly, when he arose to preach, he thought before reading his text he would comment for a moment on a verse which occured to his mind. He quoted: "And they all with one consent began to make excuse." The next he knew he found himself down by the "anxious seat" praying for and talking to twenty or more persons who were on their knees begging for salvation. He could hardly be made to believe that he had preached over an hour and a half, and had a half-dozen times had nearly the whole audience in tears. As a healer even while in church, his work was regarded by many as miraculous.

A strange train of circumstances led Mr. Hull out of the church, into Spiritualism. He now fully believes that it was his own mediumship and nothing else, that made a spiritualist of him.

He did not know what a doubt on the particular religion he preached was, until his doubts were suggested by impressions. He, to this day regards his work as an Adventist minister, as a schooling, a college, a necessary work, to prepare him for the work he is now doing; a work, which by the way is unlike that done by anybody else in the world.

In a debate with Rev. Joseph Jones, in Charlotte, Mich., in 1862, in reply to

Mr. Jones' remark that the righteous dead were in heaven praising God, he said "the dead do not praise God, for the dead know not anything." He then quoted, "They are extinct," They are quenched as tow;" they are not;" they shall be as though they had not been," etc. He then said, "According to these texts the dead are out of existence. Now, will Mr. Jones tell us how the dead, who are out of existence, can praise the Lord." He paused a moment and heard a voice say, "How can these who are out of existence be raised from the dead."

He supposed Mr. Jones and the whole audience heard the voice; it happened however, that they did not. Mr. Hull never got over that voice. When he was alone he would undertake to reply to the question it asked, but, the more he replied the more persistently the question asked itself, "How can those who are not, be raised from the dead?"

This voice was heard no more for several months. He had a debate with W. F. Jamieson, who was at that time a Spiritualist. In that debate Mr. J. presented evidence of spiritual phenomena. Mr. Hull told him he would save him the trouble of presenting further evidence on that subject by admitting all his evidence in advance; he believed it; he had no doubt that there were genuine phenomena enough to build the theory of spiritualism on, but they were not produced by the dead, as "the dead know not anything." "They are the spirits of devils working miracles." Next Mr. Hull undertook to present an argument to prove the dead could not produce the phenomena. He stated that the mind was a function of the brain, depending upon the brain for its existence. Without brains there can be no thought. In death, the blood ceases to flow to the brain and the brain does not act, therefore the dead cannot think.

Then the voice spoke again and said, "please tell the people how the devil can think and perform these wonders without a physical brain; or, if devils can do this without physical brains, why the dead cannot." This voice seemed objective, and so positive that Mr. Hull supposed every one in the audience heard it, he was perfectly sure that, Mr. Jamison, being a medium, heard it, and would tell him of it in his next speech; but Mr. J. did not.

More than a hundred times Mr. Hull went off by himself to try to reply to what he then heard, but the more he replied the more firmly he became convinced that his theory was founded on nothing better than rolling sand. The result was he, after months of prayer, much study and many tears, announced himself as a Spiritualist.

His work in spiritualism since 1863 is well known. In all this time he was never known to be idle. In 1864 he founded the *Progressive Age*. This paper he sold to S. S. Jones, and it became a nucleus for the *Religio-Philosophical Journal*.

Later Mr. Hull formed a publishing company, in Baltimore, which published *The Crucible*. He was superintendent of this company and editor of *The Crucible* for near a year, when an unfortunate circumstance induced the company to elect another superintendent, who, in six weeks squandered its funds and financially wrecked *The Crucible*. Mr. Hull then went to Boston, and revived the paper and run it six years under the name *Hull's Crucible*. Mr. Hull also founded and for two years published a large greenback paper called *The Commoner*. *New Thought* was his last journalistic venture. This was started and run six years as the organ of the Mississippi Valley Association of Spiritualists, and of its camp-meeting held in Clinton, Iowa every year. When that camp meeting became an established affair, recognized in all the papers, and no longer needed an agent, Mr. Hull sold *New Thought* to *The Better Way*, now *The Light of Truth* to which he is now a regular contributor.

While Mr. Hull has always been known, understood, and loved by his friends, he has been a terribly misunderstood man by those who have not known him. Probably he has in part, been to blame for this himself. There has never been a time wLen he could not with a very few paragraphs of explanation, have stopped the mouths of his enemies; but he took the position at the start that no enemy, or even all of his enemies combined should not extort from him any explanations. He would make any sacrifice for friends but would say or do nothing merely to gratify those who had undertaken to write him down.

In the heat of the Woodhull excitement, he took strong grounds with what he then believed and now believes to have been a terribly wronged, per-- secuted and suffering woman. He wrote a letter with the design that the letter should draw the enemies' fire from a sick woman to himself. It was a success.

While Mr. Hull, could hardly be induced today to write such a letter, he has never been known to express a regret for having written that one. He says he was led by a power higher and wiser than himself. While it has compelled him to stand comparatively alone for many years, it has taught him, that with the angels help he can stand alone. Mr. Hull has enemies, not a dozen of which he ever saw. He is glad to know that among all his enemies not one is acquainted with him, and not one can point to a man, woman or child on earth that he ever injured.

Mr. Hull's work is not done; today his calls to lecture extend from the Atlantic to the Pacific. He has several books in preparation and in press to be brought out in the near future.

At last Mr. Hull's enemies, with prob- ably one single exception, have voluntarily laid down their enmity. Many of them have confessed that they were moved in their enmity wholly by their prejudices. Many of them have asked his pardon, and, if there is a more popular man in the ranks of Spiritualism, the writer does not know who he is. His calls to preach extend not only all over this country, but throughout the civilized world.

Mr. Hull has written many books, the title of some of which are in part as follows:

' "Encyclopedia of Biblical Spiritualism." This is one of the largest, and some say, by far the most entertaining book that ever came from his pen. It contains references to *over five hundred* places in the Bible where Spiritualism is proved or implied, and exhibits the Bible in an entire new light. Besides this it contains a brief sketch of what is known of the origin of the books of the Bible. Nearly two thousand copies of this book were sold before it came from the press. Ministers, doctors, lawyers, judges, congressmen and senators read and grow enthusiastic over it.

"Two in One." A volume of nearly 500 pages, with excellent portrait of the author. There is more Scriptural, Scientific, Biblical and Historic argument in this book than in any other, Moses Hull ever wrote. It contains stores of argument which cannot be gainsayed.

"The Spiritual Alps and How We Ascend Them; or, a few thoughts on how to reach that altitude where the spirit is supreme and all things are subject to it."

"Joan the Medium, or the Inspired Heroine of Orleans. Spiritualism as a Leader of Armies." This s at once a most truthful history of Joan of Arc and a convincing argument. No novel was ever more interesting, no history more true.

"The Real Issue." This book contains statistics, facts and documents, on the tendencies of the times.

"All About Devils." Or an inquiry as

to whether Modern Spiritualism and other Great Reforms come from his Satanic Majesty and His Subordinates in the kingdom of darkness.

"Jesus and the Mediums, or Christ and Mediumship." A careful comparison of some of the Spiritualism and Mediumship of the Bible with that of to-day. An argument proving that Jesus was only a medium, subject to all the conditions of modern mediumship. It also shows that all the manifestations throughout the Old and New Testament were under the same conditions that mediums require to-day; and that the coming of Christ is the return of mediumship to the world.

"The Spiritual Birth, or Death and Its To-morrow." The spiritual idea of death, heaven and hell. This pamphlet, besides giving the spiritualistic interpretation of many things in the Bible—interpretations never before given, explains the heavens and hells believed in by Spiritualists.

Mr. Hull's residence is now in Chicago, at 29 Chicago Terrace, where he has purchased a beautiful little house which bears the name "Valhalla."

Mr. Hull says he is now determined to labor the remainder of his days for the establishment of a school, where ladies and gentlemen can be so prepared for the platform that Spiritualism shall be able to boast of a ministry which shall be fully able to compete in talent and education with the ministers in the various pulpits in the land. He sees no reason why the spirit world cannot co-operate with people who are technically educated for their work as well as for ignoramuses. All intelligent Spiritualists hope Mr. Hull or somebody else will accomplish that work.

MATTIE E. HULL.

MATTIE E. HULL.

(Written on Mrs. Hull's 52nd Birthday, June 22, 1892, by Moses Hull.)

— — —

Almost a quarter of a century has passed since I became intimately acquainted with the subject of this article, and, having lived with her twenty years of that time, I feel safe in saying I know her pretty thoroughly, both as a medium and as a woman. Mattie comes of good, honest New England stock. I was not acquainted with her father, but her mother has lived in our home several years, and I can say a more honest, conscientious and dutiful mother never lived. Mattie's sisters also are intelligent and noble women.

Mattie's girlhood was, perhaps, not much different from that of other ordinary girls, except in the early development of mediumship. She was educated at Mount Cæsar Academy, and, had not mediumship siezed her, she would probably have spent a portion of her life either as a common school teacher or in music, of which she is passionately fond, and in which her father, who was a musician, educated her.

Mediumship, which generally has its own way, spoiled the calculations of her parents and of herself.

Forty years ago mediumship seized Mattie; at that early period little was known of mediumship, and her parents were as ignorant as parents generally were, as to what it was. The best medical skill in the country exhausted itself in trying to find out what was the matter, and much nauseous medicine was scientifically poured down her throat, to cure her of "The-lord-only-knows-what," all to no purpose. The child grew worse; that is, mediumship increased. The neighbors were called in to witness the automatic writing, and to hear the child "preach in her sleep." Somebody finally suggested that they had known a medium to act very much as the child was acting, and it was learned that her disease was a chronic attack of spiritual mediumship. There was no cure; the only thing to do was to let it work itself out. It has been working ever since, and manifests no particular signs of working out. When she was only thirteen years old some of the New Hampshire and Massachusetts churches were opened, and her father was invited to take the little phenomenon there to preach, which he did. Some of these discourses were stenographically reported, and Mattie became a convert to Spiritualism by reading reports of her own discourses.

At the age of 17, Mattie married Mr. C. C. B. Sawyer, a very good and worthy man, though he was neither musically or eminently spiritually inclined. He thoroughly believed in his wife and her mediumship and music, and in every way he could assisted in her work. He enlisted in the war against the rebellion, where he contracted consumption, which carried him out of the world.

For many years Mattie, beside preaching, sat as a medium. She became as thoroughly disgusted with the average sitter as many sitters are with some mediums. She found that fully two-thirds of those who go to mediums go for anything else than a knowledge of spiritual things. Many go with the direct intention of taking the advantage of being alone with a lady, and offering an insult. Others by their very first question show that they are in Spiritualism for the "loaves and fishes,"—in other words, to prostitute it to mercenary purposes; and still others go to mediums to get the spirit world to help them out of some scrape.

So small a proportion of medium hunters wanted to learn of anything spiritual, that years ago Mrs. Hull gave up giving sittings except in very rare cases where she is especially impressed to sit. Her mediumship has long taken the phase of poetry and music, more than any other. As a speaker she is better known than otherwise, having traveled from Maine to California, and spoken in nearly every one of the Northen states, and in several south of Mason and Dixon's line. She has never been known, in her speeches or in private conversation, to say a hard thing of anybody. No matter what is said of her she never retaliates. Indeed, the worst secret of her worst enemy is safe in her hands.

Mrs. Hull has written hundreds of very readable poems, many of which have been published. Her volume of poetic and prose essays, entitled "Wayside Jottings," has passed through two editions, and the demand for it is undiminished. She has another volume ready for the press, but as yet we hesitate about bringing it out. Some time since about twenty of her songs were published on a card, over six thousand copies of which were sold in one year. Last February we issued thirty-one of her songs in a pamphlet, already we are preparing to to issue the fifth thousand. We now have in incubation a book of her best songs, together with constitution for societies, marriage service, burial service and a few other things needed by Spiritualists everywhere. All of which, except the songs, will be prepared by the writer of this.

At this time, Mrs. Hull's 52nd birthday, she is more determined than ever to use the gifts the angels hava conferred on her, in the advancement of the cause to which her life has been devoted. She asks Spiritualists everywhere to give her an opportunity to be useful in the cause.

——

P. S. It is now January, 1896. I am invited to add a little to the above. I see no reason to change anything here written. I will add that her song book has doubled in size and passed through several editions of 2,000 each since the above was written. Mattie is now in her fifty-sixth year, and, if possible, more earnestly engaged in the work than ever before.

A new development has come to her for poetry and invocations. She has gone to work earnestly for the children; in that work she seems to have found her fort, and in that work, especially at camp-meetings, she is employed and appreciated more than in anything she ever did before. Her calls to organize and teach the children at camps extend from Maine in the East to Oregon and Washington in the Northwest.

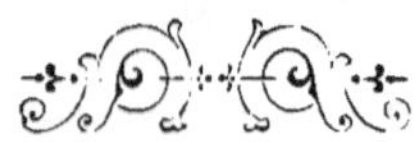

DR. N. F. RAVLIN.

DR. N. F. RAVLIN.

N. F. Ravlin, the subject of this sketch, was born in Essex county, New York, June 1, 1831. Before the close of the following year his parents moved to what was then an uncultivated region, the wilderness of Western New York, and settled in Clymer, Chautauque county. His boyhood was thus spent literally in the woods. All his early recollections are associated with the Beech, Maple, Pine and Hemlock forests, with which Chautaque county was at that time covered. His father was the Rev. Thomas Ravlin, a man of most remarkable memory and eloquence, who for nearly fifty years preached the gospel according to the accepted standards of the Baptist denomination. He was a man of progressive thought, independent judgement, and fearless utterance, far in advance of the ministers of his time in his interpretation of the scriptures. For this reason many failed to understand him. He was misjudged by some, feared by others, and persecuted by those who were jealous and envious of his power. In 1845 he removed with his family to the "Far West," as it was then termed, and settled on the, at that time, unbroken prairies of Illinois, fifty miles due west from Chicago, which town then claimed 8,000 inhabitants. One year afterwards, in the autumn of 1846, Father Ravlin died, leaving his family in fairly comfortable circumstances, though strangers in a strange land. His was the first mortal form laid in what is now the Kaneville Cemetery.

The subject of our sketch was the youngest of seven children, four boys and three girls. On the death of his father the care of the family devolved upon the brother next older than him, Hon. N. N. Ravlin, who was afterwards elected to the Illinois Legislature, and who served his township as Supervisor for twenty-eight consecutive years, and who was honored as chairman of the Board of Supervisors of Kane county for more than twenty years of that period. N. F. Ravlin was but fifteen years of age when his father died. From that time he worked his own way in the world, and labored from daylight till dark on the farm for $13 per month. When eighteen years old, he was in the woods splitting rails by the thousand to pay for timber for fence posts to fence a small farm that fell to him as his share of his father's estate. The farm he afterwards sold in order to obtain an education.

He was converted to so-called Christianity when nineteen years of age, and was induced to believe that he ought to study for the ministry. Hence, all other pursuits were abandoned, all other plans laid aside, and everything was consecrated upon the "Altar for Christ's Sake," as it was termed. Two years were spent in the University of Rochester, New York, but ill health prevented the completion of the prescribed course of study, and Mr. Ravlin returned West with a shattered constitution, and with little expectation of living but a short time. But rest from study and a change of climate partially restored his health, and he was accordingly ordained as a Baptist minister, and took a small country church "far out upon the Prairie." The meetings were held in different school houses. This church agreed to give their pastor the munificent sum of $300 per year, and his house rent and fire wood. The house consisted of two small rooms standing on the bleak prairie, without fence, flower or tree about it. The agreement was never honestly kept on the part of the church, and the relation was not of long duration. He regrets, to this day, that his first experience as pastor of a church had not been his last, for he often expressed himself that he had no business to be a pastor of a church; that he had neither taste nor aptitude for pastoral work; yet he seemed pressed into it, and there did not seem any way out of it.

Mr. Ravlin's principal pastorates were at Freeport, Illinois, Cedar Rapids, Iowa, Racine, Wis., Chicago, Ill., and San Jose, Cal. He preached in Chicago fourteen years, and during that time was called to officiate at the dedication of fifty-one Baptist churches, and he raised that number of church debts amounting to many thousands of dollars. He was very popular with the masses, and always had crowded audiences. He assailed the conventional shams of society, the pious frauds and hypocrites in the church, and the sins and crimes of the age—so widely and notoriously fostered by corrupt legislation—with a fearlessness and a boldness of utterance seldom ever heard from the pulpit. Fidelity to truth and principle as he understood it, rather than policy, controlled his pulpit utterances. For this reason he was often subjected to bitter persecutions from envious and jealous ministers who had nothing in common with righteous principle, but were governed by a time-serving policy that would not scruple, in order to serve personal ends, to make merchandise of the gospel of Christ. By pious platitudes and godless ceremonials they would assume to preach Jesus as the Christ, and yet crucify him daily between the two thieves of hyprocrisy and supreme self-interest. Mr. Ravlin was ordained when but twenty-two years of age, and entered upon the work of the ministry honestly, and without the shadow of a doubt but that all ministers were honest and just what they seemed. He learned by bitter experience that "All is not gold that glitters," and that it is possible for "A man to smile and smile and yet be a villian." His bitterest enemies have been, and are, professed ministers of the gospel, who have been most unrelenting and conscienceless in their duplicity or double-dealing, and their underhanded schemes to advance their own glory by sullying the good name of another. Of course he recognizes the fact that there are

good men, honest and true, in the ministry; men who are grand and noble exceptions to the general rule, and who are as much above the average type of preachers as an angel is above a foul "bird of night."

During the late war Mr. Ravlin ardently espoused the Union cause, and although ill health prevented him from entering the army, yet he was mainly instrumental in recruiting two regiments of men, and delivered five hundred war speeches and sermons, besides raising large amounts of money to pay soldiers' bounties. On two occasions he delivered a "war speech" where the "Knights of the Golden Circle" had sworn to kill him if he attempted it. Although being informed of the threats made, and being entreated by anxious friends not to put his life in such peril, he went boldly forward, and with burning eloquence, hurled defiance in the face of his country's secret enemies, regardless of consequences. Utterly fearless, he seemed inspired for the occasion, and no doubt did more for the Union cause than if he had been at the front in the field. Now that the war is over, all feeling of hostility toward the people of the South has been eliminated from his nature, and he recognizes that, educated as they were, they were equally honest in the defense of what they regarded as their inalienable rights.

Removing to California, in 1881, he was induced to accept the pastorate of the Baptist church in San Jose, which position he held for over four years, attracting the largest religious audiences ever assembled in the Garden City. Four months after commencing his pastorate the church edifice was burned, and Mr. Ravlin was mainly instrumental in building the finest and most commodious church in the city, containing a fine pipe organ. It has seating accomodations for 1,000 people, and not unfrequently 1,200 were convened within its walls on Sunday nights to listen to the popular pastor of the Baptist church. But his success provoked envy and persecutions from other ministers, who labored assiduously to sow discord among the members of the Baptist church, and thus break Mr. Ravlin's hold upon his people, and upon the general public. Measures were resorted to of which ordinary sinners would be ashamed, but they were only partially successful. In uprightness of life and in a character without a stain, the subject of our sketch stood invulnerable against all the shafts of his enemies, without a breath of scandal attaching to his name, or sullying his reputation. But, amid the storm of persecutions, he grew more and more liberal. Months before he resigned his pastorate he publicly rejected the whole bundle of orthodox theology, and delivered a series of discourses on the cardinal doctrines of the creed, which were published in book and in pamphlet form by the Swedenborgian Publication Society of Philadelphia, Pa., under the caption of 'Progressive Thought on Great Subjects,' and which were mailed by said society to all the orthodox ministers in the United States.

Mr. Ravlin received many bitter, vituperative letters from Divines (?) of all denominations, denouncing him, in the veritable spirit of the old Inquisition, for his "Heresy," each man supposing that the author had sent him the book. Out of hundreds of letters received, only two or three breathed a charitable spirit, or sought in any way to reclaim the "Heretic" from the error of his ways. Although Mr. Ravlin held the majority of his church firm in his support, yet he at last became tired of occupying an orthodox pulpit, when he himself had wholly outgrown its narrow limits. Accordingly, he gave up his salary, resigned his pastorate, and withdrew from all connection with the church and Baptist denomination. Although out of the fold, a liberalist and and a free man, yet he was a bitter opponent of what is known as Modern Spiritualism. He always insisted that none of his kindred would ever come to him through a third person. If they had anything to communicate they would come to him *direct*, and not through some medium. But, as the sequel shows, he was mistaken, and they convinced him of his mistake.

The first evidence of the truth of Spiritualism he ever received was by most astonishing tests of spirit return and identity through the mediumship of Dr. Louis Schlesinger, then of Oakland, Cal. The names of all his deceased kindred were given, their places of residence and the diseases with which they died, together with a characteristic message from each. The proofs were absolutely overwhelming. They came entirely unsought; for when Mr. Ravlin entered Dr. Schlesinger's office he was not aware that the doctor was either a Spiritualist or a medium. Had he known it he could not have been hired to cross the threshold of his office, so intense was his prejudice against Spiritualism. Afterwards, through others, and in his own home, spirits came, giving proof of their identity, and demonstrating the truth of immortality. There was no longer any room for doubt. All prejudice was overcome, and all opposition was ended. A smoking habit of twenty years was broken up, and a new life began. Ignorance had given place to knowledge; bigotry was dispelled by enlightenment, and blindness by understanding.

During the campmeeting in Oakland, seven years ago, Mr. Ravlin boldly avowed himself a Spiritualist, and before its close delivered three lectures in its defense. In doing this he closed the door of every pulpit in Christendom against himself, and suffered both social and religious ostracism from the denomination to which he gave the best years of his life. He really made a sacrifice for the truth to which his eyes were opened, and it required no little degree of courage to do it. Those who knew him had "cast him out," and those to whom he came did not know him. But there were no murmurings or misgivings, either on his part or that of his family. "They had bread to eat the church knew not of." "Angels came and ministered unto them." Their kindred from the realm of spirit mingled in their little family circle. To them, those loved ones, long mourned as dead, were now alive more truly than before. They proved this in many and unmistakable ways. The instructions received were always in accord with the ethics of the Golden Rule. The counsel given them from the angels were of the highest wisdom and deepest knowledge. He is much encouraged in his work by his faithful, loving wife, who says that she had rather know what they *know*, and have their experience in spiritual unfoldment, than to be back in the church with their former salary, and be in ignorance of this truth by which we understand the nature of the "world to come," and receive the sweet ministration of "angelic spirits."

On the sixth of July, 1890, Mr. Ravlin commenced his labors as speaker for the Society of Progressive Spiritualists in this city, and filled the platform every Sunday for two years, both morning and evening, discussing in a vigorous and convincing manner every phase of Spiritualism and reform. He speaks purely by inspiration, and the more intelligent and spiritual people may be, the more they are attracted by his lectures. He answers written questions from the audience, whenever desired, in the fewest possible words, and with a promptitude and directness that is truly commendable. He is intensely in earnest, and carries conviction to the minds of all that he is seeking to build up the society for which he speaks, and to defend the Philosophy of Spiritualism and the facts of its phenomena against all assailants, rom whatever quarter they may come. Having been for thirty years in the orthodox ministry, he understands every line of battle, every strategetic movement of the enemy, every argument against our position, and is fully prepared to meet the issue in open, honorable warfare.

After two years of faithful service, Mr. Ravlin was granted a leave of absence for one year, intending to make a tour of the eastern cities, visit the various campmeetings, etc., but, at the expiration of six months, circumstances arose which threatened the very existence of the society, and he was recalled to again occupy their platform. He returned to San Francisco and resumed his ministrations which continued for another year. He then accepted a call from Los Angeles, and has been engaged in that city the greater portion of the past two years.

JOHN H. LIENING.

JOHN H. LIENING.

John H. Liening was born in Germany, January 6, 1818. On his father's side the ancestry were Germans as far back as can be traced. His great grandfather was a soldier in the Thirty years' war, being in the service during all those years. On his mother's side the ancestry were Scotch, going from Scotland to Germany during the reign of William, Prince of Orange. His father was a miller and small farmer. At the age of fourteen young Liening emigrated to the United States, in the Dutch brig *Amalia*, landing in Baltimore, Maryland. After a few days in Baltimore, this adventurous youth started on foot across the Alleghany Mountains to Pittsburg. He went by canal-boat to Cincinnati, Ohio, and there bound himself to a pork merchant for three years for board and clothing, and was to receive one year's schooling during the time. He remained one year, received the board, but no schooling, and the clothing consisted of one well-worn plug hat, which he left behind him.

The same year his father, mother, ix brothers, and two sisters, and uncle, with wife and children, all came from Germany to make their homes in America. The cholera was raging in Cincinnati when they arrived. They at once hurried out into the country, where they expected to buy land, but on the journey one of his brothers died of the dreaded disease. The others reached their destination in Auglaize County, where, between Monday and Saturday, all of the two families, except one sister, died of the same disease.

The next year, 1834, the boy started on the *Chickasaw* for Mobile, where he stayed for two years, working on steamers as cabin-boy. In 1836 he went to Florida and enlisted for the Seminole War. In 1838 he returned to Cincinnati, where he was married at not quite twenty years of age. He lived in Vicksburg, Memphis, and many other Southern cities, including New Orleans, coming to California "around the Horn" in 1849. The journey occupied seven months. Arriving in San Francisco, October 20, 1849, he engaged in business here and was quite successful. In the spring of 1850 he started, in company with several others, for the mines on Feather River, just above Rich Bar, which proved afterwards so very rich, but which they failed to discover, although working on both sides of the Rich Bar for about a month. He spent about three months in hunting Gold Lake, but finally found Pyramid Lake. On the route to Feather River they passed any number of emigrant wagons deserted in the snow, the carcasses of the animals lying in the harness, the wagons containing many articles of value.

In the fall of the same year he went to Horsetown, five miles from Shasta. Having spent over three thousand dollars prospecting, he began work with only twenty-five cents clean cash and three mules. In the spring of 1851 he bought goods at Sacramento and hauled them to Shasta, taking them on to the mines on pack-mules. He came by way of Colusa on those trips, took a liking to the place, and promised to return some future day and locate, and did locate there in October, 1851. He opened a restaurant and lodging-house, commencing this business about where Spaulding's shop stands at present. At this time an incident occurred worth relating. A man came to the restaurant one evening, inquiring if a steamer had gone down the river. When told it had just gone, he exclaimed "Well, then, my money is gone!" On being asked what he meant, he said he had stopped at Moon's ranch with his pack-train, and, carrying into the house what, to all outward appearances, was an ordinary flour-sack containing a camp kit—cooking utensils, bacon, flour, etc.—had laid it on a box behind the door. In the bottom of the sack was a buck-skin bag containing over four thousand dollars' worth of gold-dust. · Now the box he had laid the flour sack on was marked for Sacramento, which he did not notice. While out attending to his mules, he heard the boat-whistle, and, hurrying into the house, looked, of course, for the sack—it had been put on the boat by mistake. Moon, on being made acquainted with the contents of the sack, at once lent him a fine horse to overtake the boat, which he did at a big bend in the river, but it would not stop for him. He tried to get someone to go to Sacramento to save his money, but no one seemed to care to take the journey, as the country was flooded with water. He cried and fretted over his loss until Mr. Liening's sympathies were aroused and he offered to make the trip. Donning an extra shirt, but without a coat, he mounted a fine California horse and started, at nine o'clock at night, for Sacramento. There was no moon and it was cloudy. After swimming his horse and getting wet to the skin several times, he finally arrived in Sacramento just as the boat was unloading its freight, and succeeded in getting the sack containing the gold-dust. Upon its return to the owner at Colusa, that individual generously paid Mr. Liening's expenses and no more.

In 1852 he was invited to witness a curious performance at Doctor Semple's home. The doctor was a particular friend, and told him that something very strange had taken place there the night before, in the way of receiving communications from the spirit world. Though born and educated as a Catholic, Mr. Liening had become an atheist.

That evening, on account of business, he did not reach the doctor's house until a late hour, and, as houses in those days were small, he found only standing-room for himself. There was quite a large table in the center of the room, with about a dozen people seated around it, equally divided as to sex. Very soon after Mr. Liening's arrival a name was spelled out for him, Henry Liening, claiming him as his father. At that time his family was in the East, and he was not known in Colusa to have a family anywhere. He had lost four children during his married life and one was named Henry, but at that time Mr. Liening did not himself recall the child's name. The incident aroused his curiosity and he set to work to investigate the subject most earnestly, as he was not satisfied with the belief of an atheist, but still hoped for more light, and at the expiration of two years from that time became convinced that Spiritualism is true, and is still firm in his belief.

In 1854 Mr. Liening returned to the East and brought out his family, and in 1856 sold out his business in town and engaged in cattle-raising, until 1861, when the war broke out. He enlisted as a private in Company D, First Cavalry California Volunteers, and proceeded to Arizona, New Mexico, and Texas. He was in various skirmishes with Indians and Confederates, and served until 1863, when he was promoted to Second Lieutenant, and returned to California as recruiting officer. Soon after, he tendered his resignation, which was accepted.

He bought the Colusa House property. He was appointed postmaster, and his most active service during the war was in the next three to five years in Colusa, as is well known in the county and State. To show his zeal for any cause in which he might be engaged or have interest in, the following incident is related. When the news of the assassination of Lincoln was brought to Colusa, someone passed a note into the postoffice stating that certain persons were taking up subscriptions to buy powder to fire a salute in jubilation over the assassination of Abraham Lincoln. Mr. Liening stepped out of the office into the room where quite a number of people were waiting for the mail, read the note, and said, "If any person or persons fire a salute in gratification over the assassination, I will kill the first man so engaged and continue shooting until the last is killed or I am shot down."

In 1870 he sold out his interest in the Colusa House property and, being broken down in health, started East on a trip to recuperate, which finally ended in a visit to his birthplace, near Hamburg, Germany, and many large cities of the Continent. He was in Paris at the time war was declared between France and Germany, and returned to Colusa on that account. He was next engaged in the Parks dam excitement, and became an active member of the party who opposed the building of the dam, and he said then that the land could not be reclaimed by dams, but must eventually have canals to carry off the surplus water during flood-time. He has held several public positions—that of Public Administrator, Justice of the Peace, etc. At present he is Town Recorder, Justice of the Peace, and Notary Public, and is a popular officer.

Although at this date Mr. Liening is seventy-two years of age, he is able to attend to every duty, and has the appearance of a much younger man than he really is, and has the promise of years to come.

DR. DEAN CLARKE.

Dr. Dean Clarke, whose name is a household word wherever our Spiritual journals have been circulated, has been before the public for nearly thirty years as a lecturer and writer upon Spiritualism. His nativity was among the Green Mountains of Vermont, where about half a century ago he drew his first vital breath, and where he was reared on a farm, and inured, even in childhood, to the hard labor necessary to sustain life upon the stony soil of New England.

His privileges for gaining an education were limited to an attendance at a rural common school about four months in a year, from the age of four to fifteen, when he attended a select school three months, and at sixteen began his career as a public school teacher. At seventeen years of of age his health failed from overtaxation by mental and physical toil. He inherherited a delicate constitution, and his ambition for knowledge and aspiration for usefulness, both to his parents and the public, caused him to labor beyond his powers of endurance, and a weakness of his digestive organs began which for five succeeding years incapacitated him for study, prevented regular school-teaching, and even disqualified him for any but very light manual labor. After suffering "the hell of all diseases," dyspepsia, for nearly two years, he was almost desparing of any relief, when, seeing in the *Spiritual Telegraph*—which curiosity had prompted his parents to subscribe for—accounts of persons being occasionally healed by spirit power, he was led to invoke that aid for himself.

Alone in the kitchen of his parents' farm-house, one winter evening, when they and his two junior twin brothers were visiting at one of the neighbors, he laid his hands on the family table, and silently invoked spirit aid, and soon felt a magnetic power which took possession of his hands, and with them manipulated his confused head and debilitated body for nearly half an hour. When the mysterious influence left him his surprise and joy were about equal to find that instead of being fatigued he was rested, and the dull depressing pain in his digestive organs was much alleviated.

This was a momentous event that began and shaped his future career as a mediatorial instrument for the use of the Spirit World. From that time to the present this beneficent power has attended him as a healing balm, a guiding hand, a quickening and illuminating intelligence, and as a comforter which has sustained him through great hardships, trials, and tribulations incidental to his public career!

But several years of discipline and experience were necessary to prepare him for his final public mission. The disease that afflicted his frail body being constitutional, yielded but slowly to the healing efforts of his attendant Indian guide, and greatly retarded his spiritual development. The necessities of life required what labor he was able to perform upon the home farm for a while, and an inborn skepticism and distrust of spirit guidance required time and trial for its overcoming. As soon as his health had sufficiently improved, his thirst for knowledge, and a determination to have a profession to rely upon for a livelihood, induced him to spend three years in the study of medicine, vainly, however, so far as that end was achieved. The spirit birth of his mother called him home from the West, where he attended his last course of medical lectures, and where he had partly arranged to enter practice.

Two years were then spent with his father on the farm, partly to recuperate his physical powers exhausted by study, then a few months were spent as a travel-

DR. DEAN CLARKE.

ing book-agent, when he met a medium through whom the spirits told him the time was at hand to begin the great work so long delayed, which *they* had for him to perform. Not long afterward an invitation came for him to attend a Spiritual meeting at Plymouth, Vt., near the earthly home of Achsa W. Sprague, the distinguished trance speaker, then four years in spirit life. Here he was invited to speak, and relunctantly yielding, the arisen Miss Sprague wonderfully inspired him to address her old neighbors and her mother, who unknown to him was present, and he spoke so pathetically and powerfully, that all were thrilled, and several moved to tears, rather of joy than of sorrow!

This occasion, the 19th of May, 1866, fulfilled for him the prophecies and promises frequently given him from spirit sources, but doubtfully received during the preceding years of preparation.

Space will not permit more than a mere allusion to his subsequent public career. Announcing through the *Banner of Light* his readiness for work as an inspired speaker, calls came from far and near. He went to Cincinnati, thence north to various places in Indiana, and to Wisconsin, where a few months of labor succeeded, whence he returned and labored in various parts of New England till the spring of 1868, when he was called by the State Missionary Association of Michigan to organize societies and lecture throughout that State. For eight months he was very successful, and won high encomiums as a speaker, then for four months assisted the President of the Association in editing the *Present Age*, a paper started to aid the Spiritual work in connection with the Missionaries.

Disagreement with the nominal editor led to Dr. Clarke's resignation and the resumption of his independent public work. He journeyed eastward and spoke a few months under the auspices of the State Spiritualist Association of Pennsylvania; then was called to a similar work by the New York State Association, spending the winter of 1869-70 principally in Western New York. From there he

returned to New England, and spent two years speaking in all of those States with increasing power and fame, though with small pecuniary returns. While there he twice presided over the only general Campmeeting then held, which assembled at Lake Walden, in Old Concord, Mass. As presiding officer he won high ecomiums from Prof. Denton, Lizzie Doten, Thomas Gales Forster. Ed. S. Wheeler, Dr. H. B. Storer and other renowned veteran speakers, who praised his graceful, dignified and happy manner of presenting them, and keeping order and harmony in all the protracted sessions.

In the winter of 1872, while stopping in New York City, Dr. Clarke was the guest of a Mrs. Baker, a well-known Spiritualist, now the wife of Colonel Kase, of Philadelphia. One afternoon she invited about fifty of her friends to meet him in her parlors, among whom were Colonel S. F. Tappan and his wife, since Mrs. Cora L. V. Richmond, Mrs. Pomeroy, wife of "Brick" Pomeroy, and her sister and husband, a son of Mr. Goodyear, of Rubber celebrity, and an Indian woman named Mary Powell. During a seance which ensued, Dr. Clarke was controlled by his Indian guide and healer, and approaching this Indian women he addressed her in a language which to him was a totally "unknown tongue," and she responded. She then translated into English what she and the spirit through Dr. Clarke had said, and thus, for a full hour, a dialogue went on between them—she translating, as they talked, to the auditors who were astonished and delighted at so marvelous manifestation of spirit power. Miss Powell informed the auditors that they had spoken in the language of the Delaware tribe of Indians, and that the spirit Indian spoke it perfectly through his medium! This was a very gratifying "test" to Dr. Clarke, as well as to all present.

In the winter of 1872 3, he went to Columbia, S. C., where he spoke a month, thence to Columbus, Ga., for another month, to Atlanta for another, thence to Nashville, Tenn., and to various towns in Indiana; then to Wisconsin, then back to Vermont, when in the fall in 1873 he came to California. Here in Charter Oak Hall he spoke for two months very successfully. But his health being poor, he had to suspend speaking here, and went South as far as San Bernardino, speaking also at Santa Barbarba and Los Angeles.

Returning, he remained in this city till the spring of 76, when he went to Humboldt county, and spent a few months lecturing with success, thence returning here, he went to Oregon, receiving there very high commendation from the press.

After a year's service there he journeyed to Puget Sound, where for two years and a half he did missionary work, awakening much interest in the Spiritual cause. He spent the winter of 1879-80 in Eastern Oregon, then labored assiduously in Portland, where he fitted up a hall, and organized a society to which he ministered six months, doing great good.

Returning to San Francisco, several months of rest were required to restore health and strength, then in 1881 he opened Washington Hall for the first time to Spiritual meetings, and occupied it about eighteen months; managing and speaking at regular Sunday meetings, when he yielded his charge to the Society of Progressive Spiritualists. which was organized out of the attendants at his meetings, and to which he gave the name it yet bears.

In 1884 he returned to the New England States, where five years were spent in lecturing in all of them with old time success; then a call from Denver took him there for six months, whence he journeyed back here to California where he labored successfully in Santa Cruz.

Dr. Clarke has been an active missionary laborer on the Pacific Coast for sixteen years doing a more wide-spread work than any other speaker. He has twice canvassed the entire length of California, Oregon and Washington, visiting most of the interior towns of each. On these lecturing tours he has received no compensation except the voluntary contributions of skeptical audiences, which, on the whole, was barely sufficient to defray incidental expenses. Those who know him best give him credit for being actuated by the highest and purest motives, and an unselfish love of his fellow-men. The desire to do his whole duty, and obey the promptings of the spirit world has been paramount to all other considerations. In his zeal to serve the cause of right, truth and justice he has been unsparing in his denunciation of imposters, fakirs, and mercenary harpies, who have "stolen the livery of heaven" in which to deceive and delude honest, confiding spiritualists. For his outspoken sentiments he has sometimes been severely criticised, but the results always justified, and demonstrated the wisdom of his course.

Probably no exponent of Spiritualism now on the rostrum excels him in clearly stating the laws underlying spirit communication. He has made this branch of his profession a special study, and is capable of answering without hesitation any question pretaining to the subject so far as the investigations of able observers have yet gone. There are of course many things connected with Spiritualism not yet well understood by even the best informed. The action of incarnate mind upon mind is in great part yet a mystery; therefore it is not to be expected that all the processes of spirit manifestation can be comprehended by investigators at this early stage of psychical research. Another half century of progress like that of the past fifty years will make clear much that is now classed among the uncertainties of the occult.

This sketch of Dr. Clarke's life is a very meager summary of twenty-seven years of public labor, earnestly, faithfully and self-sacrificingly performed by one of our most able, devoted and useful spiritual teachers. He has done heroic service for our cause with both tongue and pen, and everywhere has won high repute as a man of honor and strict integrity, and as a fearless advocate of all reforms, and of truth as his clear intuitions and vigorous intellect have discerned it.

HERMAN SNOW.

HERMAN SNOW.

BY ELIZABETH LOWE WATSON.

He was born in Pomfret, Vt., April 9, 1812. His parents were intelligent, respected, healthy and long-lived. There were ten of the children, four daughters and six sons, all of whom were married and settled in life, and with one or two doubtful exceptions, all of them, and also the parents, became Spiritualists. There was no death among these children until an average age of about sixty years had been reached, or until an aggregate of nearly six hundred years had been lived by the ten. Herman is the oldest of the seven who are still in the earth-life.

His early years were spent upon the home farm, with rather imperfect district school privileges, until on his sixteenth birthday he met with a severe accident which was supposed to disqualify him for all future severe bodily labor. Hence he turned his attention in other directions, and first served an apprenticeship of about three years in the mercantile line, partly in Boston and partly in a country village store. The business did not suit him; his yearnings were strong for a more intellectual kind of life and broader fields of action. He broke loose from business entanglements and entered a leading academy of preparatory instruction at Meriden, N. H., but his hopes of a thorough collegiate course at Dartmouth were blighted by the wants of necessary pecuniary means.

Now the allurements of the great West open up before him; he resolves to seek his fortune in that broad and still largely unexplored and unappreciated region. In September, 1831, at the age of about nineteen, he goes off leisurely and alone; takes a ride between Albany and Schenectady in the first steam railroad passenger train that was put in action in the United States, and within a week of the formal opening of the road by the State officials. At Schenectady a line boat on the Grand canal is taken to Buffalo; then a schooner passage to Portland harbor, enduring a severe lake storm for three days. Now pedestrianism is resorted to and kept up as far as Meadville, Pennsylvania; next, in company with two others, French Creek and the Alleghany River are navigated in a three-dollar pine skiff to Pittsburg, a four days' trip through much wild country and some rough adventure.

There he gets employment for a while, and then pushes on farther west and south. This was but the beginning of an unsettled, wandering life, extending west to the extremes of white settlement at the time, and which did not come to a full end for nearly eight years, when our adventurer finds himself living at Meadville, Pennsylvania, from which point a new and important change in his condition takes place. Through all this unsettled life, no real deep-seated happiness had been reached; only the changing ripples of a surface life had been his. A deeply felt yearning of his inner and better nature remained unanswered; his spiritual, religious life was in embryotic repose. But what could be done? He could not be religious in the popular sense of the term, and yet without some kind of exercise of his religious nature,

life seemed sadly insufficient, often desolate to him. But orthodox revivalism
could not move him; its hell could not
frighten him into stereotyped church
creeds and confessions. His own intuitions taught him that there must be an
overruling power of wisdom and love
pervading this wonderful universe, but
the God of the ruling systems of theology
was seen to be one whom he could not
love if he would, and would not if he
could. He firmly believed in a life beyond this, but the orthodox heaven was
one for which he had no affinity, and a
verbally inspired Bible was a perpetual
stumbling block to his intuitive perceptions; he could never endure its study
beyond the creation story in Genesis.

Until this time no opportunity had been
offered him of becoming acquainted with
liberal and rational views of Christianity;
but now, at Meadville, he found a small
and intelligent Unitarian Society, with a
good minister, through whose instruction
and guidance, especially in a rightly
ordered course of reading, he at length
gained a somewhat satisfactory view of
the Bible and its doctrines. His inward,
religious self, began to expand into a
peaceful, happy activity, and soon with
the aid and friendly advice of the minister
and others, on the occurrence of his
twenty-seventh birthday, with a joyful
solemnity he dedicated himself to the
work of a liberal and rational Christian
minister. Now follows a return to the
East and a course of theological studies,
lasting nearly five years, the last three of
which embraced the regular course of the
divinity school of Harvard University.

He was graduated in July, 1843, but
with a constitution much broken by
excessive study and the want of a wise
regard to the laws of physical health.
The change from an active, external life
at so late a period, taken in connection
with a certain degree of zeal without
knowledge, was too much for his physical
stability, especially his eye sight. This
failure began early in the course and continued not only through his preparatory
studies, but also in all his future labors,
crippling and discouraging him in many
of his higher purposes, especially in all
attempts to become a thorough student
of theology and of general literature.

It was mainly on this account that,
after his graduation, he decided not to
seek for a permanent parish settlement,
but resolved to devote himself to something like an itinerant ministry, with but
little attention to a student's life. On the
first day of June, 1845, he was therefore
ordained as "an Evangelist," in one of
the Boston churches. His engagements
were now by the year, the first one being
over an old and interesting parish at
Brooklyn, Conn., (once a part of Pomfret), preaching in the very church which
Gen. Israel Putnam was accustomed to
attend during his life-time.

Here was our friend's first experience
in the joys of married and home life, and
also a heavy weight of its sorrows, for
within the space of about twenty months,
were removed by the death-angel, the
wife and two young children, leaving him
homeless and sad. It was, doubtless,
these severe bereavements that prepared
the way for a final, faithful attention to
the claims of the new Spiritualism, in
spite of the repulsive dislike which attended the first approach toward an
investigation. It was simply as a disagreeable duty that the first efforts were
made, and the state of mind was one
almost sure to result in at least a temporary failure as, indeed, they did, but what
came of subsequent efforts was of such a
decisive nature as absolutely to compel
belief. When a full conviction was at
length reached it was with a joy unspeakable, both to visible and invisible friends
and loved ones. It was now—the "Pearl
of great price" to this zealous believer,
which having found, he was ready to give
up all else to its widespread knowledge
and support. Being soon after invited to
the regular charge of a parish, he accepted only with a full understanding of
his present state of mind in regard to
Spiritualism, and that at all times he
stood ready to aid those who wished to
investigate. Several families availed

themselves of the opportunity, circles being held with them and mediums developed. His own medial tendencies also made rapid progress, until there was a happy culmination in clairaudience, or internal hearing. He was now in direct and free communication with his spirit helpers, who were zealous in their efforts to push him forward in the good work which lay before him, and under the strong inspirational impulse thus received he was induced to prepare for circulation a pamphlet entitled, "Incidents of personal experience while investigating the new phenomena of spirit thought and action." This he had printed at his own expense, wholly for a free distribution, largely among his brother ministers, of whom not one was willingly omitted. Of about six hundred copies printed, all were soon disposed of, not a single copy being sold. This was while under a six months' engagement at Montague, Mass., (in which town are now located the well known Spiritualist camp-grounds.) By the time this engagement came to a close he had come to the resolve to give himself wholly up to the new work. He therefore declined a re-engagement, and as first move, made a visit to his native Vermont home, being then much in need of a season of quiet repose. But he was not allowed to rest long; the pressure from visible and invisible surroundings was such that he soon found himself engaged in holding circles and developing mediums among the neighbors, until not less than one-half of the families were more or less interested or decided believers in the new faith. While here he became acquainted with the author, E. Simmons, a recently developed trance medium of great promise; and, on the return trip to Massachusetts, with the consent and advice of the spirit guides, the medium speaker was taken as a Spiritualist evangelist down the Connecticut valley, speaking at the leading towns along the route, until at length the two separated, the medium continuing on to Boston, while the thus far managing helper took refuge in the pleasant So-

cialistic community of Adin Ballou, at Hopedale, where Spiritualism had already taken a deep root-hold.

There our earnest worker spent the summer, his mental occupation being the preparation for the press of a small volume entitled "Spirit Intercourse," and his bodily exercise being in the box-making shop of the co-operative companies. Early in autumn he went to Boston, got his book published, and then, still under strong spirit impulse and direction, he established a Spiritualist headquarters, at his own personal expense and under his exclusive control.

To the full enjoyment of this central office of inquiry and investigation, all sincere seekers after truth, by advertisement, were cordially welcomed, it being understood that only such free contributions be handed in from time to time as might be prompted in aid of the expenses incurred in keeping up the establishment. Most of the actual expenses of the hall were thus paid. Many important ends were answered at this Harmony Hall headquarters, and our worker would have gladly continued its occupation for a much longer period, but the drain upon his mental and spiritual forces, from a constant attention to his steady influx of visitors, that in about a year, being greatly exhausted in his nervous and general condition, he was obliged to give up his work into the hands of another earnest and faithful worker. Now, for about a year, the strength still at his command was given to aid in the establishing of the New England Spiritualist Association, of which he became the special business agent. But finally, in the spring of 1865, under wise medical and spirit advice, he was compelled to give up, as far as possible, all mental and spiritual effort, and to follow outdoor physical labors. Now, therefore, with a second faithful wife, to whom he had recently been united, he departed again for the West, and upon the outskirts of the City of Rockford, Ill., —where once in his preaching days he had aided in establishing a Unitarian Society—he purchased a few acres of land

and gave himself up to the cares and labors of mundane life, holding on still, however, to some degree of active interest in the spiritual and religious affairs closely around him. At the close of about eight years of this kind of life, he found himself the creative owner of a beautiful cottage and garden home, with abundance of fruits and flowers, hedges and shrubbery, just at the highest point of loveliness. All this he had gained, but at the expense of a further breaking down of his general condition, resulting from an excess of zeal in his gardening. He had become extravagantly devoted to this, and as he could do nothing in moderation, the natural penalty of overwork with his hands now came to him. In July, 1863, this kind of work also had to be given up, so he let his pleasant home to a stranger, and departed on a long contemplated journey as passenger of a Mormon ox-train team, over the plains and mountains of Utah—a ten weeks' solitary trip this. He spent the winter among "the Saints," watching their mode of life, and studying into their professions of faith and practice. During the winter he accumulated the material for a good-sized volume, but was prevented from eventually publishing the same by a forestallment of another writer, who published much the same kind of work, a little in advance of his own intentions. He, however, published some of his material in the public prints, as a series headed "Mormonism" by the Light of Spiritualism," in the *R. P. Journal*; also an article on "Plurality of Wives," in Vol. 7, No. 6 of the *Overland Monthly* (Dec., 1871.)

The time of the Utah sojourn was in the midst of the war, and "the Saints" were full of disloyalty and rebellion; there was a lively time also among the Indians of the plains, but in spite of all our friend made a safe return in the next spring. But no restored health came back with him, so, on rejoining his wife, who had remained at her old Boston home, it was decided to sell the place in Rockford, as something that could be no

longer cared for by its owner, though to someone else it might still be a happy home. Now followed about three years of a crippled, desultory life in Massachusetts, in which there was a partial return to the regular pulpit preaching, though always with a distinct understanding of the independent and conscientious views of the preacher in regard to the heresy of Spiritualism. His closing engagement of this kind was at Marshfield, immediately after the close of which, on the 1st of October, 1867, he departed on a long contemplated voyage to California, connected with which was an enterprise regarded by him as of great moment, the particulars of which it is unnecessary to state in detail, as "Snow's Liberal and Reform Book Store," on Kearny street, San Francisco, will still be remembered by the earlier residents. A few items of information may be added, however, for the benefit of those especially who were not then familiar with the Spiritualism of the Pacific Coast.

Mr. Snow had, while still engaged in his regular ministerial life, manifested great interest in the use and spread of the printed page as the best means of promoting the growth of a liberal and Christian faith. The works of William Ellery Channing were regarded by him as the most important instrument for this kind of work; so, at one point of his experience—having first taken means to have the price of these books reduced to a very low rate—he for a time gave himself almost wholly to the work of their extended circulation, with the result that not far from four thousand volumes were thus widely disseminated through his personal effort. This was doubtless the most important work accomplished by him while in the active Christian ministry. Having now a like deep interest in the spread of the new gospel of Spiritualism, he had long entertained the hope of being able to accomplish a similar good work for this cause, or, if not solely for this, yet for the general advancement of freedom and activity of thought in matters of deep human interest. Hence it was that he established at the central point of the great and growing Pacific slope, a small book store, where all such books could be found—of a radical and reformatory character—as were not usually kept at the regular popular book establishments, including especially and mainly a full supply of the works on Spiritualism.

The enterprise proved to be a success so far as an extended spread of liberal thought was concerned. In a few years connections had been made with independent thinkers in almost all parts of the regions of the Pacific, including the principal islands as far as New Zealand and Australia, and a regular supply of reading matter was thus sent over a vast extent of continent and island territory.

It is believed that no small proportion of the present activity in the cause of Spiritualism in this region may be traced in its origin to the seeds of thought scattered abroad from Snow's Liberal and Reform Book Store. But although a success in this the more important respect, yet in another direction the undertaking was not a success. It is true that, for a few years before the opening of the overland railroad and the largely improved mail and express connections with the coast, and also the equalization of the gold and currency circulation, a comfortable financial support was realized. But later, when conditions thus became less favorable, there followed a decided loss, and that, too, with the exercise of the closest economy, the wife being the sole business assistant. So, after about twelve years of the regular book store method, there was a change into a kind of book agency, carried on mainly through post office and express channels; and after about three years of this kind of effort, the fragment of the business still remaining was passed over into the hands of Albert Morton, and was eventually given up.

In these different methods of action, as also in various public meetings of a Spiritualist and reform character, the faithful and efficient wife was a most important helper; indeed, without her aid, espe-

cially in the close confinement of the book store, the business could not have been long kept up, as the health of the chief owner and manager, though greatly improved by the California climate, did not become adequate to a steady and close confinement to the city.

It was needful for him to spend many hours of the last part of the day in an open-air garden life, which he had secured for himself in Oakland and Berkeley. It was only in this way that he was enabled to enjoy those seasons of quiet, intuitive thought, so necessary to the advancement and usefulness of his higher spiritual capacities, which were from time to time called into activity. The most important work of this kind in which he became engaged at this time was a series of seances of a highly beneficial character, extending through a period of about eight years, of which that devoted and self-sacrificing medium, Anna D. Loucks, was the instrument employed by a band of beneficent spirits in a work of a somewhat peculiar and highly important character. Of these seances, Mrs. Snow was the appointed assistant and scribe, keeping a minute and regular record of all that took place. From this record there was published a small volume, "Visions of the Beyond, by a Seer of To-day." Also, afterwards, in the various Spiritualist papers, enough to fill another volume of about the same size. From these seances the more interested in such matters may have been able to understand, to some extent, the especial and very marked character of work thus engaged in, wholly as a labor of love for unfortunate ones on the border land between the two worlds. Mrs. Loucks gave the best part of her life to this kind of work, often amid much privation, weakness and suffering.

The final return to the East of the subject of our sketch was not accomplished until the spring of 1884.

For the next five years Mr. and Mrs. Snow resided in Boston and Cambridge. In June, 1889, Mrs. Snow suddenly passed to spirit life. The next five years were passed by Mr. Snow in the State of New Jersey; but he finally gravitated to his native State, Vermont, where he has since found a home in the family of an old friend—a fellow laborer in the cause, who is an excellent farmer of the typical New England order. Here he expects to pass the remainder of his earthly days, near the spot where he was born, and where the mortal part can finally be laid away among those of his parents and near relatives. Although now eighty-four years of age, Mr. Snow is in a reasonably vigorous condition both of body and mind. His sight is so well preserved that he does all his writing and reading without glasses, and his hearing is also quite good. The accompanying portrait is from a photograph taken when the subject was an octogenarian, and is a faithful representation of the grand old man whose life has been one unselfish labor of love along all lines of reformatory work and progressive thought.

JULIA STEELMAN-MITCHELL.

JULIA STEELMAN-MITCHELL.

Julia Steelman-Mitchell, whose face adorns this page, is one of our most earnest as well as successful "Workers in the Vineyard." Born of Scotch and Yankee parentage, in the fall of 1848, at Cassadaga—what was then called Lilydale—N. Y. Coming to earth while the "Rochester knockings" were creating so much excitement, had it predicted of her, by her mother, who was one of the pioneer Spiritualists, that "Some day Julia would be a great medium." The honored mother—whose father, a Quaker minister, has been a life-long guide of the subject of this sketch—has lived to know her prophecy is fulfilled. When quite young Mrs. Mitchell gave evidence of being a sensitive, and would often return from a lone trip through the deep forests of Wisconsin—where her parents had emigrated—and tell of the guide who always came to warn her of danger, to lead her where the wild fruit was to be found, or flowers the most profuse. Oft at dusk, she would be found perched in the top of a lofty tree, chatting to the distant clouds, touched with golden sunset—unlike other children, unconcerned that night was near. She was sent, when twelve years of age, to Cincinnati, O., for an education, remaining there until her marriage. During twenty years—while rearing her five children—she exercised her mediumship in a quiet way, making a great many believers in the fact of spirit communion.

After the death of her beloved husband and two beautiful daughters, our medium turned her entire attention to the further development of her powers, and soon found herself on the public rostrum, as inspirational speaker and test medium. In this line her advance has been very rapid.

In 1893 Mrs. Steelman became the wife of Carey Mitchell, a highly respected citizen and druggist of Covington, Kentucky.

As a speaker, Mrs. Mitchell is magnetic and attractive, and presents the Spiritual philosophy in such a clear and concise way that it may be apprehended by the child as well as the student. Her phases of mediumship are clairvoyance, clairaudience, trance and automatic writing. Describing spirits, hearing their names, or reading their messages—written in the air—answering sealed letters, describing faces and giving advice from sealed photographs, giving incidents of past life and prophecies of the future, diagnosing diseases and reading character without sight or contact, are all given before the public under strict test conditions.

Beside her spirit relatives, this medium claims as guides the ancient spirit Pakoh, Prof. Dayton, a phrenologist, Red River, one of the early Indians, and an Italian Count, who at times entrances the speaker and expresses the most beautiful sentiments in poetic verse. Mrs. Mitchell is good authority on mediumship, and teaches it from a scientific standpoint. She is engaged in writing the history of her work as a medium, which promises to be a very interesting volume; and has promised the Spirit World to devote her life to the cause that teaches man that "Truth is mighty and must prevail." Her home - which is a happy one - is in Bellevue, Ky., a beautiful suburb of Cincinnati, O.

JOHN W. REYNOLDS, M. D.

BY C. HALIFAX.

John W. Reynolds, M. D., was born at North Chatham, N. Y., March 8, 1839; the second son of Hiram and Angeline Conkling Reynolds, being of the seventh generation on the paternal and the fourth generation on the maternal side, born on American soil.

After receiving the rudiments of education at a public school, he devoted himself closely to home study, developing a strong fondness for literature.

In 1856 he moved to Albany, N. Y., and was married to Miss Mary M. Mason, of that place in 1858. On the breaking out of the Great Rebellion, he enlisted in the 11th N. Y. Independent Battery of Light Artillery, with which he served his full term of enlistment from 1861 to 1864, being in all the campaigns of the Army of the Potomac, from the second Bulls' Run to the siege of Petersburg. Shortly after the close of the war he removed with his family to Ashville, N. C., where he remained two years assisting in the work of reconstruction of the Government, and serving as an editorial writer on a Republican newspaper published at that place.

In 1869 he moved his family to Chicago, the then new metropolis of the West, where he devoted his time to various kinds of literary work, but chiefly in the line of medical literature.

In 1875 he graduated from the "Hahnemann Medical College of Chicago," and for the succeeding fifteen years was engaged in the practice of medicine and the revision and compilation of medical works.

In 1887, his health failing to the extent of disabling him from practice during the severe winter months, he moved to California, settling in Los Angeles. The soft climate and beautiful surroundings of his new home so charmed him that he resolved to make it his permanent place of residence. His character having a religious tendency, he was in early life a member of the Methodist Episcopal Church, but being by nature a logical thinker, and believing in the doctrine of mental as well as physical evolution he could not remain content with the self-contradictory theories of "Orthodox Religion." Withdrawing from membership with any church, he awaited patiently the dictates of his own conclusions, which quickly led him to embrace the doctrines of Unitarianism. In the Autumn of 1801 he became a convert to Nationalism, clubs of which were at that time organized in Los Angeles for the propagation of social, economic, and political reform, upon principles advocated in Edward Bellamy's book, "Looking Backward." Subsequently, after careful investigation, he became a professed Spiritualist, in which belief he steadfastly remained unchanged till death. The following obituary published in "The Civic Review" of Aug. 24, 1895, (a reform paper in Los Angeles) speaks his true character.

"On the 21st of July, J. W. Reynolds M. D., of this city passed from this life to the spirit world. The deceased was a firm believer and consistent expounder of the philosophy of Modern Spir-

J. W. REYNOLDS, M. D.

itualism, and was also a practical example of true manhood in its fullest meaning, the moral force of which endeared him to all who became acquainted with him. His benevolent disposition was in harmony with the breadth of his spiritual understanding which to those who knew him intimately gave evidence of purest thought. His funeral on the 23d, at Rosedale Cemetery (.L. A.), was attended by a large number of devoted friends and honest admirers, who sincerely sympathize with the bereaved family."

"Fold thou the ice-cold hands
Calm on the pulseless breast,
For the heat of the summer day is o'er,
And sweet is our brother's rest."

Almost as varied as the characteristics of individuals are their conceptions of any subject the relations of which are not immediately self-evident, and defined in such manner as to be unquestionable to the ordinary mind. The author of "The Creed of Spiritualists." J. W. Reynolds—with whom the writer had the happiness of being intimately acquainted—realizing this, and also aware of the fact that an exceedingly small minority of those who are not Spiritualists, have a correct idea of what the philosophy of said belief consists, wrote the concise and self-explanatory definition entitled, "The Creed of Spiritualists," in order that, not only those not allied, but also many who claim allegiance to said philosophy, yet understand little concerning its real mission, may have a clear definition in relation to what is —notwithstanding frequent misapplication of its true purposes—one of the grandest truths extant in the nineteenth century.

THE CREED OF SPIRITUALISTS.

As Spiritualists, obtaining our knowledge from the spirit world, and from the accepted teachings of science, we believe:—

That man is a spirit, associated with matter suited to his earthly use.

That after the process called death, the spirit is still clothed with matter, but of a more ethereal form, corresponding with and related to the conditions of his environment.

That in the spirit world his individuality is retained and the unfoldment of the mental, moral and spiritual faculties is continued indefinitely by processes not unlike the manner pertaining to the development in this world.

That the universe is an aggregate of forces and materiality governed by inherent laws; that these laws are unchangeable, but varied in their direction as they act and react upon each other, or as they are interrupted or modified to a limited extent by the will.

We believe that man is the highest personality in all the universe, and as such will always continue through whatever mutations he may pass or wherein he may be environed.

That the origin of the universe is not fully known through scientific research, nor has it been generally revealed in its entirety by the spirit world (undoubtedly for the purpose of stimulating investigation), so that for all practicable purposes it may be said to be unknown, and without special bearing on moral conduct.

That as matter and spirit are in conjunction in man, so are they found together in their proper relations throughout the universe.

That man is an animal who has progressed from the lowest form of animal matter, up through the period of consciousness, to the estate of the higher moral and spiritual faculties, similarly with the laws of evolution as understood by science.

The spirit world, as we are taught by its inhabitants, is both a locality and a state of existence, governed by natural laws, and is a fitting place for the display of human powers in their fullness; and that it is divided into higher and lower spheres, suitable to the wants and for the better advancement of the spiritual forms of life in their relative degrees of progression.

We believe that after leaving the present material body, man's moral status is the same as before the transition, and that he enters upon a high or low estate according to his attainments in this world; that while the good he does receives compensation in inherent virtue and harmonious relations to man and nature, that also evil, for the same reason, creates a state incompatible with the true order of things, and therefore unhappiness.

That the end and aim of life in the spirit world is progress in mental, moral and spiritual things, and to help the perverse or undeveloped spirits, whether in the spiritual world or in this, along the same lines of progress.

We believe, from knowledge acquired through actual demonstration, that the inhabitants of the spirit world have the power as well as the disposition to return to this world and manifest themselves in various ways, from a simple mental suggestion to a visual appearance, and also to take possession and control of the minds of mortals to an extent within the limits of the organization of the person exercised.

That the whole duty of man in his mortal life consists in taking the first steps in the attainment of all knowledge, and the perfection of his nature in a complete state of harmony with the fully unfolded spiritual state.

That all duties logically growing out of or predicated upon this primal duty should constitute the entire conduct of man, whether related to the moral, mental, or material.

We believe that the existence of man in society naturally implies the construction of certain laws for harmonious intercourse and government; that such rules of conduct have always been formulated by civilized peoples as showing the proper relations between man and man, and have been generally known as moral or ethical laws; that these laws have grown from simple principles to complex applications, according to the growth in civilization or extent of experience, and for the same reason admit of further extension or modification, so long as they do not destroy the effect of basic principles; and that the first or cardinal essential of such laws is based on the well known axiomatic precept of doing unto others as we would that they do unto us.

We are taught by the spirit world that good deeds, springing from a good heart, have a creative force in building future states of abode; and that also, conversely, the sinful create their habitations; that the wicked must undo their evil deeds, here or hereafter, and attain a state of justice before they are prepared to enter upon the path which leads to spiritual progression and happiness.

That as love is stronger than hate, and light more potent than darkness, all who are willing may, as most eventually do, (though in some cases of evildoers, through much suffering), attain a state of complete happiness.

By virtue of similar qualities and co-ordinate conditions, mankind is a brotherhood, and in this life cannot escape the good or evil which contact implies. It is therefore necessary that this brotherhood be made an efficient means of progress and happiness by the more fortunate possessors of the mental, moral and material, helping others upwards toward a proper state of equality.

In accordance with, and growing out of the foregoing principles, we affirm the following precepts:

Every person is bound to recognize the possibilities of moral growth in humanity, whatever the development may be at present, and to interest himself in all means tending towards the the elevation of the race; believing, as we do, that whatever is left undone in this life must be performed in another sphere and at the expense of an unhappy experience.

Education of the mind and body should go hand in hand, as the body and spirit interact upon one another to the extent that an injury to one is an injury to the other. All avoidable ignorance and disease is sinful.

It is a sin to take human life, whether born or unborn. The independent human spirit exists previous to the period of birth.

Unnecessary cruelty to either man or animals is forbidden by the dictates of humanity.

Every individual is an integer of the community, and for this reason should take part in the government under which he or she may reside, by endeavoring to procure laws with exact justice to all, and special favors to none.

Those who are governed should also be governors, and for this reason, men and women of suitable age should enjoy the right of suffrage and all privileges pertaining to citizenship.

Every person is under a moral obligation to prevent poverty by working for the enactment of laws for the just distribution of the products of labor,

and also to help the deserving to the extent of his means.

Idleness is a sin against the individual and the community.

We believe that it is the duty of governments and of society to oppose tyranny of all kinds—by legal means if practicable—if not, then by force; that all incorrigibles should be restrained by lawful means; and that where criminals are deprived of liberty as the enemies of society, or even as the exponents of society, they should at the same time be made the subjects of an education that will tend to turn them from evil courses. Also we believe that where individuals are threatened with loss of life, property or just rights, resistance is proper, but by constituted means in every case where possible.

Marriage without reciprocal love is a sin, entailing evil consequences on the present and future generations, and in both worlds. Marriage of all subjects of hereditary disease, or the apparently incurably vicious, cannot be countenanced by those who would make the world better. Divorce is not to be effected for light causes, or for evils which may be remedied in time; but for just cause is as much a duty as marriage.

Prostitution is an evil that bears equally upon both sexes.

Truth, from whatever source, should be sought by all; and untruthfulness, in either thought, word or deed, should be avoided.

Faith in the triumph of good over evil, and in the possibilities of uplifting the vicious; hope for the future, and courage to do right, and charity to all, are virtues to be prized and practiced.

J. W. REYNOLDS, M. D.,

Los Angeles, California.

PROF. JOSEPH RODES BUCHANAN.

Dr. Joseph Rodes Buchanan is not a man to win the cotemporary fame that he deserves, for he has not been in the pursuit of fame but of truth, and consequently is destined to be more honored after his death than while living.

The development of psychometry is enough to immortalize him, but the discovery of the functions of the brain, and of the complex relations of soul, brain, and body, is a far greater achievement, which will win the gratitude of posterity. He has been an original genius, excelling in whatever he undertook, and has kept steadily in view as the aim of his life the improvement of humanity.

He was born in Frankfort, Ky., December 11, 1814. His father was a physician, editor, and author. At the age of seven to eight he was studying mathematics, history, and science. At the age of thirteen he was studying law. At the age of fifteen, his father being dead, he was earning his living in a printing office. At eighteen he became a teacher, and was introduced by Henry Clay and President Peers, of Transylvania University, to their friends. At twenty he began the study of medicine in the Transylvania College. At twenty-one he became a public lecturer on the brain, and devoted himself to solving the problems of the constitution of man. He devoted seven years to this task, at the end of which time, after traveling through the Southern and Western States, dissecting the brain and examining many thousands of heads and skulls, he discovered and demonstrated the psychic and physiological functions of the brain by direct experiment.

It is difficult in a concise sketch to convey a complete knowledge of Dr. Buchanan to one who has not read his writings, for he differs widely from all other eminent men of the century, and to understand him intellectually one must know something of the new world of knowledge which he has introduced; for it is only by becoming acquainted with the grand results of his labors that we can realize the intellectual power which produces such results, and the profound devotion to duty that has inspired him to turn away from the paths that lead such men to wealth and honor, and devote himself to original discovery and universal reform in all things that relate to the welfare of man.

Perhaps the best description is that given by our most brilliant magazine, the *Arena*, which calls him "a many-sided man of genius," and a "really great man."

His eloquent and forceful poem in the *Arena*, on "Divine Progress," in opposition to a pessimistic bishop, his profound and novel views of education in the same magazine, and in his much-admired "New Education;" his radical discussions of great social questions—his novel researches in electricity,—his ten years' labor as a medical professor in Cincinnati at the head of a successful college for the radical reformation of the medical profession, sustaining principles which are now followed by eight or ten thousand physicians,—his original presentation in 1847 in an essay of great power, of the grand question of the nationalization of land, which he was the first to introduce, and which is now one of the

greatest questions among civilized nations,—and his publication of eight volumes of "Buchanan's Journal of Man," devoted to the great themes of philosophy and science, illustrate the great scope of his labors; and as if to complete the illustration of his versatility, he engaged for three years in managing the politics of Kentucky, as chairman of the Central Committee, when the professional politicians seemed to be paralyzed by the difficulties of the situation, with such success that he might have become Governor of the State if he had not declined the popular call for his candidacy. His ablest associate in this committee, Dr. Norvin Green, afterwards became President of the Western Union Telegraph Co., and his most resolute supporter was Gov. Charles Wicklifle, but the other leaders in politics left him to act alone.

But all these achievements are regarded by Dr. Buchanan and his most enlightened friends as a mere by-play in reference to the great purposes and achievements of his life,—the task which he assumed in 1835, and in which he is still as earnestly engaged as ever, after the lapse of almost sixty years, with unflagging energy and inextinguishable hope and philanthropy.

It seems rather a romantic story that at that early period, before our modern marvels and profoundly agitating questions had come into existence, a young Kentuckian, thrown on his own resources in boyhood, should have assumed the gigantic task of completing the unfinished science of physiology, placing medical science on a new basis, subverting all that the world has called philosophy, revolutionizing religion, education and sociology, and developing the science of the soul until it becomes a royal road to unlimited wisdom.

Such was the sublime undertaking of Dr. Buchanan in his early manhood, which he is now engaged in consummating. It is not to be supposed that he foresaw all this in 1835. He simply determined that he would not submit to

the ignorance of the medical colleges concerning the brain, which left the constitution of man an impenetrable mystery. He spent seven years in the investigation of the brain, and succeeded far beyond his own expectations by the discovery of a new and simple method of exploring all parts of the brain. This was certainly the greatest discovery in the annals of physiology,—the discovery that the function of every portion of the human brain could be ascertained, accurately located and described,—thus revealing all the psychic powers of man, their relation to each other, and their relation to the body and their wonderful interaction of the psychic and physiological faculties—thus solving the great mystery of the age, which, before the investigations of Dr. Buchanan, no one had ever attempted to explore. It was well said by the *Democratic Review*, a leading magazine in its day, that the discoveries (in reference to the brain and spinal cord) "of Gall, Spurzheim and Sir Charles Bell, dwindle into insignificance" in comparison with this great discovery of Dr. Buchanan.

Thus was revealed and established the science of anthropology—the absolute and complete science of man—the revelation of which completes the empire of science, for there remains no other great field to be explored. We may say with Berkeley, "Time's noblest offspring is the last." It has not been urged upon the public by Dr. Buchanan. He has waited for the public to come to him; but it has been indorsed by every committee of investigation, and by the State University of Indiana, and was for ten years the recognized philosophy of the leading medical college of Cincinnati.

Our limited space does not permit us to show the benevolent applications of anthropological science in the reform of education, sociology, and all departments of philosophy. Suffice it to say that it demands and shows how to realize a higher social condition than the world has ever known. The "System of Anthropology" has long been out of print, but will soon be succeeded by a concise volume entitled "The New World of Science."

The two most unique and striking departments of Anthropology are *Sarcognomy*, which relates to the body, showing all its relations to psychic life, and the new method of treating all diseases by magnetic and electric treatment of all parts of the body, and the divine science of the soul or the science of the divinity in man, which he has called *Psychometry*, though that word belongs to the methods by which the divinity in man is revealed.

Sarcognomy has many relations to art which have not been published. Its relation to the treatment of disease is shown in the imperial volume called "Therapeutic Sarcognomy, and this science is practically taught by Dr. Buchanan to his pupils every year in May and June in the College of Therapeutics.

Psychometry or the science of the divinity in man gives us a grand illumination of all the sciences, while enlarging their scope and correcting their errors. Physiology, Psychology, Geology, Materia Medica, Natural History, Political History Biography, Archeology, Paleontology and Astronomy are to become new sciences under the transforming power of Psychometry.

Religion, too, will be thoroughly revolutionized and rationalized by Psychometry, not only by making Spiritualism a positive science, with a solid foundation in physiology and anatomy, but by revealing the history of religions, showing their comparative merit and how well they correspond with the divine laws of life and the conditions of heaven, and how well they were revealed in the life of Jesus. When the discoveries in this direction shall be published it will have a startling effect upon the world.

This is a very concise and incomplete statement of the achievements of Dr. Buchanan, which will interest future centuries. They have been honored by the most advanced thinkers—by such men as Prof. Denton, Robert Dale Owen, Pres. Wylie, Rev. Dr. Strickland, Prof. Gatchell, Prof. Caldwell, Judge Rowan, the eloquent Senator of Kentucky, the poet, Wm. Cullen Bryant, Rev. J. Pierpont, Theodore Parker, Prof. Winterburn, B. O. Flower, and many others in foreign countries as well as in the United States. He presents these discoveries with undiminished ardor, notwithstanding his great age, and, as the *Kansas City Journal* well said, "he is not only the most philosophic of orators, but the most eloquent of philosophers." Editors of medical journals have spoken of him as the "highest living authority on the psychic functions of the brain," and many who are familiar with spiritual sciences regard him as the inspired leader of the great movement from ancient barbarism, superstition and ignorance to the enlightened centuries in which wisdom and justice shall rule the world.

Since the publication of his discoveries, embodying the complete science of man, ("System of Anthropology," "New Education," "Manual of Psychometry," and "Therapeutic Sarcognomy"), which reveal the organization and joint action of the soul, brain and body, and the special localities in which all the psychic and vital powers reside, and the mode of their intercourse with the higher world, as well as the basis of all medical philosophy and therapeutic treatment, with the practicability of receiving that treatment from the spirit world, and the further possibility of bringing to earth all the wisdom and love of higher worlds for human redemption. Dr. Buchanan has been greatly hindered in the prosecution of his great undertaking by exposure to malaria for two years and by contact with patients. This has hindered the preparation of his long promised works.

He is now preparing as actively as possible the full exposition of his discoveries under the title of "The New World of Science," embodying a new physiology and psychology, an exposition of the unknown regions of the brain, and of life in the spirit world, with the applications of the new science to human life.

Previous to this, however, he proposes to demonstrate the power of the spiritual faculties of man in connection with the spiritual world, to reveal not only modern sciences, such as physiology and geology, but the entire history of the human race and of terrestrial evolution.

The most important work now, which humanity has so long needed, is a revelation of the errors of what are called religious systems, and the source of the superstitions which from the very dawn of civilization have obstructed progress and prolonged ancient barbarisms, and still stand in the way of progress.

This work will show that there is but one divine religion for humanity—the religion sanctioned by science and not only endorsed but actively taught from the spirit world—the religion of love and justice.

This religion, when it made its first appearance with great spiritual power at Jerusalem, was speedily crushed by the murder of those who introduced it; and after their death, the records of the life of Jesus and the Apostles were falsified and adulterated with forgeries, to make a superstitious basis for the Papal hierarchy. None have any idea of the simplicity, purity and rationality of the first evolution of spiritual religion. The investigations of Dr. Buchanan enable him to present the real instead of the fictitious lives of Jesus and the Apostles, and to expurgate from the gospels and epistles the mass of forgeries upon which ecclesiasticism has been built—sweeping away the ancient fictions of the trinity, the eucharist, the devil, the hell, the fictitious miracles, and the endorsement of the Old Testament, and vindicating the lofty character of those who attempted but so unsuccessfully to introduce a pure religion, which mankind were unwilling to receive—the religion of the spirit world.

Dr. Buchanan proposes to present this revelation of a lost history with evidences that will compel its acceptance by advanced thinkers, and shake the foundations throughout the world of the ecclesiastical despotism under which mankind have so long suffered.

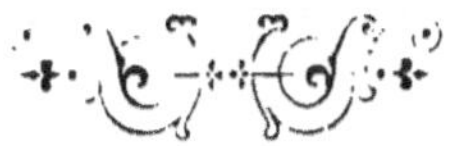

J. M. PEEBLES, A. M., M. D.

BY PROF. E. WHIPPLE.

The subject of this sketch—so well known in this country, England and the Orient, as author, lecturer, traveler and physician—was born down by the foothills of the Green Mountains of Vermont, town of Whitingham, March 23d, 1822, a few minutes past midnight, while the sign of the "Archer" was riding in the eastern horizon. His paternal lineage was Scotch, while on the maternal side he was derived from English ancestors. Peebles is a Scotch name, traceable back to the seventh century. In the eleventh century the name was one of the most distinguished in the north of Europe. Scotch blood and Scotch energy have contributed important chapters to the history of the English-speaking peoples. Dr. R. R. Peebles; of Hempstead, Texas, a relative of the Doctor, and a distinguished surgeon and physician, writing the subject of this sketch, said: "The Peebles clan, Scotch to the core, all run to doctors or preachers." The grim old "Peebles Castle," south of Edinburg, near the ancient-looking town of Peebles, on the Tweed, nearly disappeared about the beginning of the eighteenth century. It has since been repaired. The Encyclopedia Brittanica, vol. viii, page 452, says: "Peebles was, at a very early period, a favorite residence of Scottish kings, who came to hunt in the neighboring Ettrick forest." Walter Scott frequently mentions Peebles in his works, and especially describes the "energy and impetuosity of John Peebles, the Earl." The ancient cross of Peebles now occupies the centre of the court yard of the institution "Queensbury Lodge," made famous by the late Dr. Robert Chambers.

His earliest school days were spent in the "little red school house," a mile away from home, round by the pond. In boyhood he was an inveterate stutterer, of which slight traces may to this day be occasionally detected, especially when he becomes vehement in the denunciation of human oppressions. As a youth he was extremely sensitive, scrupulously conscientious, yet overflowing with exuberance, and sometimes given to mischievous pranks, which often brought him in contact with the ferrule of his teacher in school. He was a student in Oxford academy, Chenango, Co., New York, which has just celebrated its centennial anniversary.

He taught his first school at 17, in Pitcher, N. Y., boarding with an old Baptist deacon, whose prayers and worldly practice he found did not strictly coincide. While teaching this first school, there broke out in his neighborhood an epidemic—very common in those days—called a "Revival." Some of his friends got religion. James was strongly importuned. The meek-eyed girls besieged him, putting their arms round his neck, pleading so eloquently that he was induced to try the receipt; and a fat elder, who laid hands upon him, while the crowd sobbed in magnetic sympathy, completed his discomfiture. He joined his shouts to the general chorus, and it was proclaimed that another soul was saved. It was not long, however, before his sober senses resumed sway, and as the fat, long-faced elder turned out a rascal as well as a hypocrite, he learned here a sad lesson, which has remained fixed in his memory.

J M. PEEBLES M. D.

EARLY MENTAL HABITS AND RE-LIGIOUS BIAS.

Dr. Peebles inherited a lofty ideal of religion and a supreme love of truth. But in his early educational training the tares grew up with the pure grain. His mental pabulum was not always a wholesome diet, and so he early found it necessary to sift his conclusions, often throwing overboard some of the true wheat he had garnered together with the rubbish. In later years he has regained some of this pure grain which he rejected in the preliminary stages of thinking. The early reading of Hume, Paine, Voltaire, Swedenborg, Emerson, Parker and similar spirits, inclined him to a sort of atheistic infidelity, but from this he was rescued by the sober influence of Universalist ministers, and in this denomination he was admitted as a preacher in 1844. He soon found the Universalist creed too circumscribed. It had a fixed creed, and some of its preachers were as bigoted as the Calvanists. He voluntrily left the sect, warmly endorsed by his last parish. Then Spiritualism came, with its phenomena, to further unsettle him.

Theologically inclined, he married a deacon's daughter, Miss M. M. Conkey of Canton, New York, taking Oliver Goldsmith's dictum as his guide: "I chose my wife as she did her wedding gown, for qualities that wou'd wear well."

Interested in both medicine and theology, he decided to go West. At Cleveland, Ohio, he fell in with the Davenports, receiving some very striking and startling phenominal evidence of the truth of Spiritualism. From this time he has been prominently identified with the cause of Spiritualism.

Dr. Peebles has always been characterized for his genial manners, his magnetic presence, his hatred of shams, his broad and universal tolerance of opinion and expression, his sympathies for the downtrodden, his entire freedom from race prejudice, his childlike spontaniety, and for the unstudied eloquence with which he has ever pleaded the cause of the oppressed and downtrodden of every land. Nor does he belie his public teachings, as one observes his daily walk in the private relations of life. The writer has personally known him for over thirty years. He has lived in his home, worked with him, been on terms of closest intimacy with him, and he has invariably found him the same genial, magnanimous, warm-hearted friend that he appears to be before the public. His presence in the private home is a synonym for sunshine. The writer has always found him scrupulously just in all his business dealings. To the spontaneity and joyousness of the little child he adds the nobleness and dignity of true manhood.

HIS CONNECTION WITH SPIRITUALISM.

Dr. Peebles' earliest public work in the cause of Spiritualism was in the Free Church, at Battle Creek, Mich. Here he labored as its esteemed pastor about six years. He likewise gave many evening lectures in "all the country round about." While in Battle Creek he was brought in contact with Mr. E. C. Dunn, who afterwards accompanied him in some of his travels, and became his medium of communication with the spirit world.

A lecturing tour of eighteen months in California—soon after the breaking out of the civil war—gave him change and rest, and he returned to his post in Battle Creek, improved in health and enlarged in his psychic and spiritual gifts. All these many years he has maintained his own right of judgment. He listened to all that was given, weighed what was said in the balance, and rejected what he was not able to rationalize. He had his difficulties, like the rest of us, from disorderly and undeveloped spirits, and going through with that necessary piece of training, he applies sound practical common sense to the solution of this class of phenomena.

Throughout the chief cities in the United States, and in thousands of villages and country districts, he has eloquently presented the cause of Spiritualism from the public rostrum; and among all the English-speaking peoples in the Old World his earnest voice has been heard in behalf of spirit communion and general reform.

Since the year 1866, Dr. Peebles has been engaged in almost incessant medical and literary labor, in addition to his platform work. About this time he became the western editor of the *Banner of Light*. His editorials in that paper were so brilliant and popular that its circulation became greatly extended during the four years Dr. Peebles was connected with it. These editorials, for earnestness, warmth and brilliancy, bore a strong resemblance to Theodore Tilton's leaders in the New York *Independent*, when he was its leading editor. While associate editor of the *Banner*, he compiled the "Spiritual Harp," in conjunction with E. H. Bailey and J. V. Barrett, and later wrote his "Seers of the Ages." Resigning his position on the *Banner of Light* after four years' active service, he became editor of *The Spiritual Universe*, a radical paper, devoted to free thought and Spiritualism. His labor on this fully sustained his brilliant reputation as an editorial writer. Subsequently he became editor-in-chief of *The American Spiritualist*, published in Cleveland, Ohio.

Among the teachings Dr. Peebles has received from the "Summer Land," he sets a very high value upon those which were addressed to him from the arisen Aaron Nite, through the mediumship of Mr. Dunn. He regards him as a venerable and very wise spirit, with whom he was able to converse almost as one friend speaks to another, face to face; who has cleared up for him many knotty problems, and from whom he has received much wise counsel and advice.

His regard for humanity rises far above the local limitations of home and the ties of blood, beyond the limitations of country and race, and becomes universal in its expression :

"All men are my brothers; all women my sisters; all children my children, and I am every mortal's child. I have an interest in every child born into earth life. Its destiny is linked with mine. * * My country is the Universe; my home, the World; my religion, to do good; my rest, wherever a human heart beats in harmony with mine, and my desire is to extend a brother's helping hand to earth's millions, speaking in tones as sweet as angels use; thus kindling in their breasts the fires of inspiration; and aiding them up the steeps of Mount Discipline, whose summit is bathed in the mellowed light of Heaven." * * *

Hundreds of mediums are endeared to him—mediums whom he has strengthened and cheered when their path was strewn with boulders. His earnings have generally been large, but he has seldom laid by anything beyond current expenses. He is generous to a fault. He constantly expends on the unfortunate and in enterprises of public improvement.

Young speakers have been in the habit of following him from place to place, aspiring to emulate him as an example of public teaching.

Cephas B. Lynn, in a private letter to a friend, pays the following tribute :

"His kindness toward young media, more especially those struggling for usefulness on the rostrum, has been a marked feature in his career as a teacher of the Spiritual Philosophy. In fact, he is looked up to with the utmost reverence, and loved most tenderly by scores of young lecturers in our ranks. I could name ten or twelve who acknowledge that Doctor Peebles has been the leading instrumentality in advancing them into active public labors. Blessings upon him for this! I gladly affirm my indebtedness to him in this respect; and my prayer is, that the Spiritualists of the country will see the wisdom of placing funds at his command, so that through him young media suited for the Spiritual ministry may receive that discipline and culture so essential to success."

The Doctor has a strong sense of the ludicrous, while his lectures and correspondence often abound in witticisms. He is naturally controversial, and in discussions is pointed and incisive. It seemingly fattens him to corner a narrow-minded sectarian. He delights in syllogistic reasonings. He hates bigotry. He is fearless in denouncing the wrong. He despises shams; and his irony and invective are anything but comforting to an opponent. And yet, under this flame of scorching sarcasm there is a heart of kindness and tones of the most tolerant tenderness. Nor does he turn a deaf ear to the plaintive murmurs of sad hearts. "Our heart," he wrote, "is brimming with songs to-night. We would sing them to the sad. Take my hand, weary pilgrim; it is a brother's. Off with all masks! Away with reserve! Tell me of life's uneven voyage—its blighted hopes, piercing thorns, trials, losses, defeats, struggles and disappointments. There is profit in confessions that bare soul to soul. Neither of us has secrets. All lives are unrolled scrolls, open to spirit inspection. * * * Could you afford to lose the rusted links, even, from the chain that connects past and present? * * * Has thy life been stained and blemished? None are perfect. The best have their failings. Despair not. The good of earth and the sainted in the heavens delight to aid the aspirational. 'Come unto me,' said Jesus. The angels echo the song, 'Come, Come up higher.' Look not to the past, with painful regrets. In ascending a ladder, the wise never look down to the broken rounds. * * * A mother's prayers pierce dungeon bars. The philanthropist hopes for all, loves all, has faith in all." * * * Again:

"Death, a divine method, is sleep's gentler brother.

"Death, a severing of the physical and spiritual co-partnership, is life's holiest prophecy of future progress.

"Death is the rusted key that unlocks the shining portals of immortality.

"Death is the glittering hyphen-link that conjoins the two worlds of conscious existence and holy communion.

"Death is like opening rosebuds, that, in ever-recurring Junes climb up on garden walls, and, blooming, shed their sweetest fragrance upon the other side." * * *

TRAVELS.

Dr. Peebles has been a great traveler. The wonders of nature and art in all parts of the world have ever possessed a strange fascination for him. From his youth his soul had longed to tread the soil of classic and oriental lands. Hearing of his design, friends in Washington and Philadelphia procured for him a consulate to Trebisond, Asia. He at once sailed for England, whence, by way of France, Italy and Greece, he made his way to Turkey. After a brief season he resigned his official position. Routine cramped him, and the red tape of diplomatic life was as uncongenial as the formalism of ministerial office. Then followed a long tour through Asia Minor and Southern Europe—Naples, Rome, Florence, and so back to London, where, in the early part of 1870, he set to work with his usual promptitude and energy in organizing a series of Sunday meetings at the Cavendish Rooms. In this work he co-operated with Mr. Burns. These services continued several months, chiefly through the vigorous exertions of Mr. Burns. Besides his lectures in London, he penetrated to various parts of England and Scotland, drawing large and interested audiences wherever he went.

Inspired by a true missionary zeal, he was the first to deliver a series of lectures upon Spiritualism in Australia.

The opposition through the press and pulpit was bitter, but the course continuing several months, backed by Dr. Terry, of the *Harbinger of Light*, proved a great success. Upon leaving, a congratulatory address was delivered, and a purse of a hundred guineas presented the doctor.

In this first tour of foreign travel, Dr. Peebles only half completed the circuit of the globe. His intense desire to visit the far Eastern Orient remained undiminished. So towards the end of 1872 he again set out, this time for a voyage round the world, going westward by way of California, the islands of the South Sea, Australia, New Zealand, China, Malacca, India, Arabia, Egypt, the Holy Land, Turkey, and so through Europe to London once again. From this voyage he brought home with him a large collection of relics and specimens, illustrating the habits, manners, religion and general civilization of the various peoples among whom he traveled. But for what he saw and what he did, what he gathered in the way of practical knowledge, and what he suffered, the reader must be referred to his book, "Around the World." Summing up his experiences he writes of this year-and-a-half's pilgrimage:—

"It seems hardly possible that I have seen the black aborigines of Australia, and the tatooed Maoris of New Zealand; that I have witnessed the Hindoos burning their dead, and the Persians praying in their fire-temples; that I have gazed upon the frowning peak of Mount Sinai, and stood upon the summit of Cheops; that I have conversed upon antiquity and religious subjects with Chinamen in Canton, Brahmins in Bengal, Parsees in Bombay, Arabs in Arabia, descendants of Pyramid-builders in Cairo, and learned rabbis in Jerusalem; that I have seen Greece in her shattered splendor, Albania with its castled crags, the Cyclades with their mantling traditions, and the Alps impearled and capped in crystal. * * * It is difficult to realize that I have been in Bethlehem, walked in the garden of Gethsemane, stood upon Mount Olives, bathed in the Jordan, breathed the air that fanned the face of Jesus, when weary from travel under the burning skies of Palestine, looked upon the same hills and valleys clothed in Syrian spring-time with imperial lilies, and had the same images daguerreotyped on my brain that impressed the sensitive soul of the 'Man of Sorrows'— the Teacher sent from God."

Dr. Peebles' second voyage round the world was undertaken in the spring of 1877. In this voyage he also sailed westward, visiting the same countries as on his previous travels, but in addition spending considerable time in South Africa, Napaul and Ceylon. In South Africa he gave considerable attention to the ostrich farms, and was the first to suggest the feasibility of this branch of industry in Southern California.

During his second tour round the world, he devoted a large portion of his time to a study of psychological and occult phenomena in the Orient, as also the mental and physical pathology manifest in the peoples of the far East—chronic diseases in China, the prevailing fevers in India and Ceylon, leprosy in Madras, Bangalore and Kilpauk, and he further visited the more prominent hospitals in many Oriental countries.

In addition to the large volume entitled "Around the World," the Doctor has in MS. the rich results of his more recent voyage, and purposes to complete the data for a full volume by a third voyage round the world at no distant day.

Upon his return to Boston from his last voyage, the editors of the *Banner of Light* gave him a magnificent reception at one of the leading hotels, on which occasion the present able editor of the *Banner*—John W. Day—ren dered a beautiful original poem in honor of Mr. Peebles' return from his long travels.

PROFESSIONAL AND OFFICIAL LIFE.

It seems an unusual share of public honors have been showered upon the Doctor, but he has richly earned them all. In 1868 he accompanied and participated in the deliberations of the "Northwest Congressional Indian Peace Commission," appointed by Congress, and constituted of Gens. Harney, Sherman, Sheridan, Sanborn and Col. Tappan.

In 1881 he was appointed "Representative abroad" by the National Arbitration League of the United States of America, to meet the "International Peace Congress of Europe," in the interests of arbitration as against war. He continues to work with tongue and pen against war; against the infliction of capital punishment; against vaccination; against class medical legislation; against intemperance, and in favor of woman suffrage and her full equality with man.

He is a fellow of the Academy of Science, New Orleans, La. A fellow of the Anthropological Society, London. An honorary member and fellow of the Psychological Association, London. A fellow of the Academy of Arts and Sciences, Naples, Italy. A fellow of the American Akademe, Jacksonville, Ill. A member of the International Climatological Association. A member of the National Hygiene and Health Association. A member of the American Institute of Christian Philosophy. A member of the Victoria Institute and Philosophical Society of Great Britain.

These honors and fellowships were conferred upon the Doctor without his asking, and hence are the more highly appreciated. To this day he does not know who in London presented his name to the Victoria Institute for election, the members of which are said to constitute the most learned body of men in the world.

He has also become distinguished in his more recent medical practice, and lectures on Physiology and Hygiene before the medical colleges of Cincinnati and Los Angeles. He commenced the reading and study of medicine with Dr. O. Martin, one of the most distinguished physicians and surgeons in the New England States. His early medical education was "regular" or "allopathic." After attending the prescribed course of medical lectures, he graduated from the Philadelphia (Pa.) University of Medicine and Surgery, and registered at once in Philadelphia as a practicing physician. He also received a certificate of practice from the University Hospital of Philadelphia, and a number of years later a diploma from the Philadelphia Polyclinic, college for graduates only. He holds several honorary diplomas and is a member of State and national medical associations.

In October, 1892, the Doctor purchased the fine sanitarium at the West End in San Antonia, Texas. Here he built up a fine medical practice, and won some important legal battles over the local physicians, who were jealous of his success and rapidly growing influence in that section. On the night of Feb. 26th, 1894, while the Doctor was absent, this fine sanitarium was totally destroyed by fire, together with the large library which he had been collecting all his life. The property was insured for about one-third its real value.

PRESENT LOCATION AND LABORS.

With the remnant recovered from this property in San Antonio, the Doctor came to the genial climate and beautiful location of San Diego, in Southern California, arriving in March, 1894. The following August he purchased a fine residence on "Sherman Heights," near the famous "Montezuma Villa," once occupied by Jesse Shepperd. He bought during the extreme reaction from the "boom" of about five years ago, when real estate was very low. This property he has enlarged and improved, making of it a beautiful home and location for his rapidly increasing medical practice—

some of his cures, both psychic and medical seeming almost miraculous. Here prosperity smiles upon him once more. In a few weeks his good wife will join him from the East, and become installed as the matron of the institution.

The Doctor is an indefatigaple worker. Besides attending to his 167 patients (which he now has on hand), he edits the *Temple of Health*, contributes articles to various papers and medical magazines, gives an occasional discourse on Spiritualism, and performs his duties as president of the Los Angeles College of Science. He has published nine volumes of book matter, besides various pamphlets, and has others in preparation.

PERSONAL HABITS AND MODES OF LIT-

ERARY WORK.

Dr. Peebles believes what he preaches, and carries it out in the practice of his daily life. He is strictly temperate in all his personal habits, eating no animal food nor partaking of stimulants of any kind, not even tea or coffee. But his table is amply provided with the various cereals, nuts, vegetables, fruit, honey, etc. He has a passionate fondness for trees, shrubs and flowers, of which his premises is well stocked, mostly planted with his own hands; and one may observe him any morning before the sun is up, out watering and caring for these. His magnetic presence and perennial cheerfulness diffuses joy and sunshine throughout the whole house. In dress he is always neat and exact, but not dudish or foppish. He abhors the fashions. His habits are all clean and wholesome. His conversation, though often racy, pungent and abounding in witticisms, is chaste and refined. The writer—intimate with him for more than thirty years—never heard a coarse or vulgar expression fall from his lips. He is the best illustration I know of "How to grow old gracefully." At seventy-five, the lines in his face are soft and full of youthful expression. His frame is filled out, so that he is now both portly and tall. He is still projecting labors which it would seem demands a

lifetime to carry out. His mental productiveness is something wonderful. It seems like a perennial fountain, both in its amplitude and versatility,--a fountain which as yet gives no sign of diminishing its volume. His mental concepts display the various stages of inception, germination and evolution, but the processes are extremely rapid. His library may be compared to a field in preparation for a new crop, full of potential possibilities, but the crop that is to be does not present a very attractive appearance to the eye, —books, papers, scraps and unfinished MSS. lying all about. For the most part he stands at his desk while writing, but much of his literary matter is dictated to an amanuensis,—dictated rapidly while he alternately walks the floor and sits in a rocking chair. While thus engaged witticisms frequently burst forth as a by-play which serve to oil the "hinges of the mind" and keep the mental machinery in easy motion.

It was intended to speak of the doctor's attitude of tolerance towards, and qualified acceptance of the various historical religions—especially Buddhism—, and of his firm belief in the doctrines of pre-existence and tendency towards a belief in reincarnation, but since these topics are quite fully discussed in his various works, and as the limits of this article are already exceeded, no further presentation of them will be here attempted.

Our brother has indeed "fought the good fight." His years have been filled with useful labors. The golden harvest sheaves lie all about him. He has assuaged many tears of sorrow, and extended helping hands to young, aspiring souls from the summit he occupies. He never knowingly perpetrated a wrong against his fellows. His heaven consists in doing good. He believes his present duties pertain to this world, and he means to stay here until he shall be witness to some of the great social and religious changes for the better, which he believes are impending and very near. His inmost being is ever afire with the gospel—the living gospel of Spiritualism in its highest, holiest aspects. His trust in Providence is absolutely unswerving. And now, though far past seventy, and nearing life's setting sun, there is not a fragment of doubt in his mind but that the incompleteness of this rudimentary life will, in some approaching evening time, open upward into the sunlight of another and higher life of growth and ultimate completeness—one God, one law, one brotherhood, and one divine destiny for all humanity.

MRS. GEORGE ROBERTS.

Mrs. Roberts was born in Hartwick, Otstego Co., N. Y. She was a medium from her earliest recollection. Her mother was a medium of great power and her children a family of sensitives. Mrs. Roberts was married in 1851, and with her husband, George Roberts, removed to California in 1861. After their arrival in California Mrs. Roberts' mediumship became more pronounced. Spirits walked and talked with her daily and manifested through her in twelve different phases. The most remarkable of these was levitation. The first she experienced of this phase she found herself being carried through the air and a dog was barking at her. The next she knew she was extended on the hearth-rug before a bright fire in a friend's house; her consciousness returned till she did the spirits' bidding. They were then told to take the medium home; and it required careful nursing to restore her, so great had been the power over the physical. At another time she was carried across a stream and sat upright against a fence after a severe accident which caused dislocation of the shoulder and a broken arm. The broken bones were set with materialized hands. She was once sent many miles, not knowing what her mission would be, and arrived at the friend's house just in time to save his life from poison. In many ways she has been used to save life. She hears spirit voices, sees faces, and obeys their requests. She is at the present time working under the guidance and instructions of a band of wise and powerful spirits and will carry out their designs for the upliftment of humanity with all the ardor and strength of her deeply spiritual nature.

THE TEMPLE OF WISDOM.

In her beautiful and spacious home are apartments consisting of elegant parlors, set apart and consecrated to the work of divine, loving and advanced spirits. This "Temple of Purity and Wisdom" was formally opened and dedicated four years ago. On that occasion Mrs. Roberts explained to the assembled guests that the nature and objects of the Temple work was to elevate the spiritual condition of the people, to render them pure and perfect in mind; holding that one who succeeded in attaining this high degree of spiritual unfoldment would necessarily obtain perfect control over the physical organism, as the body was but the creation of the mind. If the mind was pure and elevated by the aid of spiritual perfection, the body in its action would conform to the same. The attainment of this spiritual perfection was the highest accomplishment, and should be the chief aim of life. The services attendant upon the ceremony of dedication were beautiful and impressive. The Temple and its belongings were draped in snowy white, as was also arrayed Mrs. Roberts and those who attended her.

Mrs. Roberts is the "human magnet" of the Temple, and as she says, holds converse personally with the angels, who guide her in all things pertaining to the Temple, and by their direction it was made.

MRS. GEORGE ROBERTS.

At first the room was all in white. White cashmere and lace were used for portieres, piano cover, the upholstering of chairs and sofas, the altar covers, and for the robes of those who entered the room. Nothing but white must be worn by those who hoped to be able to hold communion with the angels, even the shoes were of the same pure white. But later there has been a little transformation, and now some colors are used in the Temple. The colors introduced are: Gold, which signifies wisdom; blue, love; red, strength; royal purple, power; and green, which is nature's foundation. But the robes of all those who enter still remain pure white.

Many people have heard of the Temple, and many visit it every day, some of them coming from long distances. Some who visit it are drawn by idle curiosity, but very many more to hear the spiritual teachings which are given as freely as when Christ taught on earth. Universal love and universal brotherhood are the foundation stones of the Temple, and there is no defined membership. Everyone who wishes to come is received as a member so long as he wishes to remain, but without a white robe he may not sit in the inner Temple. Everything is free except the robe—that each one must furnish for himself. To sit in the outer temple one needs no white robe.

The principles taught are very beautiful and are aimed entirely for the uplifting of mankind. The teachings are all of universal love, love from the Father of all, and love and charity for humanity in all its phases. Mrs. Roberts believes that all things, even the most humble insects and the flowers, have within them the spark of divine life; she will take the life of nothing, and no flower is ever plucked by her before it has reached its maturity. There is a free circulating library of psychic and occult works that those who come are welcome to. On week days Mrs. Roberts is always in the outer Temple from 10 A. M. to 4 P. M., where she will receive and instruct all who may wish to learn and profit by the teachings of the angels.

As to this lady's womanly virtues there can be no question. Her creed is not as shadowy as the baseless fabric of a vision, and it delineates in its sweetness that highest of all types, a perfect woman. The belief that the ideal life can only be attained through the subjection of the body to the mind—the gross material to the intellectual, is beyond cavil true; but there must be so tireless a course of moral and intellectual evolution ere that goal is attained that only the most sanguine can contemplate it with hope.

The principles inculcated by Mrs. Roberts—the comfort she extends to those whose ambition cannot bear to be bounded by the narrow confines of this world—her clear elucidation of tangled questions where reason's light in the hands of gentleness dissipates the noxious mists of ignorant fear, appeals to the rationalist and allays the unreasoning ardor of the fanatic. The night is far spent and the day is at hand when they who do all in their power to inaugurate an era of love and banish fear from the hearts of humanity, deserve the grateful thanks and cordial co-operation of good men and women everywhere.

Besides the value of the practical teachings of the Temple, the benefits to San Jose arising from the charitable work of Mrs. Roberts is beyond estimation. Her life is devoted to her work, and with the increase of the circle of her friends it becomes more arduous. May Mrs. Roberts' hopes be realized and her zeal rewarded is the earnest prayer of many grateful hearts who have been recipients of her benefactions.

ERNEST S. GREEN.

The subject of this sketch was born near the wooded shores of Lake Waseca, Minnesota in 1866, and at the age of seven years removed with his parents to the vast and billowy plains of Western Kansas, where he spent his winters in school and his summers herding his father's flocks.

Away, away from the dwellings of men,
By the antelope's haunt, by the buffalo's
    glen—
Oh! then there was freedom, and joy and
    pride,
Afar in the desert alone to ride.
There was rapture to vault on the champ-
    ing steed,
And to bound away with the eagle's speed,
With the death-fraught firelock in his hand,
The only law in the desert land.

It was there he read "books in the running brooks," sermons in the rocks," and poems written upon the skies; saw visions of celestial cities and glories untold by mortal pen or tongue; heard voices of the prehistoric past teaching him of the mysteries that were, and were yet to be, and in this manner was developed while yet a boy to such a degree that he was able to confound collegiate "professors" with his philosophy.

At fourteen years of age he began to learn the printer's trade, which occupation, coupled with journalism, he has followed most of the time since, though some three years were spent as a musician, traveling with a band; also several tours of exploration were made among the mountains of New Mexico and Colorado, three days and nights having been spent with two companions in exploring a cave, a graphic description of which, entitled "Amid the Wonders of a Midnight World," he wrote for the *Great Divide*, a Denver magazine.

Coming to San Diego in 1891, he continued the study of Spanish, which he he had already begun, and, aided by his Spanish teacher, translated and compiled a volume of nearly 400 pages of "Mexican and South American Poems" which was published, and although highly endorsed by the literary press of both America and England, the book fell flat upon the market, causing a severe loss to the authors.

Mr. Green has also written about fifty original poems, many of which were published in the literary journals of the country, and afterwards published collectively in a pamphlet called "Poems of the Past, Present and Future." The author, however, has now a very poor opinion of these poems since coming out in the full sun-burst of spiritual truth and knowledge, which came to him since their production, many of them being influenced by the orthodox teachings of his youth.

In 1892 he married Miss Emma Jenkins, a native daughter of California, who now assists him in the publication of the *Herald of Light*.

Since the author of this book has asked me to add my "testimony," as the Methodists would say, I will do so in part, and with as much brevity as possible, in order that others may have an opportunity to give the other reasons in their varied experiences.

Although my parents were Methodists and I was raised among orthodox people,

ERNEST S. GREEN.

and first learned how to read in the Bible, yet from my earliest memory a voice spoke in my ear telling me that the first eleven chapters of the book of Genesis and many other things in the Bible were myths. I could not understand how an omnipotent and omnipresent God had to call for Adam and Eve to come forth before he could find them; neither could I understand why he had to "go down" to Sodom and Gomorrah to see if it was "altogether according to the cry of it, which is come unto me; and if not I will know." Neither could I understand why it should have scores of contradictions like the following:

*For I have seen God face to face.—Gen., xxxii: 30.

No man hath seen God at any time.—John i: 18.

And they saw the God of Israel.—Ex. xxiv: 19.

Whom no man hath seen nor can see.—I. Tim., vi: 15.

God is not a man * * * that he should repent.—Num. xxiii: 19.

And God repented of the evil he had said.—Jonah iii: 10.

Those that seek me early shall find me.—Prov. viii, 17.

They shall seek me early, but shall not find me.—Prov. i: 28.

The Lord is very pitiful and of tender mercy.—James v: 11.

I will not pity nor spare, nor have mercy, but destroy them.—Jer. xiii: 14.

He doth not afflict willingly.—Lam. iii: 33.

Spare them not, but slay both man and woman, infant and suckling.—I. Samuel xv: 3.

Thou shalt offer every day a bullock for a sin offering.--Ex. xxix: 36.

I delight not in the blood of bullocks.—Is. i: 11.

God cannot be tempted with evil, neither tempteth he any man.—James i: 13.

And it came to pass after these things that God did tempt Abraham.—Gen. xxii: 1.

*The above table was compiled by Dr. Peebles, and is copied from his answer to Dr. Kipp's Five Sermons against Spiritualism.

Neither could I believe that part of the race was to be eternally damned and part saved. In short, I found, later, that I had always been a Spiritualist but did not know it.

After these inconsistencies had been discovered, I read up on all the religions of the world, and of the numerous Messiahs of all ages, and found that Confucius had uttered the golden rule 600 years before Jesus spoke it, and that there was scarcely anything in our Bible that could not be found in far more ancient ones, and in the *Mahabarata*, the *Veddas*, and other oriental bibles, I found still more wisdom than our Bible contained.

Although I had been reading up on occultism all my life, and had read of many things that were not accounted for by the numerous books I had read which purported to be "complete exposes" of mediums, I shunned Spiritualism to the last, having never heard anything but ill reports of them as a class, especially mediums.

However, a slate-writing medium visited the city and caused considerable excitement, but of course I thought it would be no trouble for me to tell him how he did his tricks, and paid no attention to him, until one evening while sitting quietly at the table with my wife, engaged in reading the papers, a loud rap, as of a hammer, was heard on the table between us. There could be no accounting for this, as we lived in a cottage, and there was no chance for any one to get under the floor to strike the blow; besides we were in the middle of the floor, and the blow was distinctly located by both of us as on the table. After that, though we locked our doors from the inside and left the keys in them, we would find them unlocked. The windows would be unlatched in the same manner.

At last I went to the medium with my questions written in a sealed envelope. This I handed to him and watched him pass it into the lamp and burn it at once, giving him no chance for sleight-of-hand. I then took the slates, washed them thoroughly and held them firmly between my hands, upon my lap. The medium placed his fingers upon one corner of the slate, and immediately his features became rigid and the sound of rapid writing was heard between the slates, passing to and fro and working rapidly down to the bottom in about one minute—a piece of pencil about the size of a grain of wheat had been placed between the slates.

This was all done in broad daylight, and I watched the medium's fingers to see that he did not make the scratching. Three loud raps from within announced that the slates were ready to open. When I opened them I found one of them written full in very small letters. The writing resembled the peculiar style of the person to whom the questions were addressed. They were all satisfactorily answered and things referred to that no one knew this side of the Rocky mountains but myself, and none but my own people on the other side had any knowledge of.

Here was more proof of immortality than I had ever seen before. Since that time I have had abundant demonstrations in my own family that would convince any person in his right mind.

In that slate written message I was advised to start the *Herald of Light*, which I did a few months later.

In my subsequent investigations I found that many of the best, most charitable, upright and honest people I ever knew were Spiritualists, and mediums at that. I also found that many of the greatest living scientists, philosophers and statesmen living in the world to-day are Spiritualists, and that there is no other class of people on the face of the earth misrepresented and lied about so much as are our people. This may be accounted for by the fact that we are not hypocrites, and each one lets his neighbor know just what he is, while the rest of the world live dual lives, parading one before the public, and using the other in business transactions.

I also found that Spiritualism contained the key to all religions and to all science and wisdom.

The following poem was given to me in semi-trance:

DEATH OF MATERIALISM.

Earth is dying! souls awaking!
  Light is coming on apace!
Darkness flees before the morning
  Which now dawns upon the race.

Up, ye creed-bound sleeping mortals,
  For the sun-burst is at hand!
Rise to see its glory beaming
  In your golden Summerland!

Error struggles in his death throes!
  See the mist rise from his tomb!
O'er the hills a light celestial
  Breaks the long, long night of gloom!

Rise from slumber! Tell the nations
  That dark Error's reign is 'o'er!
That the light of truth eternal
  Rules on earth forevermore!

ERNEST S. GREEN.

SARAH B. WHITEHEAD.

MRS. S. B. WHITEHEAD.

The task of writing a biographical sketch is at best a difficult one. Only a long and intimate acquaintanceship, with free access to the domestic circle of the subject, will fit one for the labor. By this means you are made somewhat independent of the caprice of the subject. If he be bursting with self-conceit and be requested to furnish a few notes of his life, he will pluck a handful of needles from the cushion of his experience, and quickly manufacture them into needle guns. He will take a few mole hills from the narrow field of his labor, and placing them in a circle, cause them to stalk before you in literary garb as an interminable chain of lofty mountains of human achievement.

Should he chance to be of a modest, retiring disposition, he will suppress every event in his life of which you are unaware and belittle those with which you are familiar.

He will insist upon your viewing each good act of his life upon which you chance to stumble, through the inverted lens of your own mental telescope, that they may all be lost in the fields of beautiful nothingness.

Fortunately for me, the subject of this sketch has been well known to the writer for many years, and what is here given is from a personal knowledge, rather than from the ten or twelve lines of notes furnished for this article, coupled with the modest request that we "write nothing that will sound egotistical."

Mrs. Whitehead was born a medium and a Spiritualist in the historic town of Salem, Massachusetts. She early removed to Boston where she received many advantages of intellectual culture furnished by that progressive city—the embryotic "hub."

From her parents she imbibed a liberal spirit, they being Universalists, but she never was inclined to join any church.

In the year 1854 she learned that one of her girl friends could "get the raps." She and her sister, the late Mrs. Hutchings, determined to sit and see what would be the result. Almost from the first they were both controlled to write, and her sister soon after became clairaudient and clairvoyant. Her conversion, through her own mediumship, was complete; and though a third of a century has rolled away on the rapid wheels of time, still she has never had cause to regret this, the greatest event of her life—her spiritual birth from darkness into light.

Four years of quiet spiritual growth sped on, when the hour arrived that was calculated to show the great value of Spiritualism to her. Dear reader, have you ever watched nature's beautiful law of unfoldment as seen in the budding life of a little child? And have you also realized that the dear little darling was more to you than all the world beside? And when your mind was filled with plans for its future welfare, have you seen it turn away from all that it had loved and cherished, and as if seeking protection from the chilling winds of earth in the strong embrace of your willing arms, breathe out its last breath on your warm, loving heart? If so, then you have passed through the greatest and sweetest experience of soul refinement vouchsafed to humanity. This blessed *trial* came to the lot of Mrs. Whitehead. A darling child, a sweet little daughter of eight summers, was transferred from the breast of her loving mother to the care of the dear angel friends above.

It was then that the never failing consolation, the sweet solace of Spiritualism came to her relief. In it she found that abiding comfort born of absolute knowledge, that is not elsewhere furnished to sorrowing hearts.

In the following summer, 1859, she sought a new home and new associations in San Francisco. Her great love for children, intensified by the transition of her beautiful daughter, led her to engage in Sunday-school work. There not being any spiritual society fostering lyceum work at this time, she went into that of the Unitarian society, where she instructed her class in liberal thought, and dropped as many seeds of spirituality in their young minds as circumstances would admit. This work was continued by our sister for three or four years (to the great and lasting benefit of the church), until the arrival on the Coast of Mrs. Emma Hardinge. Her labors were a great encouragement to the Spiritualists, for shortly after a movement was made by Mrs. Whitehead and other noble souls, for the organization of the First Children's Progressive Lyceum of San Francisco.

The members of the lyceum paid a well deserved compliment to the devotion of Mrs. Whitehead and her well-known ability by electing her Guardian of Groups—a position which she continued to hold for several years with honor to herself and satisfaction to all. From that time down to the present she has been a persistent, faithful worker in the cause of spiritual progress. Being of a retiring disposition, she has never sought leadership, but has been content to labor on unobtrusively, though efficiently, in humble positions. Ever and anon she has been summoned to do battle in the front rank, at which times, we are pleased to say, she has never shown "the white feather." The Society of Progressive Spiritualists is under deep obligation to her for her wise, patient services as a director from the first day of its organization, for a period of ten years, during the greater portion of which time she filled the position either of Secretary or Librarian. She was ever devoted, faithful, honest and conscientious in the discharge of her duties and in her efforts for the prosperity and usefulness of the society. Though sometimes misunderstood and criticised by enemies, still she never swerved from the path of duty and right. To her wisdom and spiritual intuitions, that society owes largely its present prosperity, and perhaps even its existence. She is thoroughly in harmony with the progressive, practical work of this sterling, spiritual society.

She was elected as a member of the Board of Directors of the California Spiritualists' State Camp-Meeting Association, and did most efficient work there in the capacity of secretary, for three years.

On all the great questions of the day, affecting the weal or woe of humanity, she is certainly a "solid citizen," ever espousing the cause of the weak against the encroachments of the strong. Having shown that she has a mind of her own, has oft exposed her to the somewhat common but still terrible charge of being "*strong-minded.*" Though this dreadful accusation probably had the effect of excluding her from the society of the *weak-minded*, still it was a ready passport to the ranks of the woman suffragist, where she was known as a persistent worker and efficient adviser. She has lived to see the fruit of her labor in this direction.

We cannot close this article better than by making reference to the kind, patient, loving demeanor that ever characterized the gentle, faithful ministrations of Mrs. Whitehead for her aged mother. No duty to her was ever viewed in the light of labor. Nothing was left undone that willing hands could find to do. Though her mother was oppressed with the weight of over four score years, and for several years confined much of the time to her bed, still Mrs. Whitehead was her only attendant until the end came. We can only wish that when the winter of age may have whitened her brow, that that she may be fortunate in the reward of a care as tender and heartfelt from some earthly loved one, who will take a pure delight in smoothing her pathway to the beautiful home she is now building in the world of joy, when her angel friends shall have summoned her to "come up higher."

WILLIAM EMMETTE COLEMAN.

WILLIAM EMMETTE COLEMAN.

William Emmette Coleman was born June 19, 1843. at Shadwell, Albemarle county, Virginia. In 1849 his family moved to Charlottesville, the seat of the State University. Here he first attended school, and astonished all by his remarkable proficiency in study,—his teacher, in 1850, when he was only seven years old, often placing him in his seat, as preceptor, to hear the other scholars. Mr. Coleman was born with an insatiable love of knowledge, which still obtains as strongly as ever. In Richmond, Va., to which his mother moved in 1851, the same proficiency attended him. In 1854, at eleven, he left school (his teacher saying that he could teach him no more), to become assistant librarian in the Richmond Public Library, which position he retained till the library was dispersed several years after. In 1855 he prepared an analytical catalogue of the library. In 1859 came the turning point of his life,—his conversion from Orthodoxy to radical Spiritualism, at the same time renouncing his pro-slavery views for abolitionism. Since then he has been a zealous member of the Republican party, probably the first one in the city of Richmond. From that time to this he has been a supporter of every reform looking to the advancement of the human race: as woman's rights, labor, and prison reforms; dress, dietetic, and medical reforms; peace and temperance reforms; rights of children, marriage and divorce reforms; co-operative and other sociologic reforms; state secularization, abolition of capital and retaliatory punishments, etc. His thorough acceptance of the Spiritual philosophy directed his mind to scientific and philosophic matters, and also placed him on his feet morally. Mr. Coleman egards spiritualism as his saviour and inspiring guide, mentally and morally, and that all that he has since become and done is due to the revolution in his mental nature brought about by his spiritualism.

In 1863 Mr. Coleman made his debut as an actor in Richmond, and he soon became assistant stage manager; and in 1864 he was stage manager at the Wilmington (North Carolina) Opera House. He continued on the stage till 1867, during which period he was the dramatic correspondent of the New York *Clipper* and the *Mercury*. He also dramatized several works for the stage, including a successful version of "East Lynne." In 1867 he was President of the Board of Registration in Bland county, Virginia, during the reconstruction of that State, under Federal laws. From 1867 to 1870, he was clerk at the military headquarters in Richmond, Va., and when the department was abolished in 1870 he was the chief clerk in the adjutant-general's office He was a delegate to three successive state conventions of the Republican party in Virginia, in 1868-70, and in 1869 he was appointed a member of the Republican State Central Committee of Virginia In 1870 he was a prominent member of the first "Woman's Rights" convention held in Virginia, and by it he was chosen vice-president of the "Virginia State Woman's Rights Association." From 1870 to 1874 he was on the stage again, his last engagement being as stage manager in Albany, N. Y. His principal dramatic *role* was "old men;" and among his most successful impersonations were *Polonius* in " *Hamlet*," *Lord Small* in "King of the Commons," *M. Belin* in "Miss Multon," and *Don Jose* in " Don Cæsar de Bazan."

Since 1874 he has been in the Quartermaster's Department, United States Army, being made chief clerk in the chief quartermasters' office in San Francisco in 1883, in which office he is still employed. In 1875, at a pronouncing-bee in Philadelphia, he won the first prize of $50, and he also took prizes at several spelling bees. While in Philadelphia he was an active participant in the theological debates each Sunday in Jayne Hall, in which he particularly defended Spiritualism and the future life from the attacks of Materialists, and also Freethought and Rationalism from the assaults of the orthodox. Several of his anti-theological articles, on the Bible God, Jesus Christ, the Sabbath, etc., were published in the "Freethinker Tracts" from 1875 to 1879. He attended the Centennial Congress of Liberals, at Philadelphia, in 1876, thus being a charter member of the National Liberal League. He was an active member of the Executive Committee of the Liberal League in Kansas, in which state he resided from 1875 to '79, and was Secretary of the Kansas State Liberal and Spiritual Camp meeting in 1879. He is opposed to the total repeal of the laws against the transmission of obscene literature through the mails, but is in favor of such modifications as will protect the rights of all from arbitrary arrest and imprisonment.

Through Spiritualism, Mr. Coleman was a believer in evolution before he ever heard of Darwin; and a conflict between Spiritualism and Darwinism being predicated in 1876, he published an extended reply thereto, which ran through the Chicago *Religio-Philosophical Journal* for several months, and "elicited encomiums from many able thinkers." In 1878 Mr. Coleman delivered a series of lectures on "Darwinism and the Evolution of Man," before the Leavenworth (Kansas), Academy of Science, which were classed by the local press as among "the ablest and most interesting" ever delivered at the Academy. Attempts were made at the Academy, by the ultra-Christian conservatives, to silence Mr. Coleman's radi-

cal utterances, but he fought them "tooth and nail," and refused to be put down. In 1879 he lectured at the Academy twice on "Spectrum Analysis;" and also on the "Parallelism between Biologic and Philologic Evolution." At his departure from Leavenworth, the Academy passed resolutions of regret, and recommended him "to scientific and literary persons everywhere, as an able thinker, a ripe scholar, and an earnest, studious, and industrious worker." In 1877 Mr. Coleman published a number of Freethought and scientific articles in the Toronto, Canada, *Freethought Journal*, and in 1878 he conducted the "Review of Current Literature" in the *Spiritual Offering*, of St. Louis. Since 1875 he has contributed hundreds of articles to the Spiritual and Freethought journals in America and England, mostly, of late years, to the *Religio-Philosophical Journal* and the *Carrier Dove*. In 1878–9 he compiled and published two editions of an "Index of Orders of the War Department Affecting the Quartermaster's Department." He has, since 1880, lectured many times in San Francisco on Spiritual and theological subjects. For over a dozen years past he has made a specialty of Orientalism, especially of Hinduism, Buddhism, and Sanskrit literature; and he is a member of the principal Oriental societies in America and England. He also devotes special research to comparative philology and comparative mythology. He has a library of 8.000 volumes, including one thousand on Orientalism, and two thousand seven hundred on the religions of the world. The best works in all branches of knowledge form the rest of the library, which has been declared by scientists one of the finest and best-selected private libraries, for working purposes, in the country. Mr. Coleman's numerous essays on "Krishna and Christ," and on other Oriental, philological, archæological, and theological subjects, have been warmly commended for their accuracy, thoroughness, and ability, by the leading Sanskritists and comparative theologians of the world, including Professors W

D. Whitney (Yale), C. R. Lanman (Harvard), A. H. Sayce, Max Mueller, and Monier-Williams (Oxford), Abraham Kuenen and C. P. Tiele (Leiden), Albrecht Weber (Berlin), *et al.*

He was a member of the Advisory Councils of the "World's Congress of Evolutionists" and of the "Psychic Science Congress" at the Chicago Exposition of 1893. In both congresses a paper from his pen was read. Among the more important of the numerous essays and treatises which he has published are these: "The Essenes and Therapeutæ," "The Druids", "The Alexandrian Library," "The Seven Bibles of the World," "The Talmudic Jesus," "Apollonius of Tyana and Jesus Christ," "The Veil of Isis," "Sabbath Observance," "The Nicene Council and the Biblical Canon," "The Bible God and Nature," and "The Delusions of Astrology."

Mr. Coleman has an analytical, critical mind, and his writings are largely occupied with a ventilation of what he regards as the sophistries and fallacies of false theories. In Spiritualism he accepts nothing that cannot be scientifically demonstrated. For twenty years he has been especially active in attempts to place Spiritualism and the occult on a purely scientific basis, the segregation of the impure and the irrational elements therein from the demonstrably true and sensible; and the "frauds, fools, and fanatics," as he terms them, in Spiritualism, he has mercilessly excoriated. He has also vigorously denounced the bad logic and vagaries (as he deems them) of re-incarnation, pre-existance, obsession, occultism, bibliolatry, the solar-mythic origin of Christianity, and the charlatanism of many pretended mediums. "No compromise with error; the truth must prevail!" is the watchword of his endeavor. "A terror to evil-doers and evil-thinkers," he has been called by Andrew Jackson Davis.

Mr. Coleman is devoted, practically, to the reforms he advocates. He eschews the use of intoxicating liquors, tobacco in all forms, tea, coffee, stimulating condiments, profane and indelicate language, gaming, low and lewd associations, etc., and believes in purity of heart and life, integrity, chastity, and the supremacy of truth. He has a hearty detestation of all shams and hypocrisies, coupled with a fervent love of truth for its own sake. Although as a writer he is bold and vigorous, at times very severe yet personally he is mild, diffident, retiring.

Mr. Coleman has combated Theosophy as a fraud and delusion from its inception in 1875, and he has published many articles in exposure of its pretenses and of the trickery of Madame Blavatsky. For some time he has been preparing for publication a work in exposure of Theosophy in all its branchesr; and it is intended to include many facts never before published, gathered by Mr. Coleman during his prolonged researches, and his extensive correspondence on this matter in all parts of the world. Though a decided disbeliever in any form of Christianity, and many of his writings are devoted to criticisms of its claims, Mr. Coleman ever tries to be strictly just to the Church, the Bible, Jesus, and Judaism; and he has often felt called upon to oppose ard expose unfair attacks upon these by certain schools of Free thought. As the New York *Evolution* remarked, "Mr. Coleman is a devotee of science. He is one by whom truth, unadulterated truth, is preferred far above his personal whims, or passions, or desires, and regardless of the claims of party, place or power. His articles show him to be one of the most thoroughly well-read men in the country."

In 1871, Mr. Coleman married Miss Wilmot Bouton, of New York, a lady of education and refinement, beloved by all who knew her, sensitive, mediumistic, and an earnest spiritualist and reformer. She passed to the higher life in 1882. In a tribute to her memory Mr. Coleman refers to her noble qualities in the highest and most affectionate terms. His only children, a boy and a girl, are with his "Willie" in the spirit clime. He is a member of the American Oriental Society, Royal Asiatic Society of Great Britain and Ireland, Pali Text Society, Egypt

Exploration Fund, Brooklyn (N. Y.) Ethical Association, California Psychical Society, Library Association of Central California, California Camera Club, etc. He is an Honorary Associate of the Society for Psychical Research of London, and for some years was President of the Golden Gate Religious and Philosophical Society of San Francisco.

MRS. M. J. HENDEE-ROGERS.

MRS. M. J. HENDEE-ROGERS.

The subject of this sketch is a native of Maine. Her ancestors were from England. Her grandmother, on her mother's side, was a Garrison—sister of Wm. Lloyd Garrison's father. It is believed that she has the honor ot being the oldest public mediumistic evangel of the modern gospel on the Coast; that she is, in fact, the veteran medium *par excellence* of California. Long years of arduous and faithful service in the cause of spiritual and liberal truth has she spent in our midst; and fervently it is hoped that for many an additional year her snow-covered locks may be seen amongst us, as she continues to dispense, as freely as of yore, the irradiant light-gleams, descending from supernal spheres, imparted to a soul-hungry world through her beneficent inspirational gifts.

Mrs. Rogers was first led to a knowledge of the truth as found in Modern Spiritualism through conversation thereon with a friend. At that time she was an ardent Methodist. She regarded Spiritualism as a delusion, and deemed it her duty as a Christian to warn people from its snares. While engaged in warning her friend against its wiles, she felt the presence of some one in the room, though no one but her friend and herself was visible, and she heard a voice say to her, "Are you sure that you have all the truth? Is there nothing new to be investigated? 'Prove all things, and hold fast that which is good.'" For a moment she was struck speechless, feeling that she had received a well-merited rebuke for her injustice in condemning that of which she knew nothing; and she felt herself a bigot, in refusing to investigate this wondrous manifestation, and test its truth or falsity. Her friend knew nothing of her thoughts nor of what occasioned them, and was surprised, at the close of the conversation, by her inquiring when the next spiritual meeting would be held, saying she desired to attend. She did attend, and at the meeting listened for the first time to a trance speaker—a pale, feeble man, devoid of culture, but who, under control, held the audience spellbound with his eloquence. From that time she fully accepted the fact that the unseen dwellers on the thither shore return to earth and intelligently control mortals.

Although Mrs. Rogers (then Upham) so stoutly opposed Spiritualism, yet, prior even to the advent of this modern phase of supra-mundane revealment, she and other members of her family had been recipients of spiritual visitations and foreshadowings. In 1847 (a year before the ever memorable 31st of March, 1848) she had bitterly bewailed the loss of her little girl babe of four years. Its manner of death was so trying to her that she could not get over it, and often she wept herself nearly sick. In her morbid self-condemnation she felt as if she herself were to blame for its premature demise, and yet she knew that she was really innocent. One day when alone and in great distress, wishing for death, her little girl came to her and said, "Mamma, don't cry any more; it was all right; it was to be. I am happy—don't cry!" She spoke to her several times, and she fully recognized her voice, and knew that it was her sweet child, Florence. From that time she ceased to grieve for her loss, but she did not recognize *that* as Spiritualism; and when, in the next following years, Spiritualism was steadily gaining ground, based upon manifestations similar in character to those manifest in her own experience, she still refused to recognize their significancy; yet she had been taught to believe in the appearing of the dead. Her mother was a natural seer, and often saw and spoke to spirits; and prior to the death of any member of the family, she would always be warned of the approaching event by the vision of a ball of fire.

In December, 1849, her husband, Mr. Upham, came to California, at which time he and she knew nothing of Spiritualism. One night Mr. Upham awoke from sleep, when the room suddenly lighted up, and his father stood before him and said to him, "Ansel, I died to-night at 12 o'clock!" This he twice repeated, and then vanished, the room resuming its natural darkness. Mr. Upham arose and looked at the time: it was half-past 12. He noted the date, and the spirit's intelligence being fully confirmed, he became thoroughly convinced of the fundamental truths of Spiritualism.

It was about this time that Mrs. Upham became converted as before stated; and, as she knelt in prayer in church, a wondrous power seemed to possess her and all was light. The church appeared transparent; she could perceive no walls; and her friends seemed divested of their natural bodies, and were as if glorified with spiritual raiment, so angelic was their appearance. It was to her an ecstacy of joy and peace. She loved everybody; there was no sin; all was good, and God was love, pervading all things. She remained a church communicant nearly seven years, and was such when she came to California in September, 1858. She did not unite with the church here, as at that time her faith had blossomed into a knowledge of the divine realities of Spiritualism. She was surprised to find her husband a firm believer also, as he had written nothing to her concerning it.

There were no public spiritual meetings held in their vicinity, so they instituted circles, but obtained no response from the spirit country. They could find but one person knowing aught on the subject, and she told them of a lady in the vicinity who was sometimes controlled to speak. They, with others, went one evening to hear her speak, but, through sickness, she failed to arrive. The landlord of the hotel having said that he could tip the table, a sitting was held. Being disturbed by some of the men present, whom she thought were making fun of their religion, Mrs. Upham arose to leave the table, when a power seemed to sieze her, and her voice was checked. She could only make guttural sounds, and her hands pounded the table in spite of the efforts both of herself and of those present to stop it. For several days she could not talk plainly. The next day she sat at a large center-table in the parlor, which rocked and moved all around the room, and from that time her labors as a medium began.

Her mediumistic gifts have been and are of a varied character. Among them are the following: Personating death scenes and living people until they are recognized; sympathetically taking on the diseases of others and curing them; seeing writing on the wall as if written on large rolls of paper, and read as it is being unrolled; laying on of hands and curing the sick, and, under control, writing prescriptions for those diseased.

At times, for several years, she held large circles, during which period she was educated to speak while entranced, promise being given that her eyes would be opened, and that she would speak before large audiences, and, under influence, would write manuscripts for publication—all of which she was educated to do during the year she was the pupil of the invisibles.

From 1858 to 1868 her mediumship was free to all; not one cent did she charge or receive during these ten years. In Sacramento the good angels told her that she must hereafter charge for sittings as "the laborer was worthy of his hire," and if she did not her mediumship would be taken from her. At that time she was treating the sick, doing her household duties, holding circles twice a week, and lecturing twice a week in Turn Verein Hall, alternately with Mr. W. F. Lyon, afterwards one of the authors of *The*

Hollow Globe. She performed some remarkable cures, which she attributed to the good spirits, as they diagnosed the disease and restored the sufferer to health, often after being given up by the physicians.

July 18, 1868, her dear mother passed to spirit-life suddenly. While she was passing away the daughter attempted to restore her, when the mother spoke, calling her by name, saying, "I am happy! I am happy!" Mrs. Rogers afterwards saw her spirit form ascending, surrounded by a bright halo, and looking happy and joyous. The night previous to her soul's flight, the mother saw the same light that had warned her of other's departure. Her husband regarded it at first as merely a reflection of some ordinary light, but, placing his hand over it, he found that it was covered, and was, therefore, no reflection, at which he was much troubled.

A few months after Mrs. Upham removed to San Francisco, on Market street, where the Grand Hotel now stands, and there opened the first advertised public spiritual seances ever held in the city, sometimes from forty to fifty persons attending. She also gave private sittings, treated the sick, and lectured occasionally. She also held developing circles, developing a number of trance and inspirational speakers and healers. In San Francisco she, for the first time, made any charges for seances, though, during the preceding ten years, thousands had been made glad through her mediumship, with knowledge of the continued existence and loving presence of their so-called deceased relatives and friends.

Prior to her removal to San Francisco, her Indian guide, calling himself "Sunrise," had left her, so she had no Indian "control." Shortly after her arrival in San Francisco she was moved, on opening her circles and receiving the guests, to say to them, "Hichicum," and nothing else. This was not understood, until at last it was discovered that it was a "control," and finally he explained by saying that his name was Hichicum Hi, and that Hichicum meant "power," and Hi meant "here"—"power is here." From that time he assumed an active control, and has remained with her ever since. He subsequently stated that he was a Mohawk chieftain, who had lived fifty years before in the Mohawk Valley; that he had been brought to Mrs. Upham by "Sunrise," and that he was a medicine man in spirit-life. This statement has been abundantly verified in the wonderful control he has manifested to thousands of persons in healing and in giving tests. Among those cured by him was a doctor who had been given up by his physician, who told him to go home to Boston and lay his bones with his father's. Also a Mr. Thompson, said by his physicians to be afflicted with aneurism of the aorta of the neck, and who could not live—was liable to die at any moment. Hichicum told him it was not aneurism, but a strain, and the ligaments were swollen, and he, through his medium, could cure him. After four weeks' treatment he was perfectly restored, and is now, after sixteen years, alive, well and hearty.

Mrs. M. E. Morrison, residing on Howard street, San Francisco, and afflicted with inflammation of the stomach, was told by her physicians that she could only live a few hours. Mrs. Upham, being sent for, told her daughter her mother's symptoms, as she said, better than the doctors had. At the first treatment she broke the fever, and, in six treatments she cured her entirely; and Mrs. Upham now possesses her written testimonial that she cured her without one drop of medicine, or drawing a single drop of blood, and without blister or plaster—using nothing save the laying on of hands.

On another occasion she saved the life of a lady, after confinement, while she was under the doctor's care. Finding her in great pain, she was controlled, and placing her hands upon the patient's side, pulled with such force as to throw her on her knees, causing the patient to

scream a little. The cure had been effected—the placenta had grown to her
side, and was, by this means, removed.
The lady quickly recovered, and is, to-
day, one of our best mediums.

On one occasion, in sitting with a gentleman, a number of his spirit friends
came, but he said he wished to hear from
the living. She then saw and described,
in turn, (1) his wife; (2) a young man of
eighteen, whom she said would make a
good surveyor and architect, and whom
the sitter identified as his son, whom he
had just placed in a surveying school;
(3) another son, more domestic, and resembling his mother; (4) a young lady,
sitting, as it seemed, on the floor, with
one limb drawn up toward her back;—
this lady, she said, was his daughter, and
she told him the cause of her affliction,
and advised him to take her out of the
doctor's care and place her under the
treatment of a magnetic and electric healer, and that she would get well;—(5) a
young girl, ten or twelve years old, in
good health, and resembling him in appearance. The gentleman confirmed the
truth of all that had been told him, and
said he had been recommended to consult her relative to the treatment of his
afflicted daughter. He was not a Spiritualist, and had never before sat with a
medium; and he said it was the most
wonderful thing he had ever seen or
heard. His family, which had been so
accurately described, was in Chicago,
and he went on his way rejoicing.

A few weeks thereafter, the family of
the gentleman, including the invalid
daughter, presented themselves to Mrs.
Upham. The sick girl, in accordance
with the medium's advice, had been
placed under the care of a magnetic healer, and was rapidly reeovering. She
afterwards became a healthy and happy
wife and mother. The writer has seen
the written testimonial of the father, Mr.
Charles Holland, setting forth the facts
in this case as here stated.

"During my first summer in San Francisco," says Mrs. Rogers, "I felt impelled to write, and I was requested to
sit one hour each day, and the spirits
would write their experiences in the spirit
life. This request was signed, 'George
Washington.' I commenced, and the
result is the pamphlet known by that
name, written through my hand, and published by, and through the kindness of
our loved and lamented friend, T. B.
Clark, who kindly interested himself to
do the work after it had lain in manuscript nearly ten years, and who afterwards sat with me while writing the
spirit experiences of Martha and Mary
Washington. The three manuscripts
were published by him, and they have
been widely circulated.

"Spiritualism came to me in my troubles; it soothed my sorrows and gave to
me the knowledge that though my friends
passed from my sight, they were not
dead, but born to an immortal clime,
where I expect to meet them, when I am
called to go. When my husband, Mr.
Hendee, knew that he was dying, he
called all around the bed and said that
he should die, as he had lived, in the full
belief of Spiritualism; that he knew that
he should meet his mother and friends;
and, as far as his future was concerned,
he was happy to go, only being sorry to
leave his wife to the cold world. He was
a staunch Spiritualist for fifteen years—a
good and noble man. I have received
many loving tests from him in proof of
his presence and love.

While residing at Napa City, in 1865,
during my control at a seance, I saw a
funeral procession. The men walked
with their heads bowed, and dressed in
black, with black and white crape on
their arms. There soon followed a band
with muffled drums, then others on
horseback. The black horses wore white
plumes and the white horses black
plumes. Then carriages of state, then
foreigners; then the catalalque came and
was set down, and I was made to go forward and look into the casket. There I
saw the face of Abraham Lincoln, and as
I was made to express what I saw, I said,
"The head of our Nation." Then I was
taken away, and foreign ambassadors

followed in carriages, with horses highly caparisoned, all passing on in the train. Then I heard the 'Battle Cry of Freedom' played, and I looked and saw the Union troops with flags lowered and draped in black and white. They marched on out of sight. I then came to myself, when I heard them say, 'I am afraid it is Lincoln.' I had given a full description as they passed. This was on Sunday evening, at Captain West's, at Napa; and on the next Saturday noon, news came that Seward and Lincoln were assassinated. I said I did not see but one, and, as Seward lived, there was but one; and I had seen the real procession that was to be, for the processions formed at other places were meager compared to what I saw in my vision, for such it must have been. There are several now living who were present on this occasion, including Mrs. Captain West, at whose house it transpired. By this and many other testimonies regarding Lincoln's death, it certainly seems established that the spirit world is often conscious of many things before they transpire on earth, and that it was to be his fate."

Mrs. Rogers' experience as a medium and healer has extended over a period of more than twenty-five years, and is replete with interesting incidents and facts, but a few of which can be given in a brief sketch. Enough could be related to fill a large volume. Although the pioneer medium on this Coast, she is still actively engaged in public work

MRS. ESTHER DYE.

Mrs. Esther Dye, the subject of this sketch, was born on March 6th, 1852, at Athica, Fountain Co., Indiana. Her parents being strict Methodists, she was brought up and schooled in their faith. She remained loyal to her early training until overwhelming evidence of spirit power by the occult forces back of her compelled her to acknowledge the truth of Spiritualism. This, of course, cut her off from fellowship in the "church of her fathers," and she was destined, as many others have been, to run the gamut of social and religious ostracism. But she was being "led in a way she knew not," and unseen hands were shaping her future, and waking to life her latent powers. They were moulding her for use in the cause of humanity, and endowing her with the old-time "gifts of healing."

Esther Dye, or, as her spirit guides call her, "Esther the Healer," was born a medium. Though she did not understand it at first, yet she can now look back and recognize many evidences of her medial powers, such as are usually experienced in incipient development. Not until within the last six years have those gifts been utilized understandingly in the great work to which she has been set apart by the spirit world. In 1888 and 1889 her development was so rapid that she at once began to diagnose disease clairvoyantly and to heal the sick "by the laying on of hands," magnetizing garments, papers, etc., with increasing power and success up to the present time. Many very remarkable cures have been effected, through her instrumentality, of persons pronounced beyond all hope by distinguished and reputable physicians. Hundreds of testimonials can be furnished in confirmation of the above statement.

Mr. S. D. Dye, her husband, is kept busy attending to her books, answering letters from every section of the country, and sending magnetized pads to those of her patients whom she treats at a distance. She has an army of friends and acquaintances who love and esteem her for her many noble traits of character.

She is always in closest sympathy with her patients, and her large and generous heart ever throbs for the afflictions and woes of others, while with open hand she delights to give liberally to the deserving poor. The intelligences who heal through her are too exalted and humane to allow their chosen instrument to prostitute mediumship to mere money getting and feeding the insatiate greed of avarice. They recognize that "the *lust* of money is the root of all evil," and that the holy cause of human weal is sadly crippled through this debasing agency. Hence they have elevated their medium far above its baneful influence, and they propose to thus deliver her from all evil, and wonderfully augment her power for good in the years to come.

It has been Mrs. Dye's most cherished desire for years to be able to establish a healing institute in Los Angeles, her home city, where the land is watered by silver streams running through groves of golden fruit, and where the air is redolent with the sweet perfume of the lemon and orange, and ever blooming flowers. But her extreme liberality to the deserving poor has hitherto kept her too poor to accomplish the desire of her heart. However, the spirit forces promise she will yet realize her wish, and the structure be completed in the near future. The author of this brief sketch would fain paint with well chosen words her many virtues, and set them as sparkling gems in a coronet of gold, or plant them as choice exotics by the "Fountains of waters," that sweet memories like incense may rise, and the hearts be kept full, and the love fresh in those who have shared her heaven appointed benefactions. May many others of earth's sick and sorrowing ones find health and comfort through her healing ministrations, and be led to recognize that the age of so-called miracles has not passed.

MRS. ESTHER DYE.

MRS. F. A. LOGAN.

MRS. F. A. LOGAN.

Medium, Healer and Speaker.

Mrs. Logan was born in Skaneatlas, Onondago Co., N. Y., in August, 1822. Her father, a Baptist minister, settled in Wisconsin in 1841.

In the winter of 1850 she investigated Spiritualism and commenced writing communications in poetry for her friends, acquaintances and strangers, giving much consolation to the bereaved and sorrowing; but not until she withdrew from the Church and from a bondage still more severe, did she become an inspirational speaker and take the platform in 1865. After visiting New York City and becoming a member of the Progressive Lyceum, even to the promotion to the leadership of Liberty Group, did she obey the spirits' promptings, to plead the cause of human freedom from everything which cramps or degrades the souls and bodies of mankind.

She started with her recommendations and was successful in organizing Lyceums, but more frequently star armies, and temperance and literary societies.

After lecturing on the line of railroad in the principal towns and cities of Minnesota, she was made the State Missionary and ordained to solemnize marriages and to preach the gospel of glad tidings wherever she went.

After fulfilling her mission there she started down the Mississippi, lecturing in the river towns on "A Plea for Equal Rights," an original, poetical lecture. Arriving at St. Louis, she gave an original, poetical lecture, which she had memorized, on the "Past, Present and Future," which had been well received in several cities. She travelled extensively throughout Illinois and Wisconsin, and back again to New York, stopping in several towns in Canada, Michigan, Ohio and Pennsylvania; everywhere restoring some one to health, by the healing power with which she seemed particularly gifted.

The reader has but to examine her testimonials and scrap-books to be convinced of this indefatigable worker's success as healer and lecturer. We will insert one or two of the many and wonderful testimonials of cures, tendered her in her journeyings from grateful hearts.

New York City, June 20, 1866.—It is but just to the public that I state my case. I had Putrid Erysipelas all over my face and head. A council of five physicians pronounced my case hopeless; I must die! Mrs. Logan was called in to witness the dissolution of soul and body, when by her magnetic hands I was restored to consciousness, and by her treatment in a few days was able to pack my trunks and move. May God's blessing attend her wherever she goes, for if the high and pure intent be also reckoned, there can none be more truly fitted than herself to her work.

Emily C. De Lendenier

San Jose, Mason Co., Ill., August, 1870.—i had rheumatism in my left limb two years, at times very painful. Mrs. Logan came into our town as a lecturer and healer. With skepticism I employed her. In twenty minutes' time I was entirely cured, and can now walk and run as blithely as when in my youth. I am sixty-five years old.

Charlotte Kidder.

Consumption, fevers and all disease-

seemed to recede at once under her hands. Call the power by whatever name you please, mind cure or anything else, it makes but little difference about names. Mrs. L. believed that she had the assistance of angel guides, not only in healing but in her journeyings, and unmistakable spiritual power accompanied her in all her public work, until hundreds have been healed, several of the States traversed, and over 2,000 lectures given, mediums developed by the potent, silent force accompanying the application of her hands to the forehead and base of the brain. Strangers, whom she had never met before, applying to her for treatment, have been entranced at the first sitting, and described the beauties of the spirit world. Some have been developed to sing and play inspirationally, some to heal and some for speaking and writing.

One little girl, ten years old (whose elder brother had died not having been converted to the Christian religion, was mourned by the Baptist mother as eternally lost,) became entranced and described her brother as perfectly happy in his beautiful spirit home, which brought joy and comfort to the bereaved, such as they had failed to obtain in their church. Mrs. Logan has no time to idle away on foolish fashions or display, as her heart is full of sympathy for he afflicted and unfortunate ones of earth. In her travels she has visited reform schools, jails and penitentiaries, delivering addresses, distributing reform literature, and speaking words of sympathy and encouragement to the inmates.

Very many towns were visited before reaching our golden shores in 1874.

The following tribute was tendered her after her first lecture in San Francisco, which will give the reader somewhat of an idea of the subject matter of the discourse:

SAN FRANCISCO, July 13, 1874.
MRS. F. A. LOGAN:

   DEAR MADAM—Having for many years believed that a purified public sentiment and feeling would ultimate from the teachings and moral force of woman, it was with unfeigned pleasure I listened to your poetic lecture delivered in Grand Central Hall, in this city, on the 12th inst., so graphically descriptive of scenes, incidents, and illustrations of "Life in the Great Metropolis of Our Country, New York City."

A lecture so instructive and replete with interest, clothed as it is with argument, eloquence and appeal, while being fully appreciated by the thinking, intellectual and morally cultured, must also be felt as a stern rebuke to the dissipation, profligacy, shams and hypocrisy of the age.

Wishing you success in your work of faith and labor of love in this land of progress and prophetic greatness,

I remain, Yours in the bond of common humanity,   JAMES BATTERSBY,

   Late Pres. Lyceum of Self Culture.

Mrs. L. has not sought notoriety by visiting large cities only, but has gone into districts, towns, and hamlets, in the mountains and in the valleys, believing that there were jewels and pearls of immortal worth in the humblest home, or beneath a tattered coat and faded dress; and nothing grieves her more than cold formality, or the pomposity apparent everywhere, in all ranks of society. She deeply appreciates the kindly words of sympathy, the cordial welcome to hospitable hearts and homes that she has received during the twenty years of missionary life through the Eastern States, Oregon, Washington Territory, British Columbia, Nevada, Wyoming, Utah and Colorado. While in Leadville she held a public discussion with a very well-read M. D. on the conscious individuality of the soul after what is (so-called) death; not winning his point, he acknowledged that he himself had felt the presence of individualized immortal spirits.

Mrs. L. could furnish volumes of interesting incidents of her travels throughout the States and in our picturesque golden California.

During a trip to Yosemite Valley and the mammoth trees, she stopped to give a temperance lecture in Vallicito, in the church at 11 A. M., Sunday. The clergyman and his wife had made arrangements and kindly entertained and introduced her. Discovering that her audience was composed mostly of women and children she proposed that they all march down to the largest saloon and give the lecture there. Suiting the action to the word, the dignified minister, with his better half by his side, and the entire congregation, all marched to the open door of the saloon. The keeper's dark Italian eyes nearly pierced the leader of this little army through; but knowing in whom to put her trust (the power that never faileth,) she simply said: "Please allow us to hold our meeting in your place of business. We will not detain you long."

The keeper put down his billiard cue, and placed the seats around the room. His wife came in, and all being seated, the drunkards remaining also, Mrs. L., after a short invocation. said, "We have not come here to find fault with your saloon or your business, for it is a legitimate business. You are licensed by our Government to pursue it. But we would appeal to the better natures of individuals and ask them to not engage in or patronize anything that would wrong another in any way whatever, for the wrong would certainly rebound upon the wrong-doer."

During the lecture tears coursed down the faces of the most obdurate drunkards in the audience, and all expressed their thanks to the speaker, not only from their tear-dimmed eyes, but by a generous donation, which is not a small item to the one who is living and laboring for the good of souls, with no permanent home except in the hearts of the people and on the evergreen shore of the hereafter.

Mrs. L.'s spiritualistic ideas embrace all reforms, and her most popular lectures are on Spiritualism, Temperance, Cause and Cure of Disease, the Relation Man Sustains to Woman Legally, Socially and Morally, and Four Poetical Lectures, and one on Circumstances.

The subject of this sketch has indomitable perseverence to carry out her spiritual impressions against all obstacles, as instanced in getting up the first spiritual camp meeting on our shores, in October, 1884. By obeying the still, small voice, an interest was awakened in other souls on the same plane of unfoldment, and a grand, successful meeting lasting twelve days was the result.

Her only brother, Walter Hyde, presided over thirty-six sessions in such a way that harmony prevailed, mediums were developed, the humblest, the young and the old, the rich and the poor, were considered of equal importance in the mind of the chairman, as well as by the spirit helpers, and a harmonious organization was effected for future campmeetings.

Mrs. L. does not claim to be a seer or prophetess, but we find in her book of miscellaneous poems a prophecy written in 1875, of the electric lights, and form materialization, besides other gems entitled, "Poor Little Barefoot," "Mammoth Trees of California," "Companionless," and "Reasons Why I Became a Spiritualist," etc.

Mrs. Logan has a special gift for the development of mediums; and now several, who were comparatively obscure before. are giving remarkable tests from the platform, and begin to feel that they can secure halls and audiences without her assistance.

For several years past Mrs. Logan has conducted a Sunday morning meeting in San Francisco which is called the "Circle of Harmony," at which a free platform is maintained where all are allowed to give expression to their best thought, unrestricted as to time or topic, when subjects of general interest are discussed in a friendly, courteous manner. The timid and retiring have been encouraged and stimulated to put forth their best endeavors and develop latent talents. Many mediumistic gifts have been unfolded and the happy possessors gone forth to labor in the spiritual vineyard.

Mrs. Logan feels that special care should be taken to not hinder the spirit world from communing with this by arbitrary rules and ceremonies, as is often the case where none but popular speakers are engaged, and no opportunity afforded for spiritual communion such as might frequently be received through some timid sensitive in the audience. In her Circle of Harmony particular care is taken to allow free and unrestricted spirit communication through any instru-

ment the angel world may select. Sometimes such messages voice beautiful
truths clothed in beautiful language; and
at other times they express but the crudities of the spirit and the medium through
whom the message is given. In mediumship Mrs. Logan recognizes the application of the saying that "a child must
creep before it can walk," and is willing
to extend the helping hand and give the
word of encouragement to the young and
inexperienced medium who tremblingly
stands upon the platform for the first
time, fearful lest the sustaining influence
should be withdrawn, and their own
weakness become apparent to the audience. Many of our present-day workers
on the Pacific Coast are indebted to Mrs.
Logan for having opened a door and prepared a place where they could give forth
their first impressions from the spirit side
and feel assured that their feeble efforts
would meet with approval and encouragement until they grew strong and self-
confident to go out into other fields of
work and usefulness.

Mrs. Logan has published four original
poetical lectures and her sister's book of
"Prophetic Visions and Spirit communications." Her ready pen, by the aid of
invisible intelligences, has given comfort
to many hearts, and also diagnosed diseases and given a reasonable explanation
of the case as instanced in the many
communications received from patients
whom she has treated personally, and
also by spiritual science methods, when
many miles intervened between the patient and the healer. The success in
either case has always been most phenomenal.

Mrs. Logan realizes, as all writers do,
that it is impossible to put into a brief
autobiography all the struggles, trials
and triumphs of a soul laboring inces-
santly for the good of humanity. Subject
to temptations and all the ills of mortal
life, and now, when silver threads crown
the brow of this veteran worker in her
seventy-third year, she can look back
over a life hallowed with blessed deeds
and noble service in the cause of truth,
right and justice. She calmly awaits the
results of her life labors, and with Alice
Cary says:

"My past is mine and I take it all,
Its follies, its weaknesses if you please,
Nay, even my sins if you come to that,
May have been my helps, not hindrances."

Yours truly
Lois Waisbrooker

LOIS WAISBROOKER.

AUTHOR AND EDITOR.

That Mrs. Schlesinger desires to put me into her book as one of the workers in the vineyard of reform, is of itself sufficient honor, and as I desire to live more in my work than in my personality, and further, as I shrink from having my name go to posterity coupled with the too partial estimate of friends who are inclined to enlarge virtues and forget faults, I will myself say what needs to be said, but it will necessarily be more of my general than of my California work.

As to myself, I made my entrance into this life on the 21st day of February, 1826, in the town of Catherine, Schuyler County (then a part of Tiuga), N. Y., as the first of seven children born to Caroline and Grandison Nichols.

My mother's maiden name was Reed, and though their children were all Methodists, her father and mother were among the first Universalists of the country. It was my talks with my grandfather the summer of his eighty-first year, which helped to break me from the bondage of church teachings.

The death of a brother-in-law, with the circumstances attending, had prepared the way for his words to take effect. This brother-in-law, who was a good husband, son and brother, died believing he was going to hell, because he had never been converted.

The first links broken, the investigation of Spiritualism in 1856 completed the work so well begun. Among the first evidences received was a communication from that brother-in-law.

My parents were poor, uneducated, hard-working people, my father supporting his family as a day laborer—a wage slave—and as a matter of course my advantages were but few. It is the memory of my father's unrequited toil, of how much he did and how little he received, which intensifies my opposition to an opposition to an economic system which so robs the toiler.

My parents gave me the name of Adeline Eliza, but when at twenty-eight years of age I began to write over the signature of "Lois," my friends commenced calling me that, and I soon adopted it; so it is now nearly forty years since I discarded my baptismal name, as I have since discarded Christianity in all its forms. The good connected with it belongs to universal humanity, not to a sect of people who have shed rivers of blood to enforce their propaganda.

I was always called peculiar. How much of that peculiarity belongs to myself, and how much of it comes from the influence of those who were once denizens of earth, and who now hold me to the work for which they have helped to prepare me, I cannot say, but I have always wanted to write. The school composition, as it was called, while a terror to many, was a pleasure to me.

And now, dismissing myself as far as possible, turn to that in which I have lived most, to that which I have felt impelled to write. My first effort outside the newspaper column was an anti-slavery Sabbath-school book called

"Mary and Ellen; or, The Orphan Girls," which, the last I knew of it, was being extensively used in the Sabbath schools of our Congregationalist friends, I being at the time of its writing a member of that church.

My second book, "Alice Vale," was written to illustrate Spiritualism. It is now out of print, as is "Mayweed Blossoms," a collection of fugitive pieces, of which I thought more than did others, as the meagreness of its sale proved, and also, as is "Nothing Like It; or, Steps to the Kingdom," an earnest but somewhat crude effort to give a glimpse of purity in freedom, in the relation of the sexes.

Those will probably never be reissued.

"Helen Harlow's Vow" was written to show that woman should refuse to submit to the injustice which condemns her, and accepts the man for the same act—the heroine determining that she will not sink because she has foolishly trusted; that she will be just to herself if others are unjust to her. She maintains her self-respect, and in the end commands the respect of all who know her.

"Perfect Motherhood; or, Mabel Raymond's Resolve," does not trench upon the province of the physician, but takes up the conditions of society which make it impossible that mothers shall transmit, through the law of heredity, the elements of character which, unfolded, would give the world a superior race of men and women.

"The Occult Forces of Sex" is a work which is more valued each year, in proof of which I will state that the year after the last part was written, something over five years since, there were less than 200 sold with my personal effort, added to what was done by others; but during the last two years the sales have been encouraging in the extreme.

This little book consists of three pamphlets—one written in Battle Creek, Michigan, in 1873, and called "The Sex Question and the Money Power;" the second at Riverside, California, in 1880, and called "From Generation to Regeneration," (and really the most valuable of my California work), and the third at Milwaukee, Oregon, in 1889, and called "The Tree of Life Between Two Thieves."

I have good evidence that Alexander von Humboldt, his brother William, Mrs. Hemans, Lady Mary Wortley Montague, and two or three others whose names I have forgotten, assisted me, not only in writing the work prepared at Riverside, but they are still with me when I attempt to get clearer, purer views of the finer forces of the sex. I received the communication with the names given through Dr. J. V. Mansfield, and signed by Von Humboldt. Permission was given to use the names in connection with the work, but the letter being lost in my attempt to send it to Dr. J. Rodes Buchanan for psychometrization, I have never before given the name to the public. This second pamphlet is put first in the book.

"A Sex Revolution" was written in 1862. It puts motherhood to the front, demands that "women take the lead" till the conditions for a higher grade of motherhood are obtained.

Another work issued recently is the "Fountain of Life, or the Threefold Power of Sex."

I have also essayed the newspaper business or method of scattering thought. "Our Age, Ours—the Peoples'," was issued at Battle Creek, Michigan, till forty-two numbers were sent out. Then the financial crisis of 1873-4 forced a suspension.

"Foundation Principles," issued from Clinton, Ia., in 1884, and afterwards removed to Antioch, California, was carried into the fourth volume, when it suspended for a time, but was finally resumed after I had located in Topeka, Kansas.

I do not know what the future of this life has for me, but this I do know —that I shall never consider my work

done so long as I have the strength to
do, and the privilege of doing more—
and—
Whenever I'm called, I gladly will go,
My lessons of wisdom to learn over
    there;
Then back I will hasten, to help lift
    this earth
Out of its ignorance, sorrow and care—
Will aid it to cast off its sorrow and
    care,
For I could not remain in a world filled
    with bliss

While rivers of sorrow were rolling
    thro' this.
    Yours, for the Work,
        LOIS WAISBROOKER.

P. S.—I have forgotten one thing.
So many will ask: Was she ever married? I have been twice married, have
two children and six grandchildren,
but I have lived so long alone, and
there is so much questioning if marriage be not a failure, that married or
single scarcely ever enters my thought.
        L. W.

MRS. MAGGIE WAITE.

Among the mediums developed in California, Mrs. Maggie Waite is one of the most reliable for platform tests, giving names readily and correctly, and describing spirit forms accurately. When under spirit influence she is both clairvoyant and clairaudient, and gives verbal messages from the spirits without hesitation, and usually to the entire satisfaction of the investigator.

Mrs. Waite was born in the city of New York, August 31, 1561, but at five years of age was taken by her parents to San Francisco. She received her education in a convent in California, and as a child knew nothing of Spiritualism. Although it is sixteen years or more since she was first informed that she would sometime become a medium, it is only within the last few years that the development of her powers commenced. In answer to questions concerning her experience, Mrs. Waite says:

"My first knowledge of Spiritualism was received when fourteen years of age. A lady invited me to accompany her to a seance given by Mrs. Ada Foye. During the seance a pair of invisible hands encircled my waist, and lifting me from my chair, placed me on the table. I was much frightened. Mrs. Foye endeavored to allay my fear, and prophesied that I would become an instrument for the spirit world. For some weeks after attending Mrs. Foye's circle, I occasionally heard raps near me, but resolutely refused to notice them. Having been brought up from my infancy in the Catholic faith, I believed the manifestations I had

witnessed to be the work of the Devil, and consequently resolved to have no more to do with such things. I avoided Spiritualism and Spiritualists for years after that. Meantime I met Mr. Edwin Waite, whom I married in the Catholic faith, June 19, 1871. We had been married about three months, when my husband told me that his grandmother, who had passed into spirit life a year and a half previous, appeared to him and told him that in a few years everything would come out all right, having reference to the mediumistic work I am now engaged in.

"After the birth of my first child, I began to see spirits around the cradle, but did not at first recognize them as spirits. They seemed like persons in this life, and I wondered how they got there. I was afraid someone had entered the house. One night I was suddenly awakened from my sleep, and looking up, saw standing at the doorway a white-robed form. The figure made a gesture with her right arm three times in succession, as if beckoning me to come. Some of my friends, to whom I related the circumstances, construed it as a warning of my early death; but my dear friend, Mrs. Jennie Daniels, had just passed into spirit life, and although I did not recognize the form, I was assured by her mother that it was Jennie, and that she had appeared to another person at about the same time. My friend's mother was a Spiritualist, a fact of which I was not then informed. Not fully crediting the statement, I made no further inquiry; and as my visions soon ceased,

MRS. MAGGIE WAITE.

I thought no more of Spiritualism for about six years. In 1889, on passing Metropolitan Temple, one day, I noticed a poster announcing a test seance by John Slater. My curiosity being aroused, I entered the Temple, and on the following evening attended a seance at Slater's house. Among the tests the medium gave was one which puzzled me. He related a conversation which had occurred between myself and husband in our house that morning, giving some of the exact words my husband had used. I wondered what power—other than spirit—could possibly have conveyed such information to the medium, and I determined to investigate the subject.

After some inquiry, I found a medium who held circles for development. I attended, and at the first sitting my hand commenced to move independent of my own volition; and paper and pencil being given me, my hand not myself—began to write. The first message was as much of a surprise to the medium as to myself, as it was from a dear friend of his, who had passed away in Los Angeles, giving his name in full—one I had never before heard.

"More perplexed than ever, I determined to fathom the mystery, and continued my investigations, mainly by private sittings in my own house. This continued for a year or more, when, one evening, while sitting at the table with a few friends, I began to feel that I was losing consciousness. Yielding to the influence, I was soon asleep, and knew not what occurred. On awakening, my friends told me I had been entranced by the spirit of an Indian girl, who gave her name as Pohontas. This was on the 20th of November, 1890. Pohontas is one of my guides at the present time, controlling me mainly during my sittings at home.

"The next influence that came to me was that of a little girl, who passed away in Sacramento two years before, when she was five years of age. She told my friends (I being unconscious) that her name was Maude Phillips; that she was born in Sacramento, giving the street and number. Determined to ascertain if the statement was true or false, I wrote to the the person whose address was given, and to my surprise received in reply a letter from her parents, stating that they had a child of that name and age, who passed away at the time stated. Shortly afterward the father and mother came to San Francisco on business, and called on me to make further inquiry in regard to the letter I had written them. They were very ignorant of Spiritualism. I tried to explain how it was possible for their daughter to control me, but they seemed unable to comprehend, so I said that if they would sit quietly awhile, I would see if she could control me, and they might have the opportunity of talking with her through me. The father, in a very determined manner, said he would not listen to anything of the kind, and that if he ever heard again that I had called back his dead, he would have me prosecuted! They were horrified at the thought of such sacrilege, and left me with injunctions never to dare do anything of the kind again.

"This spirit continued to come to me, and not long after the visit of her parents, she stated that if I would go to a photographer and have my picture taken, she would try to appear on the plate. I did so, and when the picture was developed was delighted to find a spirit form beside my own. Afterwards, at one of my circles, a lady was present who resided next door to the parents of the little girl in Sacramento. The spirit came, and to prove her identity, called the lady by name, and told her all about herself and family. The lady had known the child well, up to the time of her transition to spirit life, and when I showed her the picture she recognized it at once as the likeness of the child. Delighted as I had been to obtain the photograph in the manner I did, its recognition by a friend of the child gave me still greater satisfaction and joy. The spirit continues to control me at times, and is always welcomed as intelligent and trustworthy, although passing away at so early an age.

"The next spirit to attach himself to me as one of my guides gave his name as William Ralston—whether "Ralston the banker" or Ralston the beggar I know not; neither do I care, so long as he renders service satisfactory to myself and to the angel world. I do not seek to know the history of controlling spirits, further than they choose to give it in proof of their identity. If they give more it is because they wish to do so for reasons of their own, or to satisfy friends with whom they communicate. When this spirit first controlled me I felt the condition of a drowning person, suffering the agonies of one struggling and suffocating in the water. This unpleasant feeling soon ceased, and now the spirit controls easily and agreeably, and has become my principal guide for platform work, assisting me with what success those who have attended my public seances know."

Mrs. Waite had no desire to become a public medium; but it was a work required of her by her spirit friends; and she consented only after becoming convinced that to do so would be giving aid and comfort to others. The communications received through her while in course of development gave such satisfaction to those in the circle that she concluded to give her time and strength to the work; but as this necessarily interfered with her duties to herself and family, she began to accept pay for private sittings. Her services as platform test medium were given freely in public until July, 1892, when she was employed by the Society of Progressive Spiritualists, in whose service she did grand work on the platform.

During the past three years Mrs. Waite has traveled extensively throughout the Eastern States, visiting many of the principal cities and attending the great camp-meetings. Her public work has been the subject of many flattering notices from the secular and Spiritualistic press. She has also received the highest commendations from the various societies for which she has labored, from the East to the West.

Mrs. Waite enters into the work assigned to her by the angel world with a sincere and earnest desire to do good, and convey to doubting and unhappy souls a knowledge of the future life that will bring peace, comfort and a satisfaction not to be found in any of the creeds or beliefs of the past. May she meet with that appreciation and support in her public labors that her gifts deserve, and never feel that her labor is in vain. That spirits and mortals may unite in upholding her willing hands, giving her the heartfelt sympathy and encouragement needful to sustain her in every trial, and thus bear her safely above the storms of persecution and sorrow that are the inevitable lot of every pioneer in reform movement, is the sincere wish of her many warm friends.

ELIZABETH LOWE WATSON.

INSPIRATIONAL SPEAKER, POET AND WRITER.

Mrs. Elizabeth Lowe Watson was born in Solon, Ohio, October 6, 1843. Her father, Abraham Lowe, was of Teutonic descent, born in New York, and her grandfather, of the Knickerbocker type, had large landed possessions in "Old Manhattan Town." Her mother was of Scotch stock. Her grandmother, Mary Daniels, was a remarkably intelligent woman, with a poetic religious temperament, possessed of psychic gifts, the nature of which was then a profound mystery.

The beginning of her knowledge of Spiritualism was at the age of seven years. One day at the school she attended there came mysterious sounds on the desks. The children wondered who made them. They were sitting with their backs to the teacher, who finally said: "Children, turn around upon your seats;" but still the raps continued.

She drew one child after another on to the floor until she came to little Libbie, and her she seated in a chair in the middle of the room; still the raps continued. As the children were returning home that day, they laid their hands upon the rocks, when those mysterious raps were heard as plainly as upon the desks at school. When home was reached they burst in upon the mother with great wonderment, saying, "I.—— is making the raps!" And the good woman did not know at first what to do; but finally said to herself, "God would not send to my innocent little child an evil one to tor-

ment her and me. I have tried to live a good life and obey His commands. Why should He let the Devil in upon my little sheep fold?" And she sat down to the table and "tried the spirits." For two weeks the mother scarcely slept, so anxious was she to know the secret of this power, and if it was really what it claimed to be. Sometimes it purported to be Libbie's little departed sister, sometimes neighbors and friends, and always claimed to be a disembodied spirit, anxious to make itself known and to tell something of that mysterious land beyond the grave. The result was the mother's conversion to Spiritualism, and a great scandal, of course, in the neighborhood. People said that the dear, good woman had been deceived, for the Bible declares the very elect are liable to delusion. Friends and neighbors gathered in to investigate; some were convinced, while some called it this thing, some that.

For several years the family lived the ordinary life of country people; hearing strange reports of spiritualistic phenomena, but not witnessing any of the mysterious occurrences, when at length there came through Elizabeth another manifestation of the peculiar power, this time in the form of trance. Sitting with her mother and sisters around the table at home, she felt a strange influence sweeping over her; the second time that they formed a "circle" she was entranced and began to quote Scripture and to discourse on various topics. It became noised abroad. Evening after evening people crowded the house to hear the sermons of the child, then thirteen years of age. But after a brief period she resisted the influence. She saw that her young mates began to look upon her as something uncanny; her great ambition to become a school teacher was going to be thwarted if she continued to serve as a medium; she begged her mother not to insist upon her yielding to the influence, and the mother consented. But finally the unseen intelligences got the mastery, and at fourteen years of age her public ministry began. It may be noted here that she never went to school more than four or five years altogether.

"I never heard a spirit rap except at home," Mrs. Watson tells us, "nor saw a trance medium until years after my own psychic development. I was compelled, by the phenomena which followed me everywhere, to leave school at thirteen years of age, and this was the first real grief of my life. My ambition was to teach; the good genius of our district school had become interested in my hopes and promised to use her influence in my behalf; my mediumship frustrated all of my most cherished plans—and I well remember the bitter tears I shed when it was decided that I must give up school, while dear, faithful, believing mother replied to my remonstrances and regrets, "My child, you will be a teacher of gray-haired men and women if you will only consent to be guided by the angels.""

"I was first entranced in a home circle and almost immediately began to speak in a semi-conscious state, from scriptural texts usually chosen by my audiences which were comprised of neighbors and friends for the first few weeks; but soon the crowds of listeners were so great that we adjourned to an old Methodist church (otherwise usually vacant) and from that day calls came to me from every direction. School-houses, barns, groves, Universalist churches and every available place for a hundred miles

around, was utilized, it being a common thing at that time for people to drive twenty miles or more to hear a morning lecture. I was at this time a frail, slender girl of fourteen years of age, whom the neighbors said would not live three months; but much to their astonishment (and I fear to the disappointment of not a few pious souls) I thrived under the tax of three lectures every Sunday and often four or five during the week, and at eighteen years had almost a perfect physique. My father relinquished farm life and devoted his time to me, as constant and ever watchful escort, and I do not remember missing an engagement in the four years during which we were never separated. Through summer heat and the most terrible winter storms we drove long distances and always found large audiences awaiting us, although it required a goodly degree of courage at that period to attend a spiritualistic lecture."

She was both too ignorant and too innocent to understand the awfulness of the tales that were circulated at this time by good souls to put down "the devil and his works." The stories that caused her friends to weep and wring their hands, passed over her head as lightly as thistle down. "The neighbors said, "She is studying her sermons," and declared that she quoted whole lectures from A. J. Davis and others, lectures of which she had never heard. Some said that she was a remarkably smart child; others that she was stupid. Questions of all kinds were sent up to the rostrum to be answered, and almost universally a committee was elected to choose a subject upon which the lecture should be based. She was told by a gentleman a few years ago that he listened to a lecture delivered by her when fourteen years of age, upon the subject of "The Relation of Matter and Spirit"—a subject which was chosen by the audience, and that it equalled any that he had heard her deliver since.

In 1861 she married Johnathan Watson, one of the oil kings of Titusville, Penn., a gentleman with five children, "rich but respectable." For severval years thereafter she retired from public work, except to officiate at funerals and lecture occasionally for charitable societies.

During those years of private life the angel ministry went on. To the sanctuary of the home the wise teachers often came, bringing messages of encouragement and needed counsel; when great emergencies arose, when the new and solemn responsibilities weighed too heavily, the heavenly light shone clear and unmistakable upon the difficult pathway; and these angelic ministrations were shared by a large circle of fond and appreciative friends.

The consciousness that the spirit mother of the children who were her chief care and anxiety, was a co-worker with her, lending her sympathy and aid whenever possible, was a constant source of comfort and inspiration.

To the vast enrichment of her womanhood were added four children, embodiments of spiritual beauty and the fruitage of true love. The following typical example of the loving watchfulness of spirit friends at this time is narrated by Mrs. Watson: "When my first-born was but a few months old, I left him to spend a few days with my husband in New York City. One Saturday night, when too late for the train to Rochester (then our home), we received a telegram stating that the baby was dangerously ill. I was young, he was my first baby, (and every mother knows what a wonderful thing that is) I was wild with grief and fear. We could do nothing but telegraph for particulars and wait until the next evening. My husband insisted that I should sit for entrancement and see what our angel friends would say, and this was their message: "There is no occasion for so great an alarm; the child is better, and now sleeping quietly. They call it cholera infantum, but it is simply indigestion; please note the time; you will soon hear." It was 10:30 o'clock. We received a telegram dated 10 o'clock that night corroborating our spirit message in

every particular, and when I reached home the facts accentuated its value, clearly precluding the possibilty of a coincidence. I could fill a volume with incidents of a similar character which have come under my personal observation, tests of clairvoyance, prophecies fulfilled. diseases healed, lives saved by angelic fore-warnings, interpositions and hearts comforted."

But the joys of maternity were quickly shaded by the death of the two youngest of the household, by that fearful scourge diphtheria, in the space of five months, and then for the first time in her life did she who had so frequently administered the blessed consolations of her faith to others under bereavement, know the full meaning of the angels' messages. Through the agonized mother heart was poured a flood of precious assurances; to her perception came revelations of spiritual truth and beauty. The deathchamber of her darlings was illumined with a light that " was ne'er on land or sea ;" the pall of grief was lifted, and angelic presences took the place of her vanished babes.

After many years of phenomenal prosperity, during which time Mr. and Mrs. Watson endeared themselves to the community in which they resided by their hospitality, liberal charities and sympathetic interest in all humanitarian efforts, financial reverses and Mrs. Watson's declining health brought them to the Pacific coast, and Mrs. Watson was immediately engaged by the First Spiritual Union of San Francisco, as its regular pastor. After several years' ministration for this society, she became the settled speaker for the Golden Gate Religious and Philosophical Society of San Francisco; and for six years she lectured almost constantly in this city, and with ever-increasing popularity. Her many womanly graces, combined with the eloquence and power of her public addresses, endeared her to the hearts of her congregation; and probably no religious teacher or pastor in the city was more beloved by his faithful flock, than was this woman-pastor by the eager-listening auditors, who each Sunday hung upon the fervid words of burning eloquence and beauty that rolled from her angel-touched lips in almost measureless streams of richest harmony and love. Mrs. Watson's sojourn in San Francisco was twice broken —first by a trip to Australia in 1882, and secondly by a tour of the East in the summer of 1885. In Australia she was most cordially received, and everywhere greeted with large and enthusiastic audiences. Her tour of the East was one continued ovation. Whether speaking in churches, halls, or campmeetings, crowds of rapt listeners hung upon the streams of living eloquence that flowed from the inspired lips of "the silver-tongued orator of the Golden Gate," as she is aptly termed; and her last address at the Cassadaga campmeeting was characterized as one of the grandest orations that the people had ever been privileged to listen to.

Owing to financial reverses in the East Mrs. Watson, about ten years ago, established her home in California. She purchased an unimproved ranch—first sixteen acres, to which was subsequently added ten acres more—in Santa Clara county, near San Jose. This she has most successfully cultivated, beautified and adorned. Her lovely home thereupon, with its beautiful surroundings, has been named by her "Sunny Brae;" and all in all, it is a charming little paradise, the admiration and delight of its every visitor, and the pride of her friends all over the country. One year she sent to market one hundred tons of the best quality of prunes, always labeled with her "Sunny Brae" brand. She also raised apricots and other fruits. She superintends the entire business herself, from which is derived an annual income of between four and five thousand dollars. With "Sunny Brae" a centre, the influence of Mrs. Watson has extended far and wide in the adjacent country, penetrating even into the conservative orthodox circles in all the country round,—addresses, talks, etc, from her on

sociological, reformatory and religious themes being constantly solicited from "all sorts and conditions of men." Her life of usefulness and goodness at "Sunny Brae" has commanded the respect and love of the entire community for many, many miles around.

One of the most potent instrumentalities to this end has been the annual gatherings at "Sunny Brae" under the grand old Temple Oak. "In the center of the lawn that in front follows its splendid sweep, stands the Temple Oak,—a noble tree, spreading its superb branches covered with dense foliage fifty feet in every direction from its trunk, making its spread about one hundred feet in diameter." Here for a number of years past, on the first Sunday in June, which, says Mrs. Watson, "we call our Memorial Day, on which we dedicate our home to spiritual services and to the memory of our dear unseen," have great crowds gathered to listen to an eloquent address from "the little preacher," Mrs. Watson, and to enjoy her hospitlity. These meetings are anticipated and planned for by hundreds of people months ahead, and many families have made it their memorial day,—bringing their offerings of loving tnoughts for their departed ones to the flower-decked altar under the great arches of the living Temple, the majestic oak. In 1895 there were about 1000 persons in attendance upon the June meeting under Temple Oak.

In 1894 Mrs. Lydia A. Coonley, President of the Woman's Club of Chicago, published a graphic description of the myriad beauties of charming "Sunny Brae," which she had visited a short time previously. Following a vivid pen-painting of the lovely house and grounds, she says, "wonderful, enchanting as is all this ministration to the senses, the keenest, most lasting joy comes through the personality of the mistress of "Sunny Brae." * * * Her earnest conversation is full of a rare personal charm, and I shall never forget our long, delightful talks. * * Few women have such gift of language and a deeply religious and loving nature continually revealed. She is poet, orator, minister, and above and beyond all a rare woman.

*　　*　　*　　*　　*

"Upon the lawn the Temple Oak
  With noble arms outspread
Breathes benediction on each one
  Who loves his green-crowned head.

" Within the home the stranger finds
  A joyous welcoming ;
Good will, the 'Open Sesame'
  At which the wide doors swing.

"But would you know the fairest flower
  That perfumes every day,
'Tis heartsease, blooming 'neath the roof
  Of blessed 'Sunny Brae.''

Mrs. Watson has only one living child, a daughter, Lucretia, now a young lady. She is ambitious, and much desirous of emulating her mother's career of usefulness as a public ministrant. Her aims turn to world-helpfulness, and she herself to that end she has for several years been taking a collegiate course at the University of California. Possibly, in the not very distant future, she may find her sphere of usefulness to be that of minister in one of the most advanced Liberal churches of America.

Immediately following this sketch, the reader will find in this volume a few choice selections from the inspired addresses of Mrs. Watson, together with some excerpts from the many poetical improvisations with which her inspiration and genius have enriched the world.

During her public career she has been the recipient of many warm encomiums from critical minds, both Spiritualists and non-Spiritualists, and the following testimonial to her worth as a public ministrant is from the Spiritualistic critic, Wm. Emmette Coleman:

"I know of no female orator in the ranks of Spiritualism comparable to Mrs.

E. L. Watson. Good, sound sense is eminently characteristic of her platform utterances. The vagaries, extremeness, idealism, and transcendental rubbish which some Spiritualistic workers indulge in, is foreign to Mrs. Watson's lectures. Instead of these, she, good, true woman as she is, with soul aflame with zealous philanthropy for all the sons and daughters of earth, ever presents in her discourses sound, sensible, rational, ethical Spiritualism,—a Spiritualism free from fads and follies, fanaticism and fallacies. It is a Spiritualism all-embracing, including all things tending to man's elevation, mental, moral, spiritual, but at the same time eminently rational. While not neglecting the basic facts of spirit communion and the phenomena in general, the philosophy of Spiritualism, in its wide-extended scope, is duly considered, including its various bearings upon the sociological reforms of the day, and upon the crying evils in our social structure. The eloquence of Mrs. Watson has long been noted. In her case, mellifluous language and sound practicality, oratorical beauty and grandeur and unadulterated common sense, are inextricably blended. Beauty of language and sensible ideas are as one in her public ministrations.

Mrs. Watson's labors are largely devoted to the edification and upbuilding of mankind morally,—the rounding out and perfecting of character, the elevation of the race in the domains of ethics, the strengthening of the moral instincts and aptitudes. Intellectual wealth is a grand thing, but moral affluence is grander. Morality is the true touchstone of human character; and seeing how largely Mrs. Watson's labors are devoted to the guidance and furtherance of the moral sentiments, my soul goes out in thankfulness to her therefor.''

EXTRACTS FROM LECTURES AND POEMS.

[Extract from a lecture on ' Come Up Higher; or, The New Year of Spiritualism.'']

The spirit world has accomplished much in establishing through these spiritual phenomena the fact of man's immortality. They have accomplished much if they have determined for you, beyond a peradventure, this question: "Shall I have further opportunity for growth after I leave the body? Shall I meet with the friends whom I have loved and lost?" But there is something beyond this in the work of the spirit world, and that is, *What does it signify to me, as a moral being?* If I go to a seance, and I am convinced that a soul whom I loved once in a visible form, who ministered to me in all sweet and divine ways, has survived the change called death, what of that?

So much as there is in me of affection, so much as there is in me to be kindled by the remembrance of that love, and make me pure; so much as that has the power to draw me to nobler action, and cut me loose from low attractions, it signifies a moral force.

But I tell you, friends, that just as primal man gazed on the magnificent phenomena of nature, unimpressed until the *spiritual man* blossomed and then drank in the beauty and was refreshed and enlarged by it, so may you, as Spiritualists, look upon this phenomena continuously, and if you do not go below the surface and find in the facts demonstrated there the roots of moral force, the inspirations to a pure life, the phenomena fall flat and dead, and do you no good. Whosoever clings continuously to them in their physical phase, and is satisfied with that, is like unto the man who will not rise to his manly estate, but continues to amuse himself with the toys of childhood, and cares not for all that genius has converted and evolved from the alpha-

bet. For, I repeat, the physical phenomena of Spiritualism are only the beginning of man's spiritual knowledge; they are only the indices of that which is of more importance, and will surely follow; and they will be meaningless and worthless to him who sees in them only an amusement—only the demonstration of spiritual power which has no moral significance—who will not go beyond these and listen to the voice that may be heard through them appealing to him as a deathless soul to come up higher.

*　　*　　*　　*　　*

The one step higher of which we speak to-night is that step which shall lead every seeker after spiritual truth to the altar of his own life. You who have felt it a necessity to seek some outside medium and outward sign in order to communicate with your spirit friend, did you ever think how great the happiness of that friend when he is able to meet you at your own fireside? Able to touch you, not through some physical sign, but to breathe into your own spirit the message full of consolation and encouragement? Can you not understand why the spirit world would plead with you to leave the childish toys and forsake the old ways of the physical world and enter into the rich possessions of the spirit, and that it is only by cultivating this sympathy between yourself and the spirit that you can be ministered unto in your times of greatest need? Do you not see how often we must fail, if we seek through extraneous channels to meet and commune with you, and how you may multiply these avenues throughout the land, by each one making his own soul a repository of angel messages of instruction and consolation?

SOUL OF NATURE.

Soul of Nature! Life divine!
Make our hearts thy holy shrine;
Let our human discords be
Mastered by thy harmony!

O, Thou mighty Architect,
Whose plans th' endless years perfect,
Building systems infinite
By thy silent, changeless might,—
Thou, whose thoughts are suns and stars,
Thou, whose law no error mars,
To thy boundless love we turn,
Toward thy perfect truth we yearn!
Very weak and blind are we,
But in trust we lean on Thee!

Soul of Nature! Everywhere
Shine the symbols of thy care,
In the sea—depths vast and blue,
In the smallest drop of dew,
In siderial spaces filled
By the beauty thou hast willed—
And earth's clods to thy caress,
Respond with pure loveliness,
Lily, rose and violet,
Gems in golden sunshine set.
From this island in the sky
Unto thee thy children cry.

Soul of Nature! Source of things!
Quench our thirst at living springs!
By the magic of thy breath
Banish bitter dreams of death!
Let its language for love's sake
Be made plain to hearts that break!

*   *   *   *   *   *   *

From the gloom of vanished years,
Speak the prophets and the seers,
Pointing to the mountain height
Whence shall come the clearer light;
And from every race and clime
At this present day of time,
Sounds a gentler undertone,
From great Nature's vast unknown.

Beloved, listen! It may be
Prelude, in a minor key,
To Love's grandest symphony—
'Th' song of Immortality!

[Extract from an Address on "Psychics and Religion," delivered June 3d, 1888, at McVicker's Theatre, Chicago, Ill.]

Question your own heart! If you set aside ancient authority, and admit the fallibility of your sacred books, though containing much truth, and listen to the oracles within—God-implanted, God-reflecting—do you not find that this doctrine of a natural, active Spirit-world is rational? Does it not accord with your hope—your need? Does it not accord with all your human experience upon the external plane? Is there anything in the discoveries of science which conflicts with the central claim of modern Spiritualism? On the contrary, every discovery in the line of the physical sciences seems to have laid the foundations of this larger truth. Glance for a moment at the subject of mesmerism, and note how far one mind can act on another, enabling the mesmerist to bridge over what was once considered an impassable gulf between mind and mind, and furnishing us with an illustration of what the disembodied spirit may accomplish. Have you any reason for supposing that the physical brain is absolutely indispensable to the thinking spirit? On the contrary, your experience with psychics proves that intelligence is at times, even in earth-life, independent of the flesh.

And what is the relationship of the psychical law to our everyday life? It frees us at the very outset from the bondage of the senses, which has been a barrier between our souls and much that is beautiful and true; it refreshes our souls with new baptisms of hope; it supplies the missing link between the bereaved heart and the departed friend; it overturns the theological dogmas that have so long been obstacles in the way of human progress.

The psychical powers of Socrates, Jesus, Paul and Appolonius inspired virtuous action; poured balm upon wounded hearts, healed diseases of mind and body, and taught that the spirit-world is a natural world; that all we need fear is the consequences of our evil acts; that even as when we mutilate the flesh we suffer pain, so if we violate the laws of virtue and fraternity, the reaction will produce spiritual suffering.

I defy anyone to prove that psychical experiences have exerted other than good and helpful influence. Ever the angel's message has been, "Fear not, fear not."

Every new revelation from that world increases our hope. Every fresh vision accentuates the fact of the natural life of the spirit, and reveals to us the beautiful truth that we may begin our heaven now and here; that the griefs with which human life is burdened are but the necessary discipline through which the soul passes in ascending to higher planes of truth, goodness and joy. And the sympathy from unseen intelligences—how it buoys us up in the midst of vast discouragements! My friend, have you ambition to secure for yourself a place of honor in this world? Have you depended solely upon outward emoluments for your happiness? One glimpse of the psychic side of life reveals the fact that the only things which endure are virtue, intelligence, truth, and the attributes of the indwelling soul. All else is but temporary—swiftly passing. "You *have* only what you *are*." All you have to fear is within yourself. You can hope for nothing too good; you cannot believe too implicitly in the divinity of life; every sweet aspiration of the soul is but a prophecy that shall surely be fulfilled.

We are enwrapped by the spiritual world. We already inhabit it. Clairvoyance and clairaudience, common experiences of the psychic, are results of the unfoldment of faculties which survive after the change called death, and reveal the fact that every effort we make toward nobler living adds to our treasures in the hereafter. Every virtuous impulse shall become a thrill of joy, while every lapse of the soul from truth and goodness is sure to bring unhappiness. To the least of us it says, "You are a Soul, inheriting all the past, heir to all the future;" and every breath of truth that kisses the face of beings here is a signal from God, leading us onward and upward.

Let us continue the writing of Sacred Scriptures. Let us listen sympathetically to the psychic experiences of others. Let us reverently remember that the greatest souls of history have been those who have defied space, and time, and things of sense, exulting in the deathless powers of the soul.

Let us strengthen ourselves for the struggles and combats of life with the thought that over all is the reign of law; and that as immortal spirits we have a right to truth, a right to to-day's experiences; and that from the proph_et's vision to the seraphic smile on the face of a dying friend; from the faintest whisper from the unseen to our inner soul, to the grandest song of spiritual triumph that was ever sung, we have need of psychical experiences; they shall be to us strength in our hours of weakness; light in midnight darkness; and when bereavements come, when our dear ones depart from us through the silent portals of death, they shall be to us the promise of reunion in years to come. They shall be to us the assurance that divinity reigns throughout the universe. And thus we shall learn that—

Our lives are one with th' rolling
    spheres,
And over all God's will hath sway;
The labor of uncounted years
    Hath brought the harvest of to-day,
    In all its many-hued array.

The Past, enwrapped in error's night,
    Was but a mighty chrysalis,
Where Truth prepared her wings of
    light,
    On which to soar from Doubt's abyss,
    And bear mankind to endless bliss.

The funeral pyres of martyred men,
    Who died for harmless heresies,
Still mark the way where truth ha
    been
    Encamped along the centuries,
    Protected by the pitying skies.

How slight the pangs Servetus bore,
    When matched with manhood's
    noble pride;
How dear the names forevermore
    Of those who have for Truth's sake
    died—
    The Christs whom hate has crucified.

Thought's golden shuttle, swiftly sped,
    As by a great, unerring hand,
Has woven Truth's unbroken thread
    Into life's pattern, vast and grand,
    Nor ever paused at priest's command;

Until at last our glad eyes see,
    As on a mighty, pictured scroll,
A sweet and tender prophecy
    Of Truth's bright future far unroll,
    Her throne th' enfranchised, deathless soul.

————

[In answer to the question: "Is Happiness the Chief Object of Life?"]

Happiness is the fruit of right living; happiness is the natural consequence of obedience to the laws of your constitution. You cannot, therefore, separate happiness from the good, and we can answer that in this sense it is the chief object of life. Not the happiness of the body—of the sensuous nature alone—for he who enjoys only the sense of the flesh, knows not great joy; it is only he who finds this a step, and uses it for mounting to higher altitudes, who knows the joy of living; he who feels that he has triumphed over sense, who has fought bravely with temptations and won the victory. Then, sweeter than the shout of happy soldiery, when victory for them is declared; prouder than the trumpet-blare, which cries a great man's power, is the consciousness of that man who has seen what is good and true, and been able to climb to it, and live it in his soul. To feel one's self attacked by a thousand malignant enemies that make raid upon our virtues—beings that strive to bind us through our passions, and drag us from that high estate to which we all are heirs—to feel ourselves proclaiming victory over these; to stand upon a battle-field so proudly and nobly won—this is to know true happiness. This must be the grandest object of our life; to conquer that which is pernicious in ourselves, and that which militates against the highest nature of the soul; to conquer all things below us, convert chaos into beauteous forms of life, and bring from discord sweetest harmony. To work all life's fallow ground; to tear up the virgin soil, where now may grow only weeds, and sow it thick with golden seeds that abound with life most beautiful, impatient to burst forth into bloom and sacred fruits; and where there are desert wastes afar, o'ersweeping which are scorching winds of bitter passion; to turn into these the fresh, full, silvery tides of spiritual being, until the banks shall overflow and water all those scorching sands; until the very atmosphere shall call from the flashing music of the tides their soft tributes to send them back again in sweet baptismal rain, and from this mighty labor of the soul to see those wastes made to blossom like the rose! At last to wrench from Nature crude her wondrous secret; to convert her ores and precious stones into things more fair, that shall stand for attributes of spirit life; to see the chill, dull atmosphere of mortal being glittering with ten thousand starry thoughts that have their birth in God's own bosom—this is to labor well, and to earn rich happiness. And this, whether we know it or not, is the object and aim of every human soul. Though now we lose our way; though we now see not into the mystery by which we are surrounded; though vain seems all our labor, and impossible to attain the heights and the vast plains outlying there beneath the gorgeous sun of wisdom's day, still the

steps are possible—they were carved by the law of God.

By and by the mist will melt away, and the rough stone of life, which, like that quarried there in Nature's mighty warehouse, awaits the artist's hand to give it form, will, by the slow dropping of our human tears, reveal a diviner shape. And in these ways, so wondrous and so little known by us, God works His will with men, until at last that blessed vision which glows before us all and which we name our happiness, shall be fulfilled, and each soul know why it is here, why it has waited long, why toiled and struggled against a cruel fate—a fate that at last becomes its servant, and shapes the higher life to which it was born and of which it is the natural heir.

Judge not your life by th' little part
　That lies too near to view aright,
But with a calm and trusting heart
　Await the future's clearer light.

By looking at a tiny seed
　How can we prophecy the flower?
Who knows how far a trifling deed
　May yet extend its subtle power?

Take not your journey's reck'nings while
　Within the valley's veiling mist,
Nor in the mountain's dark defile,
　Where light of sun hath never kissed,

But press straight on, without delay,
　And what has seemed a trackless wild
Will open up a flower-strewn way,
　On which God's tender thoughts have
　　smiled.

Through winter's storm and rayless night
　The earth in perfect safety rolls,
Guided by her attractions' might,—
　And thus it is with human souls!

When all life's surface writhes in pain,
　And by some cruel fate seems driven,
We still are held by love's bright chain,
　Safe sheltered in the breast of heaven.

We cannot controvert God's will,
　Within its circle all abide;
There is no depth He does not fill,
　There is no height to us denied.

As atoms into crystal build,
  Moved by a silent, unseen power.
Or sunlight's fairy pencils gild
  The satin cheeks of opening flower;

So does the weakest man obey
  A law of life that slowly brings,
From all his fellowship with clay,
  A shining soul that soars and sings.

Then, though we may not understand
  The mighty, veiled Alchemist
Whose sweet, unuttered thoughts com-
    mand
  The birth of pearl and amethyst,

O! let us fill, with heart content,
  The place He deems for each the best,
Of Love a willing instrument,
  Trusting to time and God the rest.

CHARLES DAWBARN.

CHARLES DAWBARN.

Mr. Charles Dawbarn is a well known thinker, writer and lecturer, whose life and labor is that of a level-headed Spiritualist. Ornamental Spiritualism has had little attraction for him. To discover a fact, then learn and teach the lesson of that fact, has been his object; and carried out so fearlessly that he often startles and alarms the worshipper of phenomena.

Mr. Dawbarn is from England and from old Baptist stock. His ancestors of three generations have preached many a solemn sermon warning sinners 'to flee from the wrath to come.' Born in 1833 amidst the narrowest of all religious surroundings, he grew to early manhood unconscious of the scientific agitation that was even then bringing light out of darkness. He was trained to accept 'faith' as divine; but 'human reason' as a deadly snare.

It is now about forty years since Mr. Dawbarn came to America, where for a year or two he did Sunday work in Baptist pulpits at the request of the church he had joined. He says that it was reading "Buckle's Introduction to the History of Civilization" that first stirred him to independent thought. Carefully reviewing the grounds of his religious belief, he became convinced that a personal devil and an' endless hell were not taught in the Bible; so he left the Baptist and joined the Universalist church.

Of course his old friends were wounded, and left him to win a position amongst strangers as best he could. But he soon gained favor, and once again lectured and preached and was active in Sunday-school work. Phenomena occurring in his own home induced him to investigate Spiritualism, with the result that he became an avowed believer. Once again he was almost friendless, for there is a bitter antagonism to progressive thought amongst many so-called liberal Christians that was not surpassed by the Mayflower puritan. Even by the most charitable of his Universalist friends he was counted as afflicted with softening of the brain. But such animosity neither embittered him, nor caused him to swerve from avowing his belief, although for a time it destroyed his domestic happiness.

Mr. Dawbarn has been a widower for twenty years, and has devoted his leisure to a most earnest investigation, both of phenomena and philosophy; but a very active business life held him from public work for a number of years. He then gave a course of lectures in Frobisher Hall, New York, on social and religious subjects, which led to his being invited to lecture at the well-known Lake Pleasant Camp the following summer.

Mr. Dawbarn early attracted attention amongst thinking Spiritualists by his articles published in various papers; but chiefly those in the *Religio-Philosophical Journal*, of Chicago. "Manhood versus Anthood," "Mistakes of Investigators," "Gospel of True Manhood," "Unborn Man," and a lecture published in the *Banner of Light* on "A Warning from East to West; or, Spiritualism in India," were among his earliest productions, and had wide circulation and aroused earnest thought. An anniversary address, "A Review of Modern Spiritualism," which was reported for and published in the *Carrier Dove*, was an admirable specimen of his fearless criticism and outspoken indignation against everything he deems unworthy of the cause.

In 1888 Mr. Dawbarn came to California, making his home in the beautiful little city of San Leandro. For more than a year he lectured to large audiences in San Francisco, and for another year he accepted engagements in various cities on the Pacific Coast, from Victoria in the north to San Diego in the extreme south. His lectures were highly esteemed everywhere, and it seemed as if the demand for his scientific and philosophical addresses would hold him permanently to the Spiritualistic platform. But his value as a citizen became recognized, and he was claimed for public service. For a time he served as a county health officer. He was then chosen as City Trustee, in which position his care for the health of his adopted city led him to demand and finally complete a most successful system of sewerage. And yet more recently his services have been sought to help in establishing a plant for the electric lighting of both the streets and homes of San Leandro.

Amidst the cares and duties of a very busy life he retains all his interest in the cause of Spiritualism—demanding only that it shall be accompanied by approved phenomena, and freed from the credulity which so often endorses fraud. Mr. Dawbarn finds time for articles in the Eastern press, which are always welcomed by thoughtful readers, and have helped to compel the present general respect for Modern Spiritualism that has been conspicuous by its absence during many of the forty-eight years of its history.

Mr. Dawbarn is still in the full vigor of manhood, both physically and intellectually, and proposes to continue to maintain and support his belief by his pen as often as he can find leisure.

Whether he will appear upon our platform is a question that he cannot now answer, but at the present time he is obliged to refuse all invitations to lecture.

MRS. GEORGIA COOLEY.

MRS. GEORGIA COOLEY.

I was born in Portland, Oregon, where my parents are still residing. I was the youngest of ten children, five of whom are still in earth-life, the other five having passed to spirit-life.

No special religious belief was instilled into my young mind, as father was an independent thinker, bordering toward materialism. When I was a child my mother attended the Methodist church, consequently I became a member of the same Sabbath-school. After a time I tired of this one, and became a member of the Presbyterian Sabbath-school, which I attended until I was about sixteen years of age.

As I now understand the phiiosophy of Spiritualism, I find I was always a medium, yet among those who understood me not. Being very delicate, I was compelled to remain at home from school a great part of the time, and while suffering from malaria and other physical ills—all being given a different name by the various physicians—I would begin to speak in a manner quite foreign to my accustomed way, and was naturally considered "out of my head." Very often during the night, the other members of the family would be aroused by what was called "Georgia's night-mare of preaching." On some of these occasions I would realize what was transpiring, but found it impossible to prevent the same. At other times I knew nothing, and on being told what had happened, felt inclined to disbelieve. These spells occurred oftener and lasted longer as I grew older, and all possible remedies were used to quiet me, but without avail, until at last, by some unknown means, salt was thought of, and my mother would watch her opportunity to throw some into my mouth. This seemed to break the spell for the time, and longer periods gradually intervened, until at last I began to feel I had outgrown the terrible unnamed malady. During all my childhood days I was exceedingly clairvoyant, seeing spirit forms, yet could not hear what was said, although their lips moved. I also took "Trips to Heaven," as I then termed it; but of late years find it is my spirit leaving the body, and going out into space—sometimes visiting the "Spirit World.' While attending Sabbath-school, I frequently saw writing on the walls, names over the people's heads, visions, etc.; and becoming interested in this, when the time came for me to read my verse from the Bible, I had lost the place, and would have to be shown it by my teacher, which was very embarrassing. I often wished to tell the teacher, yet felt intimidated. This continued until I began to feel a restlessness coming over me, which finally grew into a distaste for Sabbath school. I then went to the Baptist church for a time, but emptiness seemed connected with all, and I ceased going to church altogether, and saw but little clairvoyantly for several years, but was very impressional—so much so, that it became my sole means of guidance.

I knew nothing of Spiritualism until I met Mr. Cooley. He spoke of his father being a medium, and I felt very much annoyed; consequently very little was said upon the subject until after we had been married about two years. Then strange noises were heard about the house—loud raps, as though some one was at the door—and on opening it, to my astonishment no one was visible. Raps would then be heard on the window, my stove covers would rattle, oven doors open and close with a bang, and coal was shoveled without visible hands. As I was much alone— Mr. Cooley working at night—I became very much alarmed, and we sought another house, feeling the one we occupied was haunted. My husband reasoned with me, saying: "Our spirit friends are making these disturbances, as they wish you to know they are here. Why do you not talk to them?" etc. But he reasoned without avail, and we removed to another home. But the noises followed me, and I again became clairvoyant and also clairaudient. The spirit friends explained to me that I was an instrument the spirit world desired to use for humanitarian work. I rebelled against this, fearing that if I gave up to these influences, my individuality would be destroyed, and I would become a slave.

I was influenced by my husband to attend a camp-meeting at New Era, Oregon, but went more for the purpose of visiting with his people than from any interest I took in the proceedings. The first day passed quietly. The second day I thought I would walk around the grounds and take a good look at the people calling themselves Spiritualists. I had only gone a short distance from our tent, and was saying to myself, "They look very much like other people," when I was entranced by a spirit friend of a lady who was passing me. From that on, I was not myself but a few moments at a time for the remaining ten days of our stay on the grounds. As soon as one spirit left me, another took possession, personating, passing through death scenes, talking in their old, familiar way—much to the satisfaction of their earth-friends, and very often to the amusement of those present. I was very delicate at the time, having just recovered from an attack of typhoid fever, and found it impossible to prevent the various spirits that desired from taking possession of my organism. Naturally the variety of such influences caused much merriment— especially when one who made himself

known as "Pat" would control. He was a typical representative of "Old Erin," and in his witty, yet earnest manner, caused quite an excitement. On being told of this I felt very much hurt, and endeavored to leave the ground, but found it impossible to get away. On returning home, we found "Pat" had followed us, and to this day he is still in the band, as one of the most earnest workers, being a good test guide as well as a proficient character-reader. When lack of enthusiasm or harmony is felt, "Pat" is always at hand, and with his harmonizing influence sets all present at ease.

After returning from the camp-meeting, I again began to fight against my development, and only after a long period of patient waiting and earnest persuasion by my Guides did I consent to do the work the angel friends desired. I have never regretted my decision. I have not lost my individuality, but have become more fully individualized; and as I follow the instructions of the higher intelligences I find life grows more beautiful each day. By being cautious, exacting and earnest, and with the help of my husband's influence, I have attracted a band of truthful, earnest and enthusiastic workers from the world beyond, who never tire of giving their aid to mortals.

Through the magnetic influence of my Indian band, of which "Red Fox" is the leader, I find myself growing stronger each day. My mediumship has changed very much since the beginning. Different phases have been developed, such as trance and inspirational speaking, public tests, writing, etc. I have had much experience with what is known as "dark spirits," and find that some of my best work has been in that direction, breaking obsession, causing both mortal and spirit to be lifted into a higher condition.

As we educate and familiarize ourselves with the grand and beautiful philosophy of Spiritualism, we become more helpful and useful in this world, and find no moments to spare; for as we learn, we can always find others to instruct and assist. May we all grow into the light of truth, and as we gain strength and knowledge therefrom, never weary of sowing the seed that will thrive throughout all time, and yield a bountiful harvest in the golden fields of eternity.

A REMARKABLE TRANCE.

The following is a statement made by Mrs. Georgia Cooley, who was living in Summerland, Cal., at that time. She says :

"On the 13th day of March 1895, about 2.30 P. M., I had just finished giving a sitting, and being in a very sensitive state, everything around me seemed illuminated. As soon as I opened my eyes I saw the name Carrie Van Horn written out, and at the same instant a voice whispered, 'Go to her as quickly as possible. We wish your help to relieve the spirit.' I found the lady very low, and the friends who had gathered around her bedside seemed anxious to learn what I thought of her condition and urged me to do all I could to help her regain her senses and bring her out of the unconscious condition she was in. There were two windows in the room ; one near the head of the bed, the other nearly opposite. I raised the one farthest from the bed and looked out ; when I turned around I saw a light vapor rising from the head of the sick woman. This seemed about the size of a person's hand. She could not speak and did not seem to recognize anyone in the room. The atmosphere was heavy and stifling and I suggested that the window be raised near the bed. This was objected to by some spirit, for I heard a voice saying, 'Do not nurse the physical. Please sing.' None present could, or at least felt inclined to do so, and the sensations that passed over me were very disagreeable. I tried to leave the room, but could not. The small vapory-like cloud was changing rapidly, and in its place came a spiritaul counterpart of the dying woman, which seemed to rise a few feet from the body.

could only see at this time clearly—the head, neck, and part of the chest. The lips of the physical moved as if talking and the same was noticeable of the spirit, both moving in unison with each other. I here noticed what apparently was a struggle going on between the physical and the spiritual. The latter seemed making a desperate effort to free itself from the body. Again I heard a voice say, 'You must now create a vibration.' My hands at the same time were lifted above my head and descending with a slow steady motion. Those present joined in this movement and we all felt much relieved. I saw a number of spirit hands at this time doing precisely the same thing. They, however, were working directly over the dying woman. I saw also the spirit form of an elderly lady step up to the bedside and place both her arms under the reclining spirit and raise it gently upward. At the headboard and surrounding the entire front of the bed was a beautiful vapory-like lace that hung in folds, while the centre was studded with some of the most beautiful roses I had ever seen. I began to feel sick and weak, and arose to go, when some one asked me when I thought Miss Van Horn would pass out. Like a flash there came nine marks on the head of the bed. I did not feel sure as to the meaning and said, 'I saw nine marks but do not know what was meant by it.' Once more I heard a voice say, 'By nine o'clock all will be over. You can go now, but we will remain."

"I went home and was busy with my household duties until a few minutes past seven, when I felt a smothering sensation come over me and a strong spiritual influence. I went to the cabinet with my husband and sat a few moments, and went into a trance. I soon became aware of moving in the direction of the Van Horn residence ; but while the sensations of moving were somewhat like the physical act of walking, I moved with more ease and rapidity. As soon as I reached the house there appeared to be an opening I had not before noticed, through which I passed into the room of the dying woman. I immediately saw that the spirit had freed itself from the body and was in the act of passing out of the room through the window. There were several spirits who attended this new born one, and were of both sexes. I followed them out of the room and saw them gradually rising upward—going out over the ocean.

" The town of Summerland is situated on the beach, and the body was borne for quite a distance out and above the water. I now began to feel myself ascending, and also became aware of the presence of my guide. We were following the group, but were some distance below and back of them. I could see quite a distance beyond them a cloud of white vapor, which parted as we neared it, and we all passed through without any inconvenience. I soon began to feel much better, as the atmosphere seemed lighter and purer. I noticed Miss Van Horn raised her hand to her head as if in pain. Then an attendant spirit stooped over her, and made a few passes in the direction indicated, saying, ' Never mind, that is all right.'

" As my attention was drawn to this part of the body, I saw a silvery cord attached to the neck or base of the brain ; and to my surprise, in following it up, found it still attached to the body. By this time we had reached a plane that appeared circular, the dimensions of which extended as far as the eye could reach. The surrounding objects seemed as tangible as anything I had ever seen on earth, and the whole area was covered with cots or beds (for they had no head or foot board). The covering was of a beautiful texture resembling lace, and

hung in folds around each bed. There was no roof over this place, which I thought was a hospital, and thousands of spirits flitted hither and thither, attending to the weak and suffering spirits who were brought here. Miss Van Horn was placed upon one of these beds and given a vigorous treatment. To my question as to what place we were in, my guide said : " We are in the sphere of strength. Soms remain twelve hours ; others longer. Much depends on the condition of the spirit.'

" I do not remember how much time I spent in this invigorating atmosphere, but at the request of my guide I again started earthward, and soon stood in the presence of my friend's body. Her lips were moving, and she gasped for breath, while a deathly pallor overspread her features. I remained but a few minutes and returned to my home, and next awoke to find myself in about the same position as when I left, or rather went in the trance. It was then about 8 o'clock. I went to bed, but was again drawn to the chamber of my friend ; and as I stood looking at the body which was still breathing, I saw the cord break, and like a flash disappear. I awoke with a start, and when I looked at my watch it was nine o'clock. I learned since it was near that hour that she ceased breathing.

" It seemed strange to me that the spirit could be absent over an hour from the body, and still the latter showing signs of life. But is it any more wonderful than the trance condition in which mediums leave their bodies and visit distant places while the physical body is apparently in a condition resembling sleep. Oh, how grand and uplifting are the scenes in spirit life, and the power of the unseen forces that are around us. We think life a hardship, but does not the blessings of our spiritual gifts carry us far above and beyond the trials of this life? Friends and co-workers, lift up your heads ! Your gift is a blessing and not a misfortune. Open the door to the unseen world, and you will receive the richest blessings the spirit world can give."

CHARLOTTE MacMEEKIN.

MRS. MacMEEKIN.

The subject of this sketch was born in England, Nov. 5th, 1837. On her father's side her ancestors were English, and on the mother's side they were Scotch. Her father was a wholesale merchant. Her mother was a medical doctor, and for a long time held a position as such in the Glasgow Infirmary.

In the year 1857 she married; five children were born in the British Isles. Three beautiful girls passed to spirit life at an early age. The family came to New York in 1869, and from there to California in 1870 and settled in San Jose, which at that time was a small village. She grieved very much at leaving home, and not understanding her new surroundings kept a great deal to herself, and being of a very sentitive nature would sit by the window for hours alone, and would there see panoramic visions passing before her. Thinking she was becoming demented her physician was sent for, but he could discover no disease, and he said there was nothing whatever the matter. He tried. however, to stop the deep intense breathing; but as both the doctor and herself were ignorant of the laws of spirit control they could not understand what was the matter. Her husband at that time was investigating the phenomena of spiritualism.

Being a doubter she would not have anything to do with mediumship, spurning it from her; and not until the year 1889, when questioning within herself one day when alone concerning the phenomena and philosophy of Spirit. ualism, she became enveloped as it were, in a cloud of white mist when she saw the form and heard the voice of an old time friend, named James Ferguson who was a lawyer when in this life. He told her to doubt no longer, as he with many others would aid and prepare her for the work that was in the future before her. From that day hundreds of broad minded spirits have controled her brain, and she is always ready to join hands with those who are striving to advance poor humanity. Her natural inclination leads her to the whole, and not to individualities. Her experience in Spiritualism has been a marvel to herself and many others. Her phases of mediumship are clairvoyance and clairaudiance, inspirational speaking and psychometric reading. She has also diagnosed and cured disease through her guides for a number of years free of charge, and held parlor meetings at her home for many years for those who were seeking after truth. Those who are acquainted with her guides and teachers know what spiritual truths they have given through her as their medium.

CHARLES H. FOSTER.

TEST MEDIUM.

—

Charles H. Foster was one of the early test mediums whose name became prominent wherever spiritualism was known full forty years ago. He was called "the skeptic's medium" from the fact that his tests were of such startling and convincing character that they carried conviction with them. To have a "sitting" with Mr. Foster was equivalent to an open acknowledgement of the facts of spiritualism. Few, if any, ever left his presence doubting or disbelieving. They were forced to accept as true the unmistakable evidence given them of spirit communion through this remarkable man's psychic powers.

Mr. Foster was born in the historical town of Salem, Mass., and had that event occurred two hundred years earlier he would probably have shared the fate of many other psychics of that time who were put to death by an ignorant, bigoted people who charged them with the unpardonable crime of witchcraft. However, our medium did not put in an earthly appearance until it was safe and proper for him to do so ; consequently his life was spared and his mission as a medium accomplished.

Mr. Foster's mediumship began to develop when he was about fourteen years of age, his attention being called to it by hearing raps on his desk in school. Physical manifestations occurred in his room at night, and his parents would find the furniture scattered about in great confusion.

Such demonstrations gradually gave way to an organized and systematic presentation of these phenomena in the light, and the medium soon attained a world-wide reputation. At an early stage of his mediumistic career, Mr. Foster visited England and created a great sensation among all classes through the wonderful manifestations of spirit power occurring in his presence. It is said that during that visit he was the guest at Knebworth, of Lord Bulwer Lytton, and so greatly was the distinguished author impressed with what he witnessed, that it formed the foundation of "A Strange Story" in which Mr. Foster figured as "Margrave."

He was treated royally, and received everywhere. People of rank and social station visited him, and even Queen Victoria attended one of his seances. In Paris he was the object of distinguished attention. He was an invited guest and had frequent sittings with the Emperor Napoleon, the Empress Eugenie and other members of the Imperial household. In Belgium he was also highly favored, receiving from King Leopold a magnificent diamond pin as a token of his regard.

He also visited Havana, and the communications received at his seances were many of them given in Spanish and French, although Mr. Foster knew nothing of either language. He traveled extensively throughout the United States visiting all the principal cities, convincing skeptics wherever he went of the truth of spirit return.

An illustration of the nature of Mr. Foster's wonderful mediumship was published in the *New York Graphic* a number of years ago which is copied here.

"One night a total stranger to Foster called at his rooms and said :

"Foster, I do n't believe in your humbug. Now, you never saw or heard of me, and I will bet you twenty dollars

CHARLES H. FOSTER.

that you can't tell my name ; I do it to test you."

"Twenty dollars," slowly repeated Foster ; "twenty dollars that I can't tell your name? Well, sir," putting his hand to his brow, "the spirit of your brother Clement, tells me that your name is Alexander B. Corcorane."

Mr. Corcorane was astonished, and took out his money to pay the medium' who pushed it back with a laugh. "One day," said Mr. Frank Carpenter, when we met at Mr. Foster's—"one day a lady, an utter stranger, came into Mr. Foster's room with a lock of coarse hair in her hand. It looked like fine bristles. Holding it up, she asked the medium whose hair it was. Foster took it in his hand a moment, pressed it to his brow, and exclaimed : 'By the eternal, this is Andrew Jackson's hair.'"

It turned out that the lady's mother was an intimate friend of General Jackson, and that the bunch of bristles was really an heirloom from the head of old Hickory himself.

One day, Alexander McClure of Pennsylvania, came into the Continental Hotel with Colonel John B. Forney. Mr. McClure was very sad, for he had received news that his son was drowned at sea. "What do you think about it, Foster ? " asked Colonel Forney. "Why, sir, the boy is not drowned at all," replied Foster. "He's alive and well, and you'll have a letter from him in a day or two, and then he will come home."

Two days afterward McClure met Foster and said with tears of gratitude :

"Why, Foster, you were right. My boy is all safe. I had a letter from him today. * * *

Next to this gentleman sat another, a person well known in political circles. Foster suddenly turned to him and said : "Wilcoxson—is that the way you pronounce it? His spirit is here." The gentleman spoken to said : "This is most singular. Wilcoxson is right. Where did he die ? " Said Foster : "The power is in my arms ; I will write. He seized a pencil and wrote in a scarcely legible scrawl, very rapidly : "Died at Fordham." The gentleman shook his head. "Is it anything like Fordham ? " asked Foster. "Suppose you write it, and on the other pieces of paper write the names of other towns."

This was done, and the bits of paper were folded up and thrown on the table. The correct slip of paper was immediately selected—the name being "London."

"This is indeed singular," said our friend. "I this morning received a dispatch by cable announcing the death of that person yesterday in London."

During Mr. Foster's visit to the Pacific Coast many years ago, he made hundreds of converts to Spiritualism, and gave some of the most remarkable tests ever given by any medium.

Epes Sargent is given as authority for the statement that on one occasion two skeptical gentlemen who had witnessed the mysterious red writing in process of appearing on the medium's arm, seized hold of it to discover his trick as they called it, and said : "We know nothing will come while we hold it." "What will you have?" said Foster. "Something that will be a test—something that will fit our case," said they. Immediately while they held his arm as in a vice, there appeared in large, round, blood-red letters the words "Two Fools."

Many similar tests could be given, but the above are sufficient to illustrate some of the various phases of his wonderful mediumship, and the almost absolute certainty of the statements made by him when under the influence of his spirit guides.

Mr. Foster passed to spirit life on Dec. 15th, 1885, at the age of fifty-two years. He was the victim of typhoid fever which resulted in a nervous difficulty from which he never fully recovered. He had always been a devoted son during all the changes and exciting events of his remarkable career, and when affliction came, they in turn ministered unto him and sought to stay the ravages of mental decay. After years of suffering he recovered his spiritual perceptions, and with them came a deeper spirituality,—an unfolded, chastened manhood. He was always generous and noble in giving, having no thought of accumulating wealth ; but earning money and spending it freely he made many hearts glad through his benefactions. The good he did far over-balanced his faults and left his life page written over with blessed charities and tender, fragrant memories. He passed away at the home of his aunt, in the place of his birth, Salem, Mass.

WILLIAM MacMEEKIN.

WILLIAM MacMEEKIN.

Wm. McMeekin, was born in Scotland in the year 1838, his father and mother being Scotch, and of the lineage of the old Scotch reformers. His father was a very religious and moral character, and so sensitive that he was called a crank. He was always searching after truth while on earth, and is now one of the principal spirit controls of his son for inspirational writing. He always eschewed the use of intoxicating liquors, or tobacco in any form, believed in purity and integrity, he had a detestation of hypocrites, loved truth wherever he could find it, and transmitted those qualities to his offspring.

Mr. Mac.Meekin has been a teacher of music for the last twenty-five years in San Jose, and his family are all musicians. He began his investigation of Spiritualism in 1870, and at that time was sexton of the Episcopal Church of San Jose, which position he had held for 15 years. From the spirit of his mother he received his first message through planchette, and since that time has been a spiritual worker as far as circumstances would permit him; and by holding developing classes has brought a great many to the light. He was president of the First Spiritual Union of San Jose, in the years 1892 and 1893, and held said position until he went to the Sandwich Islands with his youngest son and remained there during part of the troubles and insurrection in Honolulu. He returned in 1894 and resumed his work in San Jose. Mr. Mac.Meekin and his wife are both exemplary spiritualists, and faithful, conscientious mediums, giving freely of their spiritual gifts wherever they can benefit a poor, unfortunate fellow creature. The cause has in them two faithful and efficient workers, whose good deeds entitle them to loving remembrance.

ADDIE L. BALLOU.

POET, PATRIOT, PREACHER AND PAINTER.

The author of "Workers in the Vineyard" is indebted to Mr. Albert Morton, for a portion of the notes comprising the sketch of one of the most efficient and practical workers along reform lines on the Pacific Coast. Mrs. Ballou is untiring in her philanthropic labors, and is the leading spirit in a number of societies and enterprises for the aid and betterment of those in need, for social purposes, and individual upliftment and culture.

The Western Reserve in Ohio has been the nursery of many eminent workers in the reform fields of labor, among whom were the prominent Spiritualists, Joshua R. Giddings, M. C., for many years, Senator and Vice President, Benj. F. Wade and President James A. Garfield.

In this section, where the very atmosphere was impregnated with Anti-Slavery and rigid theological beliefs, our heroine, Addie Lucia, the daughter of strictly orthodox parents, was born, and when about thirteen years of age became a member of the M. E. church, although she rebelled against its doctrinal restrictions, which she felt to be horrible and terrifying. Directly after becoming a church member her mediumistic tendencies were discovered while attempting to play at ghosts and summon spirits for the edification of the son of a deacon—her juvenile sweetheart—she was suddenly controlled and made to do remarkable things, greatly to the consternation and displeasure of the good deacon and members of the family with whom she was visiting, and was made the object of vehement prayers till the spirit was exorcised—temporarily.

For years thereafter she was used mediumistically in various ways, writing, healing and seeing while in a semi-conscious state. Soon as she decided to enter the lecture field, all her mediumistic powers were concentrated upon speaking and writing, and she traveled widely and became celebrated for her faithful services as a writer and speaker on all reformatory subjects. The secular papers in commenting upon her grand work in the many reforms she has ably advocated, and in referring to her artistic achievements have generally ignored her work for pure Spiritualism.

In "California, Her Industries, Attractions and Builders," the following biographical sketch appears:

"The life and honored career of Mrs. Addie L. Ballou, artist, orator, writer and notary public, of San Francisco, is a representative type of self-made women of the West. Born on the Western Reserve in Northern Ohio, during the exciting days of Anti-Slavery agitation, of parents devoted to the abolishing of slavery, and other humanitarian reforms. Her inherent tendencies drifted her into advanced fields of thought and activity, identified with which from her earliest years, she is so well-known throughout the United States and the Colonies as a forcible, eloquent and ready speaker and writer of both prose, verse, and as a philanthropist in reforms. The early

ADDIE L. BALLOU.

death of her mother, and the removal of her family to the frontier in Wisconsin deprived her of the opportunity of even a common school education, as the care of other motherless children devolved upon her in a neighborless region of the far west for some years, and where, at the early age of fifteen years, she was married.

By studious application and remarkable energy and courage, she succeeded in overcoming monumental obstacles and inopportune environments, grasping every suggestion for improvement. Sometimes with feet on the cradle, and needle in hand, applying the lesson from the book neat at hand, and never despairing of the ultimate success in the uncertain future. Her first literary contribution was composed while doing her family washing—written upon scraps of brown paper and stealthily transcribed in a wretchedly cramped hand that night, after every one else slept, then she walked a mile to post it to the county newspaper, lest her secret might be discovered, and then she suffered a week of honest remorse and torture for doing so, at the end of which time a highly flavored editorial announced the simultaneous birth of a local poet and the publication of the exquisite gem " Contentment," and gratuitously prophesied the brilliant future of the author. The poem was widely copied, and each announcement of the fact threw the writer into violent ague, but succeeding ones have continued to evolve, until at present a large volume is in contemplation for the publisher. Some of the later poems appear in a compiled work of an eastern house in "Poets of America," and a late local publication as well. The author has been a successful writer of short stories and essays, and has for many years been recognized as a terse writer and ready journalist.

During the late war of the sixties she distinguished herself in the service of the government by enlisting, and afterward received a commission from Surgeon General Wolcott, as nurse and matron of the 32nd Wis. Vols. Inft., by whom

of the surviving members she is held in affectionate and revered memory still, as she is also esteemed by the G. A. R. wherever found, as a comrade."

Mrs. Ballou, through many vicissitudes and at cost of many privations, took up the study of art, writing and speaking in the intermediate spaces between study hours, and has succeeded in making a name among Californian artists beyond her most sanguine and earlier hopes. Several of her largest and best pieces fill places of honor in the celebrated Stanford Gallery at Melbourne, Australia. Mr. Stanford (younger brother of Leland Stanford) having secured the entire productions of her brush during her three years' stay in Australia. The place of honor in the entire collection numbering some 300, being given to the painting now celebrated in both countries— "Morning "—rejected at the State Fair in Sacramento.

Among the successful bills of Mrs. Ballou's championage, was the one introduced and acquired through her efforts at the Legislature of California three years ago, which provides for the appointment of *women* as notaries public in and throughout the State. Many women, at present in California, are since made beneficiaries through appointment to the office, among them recently and to the gratification of her many friends, the author of the bill.

Mrs. Ballou is inordinately fond of the little people, and enjoys their sports or their sorrows with their griefs as if they were her own, and always has a tender word for all, and enjoys a romp or a season in their companionship as the one restful and happy incident in life to anticipate. She has three sons and one daughter at the head of their several homes in honorable and honored manhood and womanhood, and for whom her efforts and upon whom has centered the hopes of a hard-wrought, self-sacrificing and devoted life

In answer to a call from California Mrs. Ballou came here in Feb. 1871, and after filling her engagements in San Jose, San

Francisco, Sacramento and elsewhere, in May she attended the New Era camp-meeting near Portland, Oregon, thence to Salem where she became interested in the boy, Thomas Gerrand, condemned to be hanged in a short time, visited him in his cell and learning the circumstances below, and being moved by his tender years determined to save him if possible. Public prejudice was very bitter against him principally owing to the fact of his being a half caste, his mother being a squaw of more than usual intelligence. He seemed not the hardened criminal represented to be, but the child of untoward and unfortunate circumstances and was dejected, forlorn and friendless.

Having but a few hours to remain in Salem before leaving for other engagements, she hurriedly drew up a petition presenting a strong plea for the prisoner and urging executive clemency by a commutation to life imprisonment, and went in person to Gov. Grover who gave the matter serious consideration and both the petition and his answer were printed in the papers all of which were favorable to the boy. The Governor refused to commute the sentence but ordered a stay of execution, and that allowed of a new trial which was had later on but with a second sentence of legal murder. In the mean time through the free columns of the press, from the rostrum, and in circulating petitions, she succeded in arousing public opinion throughout the entire country reaching as far as New England, from which letters were daily pouring in, and by a constant effort, speaking almost daily on a tour up the Sound, from every point on the line of which she wrote descriptive and amusing letters for publication to keep before the Oregon public until the Legislature should convene in Salem in September. Then she prepared a Bill to prohibit capital punishment in the State, which was introduced by Col. C. A. Reed, who worked assiduously for its passage. The Bill became the sensational one of the session, as in the event of its passage Gerrand would not be hanged. The Legislature tendered a seat within the bar, and the judiciary gave a hearing on the merits of the bill. With the exception of a few dollars that she raised on the train and handed to the mother of the condemned boy, no one contributed one dollar to help her bear the expenses incident to all the time and money necessarily spent to carry on the work of saving the boy, and she wrote her own son at college that it would hardly be possible to contribute to his expenses during the time the case was making such demands upon her. He managed however to get along without her aid by working for his board and in other ways helping himself, and did not have to leave school till graduated.

The Bill referred to failed to pass by three votes, so the case went on to what seemed a forlorn ending. The Governor was inflexible, the gallows were in process of erection, and only two days remained to the execution when such a tide of public disfavor set in as to overwhelm him, and he at the last moment commuted the sentence to imprisonment for life; the best course and about the only one there seemed for him to pursue if he would keep any faith or favor with the people who had elected him. Mrs. Ballou had furnished the boy with drawing-slate, pencil, paper, and other things to make life less terrible, and his improvement was marvelous; and the letters he wrote her, some of which I have seen, were full of genuine gratitude, and evidenced great pains and intelligence.

Gerrand became one of the best disciplined prisoners at the penitentiary, and after remaining for a term of some seven or eight years there was but little difficulty in getting him pardoned out. He then went to Vancouver where he engaged in saddle making, a trade acquired at the penal institution, and at the last time heard from was providing for his old mother as well as himself, as an honorable citizen.

One more instance of the beneficial results following Mrs. Ballou's indefatigable philanthropic labors was in the case of Jesse Pomeroy, the noted boy murderer, who was sentenced to be hanged for murders committed near Boston. Being well versed in the laws of pre-natal conditions, she was shocked by the monstrous laws which by a legal murder are supposed to atone for a murder perpetrated by a boy whose mother had frequently assisted her husband in butchering cattle while the unborn boy was beneath her bosom. Her persistent efforts with the Governor of Massachusetts, by gaining the assistance of others through correspondence and the press, resulted in the commutation of Jesse's sentence to life imprisonment.

The investigation Mrs. Ballou made of the Jesse Pomeroy case opened up some startling testimony in the matter, and laid bare many falsehoods that a morbid public had taken for truth relative to the boy and his family, together with which and the story as told by himself, and the Gerrand case also she has in preparation to present in a new coloring to the public in a not distant day.

An extract from one of our journals descriptive of an art gallery recently opened, contains some items of interest relating to Mrs. Ballou's artistic work. It said : "This picture gallery will be the attraction for all visitors. Paintings of great value have been secured, the most costly and unique of which will be the companion paintings of Addie L. Ballou, representing "Morning" and "Night." These paintings have quite a history. Their perfection has not been questioned by the most severe critics. The attempt to place them on exhibition at the State Fair and the Columbian Exposition was repelled by those who questioned the propriety of doing so. The Sacramento *Bee*, in speaking of " Morning " said : "It is possible that the approach to Nature by the artist was too close for the fastidious, but Nature's model is perfectly copied, and the coloring turned to suit the subject." In speaking of "Night," the San Francisco *Post* said : " The figure is of a nude young woman, standing on the crest of a globe, with hands gracefully poised above her head, the perfect coloring giving it the glow of life." These paintings, being the product of a San Francisco artist, will invite special attention and interest."

The *Searchlight*, organ of the equal-suffragists, said of Mrs. Ballou : " As a writer of prose and verse she has achieved national fame. She is President of the State Republican Club, and to no woman in California does the Republican party in the last campaign owe more than to this distinguished author, artist and woman-suffragist."

The same paper also gives a report of a justly merited scoring given to one of our Solons—who evidently had little respect for his mother and less for himself —in artistic touches more vigorous than finished, a *realistic* word painting. Mrs. Ballou said : "The surest indication of the approach of the hour's great need of woman's voice and influence in the making of laws that embrace her welfare and that of her children, is the possibility of such forgetfulness on the floor of legislation, (of a member who speaks, and others who listen, with levity,) of the first sense of honorable manhood in the reverence and respect due all womanhood in the relation of that office through which his own mother, in common with all motherhood, had periled life and endured maternal anguish that he might be.

There is no man of intelligence but holds in reverence the holy condition of maternity, no matter what the station, or the race of her to whom it comes. No man who lacks the instinct to revere, or the tenderness to consider that condition through which the mothers of our race, in unspeakable anguish, often lose their lives in perpetuating life—should find an honored place in the halls of legislation. It remains the duty of self respecting womanhood to continue her insistance to a seat beside him, if for no other reason than to guard the sanctity of maternity from the vulgarity of profaning and contemptuous lips.

No wonder that nations decay and men

deteriorate, when the halls of the Solons are made the vulgar jesting places of sons of women whom they debar ; to defile by making merry over, and insulting the shrine before which they should reverently kneel with uncovered head."

In her literary work Mrs. Ballou has been highly complimented in the same way as the writers of " Beautiful Snow" and "Curfew must not ring to-night." Her touchingly beautiful poem entitled " Where is my boy to-night ? " has been appropriated by several literary pirates.

It is pleasant to rehearse the achievements of the faithful workers, but the limitations of space demand that much remain unsaid that could be told concerning the valuable services of one whose life has been consecrated to high and lofty purposes for the advancement and upliftment of humanity.

STEPHEN D. DYE.

S. D. DYE.

S. D. Dye was born on the 19th of June, 1836, in Troy, Miami Co., Ohio. His mother, Catherine Cappock, belonged to the old Quaker stock who were banished from England, and their property confiscated, while they were made to suffer all the curses that could be heaped upon them by fanatical, creed-bound religionists, who, in their blind zeal to serve God, made it a crime to give a Quaker something to eat. Coming to America in 1709, they met much the same treatment at the hands of those who themselves had fled from religious intolerance in the old world, for they seemed to think they were doing God's service by whippings, fines, imprisonment, and banishing from the commonwealth of Massachusetts, Baptists and Quakers. The dark history written in blood, and the charred remains of the victims burned at the stake, both in the old world and the new, cruelly murdered by the professed followers of the compassionate, meek, and lowly Jesus, created a prejudice in the mind of Mr. Dye, that can never be eradicated. His ancestors had suffered these persecutions mainly at the hands of Protestants, and it would be simply impossible for any religious sect to ever reach him, even though all the Christian (?) Endeavorers in the country should turn the focus point of prayer upon him. And yet, he is not a hardened sinner. He is a good man, a man with a noble generous nature, indomitable courage, perseverance, energy and pluck, and like the Yankees of 1776, never presumes to know when he is whipped. In whatever he undertakes, he rests his eye on victory, and works to that end never stopping to look at the difficulties that lie in the way. When the war broke out in 1861, Mr. Dye responded to President Lincoln's first call for troops, and became a member of Company A, 44th Regiment of Ohio Volunteer Infantry, serving faithfully through the war. He was then and still is a consistent spiritualist. After the war he personally engaged Moses Hull to deliver three lectures in West Milton, Ohio, paying him seventy-five dollars for his services.

Removing soon afterwards to Iowa, Mr. Dye took his principles along with him to the new country, and it was mainly through his energy and perseverance that the first meeting of Spiritualists was held in Tama City, Iowa, for the purpose of effecting a State organization. He was then publishing a liberal, spiritual paper in that place, and was the author of a pamphlet entitled "The Crusade" which has passed through six editions. With his pen he dealt sturdy blows against hoary-headed superstitions that have usurped the name of Christ to serve their nefarious and selfish purposes. With tongue and pen, with brain and brawn, the subject of this brief sketch is ever ready to serve the cause of humanity. When the history of Spiritualism on this coast shall have been written, and each worker shall receive his or her just mead of praise for service rendered, that will not be a stinted portion bestowed upon Stephen D. Dye. Spiritualism in Los Angeles has come to the front as an acknowledged power, largely through his labors and influence.

From one weak struggling society two

years ago, they have grown till now there are three societies besides two or three independent meetings. Instead of occupying some "out of the way" hall over some saloon as is too often the case, they have converged to the very center of the city, one occupying Music Hall with a seating capacity of 1400, while the last and newest society of which Mr. Dye is President, is ensconced in Los Angeles Theatre, one of the finest in the State, with a seating capacity of 2000. It was to Mr. Dye's foresight, energy and perseverance more than to any other agency, that the Southern California Camp-meeting Association was inaugurated and its first meeting made a grand success, during the summer of 1895. As others weakened, he grew strong. As the prophets of evil cried failure, he shouted success. While rich spiritualists tightened their purse strings, he loosened his and out of his own pocket advanced the money to make the first payment on the tents and the pavilion.

He assumed great responsibilities, for he is not rich in this world's goods. Speakers and mediums were engaged at a stipulated sum for each appearance on the platform. Many other expenses were to be met. All sorts of evil prognostications were indulged in by the wiseacres who knew it would be a failure. Some feared it would be a success, and Mr. Dye get more than his share of credit. Others did not believe in a "one man power" although there was no attempt at any such exercise of power ; but in certain emergencies somebody had to shoulder the responsibility, and our subject did it with results that have passed into history, and that have also been recorded above.

Walking in harmony with his companion and yet working along different lines, they form a combination not easily broken, and destined to do much for humanity in sowing the seeds of truth in a prepared soil, that shall by and by spring up into everlasting life, and their labors be crowned with the fulness of a blessed Immortality.

BISHOP A. BEALS.

BISHOP BEALS.

In answer to questions concerning his early mediumistic experiences, Mr. Beals says : "I do not recollect the time that I was not visited with strange, prophetic dreams and trance-like visions. I have always been conscious of the nearness of the spiritual world. I was even in childhood a worshipper at the shrine of nature, and later in life I found her sweet influences far more in harmony with my religious aspirations, than were the religious doctrines of the popular churches."

Mr. Beals was born in the village of Versailles, in western New York. His father, a physician, was a member of the Universalist Church, with which denomination Bishop also allied himself. In 1856, while residing in New York City, he united with the congregation of Rev. E. H. Chapin, at that time one of the most popular pulpit orators in America. It was here that he first became interested in the facts and philosophy of Spiritualism, through the columns of the *Banner of Light*, in which the sermons of Chapin and Beecher were then published. In 1857, during a visit to his native village, he attended lectures by Miss Libbie Lowe (now Mrs. E. L. Watson, of San Jose, Cal.) who, although an unsophisticated girl of fourteen years, gave utterance in the trance state, to thoughts so profound and of such sublime spirituality that all who listened to her were struck with wonder and admiration. Of the effect on himself, Mr. Beals says : " Her eloquent trance utterances touched a responsive chord in my soul, and awoke within me the latent power of mediumship."

It was not until some years after this awakening that Mr. Beals began his career as a public speaker and teacher. The ultimate incentive to his public work was the death of his mother. This event seemed to bring him more than ever into rapport with the higher life. At his mother's funeral he came under spirit influence and in an unconscious condition played [on the organ, sang, and improvised a poem in which the names of members of the family were given, and the guardian spirits were invoked to protect and shield him in his future public work as a medium. From that day to this Mr. Beals has been engaged in the work of spreading a knowledge of the spiritual philosophy, traveling from point to point, and ministering wherever there seemed most premise of doing good. He speaks rapidly, and frequently goes from one topic to another in the same discourse. On this account his lectures have by some been called illogical ; but he gives pleasure to a large class of spiritualists, and as his utterances are characterized by spirituality and moral purity, they are the means of accomplishing great good. Mr. Beals is an accomplished musician, and many lovers of music are attracted to his lectures, who, except for the sweet spiritual songs and the artistic instrumental performances of the medium, would never attend a spiritual meeting.

Mr. Beals has traveled extensively and lectured in all the prominent cities of the Pacific Coast. He recently married an estimable lady of Summerland, Cal., and has located in that beautiful little city by the sea. He frequently lectures for the different societies of that place, and is held in very high esteem by a large circle of friends. His contributions to the spiritualistic press are widely read and greatly appreciated. Among his poetic contributions are many beautiful gems of thought and inspiration. The following, written a number of years ago, breathes the same fond spirit of filial love and tender reverence for the memory of his sainted mother, that characterized his earlier writings and poems. It also shows the deep appreciation and love of nature that ever dwells in the soul of the true poet and inspired writer.

I gazed at the sun's bright path in the
    West
  'Till the earth seemed flooded with
    glory,
And I thought of the dear ones happy
    and blest
  Held sacred in song and story.
And I longed to climb the star-steps of
    night
  To that beautiful city of gold,
Where the morning returns with infi-
    nite light
  And whose splendors can never be
    told.

I thought of my mother's dear sainted
    eyes
  That beamed with such tenderness
    here,
And I musingly asked if still from the
    skies
  They reached earth's shadowy sphere.

And if on missions of mercy and love
  To guide and counsel she came;
And to picture in dreams that city
    above
  Where our heart's dearest treasures
    have gone.

Dear Mother, once more earth tenderly
    weaves
  Her mantle of sunset with gold,
And wrapped in its glory my spirit
    still grieves
  For thy sympathy sweet as of old.
The zephyrs are laden with messages
    sweet.
  From the lips of many a flower,
In the innermost shrine of my heart,
    there's a seat
  That waits for thy presence this
    hour.

I know that the morn will spangle the
    earth
  With pearls in the trembling dew,
And break into songs and rapturous
    mirth
  With many a radiant hue.
Yet in the low west where the firelight
    burns
  The hush of a vision is seen—
Through the vista of years my spirit
    oft turns
  To my childhood, sunny and green.

JAMES G. CLARK.

JAMES G. CLARK.

James G. Clark, though for thirty-five years an earnest believer in the facts and philosophy of Modern Spiritualism, can hardly be classed among mediums and special workers in the cause. He is known rather as a writer on general lines of reform, and as a helper and inspirer in every good work and cause without regard to creed, party, or faction. He has long been known and loved by all classes for his inspired songs and poems. Many of his reform lyrics have been quoted and recited all over the English-speaking world. This has especially been true of "The Voice of the People," by all odds the most stirring labor poem ever written in any language. As a writer, composer, and singer of spiritual and reform songs, he stands without a rival.

Mr. Clark, while intensély radical and pronounced in his convictions and opinions, is, nevertheless, generous and catholic in his treatment of all creeds and beliefs. He may be termed a "Christian Spiritualist," as he never hesitates by speech and pen to declare his faith in the Nazarene as the Master Soul of all time, worthy of emulation, love, and homage as the divine Ideal Man. And he defends his attitude with arguments that are not easily refuted by those who take a different view of the great Galilean Medium. B. O. Flower has, in the past two years, written and published in that greatest of our popular magazines, *The Arena*, two sketches of Mr. Clark, from which we quote the following passages, as they give a better idea of the man and his general work than anything we have found elsewhere in print:

"POET OF THE PEOPLE.

"In the present paper I wish to give a brief outline of the life and work of the poet, composer, and singer, James G. Clark, whose fine lyrical and reformative verses have been an inspiration to thousands of lives.

"Mr. Clark was born in Constantia, N. Y., in 1830. His father was a man of influence in his community, being recognized as intelligent and honorable, and possessing that cool, dispassionate judgment which always commands respect. The mother gave to her son his poetical gift and his intense love for humanity, his all-absorbing devotion to justice and liberty, and a nature at once refined yet brave. When but three years old, the little poet had learned from his mother "The Star of Bethlehem," sung to the air of "Bonny Doon," and could sing the entire piece without missing a word or note. When twenty-one years of age, he was well known in his community as a concert singer of rare ability. At this time Mr. Clark attracted the attention of Mr. Ossian E. Dodge, who, in addition to publishing a literary journal in Boston, had under his management the most popular concert quartet in New England. Mr. Dodge was a man of quick perception; he readily saw that the young poet and singer would prove a valuable acquisition to his already famous troupe, and promptly appointed him musical composer for his company. Into this work Mr. Clark threw all the enthusiasm of youth, composing such universally popular songs as "The Old Mountain Tree," "The Rover's Grave," "Meet Me by the Running Brook," and "The Rock of Liberty." "The Old Mountain Tree" was for some time a reigning favorite through the land, it being sung for months in theaters and concerts. At the Boston Museum, then the leading theater of Boston, it was no unusual thing for it to be called for as many as three times in a single evening.

"One day, during this period of popularity, his mother, who was a very religious woman, said to him, 'James, why cannot you write a hymn?' He loved his mother devotedly. There was between them more than the strong ties of mother and son. She had fostered and encouraged his every poetical and musical aspiration, and it was his most earnest desire to gratify her wish, but thought along this line came slowly, and almost a year elapsed before the young man placed a penciled copy of his hymn, "The Evergreen Mountains of Life," in his mother's hand. She read it through silently, too much overcome to speak, while great tears coursed down her wrinkled cheeks. At this period he composed several songs and hymns which have been universally popular, such as "Where the Roses Never Wither," "The Beautiful Hills," and "The Isles of the By and By." Of these poems, Dr. A. P. Miller, himself a poet of more than ordinary power and an admirable critic, writes: 'These songs have for thirty years been received by all classes as forming a group of original and perfect lyrics adapted to every platform and hall, whether sacred or secular. To say this,' continues Dr. Miller, 'detracts nothing from his songs of love and freedom. It is only saying that they are the St. Elias, the Tacoma, the Hood, and the Shasta, which out-tower all other song peaks and reach those heights where the sunshine is eternal and the view universal.'

"It may be well to note at this time the singular fact that in his poetical life Mr. Clark has appeared in three distinct roles, although he has always been the poet of the people. During his youth and early manhood the popular lyric and ballad claimed his power. It was the work of this period which won for him the name of the Tom Moore of America; and had he not taken the other upward steps, the appellation would not have been so palpably inadequate to describe the man who for thirty years has been the poet of reform and the prophet of the new day. When the sixties dawned, the first song epoch of his life was drawing to a close, and the mutterings of the Rebellion were oppressing age and stimulating youth throughout the North. Mr. Clark had given his country a collection of songs and ballads destined to live long after his body had returned to dust, and he had sung his melody into the hearts of thousands who had listened to the poet composer and singer with that rapt attention which is the tribute of manhood and womanhood to genuine merit. The clouds of rebellion were gathering around the horizon; but ere the shock of arms thrilled the nation, Mr. Clark was summoned to the death bed of his mother. Sitting at her side as the spirit was poising for flight, and catching inspiration from her words, there came to him that exceedingly popular and touching poem, "Leona," which was first published in the *Home Journal* of New York, then edited by George Morris and N. P. Willis. This poem, Mr. Morris afterwards declared, had been more widely copied, admired, and committed to memory than any other composition of its class ever published in America.

"The divine afflatus which fills the poet brain, and weaves itself into words which thrill and move the profound depths of human emotions, was next manifested in Mr. Clark's soul-awakening songs of freedom. The sweet ballads and lyrics of love and home disappeared before stern Duty's voice. While Whittier, Longfellow, and Lowell were firing the heart of New England, Mr. Clark sent forth "Fremont's Battle Hymn," one of the most noteworthy poems of war times, and a song which produced great enthusiasm wherever sung.

"During the early days of the war the poet traveled from town to town, singing the spirit of freedom into the hearts of the people, and arousing to action scores and hundreds of persons in every community visited, who had heretofore taken little interest in the pending struggle. In this way he raised many thousands of dollars for the Sanitary Commission and

Soldiers' Aid societies. In addition to "Freemont's Battle Hymn," this period called from his pen a number of war songs and poems, such as "Let Me Die with My Face to the Foe," "When You and I Were Soldier Boys," "The Children of the Battle-field," and "Minnie Minton." The history of this last-mentioned poem is peculiarly interesting, and reveals the fact that at times coming events have been flashed with singular vividness on the sensitive mind of our poet. The pathetic facts connected with the poem are as follows: Mr. Clark was visiting a family by the name of Minton. In the home circle was a young lady named Maria, who had a lover in the army. One day Mr. Clark said, 'If your name were Minnie, it would make a musical combination for a poem.' The young lady blushed and replied that her friends often called her Minnie, and doubtless at this moment her thoughts went out to the soldier boy for whom she daily prayed. Some months passed, when one night, while the poet was riding in the sleeping-car, the words of the ballad "Minnie Minton" forced themselves upon his brain, so haunting his mind that he could get no sleep until he had transferred them to paper. This was done by drawing aside the curtain of his berth, and writing in the faint glimmer of the lamps, which had been turned low for the night. It is probable that the poet did not dream, as he penciled the following lines, that he was writing a prophecy which a year later was to become history. Yet such was in fact the case.

Minnie Minton, in the shadow
I have waited here alone,—
On the battle's gory meadow,
Which the scythe of death has mown,
I have listened for your coming,
Till the dreary dawn of day,
But I only hear the drumming,
As the armies march away.

O Minnie, dear Minnie,
I have heard the angel's warning,
I have seen the golden shore;
I will meet you in the morning
Where the shadows come no more.

"We come now to the third epoch in the history of Mr. Clark's poetry. The war was over. His thoughts turned to the toiling millions of our land, for from early manhood his heart had ever kept rhythmic pace with the hopes, aspirations, and sorrows of the masses. Now, however, the ballad singer, who in the Nation's crisis became the poet reformer, becomes the prophet poet of the dawning day. And with advancing years came added power; for it is a notable fact that with the silver of age has come a depth of thought, coupled with strength and finish in style not found in his earlier work. Take, for example, the following stanzas from "A Vision of the Old and New:"

'Twas in the slumber of the night—
That solemn time, that mystic state—
When, from its loftiest signal height,
My soul o'erlooked the realm of Fate,
And read the writing on the wall,
That prophesies of things to be,
And heard strange voices rise and fall
Like murmurs from a distant sea.

The world below me throbbed and rolled
In all its glory, pride, and shame,
Its lust for power, its greed for gold,
Its flitting lights that man calls fame,—
And from their long and deep repose,
In memory and page sublime,
The ancient races round me rose
Like phantoms from the tombs of Time.

I saw the Alpine torrents press
To Tiber with their snow-white foam,
And prowling in the wilderness
The wolf that suckled infant Rome.
But wilder than the mountain flood
That plunged upon its downward way,
And fiercer than the she-wolf's brood,
The soul of man went forth to slay.

Kingdoms to quick existence sprang,
Each thirsting for another's gore,
The din of wars incessant rang,
And signs of hate each forehead wore.
All nations bore the mark of Cain,
And only knew the law of might;
They lived and strove for selfish gain
And perished like the dreams of night.

*　　*　　*　　*　　*　　*　　*

I woke: and slept, and dreamed once
more,
And from a continent's white crest,
I heard two oceans seethe and roar,
Along vast lands by nature blest;

All races mingled at my feet,
  With noise and strange confusion rife,
And old World projects—incomplete—
  Seemed maddened with a new-found
    life.

The thirst for human blood had waned;
  But boldly seated on the throne,
The grasping god of Mammon reigned,
  And claimed Earth's product for his
    own.
He gathered all that toilers made,
  To fill his vaults with wealth untold.
The sunlight, water, air, and shade
  Paid tribute to his greed for gold.

He humbly paid his vows to God,
  While agents gathered rents and dues.
He ruled the nation with a nod,
  And bribed the pulpit with the pews;
Yet, over all the regal form
  Of Freedom towered, unseen by him,
And eagles poised above the storm
  That draped the far horizon's rim.
At length, the distant thunder spoke
  In deep and threatening accents; then
The long roll of the earthquake woke
  From sleep a hundred million men.

   *   *   *   *   *   *   *

I woke: and slept, and dreamed again:
  A softened glory filled the air,
The morning flooded land and main,
  And Peace was brooding everywhere;
From sea to sea the song was known
  That only God's own children know,
Whose notes, by angel voices sown,
  Took root two thousand years ago.

No more the wandering feet had need
  Of priestly guides to Paradise,
And banished was the iron creed
  That measured God by man's device;
No more the high cathedral dome
  Was reared to tell His honors by,
For Christ was throned in every home,
  And shone from every human eye.

No longer did the beast control
  And make the spirit desolate;
No more the poor man's struggling soul
  Sank down before the wheel of Fate;
And pestilence could not draw near,
  Nor war and crime be felt or seen—
As flames, that lap the withered spear,
  Expire before the living green.

And all of this shall come to pass—
  For God is Love, and Love shall reign,
Though nations first dissolve like grass
  Before the fire that sweeps the plain;
And men shall cease to lift their gaze
  To seek Him in the far-off blue,
But live the Truth their lips now praise
  And in their lives His life renew.

There yet shall rise beneath the sky,
  Unvexed by narrow greed for pelf,
A race whose practise shall deny
  The heartless creed "Each for him-
    self."
There is no halt or compromise
  Between the ways all life has trod,
'Tis downward, with the brute that dies
  Or upward with the sons of God.

"This poem was founded on a vivid dream which came to the poet and so impressed him that he found no peace until he committed the verses to paper.

"The poet's loyalty to the toilers is voiced in most of his latest poems and songs. "The People's Battle Hymn," published last autumn, was sung with great effect at the industrial gatherings throughout the West. Of this song, General J. B. Weaver, the candidate of the People's Party for President in 1892, said: 'It is the song we have been waiting for. It is an Iliad of itself.'

"The following stanzas from this song will give an idea of the exaltation of thought, which, when accompanied by Mr. Clark's soul-stirring music, arouses an almost indescribable enthusiasm among the people wherever it is sung:—

THE PEOPLE'S BATTLE HYMN.

There's a sound of swelling waters,
  There's a voice from out the blue,
  Where the Master His arm is reveal-
    ing,—
Lo! the glory of the morning
  Lights the forehead of the New,
  And the towers of Old Time are reeling,
There is doubt within the temples
  Where the gods are bought and sold.
  They are leaving the false for the true
    way;
There's a cry of consternation
  Where the idols made of gold
  Are melting in the glance of the New
    day.

CHORUS.

  Lift high the banner,
  Break from the chain,
    Wake from the thralldom of story.
  Like the torrent to the river,
  The river to the main,
    Forward to Liberty and Glory!

There is tramping in the cities,
  Where the people march along,
  And the trumpet of Justice is calling;

There's a crashing of the helmet
  On the forehead of the Wrong,
    And the battlements of Babylon are
    falling.
O! the master of the morning,
  How we waited for his light
    In the old days of doubting and fear-
    ing—
How we watched among the shadows
  Of the long and weary night
    For his feet upon the mountains ap-
    pearing.

He shall gather in the homeless,
  He shall set the people free,
    He shall walk hand in hand with the
    toiler;
He shall render back to labor
  From the mountains to the sea
    The lands that are bound by the spoiler.
Let the lightning tell the story
  To the sea's remotest bands;
    Let the camp fires of freedom be flam-
    ing,
While the voices of the heavens
  Join the chorus of the lands,
    Which the children of men are pro-
    claiming.

"Mr. Clark is not only a poet, musical composer, and singer of rare ability, he is a scholarly essayist, and, during recent years, has contributed many papers of power and literary value to the leading dailies of the Pacific Coast.

"The wealth of poetic imagery, strength, and deep penetration which characterizes the recent work of Mr. Clark is very noticeable in some of his later poems, and reaches altitudes of sublimity in thought rare among modern poets. This characteristic is well illustrated in "The Infinite Mother," which I give below. It is considered by many critics as Mr. Clarke's masterpiece.

THE INFINITE MOTHER.

I am mother of Life and companion of
  God!
I move in each mote from the suns to the
  sod,
I brood in all darkness, I gleam in all
  light,
I fathom all depth, and I crown every
  hight;
Within me the globes of the universe
  roll,
And through me all matter takes impress
  and soul.
Without me all forms into chaos would
  fall;

I was under, within, and around, over all,
Ere the stars of the morning in harmony
  sung,
Or the systems and suns from their grand
  arches swung.

I loved you, O earth! in those cyles profound,
When darkness unbroken encircled you
  round,
And the fruit of creation, the race of
  mankind,
Was only a dream in the Infinite Mind;
I nursed you, O earth! ere your oceans
  were born,
Or your mountains rejoiced in the gladness of morn,
When naked and helpless you came from
  the womb,
Ere the seasons had decked you with
  verdure and bloom,
And all that appeared of your form or
  your face
Was a bare, lurid ball in the vast wilds of
  space.

When your bosom was shaken and rent
  with alarms,
I calmed and caressed you to sleep in my
  arms.
I sung o'er your pillow the song of the
  spheres
Till the hum of its melody softened your
  fears,
And the hot flames of passion burned low
  in your breast
As you lay on my heart like a maiden at
  rest;
When fevered, I cooled you with mist
  and with shower,
And kissed you with cloudlet and rain-
  bow and flower,
Till you woke in the heavens arrayed
  like a queen,
In garments of purple, of gold, and of
  green,
From fabrics of glory my fingers had
  spun
For the mother of nations and bride of
  the sun.
There was love in your face, and your
  bosom rose fair,
And the scent of your lilies made fragrant the air,
And your blush in the glance of your
  lover was rare
As you waltzed in the light of his warm
  yellow hair,
Or lay in the haze of his tropical noons,
Or slept 'neath the gaze of the passion-
  less moons:
And I stretched out my arms from the
  awful unknown,
Whose channels are swept by my rivers
  alone,

And held you secure in your young
    mother days,
And sung to your offspring their lullaby
    lays,
While races and nations came forth from
    your breast,
Lived, struggled, and died, and returned
    to their rest.

All creatures conceived at the Fountain
    of Cause
Are born of my travail, controlled by my
    laws;
I throb in their veins and I breathe in
    their breath,
Combine them for effort, disperse them
    in death;
No form is too great or minute for my
    care,
No place so remote but my presence is
    there.
I bend in the grasses that whisper of
    spring,
I lean o'er the spaces to hear the stars
    sing,
I laugh with the infant, I roar with the
    sea,
I roll in the thunder, I hum with the bee;
From the center of suns to the flowers of
    the sod
I am shuttle and loom in the purpose of
    God,
The ladder of action all spirit must climb
To the clear hights of Love from the
    lowlands of Time.

'Tis mine to protect you, fair bride of the
    sun,
Till the task of the bride and the bride-
    groom is done;
Till the roses that crown you shall wither
    away,
And the bloom on your beautiful cheek
    shall decay;
Till the soft golden locks of your lover
    turn gray,
And palsy shall fall on the pulses of Day;
Till you cease to give birth to the chil-
    dren of men,
And your forms are absorbed in my cur-
    rents again—
But your sons and your daughters, un-
    conquered by strife,
Shall rise on my pinions and bathe in my
    life
While the fierce glowing splendors of
    suns cease to burn,
And bright constellations to vapor return,
And new ones shall rise from the graves
    of the old,
Shine, fade, and dissolve like a tale that
    is told.

"Like Victor Hugo, Ralph Waldo Emerson, Robert Browning, and, indeed, a
large proportion of the most profoundly
spiritual natures of the nineteenth century, Mr. Clark, while deeply religious, is
unfettered by creeds and untrammeled by
dogmas. In bold contrast to the narrow-
minded religionists, who, like the Phari-
sees of Jesus' time, worship the letter,
which kills, and who are to-day persecuting men for concience' sake, and seeking to unite church and state, Mr.
Clark's whole life has been a protest
against intolerance, persecution, and
bigotry. Living in a purely spiritual
realm, HE LOVES, and that renders it impossible to cherish the spirit of bigotry and
persecution manifested by the American
Sabbath Union, and other persecuting
un-Christian bodies, whose leaders have
never caught a glimpse of the real spirit or
character of Jesus. He is a follower of
the great Nazarene in the truest sense of
the word, and thus cannot understand
how professed Christians can so prostitute religion and ignore their Master's
injunctions as to persecute their fellow
men for opinion's sake. On this and
kindred subjects he has written very
thoughtfully and with great power.

"The light of another world has already
silvered and glorified the brow of this
poet of the dawn; and, as I have before
observed, with advancing years comes
intellectual and spiritual strength rather
than a diminution of power. Such men
as Mr. Clark wield a subtle influence for
good in the world. Their lives and
thoughts are alike an inspiration to thousands; their names live enshrined in the
love of the earnest, toiling, struggling
people—the nation's real nobility.

"Mr. Clark, like William Morris, Mr.
Howells, and many other of our finest
contemporary thinkers, has become an
ardent social democrat. Perhaps he is
not quite so extreme in his views as the
English poet, but I imagine he holds
opinions much the same as those entertained by Mr. Howells, and he is even
more aggressive than the American
novelist, which is saying much, when
one considers Mr. Howells's fine and
brave work of recent years, and espe-

cially his bold satire on present-day injustice, in "A Traveler from Altruria."

"Against the aggressiveness of wealth in the hands of shrewd, cunning, and soulless men and corporations, Mr. Clark raised his clarion voice, even more eloquent than in the old days when he wrote, composed, and sung for freedom and the Union before the black man had been freed. It is difficult to conceive a picture more inspiring than this patriarch of Freedom, whose brow is already lighted with the dawn of another life, fronting the morning with eyes of fire and voice rich, full, and clear, now persuasive, now imperious, but never faltering, as he delivers the messages of eternal truth, progress, and justice."

GEORGE HAZELTON HAWES.

Among the hills of western Massachusetts the well-known shorthand reporter of the Pacific Coast passed the early years of his life. His native town is Middlefield, in Hampshire County, and he was born December 4th, 1849. He descends from the names of Hammond and Hazelton, Hawes and Bird. He is the youngest of six children. He was favored in being the offspring of parents happily united, devoted to each other and to their children, and who had the fullest confidence and respect of the community. His father was a schoolteacher and farmer. He lost his life through an accident when George was but two years of age, and it is quite a remarkable circumstance that since that time, forty-four years ago, death has not invaded the family circle he left behind.

When Mr. Hawes was six years old his mother married Ebenezer Smith, who possessed a snug little farm on the eastern outskirts of the town, sheltered by hills and maple woods, but rather a lonely and secluded spot, the nearest neighbor a mile distant. Mr. Smith possessed many fine qualities, and was one of the staunch men of the community. Although a good Baptist deacon, he was very liberal in thought, took a number of newspapers, and was well posted on all the stirring events of the day. He was among the first to adopt improved machinery in farming, and was always ready and patient to consider new ideas. No doubt this state of mind took deep root in the receptive nature of the young boy, and prepared the way for the comprehension and adoption of those great vital principles which have so enriched his later years.

Notwithstanding a comfortable home and fostering care of parents, the stern necessity for unceasing and rugged toil in that particular portion of the country to win from the soil a livelihood, makes a bondage of childhood which absorbs nearly all its sunshine, and the toiling years wore deep resolves in an earnest character that the labor of his manhood should yield more results than he saw were possible around him. He disliked farming, and repeatedly declared he would not make it his occupation. Up to the age of ten he attended the little district school three months in summer, and three in the winter. He then entered into the work of the farm, laboring nine months of the year with all the regularity of a hired man, going to school three months in the winter.

Mr. Hawes claims there was nothing striking about his youth, but that something within him continually caused him to long for greater opportunities. He was quiet in manner, studious as a scholar, gave but little trouble to teachers or parents, and seldom quarreled. His parents were members of the Baptist Church, and he was a constant attendant at its meetings and Sunday School.

At eighteen years of age a marked and complete change took place. About three years before a sister had married and settled in California, and through her efforts and the hearty encouragement of an older brother, he decided to make the Golden State his future home. The gentle mother made but little objection, but as the day of farewell drew near, would frequently drop the daily duties to throw her arms around his neck and press him to her heart in silence, as though she would forever hold in her embrace the child who had never left her side. It is one of the singular workings of events that this brother, sister, and mother, having lost their companions by death, have for some time shared a happy home together with Mr. Hawes in San Francisco, he having remained single.

GEORGE H. HAWES.

A journey of twenty-six days by water and the country life of New England was exchanged for the great metropolis of the Pacific. Mr. Hawes reached San Francisco September 2, 1868, and most of the time since has resided here and in Oakland.

For a few years he was engaged in ordinary work of different kinds as an employee, and resided with his sister. The charm of her home and the atmosphere of a happy marriage relation were the stronger attraction during the most dangerous years of temptation when the character was forming and the mind unfolding. Here in the home and under those favorable influences were born that deep love for spiritual truth, and confidence in spiritual power to bless mankind, which have shone forth so vigorously in later years. But to eradicate many of the old teachings was a work of time. While ever ready to reverently consider new ideas, he is slow to adopt until he thoroughly comprehends and discovers they are valuable. He had somewhat outgrown creeds, but finding a religious body that required only a belief in Christ and an acknowledgment of the Bible as the rule of faith and practise, he felt he could go as far as this, and about 1872 he united with a denomination in Oakland called "Disciples of Christ," or perhaps better known to those outside as the "Campbelites." To his great surprise and pain he found himself allied to an orthodoxy so rigid that the question of whether instrumental music in worship was sinful, or praying in any other position than on the knees was acceptable to the Lord, caused such dissentions, that not many months had passed when the little flock were compelled to discontinue public services. Mr. Hawes, however, would throw no discredit upon this denomination, and while the above was strictly true, it is only its extreme, and even at that time, unusual manifestation. He never renewed this relation, for he realized at once that his noblest feelings and richest experiences must be suppressed, and he resolved that no organization should ever stifle the deepest convictions of his heart.

At the age of twenty-seven his brother-in-law died after a short illness, leaving his wife in feeble health, and three young children. Their means was slender, save a life insurance policy, and this was never collected owing to the breaking up of the company. Mr. Hawes did not hesitate as to the course he should pursue. The helpless ones were never allowed to be separated or suffer for what his hand could supply. He had the great satisfaction of seeing the mother finally restored to good health, and two of the children live to mature into useful members of the community, and become his loving companions. With this new and serious responsibility he saw how important it was to have a distinct and definite line of work, and he commenced the study of shorthand. It is somewhat significant that his mind was first directed to this work from hearing some beautiful utterances by trance mediums, and feeling a great desire that they might be preserved in the language in which they were given. Those who have seen his trained hand gliding gracefully over the pages of his note book, and the thousands who have read the magnificent discourses he has reproduced, are little aware of the difficulties he overcame, and the patience and perseverance he exercised to perfect the art of verbatim reporting. Without a teacher and after the heavy labors of the day, he took up the self-appointed task, and without faltering and unassisted, carried it to success.

He now has one of the best equipped offices of his profession in the city, and has able assistants. His reporting has taken a wide range. He has served a term as official reporter in one of the courts, and during the past two years has reported on some of the most important cases tried in the United States Circuit Court. He has also reported extensively for the religious and secular press sermons and lectures of distinguished people visiting the Coast. Among these may be mentioned Professor O. S. Fowler,

D. L. Moody, the Evangelist, Reverend Sam Jones, Reverend J. A. Dowie, the great Faith Healer, Reverend A. B. Simpson, Father McGlynn, Robert G. Ingersoll, and John B. Gough. In 1890, he reported a series of Sunday evening lectures on Roman Catholicism by Reverend Richard Harcourt at the Howard Street Methodist Church, which were published in book form and illustrated by Thomas Nast.

But the work which Mr. Hawes looks back upon with the greatest pleasure and satisfaction, he says, is the reporting he has done under the name of Spiritualism. So far as is known, he is the pioneer reporter in this field on the Coast. His first work appeared in *Light For All*, October, 1880. It was a lecture delivered by the eloquent Mrs. E. L. Watson, entitled "Our Treasures in Heaven." He has reported extensively the inspired thoughts and sayings given through this gifted instrument of the spirit world, as well as the utterances of all the noted speakers who have visited San Francisco. He was the regular verbatim reporter for the *Carrier Dove* and the *Golden Gate*, and also furnished many lectures for the *Spiritual Offering*, *Religio-Philosophical Journal*, and *Banner of Light;* also many reports of important meetings and events.

Early in 1884 he published a pamphlet of a series of fifteen discourses by the Guides of Mrs. Cora L. V. Richmond, upon "The Nature of Spiritual Existence and Spiritual Gifts." It found a ready sale, and the edition was soon exhausted. He received from the hand of Mrs. Richmond the following approving words:

"I am pleased to acknowledge receipt of the beautiful pamphlet of discourses. My husband and myself consider it the best piece of work, including reporting, editing, and printing, that has ever been done in connection with any published discourses of my Guides; and the modest, yet appreciative preface could only have emanated from a mind thoroughly imbued with the spirit of what the discourses contain, and what lies beyond them in the realm of soul."

In 1888 Mr. J. J. Morse published a work entitled, "Practical Occultism," which was a series of parlor lectures on mediumship and certain phases of life in the spirit world. The reporting of this was also the work of Mr. Hawes. A second edition of this able work has just been published, but under a new title. Mr. Morse says that Mr. Hawes is one of the most skilful reporters he has ever met, and upon his late engagement with the California Psychical Society, he secured the appointment of Mr. Hawes to report the public ministrations given through him from the rostrum.

During the existence of the California Spiritualists' Camp Meeting Association, Mr. Hawes was one of its active members, acting as its Corresponding Secretary, and a portion of the time as a member of its Board of Directors. For years he has been identified with some Spiritual society. At the present time, he is a member of the Society of Progressive Spiritualists. He has been urged to accept a position on its Board of Directors, but, owing to the demands upon his time by his profession, has felt compelled to decline. It is his cherished desire to soon turn his energies into spiritual work more fully than he has hitherto been able to do.

Mr. Hawes' name has become familiar to the spiritual public, chiefly through his reports of the thoughts of others—a work which has been for him largely "a labor of love." But those who know him best know that he wields a facile pen for recording his own inspirations, with occasional evidences of poetical fire.

At one time he was offered the position of assistant editor of one of the prominent spiritual papers in the East. None who have read his tastefully worded introduction to the volume above referred to can fail to have been touched by a sense of his rare love of truth, thoughtfulness, and spirituality. Quiet in manner, genial in conversation, with a strong vein of humor which renders him an agreeable companion, and softens the sharp edge of many outward expressions, his clear brain and true heart have endeared him to all who know him. Though not generally known, his most intimate friends are aware that Mr. Hawes possesses some interesting phases of mediumship, which, when he is permitted to give more time to their manifestation, may prove of interest and value to a wider circle. It has been said that but for war there would be no history. It is equally true that the most external characters occupy the most voluminous biographies.

Lives such as that of this spiritually minded man seldom have their due appreciation in their own day and generation. Spiritual forces are silent, but potent; and a virtue goes out from such characters that stamps its impress upon the coming time; but it is an impersonal impression, lifting up the divine qualities of truth and virtue, and overlooking the humble embodiment and example.

Mr. Hawes' merits entitle him to a more elaborate tribute; but in view of his own characteristic modesty, it seems fitting to offer only this brief but sincere testimony to the worth of one well entitled to a place among the really spiritual workers upon the Pacific Coast.

WILLIAM CLAYTON BOWMAN.

William Clayton Bowman, now a resident of Los Angeles, Cal., was born in the year 1833 in Western North Carolina, Jacob Bowman, his grandfather, being a pioneer of the mountain region of that State. His father, Joseph Bowman, as the settlement of the country advanced, in order to gratify his preference for life amid Nature's wilds, made repeated moves still further away from "the busy haunts of men." Born to the freedom of rural life, nurtured in the atmosphere of, the highlands, accustomed to outlooks from mountain peaks over wide expanses of country, young Bowman imbibed and insensibly incorporated into his very nature the spirit of freedom which, in later years, enabled him to break away from the thraldom of a narrow religion, to welcome the broader teachings of Universalism, and, finally, to embrace the still more advanced ideas of the Harmonial Philosophy, until now, as the founder and pastor of the "Church of the New Era," he is among the foremost advocates of religious liberty, and of moral, social, and political reform. An earnest exponent of the philosophy of spiritual unfoldment, a worthy teacher of the art of right living (which is the essence of true Spiritualism), he is devoted to the emancipation of humanity from all hurtful restraint and from every debasing condition, and the induction of mankind into a higher life on earth—the fraternal love, freedom, purity, and justice of the new era.

Mr. Bowman's mother, whose maiden name was Sarah Garland, was the daughter of Elisha Garland, a Methodist preacher, of whom it is said: "He was habitually filled with the Holy Ghost," which, in the Methodism of those days, meant not only the occasional ecstasy of deeply religious feeling, but on all occasions great solemnity of manner and awfulness of discourse—an austere bearing and words of deep seriousness being at that time considered as specially befitting an ordained preacher, who must never forget that his holy calling, as the representative of an angry God, required from him a demeanor in the presence of his people that would continually remind them of the terrors of divine wrath. Yet Mr. Bowman writes: "Dreadful as were the visits of my grandfather, I revere his memory because he was sincere, and his somber life was in honest keeping with his faith."

Sarah Garland Bowman, though a woman of limited education, was liberally endowed by nature, intellectually and spiritually. Her secluded life, and the simplicity of the times in which she lived, prevented the full development of her intellectual faculties, yet the earnestness and sincerity of her character left a lasting impress on her children. Having no newspapers and very few books, she became a devoted student of Scripture, especially interested in the prophesies, and a believer in the speedy coming of the end of the world, when "the heavens shall roll up as a scroll, and the elements melt with fervent heat." Having no access to any rational interpretation of the Scriptures, her sensitive spirit was oppressed with the dread of a coming catastrophe. As the Jehovah of the Jews visited the iniquities of parents upon the children to many generations, so the God of her imagination was a being of awful majesty and power, whose wrath might at any time be wreaked on the children of men. Death, to her, instead of being the decree of nature, was the direct act of God. As a consequence, young Bowman became subject to fears of impending evil and gloomy thoughts of death, which even the beauty and brightness of nature could not at all

WILLIAM CLAYTON BOWMAN.

times dispel. In relation to this early experience, he writes:

"Religious teachings are fastened upon the minds of children at an age when they are incapable of distinguishing between truth and fiction, and are enforced under the awful name and authority of God, written in a book they are taught to revere as divine and infallible truth. Add to this the fact that religious prejudices and superstitions are the deepest and most ineradicable of all the prejudices which enslave mankind, it ceases to be a matter of astonishment that thousands of intellects, otherwise clear and cultured, are still in bondage to the myths and fables of the world's childhood."

The Bowman family consisted of eleven children, of whom William C. was the fourth. There were ten boys and one girl. The head of the family, Joseph Bowman, was a moral but not a pious man, therefore there were no family prayers, except when a preacher or other zealous Christian visited them. They lived too far from churches for frequent attendance, and Sunday Schools were then unknown in that part of the country, so the children, in spite of their mother's influence, grew up comparatively free from the early religious bias which priests consider so essential in moulding the minds of the young so as to fit them for future service in the church. From an account of his early religious experiences written by Mr. Bowman, the following is taken:

"The little preaching I heard was about equally divided between three sects—Methodist, Baptist, and Tunkers or Dunkers (usually called Dunkards), more properly 'Christian Brethren.' The preaching consisted mainly of doctrinal controversy, alike unprofitable and uninteresting to those not members of the church. 'Soul-saving' seemed only an incident connected with questions of baptism, the Lord's supper, 'feet-washing,' etc. The Dunkards differed from the other two sects not merely in ritual forms, but on the subject of conversion,

commonly called 'getting religion.' The Dunkard preachers maintained that the process of 'getting religion' under revival excitement was unscriptural. Having a number of relatives on my father's side who were preachers of that denomination, and noticing that their arguments seemed more plain and scriptural than those of their opponents, I inclined to their views; yet, when I attended the Methodist revivals, where my mother's people were largely represented, I sometimes found my Dunkard principles severely tested by the earnest exhortations of relatives and friends urging me to go to the 'mourner's bench' and 'seek religion.' While I did not doubt the sincerity of those undergoing these 'religious' experiences, my doubts as to such being the genuine way of salvation made me stubborn to withstand their entreaties.

Up to the age of nineteen years, young Bowman's facilities for obtaining school training had been slight indeed. In that region, at that time, boys learned to read, write, and spell imperfectly, and some acquired a knowledge of the fundamental rules of arithmetic. Nothing beyond this was thought of in the free schools of that mountain country. Concerning this period of his life, Mr. Bowman writes:

"I had never heard an educated person speak. But, attending a Methodist meeting one Sunday, I had the pleasure of hearing a preacher named Adams, who had just opened a 'high school,' at the county-seat, twenty miles away. He was a man of culture, and I was so captivated by his manner of speech, and the strangely beautiful words he used, that I then and there said in my heart, 'I must go to school to that man.' The revelation of this purpose to my parents was a surprise to them, and my sudden resolve a mystery they could not understand. For awhile they treated my request for permission to go as a most unreasonable proposition, but perceiving that I was determined they finally consented, my mother going with me, as I had never been to the village. I attended the school three years, paying my way at first by chopping wood, and afterward by teaching, at intervals, in the district schools.

"It was while attending this school that I passed through the experience of 'conversion;' a psychological phenomenon of much interest to the student of mental science, although easily accounted for by the well-known laws governing the action of mind upon mind; it is still held by revivalists to be of supernatural char-. acter due to conviction of sin and faith in Christ as a Divine Savior. It was a reality to me, as it has been to thousands. In my subsequent progress of observation and thought, though never doubting for a moment the moral and spiritual change wrought in me by that experience, I have been compelled to adopt a theory of its nature and causes widely different from that of the revivalists. My first doubt of the truth of the revivalist theory came very soon after my 'conversion,' long before my general revolt from orthodoxy. This doubt arose from the want of harmony between the facts of my experience, and the theory of faith in Christ by which the facts had to be explained. I knew there was a change. The transformation was marvelous. It was darkness changed to light, sorrow to joy, hell to heaven. I knew there was no mistake as to that, yet I also knew that *there was no preceding faith in Christ* on my part. On the contrary, all had been doubt and utter inability to exercise such faith.

"The principal of the school at that time was Reverend R. N. Price, a Methodist preacher, who had succeeded Reverend Mr. Adams, the founder of the school. For both these men I still cherish a memory akin to reverence. Under Mr. Price's ministrations a revival was started in the school, the students being required to go on with their school duties as usual, and attend the revival services at night. Having been, years before, familiar with revival proceedings, and skeptical as to the real character of such experiences, I at first took little interest in the revival further than to attend the meetings, as required, and look on with indifference, while my schoolmates were yielding to the appealing sermons, the earnest prayers, and heart-stirring songs. From what I have since learned of the laws of mind, of the psychological influence exerted by magnetic persons and the effect of long-continued excitement, together with the appeals of friends and my natural desire to yield to their wishes, it seems remarkable that I held out·so long, especially as I was not at that time fortified by a knowledge of the natural laws underlying such phenomena. But the process is plain enough now. Persistent concentration of mental and moral effort, with one accord, in one place, and for one purpose, can always be relied upon to produce the desired result, in some degree at least. Such result (depending on laws inherent in the mind itself) will follow independently of the truth or error of the beliefs or theories on which such efforts are put forth—just as the rock is broken by the accumulated blows of the hammer, no matter what the purpose for which the blows are wielded, even though it be under the delusion that the rock is full of gold.

"Here seems to be the true explanation, not only of the puzzle of real conversions under the delusions of a fictitious and absurd theology, but of the entire class of religious phenomena so numerous, and otherwise so unaccountable, including 'jerks,' ecstasies, and extravaganzas of revival work. Some phases of the trance, also the numerous forms of religious healing, and 'mind cure' in the various names of Magnetism, Spiritualism, Mental Science, Christian Science, etc., may be included. In all these phenomena it is evident to the unprejudiced mind that the effect is independent of the theories held by the various schools of religious faith practising these diverse methods of revival and healing. The phenomena are the result of well-understood causes, being plainly due to the operation of natural law under certain conditions, such as mental suggestion, concentration of influence, persistent effort, abnormal excitement, intense expectancy, exhaustion, reaction, etc.

"It may here be pertinently asked: In a case like my own, where there was *no* faith to begin with—in fact, a positive disbelief in the whole business of 'getting religion' in that manner—how was it possible to even make a start in that direction? My answer is in one word—hypnotism. I was intently listening to the sermon. It was full of 'holy unction'; it was pleading, inspiring, sympathetic. The speaker, the people, and the very place in which they were assembled had become magnetized with the spirit of the revival work. My attention became absorbed, and I was thus held captive. The eye of my soul was fascinated to one spot, focused to one point—that spot where the preacher stood; that point, the preacher's mind. My personality had become lost in the oversoul of the magnetic man, who overmastered me. I could think only his thought—could do only his will. I was mesmerized, and, at his bidding, went to the 'mourners' bench' as helplessly as any subject who obeys the command of the hypnotist. But when I knelt with the other mourners where the magnetic eye of the preacher no longer gazed into my own, and his pleading voice no longer seemed to appeal to me—especially to *me*—to surrender my will to his—the spell was broken, and my normal condition of mind, with all its power of reasoning, was restored. Freed from the influence which had bound me, my doubts were as strong as ever. What was I to do? Thus openly committed to 'seek religion,' my self-respect would not permit me to turn back. And there I was—kneeling at the altar—with no faith in what I was apparently professing. After a few moments' thought, I decided to persevere, because failure after perseverance would be less disgraceful than to stultify myself on the spot. So, although I despised myself for the part I was playing, I remained with the mourners

as if, like them, 'under conviction,' and continued to go to the 'anxious seat' night after night, hoping that I might, by prayer and earnest endeavor, work myself into a different state of mind. After several nights of praying and crying, with no other result than a greater dissatisfaction with myself, an increasing sense of gloom, and, finally, a feeling of utter despair, after a long struggle in my accustomed place at the mourners' bench, I became exhausted, and sank into a state of profound sleep, a condition of entire unconsciousness. Though there was a great noise of singing, praying, and shouting all around me, there was to *me* a stillness as deep as death—a blankness of mind as profound as nonentity.

"The intelligent reader will note that this part of my 'religious experience' was due to a cause entirely different from that which controlled my will when I first went forward to the mourners' bench. *That* was the result of the mesmeric influence of mind over mind; the swooning was the result of mental and physical exhaustion from excessive and long continued excitement and mental agony. The profundity and duration of such syncope are proportionate to the violence and prolongation of the strain which causes it. I have witnessed revival swoons which lasted several hours. In my own case, the time was probably an hour. The return to consciousness can never be forgotten. To the ear, it was like the gradual awakening from sleep by the music of a midnight serenade, the soft strains lulling the mind to quiet enjoyment while arousing it to happy consciousness; and to the eye the resuscitation was like the slow forming of pictures on the canvas in a panorama of dissolving views. Every sound was melody, every scene beauty, and every thought and feeling full of sweetness, harmony, and love. Why was this? From whence came the great happiness, the feeling of peace and joyousness glorifying the very existence of one whom an hour before all had been discord and wretchedness? No wonder in the world's ignorance of the laws of nature such experiences have been deemed supernatural, but in the light of the psychological science of our day, the supernaturalism of modern theology is fading away, as the supernaturalism of ancient mythology disappeared before the advance of physical science hundreds of years ago.

"But it may be asked, 'If these religious experiences are real, and if they change men's lives for the better, why are they not good for the world, and why attempt to undeceive the mind as to their nature, and thereby dissipate the charm and hinder the good accomplished by it?' The answer is: Truth is better than error; the true interests of mankind are better subserved by knowledge of the truth than by any accidental advantages which may arise from the delusions of error. Besides, a bliss which depends upon ignorance is not enduring in its nature, neither is it worthy of rational beings.

"After my conversion naturally came the 'call to preach.' I say naturally because nothing is more natural for one under the influence of excitement based on a belief in the orthodox hell than to feel a strong impulse to rescue sinners from such awful peril. So I became a student of theology, and at the same time a traveling Methodist preacher, and continued in the business fifteen years, meantime passing through the Civil War, serving a part of the time as a chaplain in the confederate army. I fully believed in the divine right of slavery and the justice, (the necessity even) of secession, for I had been so taught. Our politics and our religion—the result of early teachings—are mainly dependent upon locality; so in a sense they may be said to be geographical questions; and later in life, when I began to think about the reason of things I doubted whether a God of justice would send people to hell for purely geographical reasons. When I spoke of my doubt to some of my brethren in the ministry, they informed me that the heathen would be saved through ignorance, whereupon my missionary zeal began to cool, for it seemed to me hardly the proper thing to enlighten the heathen if nine-tenths of them were to be eternally damned in consequence."

Near the close of the war, in 1864, came the main turning point of Mr. Bowman's life, his marriage to Sarah A. Colbert, of Virginia, who, like himself, was an early believer in orthodoxy and who, like him also, by fearless questioning of its correctness, has come out of the shadow of that cold and cheerless religion into the warmth and sunlight of rationalistic belief. One in spirit and purpose through all the joys and sorrows of more than thirty years, and in spite of the struggles and trials that always attend those, who, regardless of material reward, choose the right because it *is* right, this happy couple have ever kept even step in the march of progress. Happy is the man, who, no matter what wrongs he receives from his fellow men in the struggles of life, can, at the close of each day, turn to his own home, knowing that whoever else is false, there is *one*, at least, who is true and whose loving faith in him never fails. Especially does the worker in the field of reform need such a place of refuge, where he can get renewed faith in human love, renewed confidence in human integrity, renewed hope in the ultimate triumph of the right, and consequent renewal of strength for the labor yet to come. Fortunate is the man who is blessed with such a home—doubly fortunate he who appreciates his great blessing.

Young Bowman's high school education, though better than, in his early youth, he had hoped ever to receive, was not satisfactory to him. It served only to show the vast fields of inquiry that lay beyond, and which he could not explore unless better prepared by mental discipline. He accordingly entered upon a three-years' course in the University of Virginia, which he found of incalculable value in his future career. Besides preaching, Professor Bowman devoted himself to the cause of education in his native State, including two years' service in the Asheville Female College. He was about to establish an educational institution of his own in Bakersville, N. C., to be called "The People's College," when his theological views so changed that he gave up his plan, knowing that he would not be sustained by the people of that orthodox community. The following is from a statement recently made by Professor Bowman, concerning his growth out of orthodoxy. He writes:

"Reasoning as to the love and the goodness of God in connection with a hell of endless torment, I said: 'Had I foreseen that a certain number of my children would be miserable to all eternity, I would not voluntarily have become their father. Had God foreseen such a destiny awaiting any of his creatures, would he have brought them into being? If so, then I am more merciful than God.' For various other reasons, equally conclusive, I was compelled to abandon the doctrine of endless punishment. I had been taught that it was wrong to reason about such things, but I could not help it. Believing, as I then did, that such use of reason was an act of enmity to God and a peril to the soul, I prayed earnestly that my tendency to so reason be taken from me. But my prayer was not answered. I continued to reason. The result was, I found it necessary either to abandon the Bible or to put another interpretation upon its teachings. I chose the latter, and in the light of the 'higher criticism' I became a Universalist. I still held to the Bible as the infallible word of God, but it was redeemed in my mind from the horrible meanings given to it by orthodoxy. This was a long stride toward liberation— a great change for the better. The difference between a universe with an orthodox hell in it and one without that foul blot is a difference of vast significance to the benevolent soul."

But this new and pleasanter view of things had its drawbacks, as the Professor soon learned. He was no longer consid-

ered a safe teacher for the young, and no longer was he a well-paid sermonizer, for young or old. He commenced preaching Universalism—working for people who hold fast to the hope that all will be saved. Such never pay as liberally as do those who are striving by aid of the priest to escape the damnation of hell. Professor Bowman therefore was obliged to earn his living by the labor of his hands. He cleared off some wild land, cutting the wood, grubbing up the roots, and preparing the soil, until he had a well-cultivated farm, on which he sustained his family by hard labor during the week, and on Sunday pointed out to his Universalist brethren the way toward a higher and better life on earth. After five years of such work, he went to Atlanta, Ga., and organized the first Universalist Church of that city. He was successful in his new field, but after a few years, becoming interested in the writings of Andrew Jackson Davis, and having now time for study, he began an investigation of the Harmonial Philosophy, and without much aid from the phenomena of Spiritualism, he became convinced of its essential truths. With him to be convinced is to act. He therefore severed his connection with the Universalists, and in 1881 organized a Spiritual society in Atlanta. He also edited a Spiritual magazine called *The Progressive Age*, and later a weekly publication called *Light For Thinkers*, which was afterward combined with *The Better Way*, now *The Light of Truth*, Cincinnati. After speaking for the Spiritual society in Atlanta a year, he accepted an invitation to go to Cincinnati, where he remained as speaker for the Spiritual society a year and a half. Concerning his growth out of Universalism, Professor Bowman writes:

"After eight years of thought and preaching as a Universalist minister, notwithstanding the great breadth and brightness of my new faith as compared with the old, I found myself again hampered with limitations which had to be broken. These limitations were the One

Book and One Savior ideas. Although the change from the orthodox to the liberal theology was a very decided change, yet it was still theology—a binding of the mind and conscience to traditional sources of authority, and supernatural revelation. I saw that the theological plane had to be wholly abandoned, and that I must henceforth trust to absolute liberty of thought and conscience, untrammeled by authoritative limitations to any one book, savior, creed, or system of religion. | Authority must not be accepted as truth, but truth must be made the basis of authority. This second transition (the change from theology to philosophy) was made, and I found myself with the universe for my Bible, the soul of the universe for my God, obedience to its laws for my Savior, and the dictates of conscience, reason, and experience for my authority. I am free to confess that this surrender of the personal for the impersonal, the definite for the indefinite, the narrow for the boundless, is to launch the barque of an ordinary mortal upon a very wide sea. But every sailor knows it is safer on the bosom of the great deep than in the shallows of the shore, though the sailing may be less spirited and the voyagers less boisterous, because the waters are calmer, and the storms less violent, than along the surfy coasts and the narrow channels of dogmatism!"

In 1884, Professor Bowman left Cincinnati with his family and went to New Mexico, where he expected to join a cooperative colony (since disintegrated), but on investigation he concluded to not do so, and engaged in other work, first as a laborer, then as clerk, then studied law, practised three years in the courts of Las Cruces, and finding such employment uncongenial, he went to Tucson, where he became Principal of the High School and City Superintendent of Public Schools. In 1890, he came to California, lectured for a Spiritual society in Los Angeles two years, stumped the State for John B. Weaver in 1892, returned to Los Angeles and organized the church of the New Era in 1893, was the People's Party candidate for Congress in the sixth district in 1894, and has since resided in Los Angeles, most of the time in charge of the Church of the New Era.

Professor Bowman has six daughters and one son—all bright, active, progressive young people. Three of the daughters are married, the eldest to James G. Clark, Jr., son of the people's greatest reform poet and singer.

As a fitting close to this brief sketch of the reform work of Professor Bowman, the following extract is taken from an account written by him concerning his present position in relation to religion, and the circumstances that led to the organization of his reform church. He writes:

"In the transition from the theological to the philosophical plan, I have not abandoned religion. I only view the subject from a different standpoint and treat it in a different manner. Under the philosophic regime, I am free to investigate, criticize, and judge in matters of religion as on all other subjects. Under theology, one cannot do this, but must accept and believe—the penalty for failure being eternal death. Theology assumes to be identical with religion, but philosophy discriminates between the two. Religion is something essential and permanent in the very nature of man. Theology is but a system of doctrines and theories growing out of religion. Religion is innate in man's spiritual nature; theology is an exotic planted in the mind by education, drawing its life and nourishment from the religious sentiment, but shaped according to environments. Religion, subjectively, in man, is a constant quantity; objectively, its external expression in theological dogmas and rituals is a variable quantity, differing according to the ethnic and historic peculiarities of each case.

"The abandonment of any particular scheme of theology or form of worship is not the abandonment of religion any more than would the rejection of any particular theory of government, therapeutics, or morality be the repudiation of the science of sociology, medicine, or ethics. The so-called liberalists, who make war on religion itself because of the errors and absurdities of theology, are as unreasonable as if they should war against chemistry or astronomy because the ancients held such crude and unscientific views on these subjects. The art of building must not be destroyed because our ancestors built so rudely. The true reformer comes not to destroy, but to fulfil. Religion, innate in man, has found expression in accord with human development. Modern religion is a branch of civilization, not an unnatural excrescence upon it. It should, therefore, be treated as all other branches of civilization are treated—not warred against, but improved upon. The primitive gods and primitive religions need civilizing as much as primitive modes of agriculture or navigation. As a spiritual being, man can no more abandon religion than he can, as a physical being, abandon the atmosphere or the sunshine.

"So, although I have been compelled to relinquish my faith in the entire system of theology or 'plan of salvation,' yet I hold on to religion as a necessary factor in human life, and to a church as necessary to represent the claims and conserve the interests of religion in the world, believing such to be the highest claims and the most important interests of humanity. But, having rejected the theological foundations on which existing churches stand, it became necessary, before a church could be inaugurated under the new idea, that a new plan on a new basis should be devised for the new church. This new plan was the outgrowth of many years of experience, but more especially of my California experience. After lecturing two years in Los Angeles on Spiritualism, and on religious, social, and political reforms, and becoming deeply interested in the great third-party movement, I became convinced that all reforms aiming at the overthrow of wrong and the establishment of justice are, in their deepest meaning, essentially religious, and, as such, should be taken into the church as a part of its practical work, and as a necessary part of true religion. This conviction was followed by the thought: We must have a church of the new era to realize this ideal—a church broad enough and fearless enough to advocate all righteousness and all truth, irrespective of ecclesiastical customs and theological traditions. My thought was communicated to kindred minds, and the result was the organization of 'The Church of the New Era,' devoted not to the propagation of any creed, but to the advancement of universal truth for the truth's sake, and for the promotion of every human interest, social, intellectual, moral, civil, and religious. The Articles of Incorporation provide that in matters of belief and opinion there is to be absolute liberty of mind to accept whatever is proved or seems probable, and to reject whatever is disproved or seems improbable, unprejudiced in all matters not yet investigated—truth alone being the object sought, and the only authority relied upon."

MARY DANA SHINDLER.

Through the kindness of Herman Snow the author is enabled to present the following interesting sketch of the life of an earnest, aspiring woman. The sketch was prepared by Mr. Snow several years ago for publication in the CARRIER DOVE:

"Mary Dana Shindler was the daughter of Reverend B. M. Palmer, D. D., a leading Presbyterian minister of Charleston, S. C., having been born into this life in the year 1810. Here, at the very center of a conservative and slave-holding oligarchy, she received her earliest impressions, social and religious; yet, starting from such a point in her earthly career, she eventually not only freed herself from the old theological shackles, but with her large intuition and earnest aspiration she advanced onward, first into a liberal Unitarianism, then into Spiritualism, and finally into the position of an earnest worker into the Labor Reform movement, one of her latest literary efforts having been the publication of a book of songs for the working people.

"My first knowledge of the subject of this sketch dates back to about the year 1839, when a copy of her 'Southern Harp' fell into my hands and at once interested me, particularly from the depth and tenderness of its religious thought and aspiration. The author then bore the name of Mary S. B. Dana, from her first marriage, she being a widow at the time. The main feature of the work is the adaptation of words of religious significance to music already popularly known and loved. The following is a quotation from the introductory lines:

There was a time when all to me was light;
No shadow stole across my pathway bright.

I had a darling sister—but she died.
For many years we wandered side by side,
And oft these very songs she sung with me;
No wonder, then, that they should plaintive be.
I had an only brother, and he died,
Away from home and from his lovely bride.
And not long after, those I loved too well,
Pale—cold—and still—in death's embraces fell;
In two short days on me no more they smiled,
My noble husband and my only child!
'Twas sorrow made me write these plaintive lays,
And yet if sad they are, they end in praise.

* * * * * * *

"The volume contains nearly fifty songs, all written by our friend in her early years, and adapted to music chosen by her. Most of these are of a plaintive character, but occasionally there is one of a cheerful, even of a joyful, strain.

"I have thus spoken somewhat fully of this early work of our friend, under the impression that it is now out of print, and not likely to be seen by my readers; also because it signally illustrates the condition of one of gentle and affectionate make whilst laboring under the double burden of false religious ideas, and of deep personal sorrow.

"But the time was at hand when our friend was to find deliverance from the dark shadows of the old theology. Urged on by her sincere love of the truth, and aided, doubtless, by unseen helpers through her large inspirational capacity, she was enabled successfully to investigate and reject the accepted orthodoxy with which she was surrounded. She began upon the doctrine of the Trinity, but eventually extended her investigation throughout the entire system of Calvinism. The result was, that in spite of the powerful adverse influ-

ences of her social and church surroundings, she became satisfied of the falsity
of the distinctive doctrines of the church
in which, as the daughter of its minister,
she had been brought up, and became
publicly known as a Unitarian. A great
commotion this created throughout her
widely extended circle of relatives and
friends. She was at once beset with
opposition in all its varied forms. Letters of remonstrance, of rebuke, and of
entreaty came in upon her like a flood;
but the brave woman stood her ground
nobly; she did not suffer herself to be
driven or coaxed from her advanced
position. She could not, however, answer in detail the large influx of letters
thus coming to her ; she, therefore,
decided to publish a volume embodying
the substance of her defense against the
attacks of her opponents generally. This
was entitled, ' Letters to Relatives and
Friends on the Trinity.' It was written
in a good spirit, and with marked ability,
so much so that it eventually came to be
used quite extensively by Unitarians as a
means of extending their faith.

"In the year 1848, whilst still living in
South Carolina, the subject of our sketch
was again married, this time to a clergyman of the Episcopal Church, which
event somewhat disturbed her relations
with her many Unitarian friends, because
it was reported that she had also renounced her Unitarianism and joined the
Episcopal Church. Her own explanation
of this passage of her life, as given in a
letter of our subsequent correspondence,
is as follows:

I should probably never have married
again, nor left the Unitarian ranks, if I
had not been suddenly deprived by what
is called death of both my parents, which
left me so much alone in the world, that
when Mr. Shindler and myself were
thrown together I was persuaded to unite
my earthly lot with his. He married me,
knowing that I was an honest Unitarian;
but his Bishop and the South Carolina
clergy, generally, were surprised at his
choice, which I believe neither he nor I
have ever had occasion to regret.

"At the close of the war Mrs. Shindler
with her husband removed to Nacogdoches, Texas, where, until his departure
for the higher life, they seemed to have
lived in the quiet routine of home and
parish life. After that event, a son, Robert C. Shindler, was the only near relative left to our friend; and, unhappily for
her future peace as a Spiritualist, that
son, though otherwise dutiful and promising, proved to be a bitter opponent of
the new faith. It was this that constituted the great trial of her later life,
sending her often away among Spiritualists at the North, when otherwise she
might have chosen the quiet of home.

"In our successive glances at the life
career of our friend, we have now arrived
at the period of her positive activity as a
Spiritualist. She had diligently investigated the claims of her new faith, traveling extensively to visit mediums and to
compare experiences with others. The
results she had published in a book,
entitled, 'A Southerner among the Spirits '; a volume which is still accessible to
the public. Having now reached the
time of the opening of my correspondence
with her, I shall shape this sketch almost
into the form of an autobiography, giving my own comments only when needed
to keep up the connection.

MEMPHIS, TENN., April 19, 1877.
I published my book here at my own
expense. I wrote it to give my testimony
to what I believe—yes, know—to be the
truth, and I want to be heard....
I am now residing with Mrs. Hawks, a
very fine trance lecturer....She attracts
large audiences of the most high-toned
and intelligent people of this city. I
mention her to you because I want to tell
you of a project we have in view, not yet
announced to the public. Her spirit band
and mine are anxious that we should
establish a weekly spiritual paper, to be
called *The Voice of Truth*... I think that
between us, she with her inspired lips,
and also her pen, and I with my pen, we
could edit a pretty fair paper ; and a
weekly is much needed at the South....

"It will be remembered that a monthly magazine had for some time previous
been published at Memphis by Dr. Watson. Eventually this became merged as
a department of the new weekly.

"Under the date of May 22, 1877, Mrs. Shindler writes:

I am about starting for my Texas home where I shall probably remain till October.... My only son is bitterly opposed to Spiritualism, and is very unwilling for me to leave home. It is very sad, and is my "thorn in the flesh." May his spiritual eyes be opened, is my constant prayer. He is one of the best, most moral young men I ever knew, and is a very affectionate son; but a wall has risen up between us which is very painful.

NACOGDOCHES, TEX., July 28, 1877.
My Good, Kind Friend and Brother: If you only knew how much good your letters do me—how your heart's warm tide flows into mine—you would rejoice that you have it in your power to do so good a work as to comfort the one who is at present living in a benighted region with not one human being near who can understand or appreciate the only subjects of thought in which she is interested....

I will tell you all about our projected paper, *The Voice of Truth.* From first to last I have been led along; and even about the publication of my book I was dubious till the last moment, not being absolutely certain that I was doing right. I spent the last two months in Memphis with Mrs Hawks, an inspirational medium of rare powers, and of great purity and spirituality of character. Her guides proposed and urged the project, and were particularly positive in the direction that I should be associated in the editorship; and then I had intimations from my spirit band to the same effect; and these intimations came to me so in many ways, sometimes really startling, that I was forced into a conditional consent.... I suppose my portion of the work will be to write, write, write; and select such matter as I think interesting and profitable.

Sept. 16th . I have been trying to get to Memphis for the last month, for I am very much needed there to assist in the issue of our first number of *The Voice of Truth,* but my presence at home seemed almost indispensable.

I have not been idle this summer. I have been collecting matter for the paper, both original and selected, and have quite a store of material on hand. Though my brain is not large, it is terribly active; if it were not for that I might become mediumistic enough to receive help through my own organism; but I am never "passive" a moment when awake. But let me tell you something funny. Every night, before retiring, I

'sit with a pencil and paper and write to myself as from my spirit friends; but cannot, for the life of me, tell whether I am not doing it all. Sometimes I can write, and sometimes not. At any rate, reading over these communications is a comfort to me, and that is something.

"Not long after, Mrs. Shindler found herself regularly harnessed into the editorial life at Memphis. She must have been very busy, working hard as leading editor of the new Spiritualist paper, the numbers of which came out regularly for about six months, containing an unusual proportion of editorial matter, written in the free, flowing, and interesting style of the leading editor. I think that the paper was becoming quite extensively popular, and might have continued with some degree of permanence, had it not been for unforeseen adverse conditions, soon to be noticed. Owing to this very busy life in which she was engaged, several months elapsed before I received another letter from my friend. But under date of February 28, 1878, after apologizing for the delay, she wrote:

I knew I was undertaking an arduous task when I consented, after the earnest solicitations of my earth—and so far as I can judge, my spirit—friends to engage in the editorship of a weekly journal; but if I can only go on with it, I shall feel thankful for the opportunity of pouring my little bucketful on to the tidal-wave which is now sweeping over the earth, bearing away the rubbish of old systems which are tumbling and falling all around us.

"The following extracts are taken from a letter dated at Memphis, April 23, 1878:

I am receiving cheering letters from many quarters, and feel thankful that my first attempt at editorship has been so favorably received. It is pleasant work for me, only my task is rather too severe. I do not mind writing the articles, that is the part I love; but the responsibility of filling the paper with a variety of interesting matter, worries me considerably. The proof-reading also is no easy work. You need not be uneasy about my vacating the editorial chair for a while, for I shall continue to write, especially on certain subjects, and send matter to the paper by mail. But my brain has been on the strain too long, and

I am admonished that I must break away and enjoy the quiet of home for a season.

"Soon after, leaving the immediate management in the hands of her assistant editor, Mrs. Hawks, whose husband was the business manager, and upon whom also rested the pecuniary responsibility of the enterprise, Mrs. Shindler returned to her Texas home, intending to spend the summer there. The passages from her letters which follow will sufficiently indicate the course of succeeding events:

June 3, 1878.
I nearly broke myself down before I left Memphis, and ever since I have been at home I have found even the writing of a letter a grievous burden; yet occasionally a thought or a series of thoughts comes to me with such power that I am obliged to give them expression in a hastily penned article, which the next day I would not know to be mine, if it had not my signature. What kind of writing do you call that? Inspirational or what? .... My home looks lovely. I have white, pink, and red tea roses in bloom, and many other flowers, which make the garden gay, while the mocking birds keep up a constant serenade. It will be very hard for me to break away when it becomes necessary for me to return to Memphis; but by that time I suppose I shall begin to long for the society of spiritualists.

"In her next letter of June 22d, Mrs. Shindler begins to manifest trouble and alarm at the state of things at Memphis. Mrs. Hawks had been taken dangerously ill, in view of which state of things is found the following anxious inquiry:

What is to become of the *Voice of Truth?* In the present wearied condition of my brain I would not again undertake to carry it on alone......

"However, from the exigency of the case, it was found necessary to suspend the publication for three months. Then came on that terrible prevalence of the yellow fever, the remembrance of which is still fresh in the public mind. This put an end to the noble enterprise of our friends, as it did, for the time being, to almost every enterprise of that devoted city.

"Under date of November 23d Mrs.

Shindler thus writes of the final catastrophe:

I have had two or three letters from Mr. Hawks—*she* is not able to write a line. They are still sick and thoroughly discouraged. The whole family had the yellow fever and it has left both Mr. and Mrs. H. in a very nervous condition; and he writes that from financial and other considerations, there is no probability of resuming the publication of the *Voice of Truth.* It is one of the great disappointments of my life, for I had formed a broad and comprehensive plan of action which was but just begun to be fulfilled; especially was this the case in regard to the topics of "Co-operation" and of "Woman and her Work." But I think I shall still go on writing upon the latter subject; and perhaps, if times grow better and I have a favorable opportunity, I may offer the result to the public in a book form.

"Our friend now, for a time, felt that her occupation was gone, and that she was doomed to an unwelcome extension of her time of inaction and exile in the uncongeniality of her Texas home. But soon there were indications in her letters that her intensely active mind was at work on other projects. She writes:

I have been writing for the working people. My articles are not so much on the finance question, about which there are such differences of opinion. They are directed more to the hearts of those who can feel for the poor, and who hate monopoly, bribery, wicked legislation, and fraud of all descriptions. Letters are pouring in upon me from working men, thanking me for my labors in behalf of the laboring classes, and I feel that a higher power than mine has been my guide in this matter.

"We soon after find Mrs. Shindler in New York, where she remained till near the close of the year, keeping herself quite busy, especially with the pen, in the new work she seemed to have before her. From letters received during this period, I must limit myself to the extracts which follow:

Before I left home I was writing songs for the working people's party; and I also wrote a great many prose articles, which were extensively copied into the labor reform papers, till now I find myself quite popular with the common people....I feel sure that this work has been chosen for me by my angel friends, who seem to be leading me along, opening for me doors of usefulness all the time....I am at all times conscious that I am watched over and guided by the wise and good who have passed on before me; and I believe that they will preserve me from contamination while leading me into rough paths and to acquaintanceship with strange companions...Letters come to me from perfect strangers in all parts of the Union, gratefully thanking me for the sympathy expressed in my writings for suffering humanity, and I cannot help hoping that I am doing a good work; but be this as it may, I cannot choose for myself; I have been obliged to enter this field, and here I must stay until I can get leave of absence....

"Soon after, Mrs. Shindler returned to her home in Texas, and remained about a year; but early in the year 1881, being then past seventy years of age, she made another and a final visit to New York. Upon her final return to her Texas home our correspondence continued until the closing months of her earthly career, when her letters ceased. The announcement of her death, in February, 1883, reached me through the columns of a paper, but no particulars of the final hours. But we may safely infer that when the closing crisis came, whatever may have been the uncongeniality of the visible surroundings, there was an abundant concert of harmonious blendings close upon the borders of the two worlds where now was transpiring a most joyful transition.

"Since her entrance into the unseen world I have had two interviews with her who is now my spirit friend, in the presence of a mediumship of the most excellent and reliable character. During the first of these she said: 'I have had in mind continually almost since my passage into this life to come *en rapport* with you and the medium through whom so many beautiful communications have been given. I thought first of the help it would be to me, and thought, too, of the pleasure. Tears are compensated for in this hour. So much that is grand and beautiful beyond expression opens to my vision! I am filled with the influence, but may not give expression to a tenth part of my feeling....I am with you now as ever in the wish to benefit others. Whatever I can do to assist in your work, I shall be privileged, I trust, to do....A light is shining as far as the spirit eye can reach, and to me it seems that the whole universe must feel its power. Joy unspeakable is mine. I would that the whole world were so blessed.'

"At our second interview, after I had nearly completed this article, it was said: 'I am here to-day to speak of self. My earthly career is ended, and yet not ended. I am possessed of clearer perceptions of life and its duties than ever before. And, oh! how I long to be able to straighten out all the crookedness of my past! For sometimes I have been blinded by a zeal and enthusiasm not enlightened by wisdom. Yet, on the whole, I am happy to be able to say that I did the best I could. Your attempt to bring before the public a notice of my humble self, would flatter me, did I not know my many imperfections. If I had had more self-confidence, I might have used my powers more forcibly; so please pass lightly over the past, and say of her of whom you have been writing, that since her entrance into the spirit life, she, like others, has become aware of the possession of powers far beyond her own conception of her real self; and would gladly, had she the instruments so to do, devote years of time in humanitarian work; for her heart still lingers with those she knew on the earth-plane, who were enslaved by circumstances and conditions, and in need of powerful helpers on this side of life.' "

ANNA D. LOUCKS.

The subject of this sketch was one of the pioneer mediums on the Pacific Coast, and did much for the education of both spirits and mortals during the years of her mediumistic work. Mrs. Loucks passed to the higher life from the Kings Daughters' Home in San Francisco, May 21, 1893. Of her mediumship and its value to the world, there is no one more competent to decide than that veteran Spiritualist, Herman Snow, who was at one time associated with Mrs. Loucks in the capacity of scribe, reporting her seances, and publishing much valuable and interesting matter given by the spirit friends during her entrancement. The author can do no better than make extracts from a sketch written by Mr. Snow, and published in the CARRIER DOVE some nine years ago, which will give the reader a clear idea of her noble, unselfish life and work. Mr. Snow says:

"Among the many striking phases of our modern Spiritualism are some which go to show that we of this life are by no means the sole recipients of the more important benefits resulting from a close mediumistic relation between the two worlds. It is now well understood by the more experienced in matters of the kind, that there is a mutual exchange of helps between spirits in and out of the earthly body; and many of our most devoted mediums have given largely of their capacities in aid of necessitous ones on the spirit side of life. Of medium-helpers of this kind may be ranked—pre-eminently I think—Mrs. Anna Danforth Loucks, who is well known to many of the earlier and well-established Spiritualists of San Francisco vicinity, including the present writer, with whom during a period of about eight years, she was engaged in a series of seances in aid of unfortunate ones upon the borders of the spirit world. This work was under the control and guidance of a band of beneficent spirit workers, who were constantly seeking new methods of advancing their work, and to which Mrs. Loucks had given herself up unreservedly and unselfishly. My own part of the work consisted in acting as the scribe of our seance, and otherwise aiding in their harmony and efficiency; also it belonged to me to publish to the world some of the more striking results. A regular record was kept of our proceedings from which was eventually published our volume, "Visions of the Beyond, by a Seer of To-day"; and also, afterwards, there was contributed to the different Spiritualist papers enough to fill another volume of like size had it been deemed best to publish another. It has been from my journal of the seances that I have gathered the materials for this brief sketch of the life work of the medium.

"Mrs. Loucks is a native of New Hampshire, and in that State her childhood and youth were passed, her family name being Danforth. Later, she lived much in Boston, but came to California whilst yet in youthful vigor, and here she lived many years, mostly in San Francisco. She was married here, and for several years enjoyed a happy home-life, until, during the prevalence of one of our virulent epidemics, her husband was suddenly taken away, leaving her sadly alone and dependent. In all the many years since that time, she has given the strength of her life to the specialty of her mediumship, the demands upon her being of so exacting a character that she had but little strength for such other purposes as might have enabled her to earn for herself the means of a comfortable support. But having a strong, personal dislike to engaging in anything like a regularly paid mediumship, and being encouraged in the same direction by her band, she was induced to depend upon voluntary contributions of friends to support her in her work. These, though at times liberal and sufficient, yet often failed, so that she sometimes suffered privations and want, all of which she was ready to endure rather than shrink from a work of relief to those in the spirit form, which to her seemed so real and important. She once told me that she would rather live on bread and water than give up this work.

"Mrs. Loucks was a medium-seer, that is, she could see clearly spirit forms and scenery, and, when conditions were favorable, as was generally the case with us, she could convey to me in clear and compact language, the thoughts of spirits with whom she was *en rapport*. She could also, at the same time, converse with me in answer to my questions, thus enabling me to exchange thoughts with this controlling band, or with the special objects of our relief; and sometimes such spoken words from one in the bodily form, prove to be of great importance as a starting point of relief. Important symbolic instructions were also sometimes conveyed through this medium, as may be seen in the volume already alluded to. This mediumistic gift seems to have been a native endowment, though something was done for a further development in later life. On two occasions, as a part of seance proceedings, while Mrs. Loucks was still partially in her abnormal condition, the following concerning her earlier mediumistic experiences, given in her own language, will, I think, be found of special interest to the reader, although much abridged through lack of space. She says:

I did not see much of special interest until I was about eight years of age. There, I see myself extremely restless and unsatisfied, especially with my want of opportunities for gaining the mere rudiments of a common school education. But I now see that this deficiency in my early training was not, perhaps, a loss, for in proportion to the want of external advantages, so were my inward capacities of an intuitive character deepened. At times, a perfect flood of joy would fill my being, and yet I knew not why nor whence it came. Then the tide of my

life would flow back to the other extreme of a restless dissatisfaction. I can now see that all this was of an educationary character, stimulating and enlarging my inward growth, and preparing me for the kind of work I had to do, far better than a store of general education, the want of which I was accustomed so deeply to deplore, would have done.

The first remembered use of my vision-seeing was not far from the time of the death of my mother, I being then about twelve years of age. I clearly foresaw her death, even to the very position in which she was afterwards placed in the coffin, the infant child whose birth was her death being laid upon one arm at her side. About a month after, when most of the family were away, she came and partly showed herself to me, but the effect upon me was such that, as I have since been told, she withdrew herself from my vision. The earthly members of our family were greatly troubled when I told them of what had taken place, and said they should not again leave me so nearly alone.

With my present illumination, I can look back and trace the wisdom-hand that has led me *all* the ways, being now recognized as the ways of wisdom and love, though at the time much has come to me in dark and doubtful forms. My father, who is now near me in his spirit form, says that in such cases we are " the blind led, but not by the blind."

All along my life-course I have had this especial annoyance: I would seem to have a vivid consciousness of the active, inner state of those with whom I come into near relations, and so large a part of such inward life being of an evil or perverted character, I have often been impelled into apparent harsh judgments of those around me, although I have tried hard to curb myself in this tendency. Many a severe reproach have I thus incurred when, as I now see it, I was no more blame-worthy than I am when, with the external eye, I see bodily deformities directly before me.

Another tendency has greatly troubled me: All great sufferings and sorrows have been so far forshadowed that I have been made to tremble, and sometimes to cry out in an agony of apprehension, although the exact nature of the coming calamity could not be seen by me. This was especially the case at the time of my husband's transition which came suddenly upon me. Even in that case, the great suffering was whilst I was under a cloud of apprehension foreshadowing the calamity. When it was actually at hand, I was comparatively calm and sustained.

"At a later period, while in her normal conversational condition, Mrs. Loucks gave me some of the more interesting particulars of this departure. It seems that she herself took the almost exclusive care of her husband, and was entirely alone with him when the final crisis was reached. As she stood by the bedside, she clearly saw the process of the separation of the spirit from the material body; and when it was fairly over, her dear one beamed upon her a genial and loving smile, playfully waving his hand toward her, but did not leave her near presence until he had advised her somewhat in regard to the disposal of the body, and other matters of immediate interest.

"Before closing, some effort should be made more clearly to define the peculiarities of this mediumistic work of Mrs. Loucks. It was, I think, different in at least one important respect, from what had been generally known, even among advanced Spiritualists. All such, from an early date, have been familiar with aiding ignorant and vicious spirits through mediums. But our work was by no means confined to aiding this class, for often individuals of advanced intelligence were made participants in the wise helping influence of our band. In such cases, the efforts were largely of an experimental character, aimed at once to a better understanding of the condition of a natural and easy transition from the earthly to the spirit life, and to a needed relief in certain instances wherein worthy persons had become victims of imperfect knowledge in this respect. Of course, such should be regarded as exceptional cases, the general order of the death transition being natural and of brief duration. Of the nature and action of these occasional obstructions in the passage to the life beyond, but little can be known by any of us, much less be clearly conveyed to others. But perhaps an imperfect conception of special cases in view may be gathered from the following descriptive headings over the condensed accounts of some of our more recent seances published in the Spiritualist

papers: "An Esthetic; How He Was Helped in Spirit Life"; "Fashion's Victim"; "The Marble-Worker, His Head Crushed Beneath a Falling Column"; "A Negative Innocent"; "The Hypochondriac"; "A Maniac Restored"; "Death by Starvation"; "A Warning to Mesmerisers"; "Killed by Drugs"; "Effects of a Violent Transition"; "A Slave to Drink"; "A Sympathetic Subject"; "The Buried Miner; Crushed by the Falling Rock"; "Release of a Spirit Long Confined in a Stone Burial Case"; "Lost and Starved in the Adirondack Forest"; "The Happy Sleep of an Aged One"; "A Victim of Ante-Natal Ills"; "She Fell from a Swing and Lost Her Physical Body"; "Waiting for the Resurrection Day." During my entire experience probably some hundreds of cases of a similar character have passed before me, and what has most forcibly struck me has been the constant variety as well as the novelty and dramatic naturalness of each case. There has been but little repetition, each individual exhibiting characteristics of his own, almost as much so as if a procession of marked individuals in the bodily form had passed in review before me; and, yet there have been certain characteristics in conduct belonging to these cases generally, and this is what ought to be, since the action of natural law should be uniform on the borders of the two worlds as well as in them. It has been found, for instance, that whenever a dormant or bewildered spirit first enters upon a course of recovery under the influences brought to bear upon him by the methods of one band, it has invariably followed that the thread of natural life has been renewed at the point of the lost earthly lucidity or consciousness. It is very much so in those cases of our earthly life wherein from accidental concussion of the brain the unconsciousness, when at length ended, results in the taking up of the thread of thought or speech at the precise point where it was interrupted by the accident. It is from such points of renewed contact with earthly conditions that the long dormant or bewildered spirit gains a foothold for advancing into the actualities of the spirit life and its open ways of progress.

"It was not claimed that the methods of our band are the only means of such deliverances; it was only implied that some such action through an earthly medium is more prompt in its results than that which comes through the natural operation of law as it acts in the spirit spheres. It was said that, without some such action, ages might elapse without a full deliverance; also, that what was now being done was not a tithe of what might be done through mediums if rightly employed in this direction. Hence it appears that this especial work was comparatively and necessarily a limited one, and in seeking out the especial subjects of its action, reference was constantly had to those who were naturally best fitted to become useful workers for humanity, when they should become fully established in the ways of the new life."

AARON W. PRATT.

AARON W. PRATT.

Mr. Pratt was born in the town of Williamson, Wayne County, New York, November 24, 1819. His birthplace was, at that time, in the "Wilds of the West," a heavily timbered country requiring hard labor on the part of the pioneers who penetrated its forests to fell the trees, clear the land, and make the wilderness yield place to fruitful farms and fragrant orchards. Such was the home life and material surroundings into which was ushered the subject of this sketch making his early life one of toil and privation. His only schooling was hard labor and good moral training. As he approached the years of manhood he was led to investigate and inquire into the claims of Christianity which, after a time, resulted in his acceptance of the "terms of grace" according to theological standards, and rejoice in the confidence of a soul-conversion or new birth as taught by his spiritual advisers. This change of heart was followed by zealous and active work as a Christian for three or four years; but careful observation and note of what seemed to characterize high professions in the various churches led him to gradually become an agnostic in regard to religious teachings. Yet, his aspiring nature could not be satisfied with a doubtful or neutral position; he must know the why and wherefore of life —its purposes and their fulfilment. With earnestness of purpose, strong determination, and a desire to know something of the way in which the All Father designed His children to walk in their journey through earth life, he began his investigations along new lines, and with different motives. The one prayer in his heart by day and night was the prayer for light and knowledge. The answer came with a spiritual illumination in which he saw the faces of shining angels, and a scene of transcendent glory and loveliness was unveiled before his astonished and wondering eyes. His soul was flooded with unutterable joy and peace; the great truth of immortal existence— the solution of the mysterious problem of death—why we live and for what purpose is living—all had answers.

Spiritual influx comes in great waves. It has its periods of ebb and flow—its low tide and its flood. While all the world were discussing the wonderful "Rochester rappings," on the quiet little farm at Williamson, the young farmer was receiving the marvelous revealments that settled the question forever in his mind as to the reality of the future life, and the conscious existence of man after the change called death. His views of life were broadened, the terrible dread of death vanished, and living became a joy to him, even if occupied with hard work and tasks disagreeable and uncongenial. As the new light dawned more fully upon his consciousness, his sensitively attuned nature absorbed, assimilated, and made it a part of his character. He fully recognized the fact that all reform must begin with self; and he lived his humble life for its own perfection, always ready to assist others, seeking by every means to educate them, and in his humble sphere to do all the good, alleviate all the suffering, and give all the assistance in his power. At times his inspiration has been prophetic, and the clouds lowering in the horizon cast ominous shadows upon the sensitive dial of his soul as he foretold their significance.

Like all others who have dared to step out of the old and beaten paths of accepted theological error, Mr. Pratt was destined to meet with opposition and derision among those of his own household. But nothing could chill the ardor of his purpose or shake his determination to stand by the truth as revealed to his understanding, as it was based upon, and in harmonious accord with, universal law as demonstrated in nature.

Mr. Pratt is not a medium for physical phenomena, and can convey to others but a small fraction of what he receives interiorly; yet a silent, potent influence or power attends him, which is felt by all with whom he comes in contact, that is sufficient to cope with all opposition. This power seems to command for him a large blessing, as he constantly strives for the highest and best attainable, and receives, therefore, spiritual gifts and illumination as the gentle dews descend from Heaven and are absorbed into the bosom of the thirsty, expectant earth.

Mr. Pratt resides in Edgar, Nebraska, where he maintains himself by labor on his farm, although now past his seventy-sixth year. He is still in perfect physical health, as elastic as in youth, and the perfect expression of a harmonious life in accord with the teachings of the divinity within his own soul, and as revealed from the higher shores of life and the realm of causation. He is truly an embodiment of the principles of the spiritual philosophy, and one of the few surviving pioneers who dared to brave the sneers and scorn of the world for its vindication.

MRS. S. COWELL.

MRS. S. COWELL.

Among the many mediums who have come to the front in Spiritualism on the Pacific Coast during the past few years, no one stands more conspicuous in the work than does the subject of this sketch. Since her first appearance upon the Spiritual rostrum, seven years ago, she has been kept constantly engaged, both in public and private, and her work has received the highest indorsements from societies and individuals who have been the recipients of her ministrations. Mrs. Cowell made her first appearance as a platform test medium in the City of Oakland, where she has resided many years, and where she has a beautiful home, and a large circle of true and devoted friends. It was no wonder that the Spiritual gifts which had been hers from earliest childhood, although not understood or comprehended by herself or her parents until they had been the source of much suffering, both physical and mental, should at last, under the pleasant surroundings and harmonious influences of her married life, blossom forth into the beautiful fruition of a grand and holy mediumship, that was destined to fill all her mature years with a joy and peace unspeakable, and bring comfort and happiness to thousands of earth's weary and benighted ones. It was but a just and fitting compensation for all that she had suffered as a child on account of being possessed with powers not in common with other children, but belonging to the class of superphysical senses, which enabled her to see clairvoyantly, and hear clairaudiently, even when too young to understand the meaning of the sights and sounds coming to her from the spirit side of life. These strange experiences were the cause of frequent punishments and reproof from those who, as ignorant as herself of their true source, attributed them to Satanic influence, and as such to be condemned and "cast out" if possible. Notwithstanding the trials and hardships of her young life, still the angel teachers did not abandon their favored instrument, but patiently waited until the time should come when they could unfold and use her wonderful powers for the good of humanity and her own highest development.

Mrs. Cowell is well known throughout the State of California, having received calls to lecture and give platform tests from all the leading societies in the principal cities from San Diego to San Francisco. She has been the recipient of many valuable testimonials from individuals who have received remarkable tests, both public and private, and has been highly indorsed by societies wherever she has appeared. The leading societies of Los Angeles, San Jose, and Oakland keep her almost constantly engaged upon their respective platforms, with but short intervals of rest between engagements. She has also had a number of calls from Sacramento, and filled the engagements with great satisfaction to all concerned.

During the various camp-meetings held in Oakland, Mrs. Cowell was always a conspicuous worker, and whatever of success has attended such efforts of late years has been largely owing to her indomitable energy and perseverance. She was one of the most prominent of the leading speakers and mediums at the first camp-meeting held by the Spiritualists of Southern California at their Convention at Santa Monica during the summer of 1895, and, at the close of that meeting, Mrs. Cowell united her forces with other prominent mediums, and held a Spiritual Congress in Music Hall, Los Angeles, which attracted large audiences, and aroused a public interest in Spiritualism never before known in that City of Priests and Masses. After the Congress closed its sessions, Mrs. Cowell, Doctor Schlesinger and Mrs. Frietag formed a mediumistic combine, and, with the assistance of Mr. S. D. Dye and Mrs. Schlesinger, they engaged the Los Angeles Theater and commenced a series of most successful meetings, which continued seven weeks, and resulted in the organization of The Harmonial Spiritualists' Association, which retained the Theater, and held very large and popular meetings, with the best talent available on the platform, after the projectors of the movement had been obliged to return to their respective homes to fill other engagements. That Society is now the leading one of Southern California. Since its organization both Doctor Schlesinger and Mrs. Cowell have been recalled to occupy its platform, and others long prominent in the work have been engaged for the near future.

Mrs. Cowell's tests regarding business matters are remarkable for their clearness of detail and accuracy. Many testimonials of a private nature, and otherwise, are in the possession of the writer from grateful souls who have been helped materially, as well as spiritually, through the advice they have received from spirit friends through this grand medium. One instance of this kind occurred in Oakland, where parties were told concerning matters of business pertaining to an inheritance due them in England, which resulted in a trip to the Mother Country by the gentleman interested, and of his coming into possession of his property amounting to twenty thousand dollars. In this instance Mrs. Cowell's guides managed the entire matter, and gave explicit directions as to the proper course to be pursued by the parties interested, in order to obtain their rights.

During the camp-meeting at Santa Monica, Cal., Mrs. Cowell, while giving tests from the platform, said to a young man in the audience that his father, who lived in England, had recently passed to spirit life. The young man admitted that his father was in England, but that he believed him to be alive and well. A few days later the gentleman sought an interview with Mrs. Cowell at the close of an evening meeting and stated that he had just received news from home saying that his father had died, the time of his death corresponding exactly with the date fixed by Mrs. Cowell at the time she gave the test.

The Herald of Light, of San Diego, speaks of Mrs. Cowell's visit to that city as follows:

Mrs. R. Cowell and her genial husband made a host of friends during their three weeks' visit to San Diego, and it was with regret that we bid them farewell. During her brief sojourn here, Mrs. Cowell's clairvoyant eyes have brought to light hidden documents of much value to the owners, and in some cases, keeping them out of the courts; they have unraveled mysteries and brought peace and comfort to sorrowing souls.

The Medium, of Los Angeles, speaks of her first appearance before a Spiritual Society in that city in a pleasing paragraph. It says:

Mrs. R. Cowell of Oakland occupied the platform of the First Spiritual Society last Sunday afternoon and evening, and made a fine impression upon all. The lady is a powerful medium and a pleasing, eloquent speaker, both while under control and in her normal state. Her discourses are given under control and she never knows beforehand what the subject is to be. Her tests, to which she devotes most of the time, are given with great rapidity and wonderful accuracy. She will remain with the Society during this month, and those who miss the opportunity of hearing her will surely regret it.

In the same paper, a few months later, Mrs. Amanda Wiggin, a pioneer medium and speaker, pays a just and fitting tribute to genuine mediumship in the following words:

Editor *Medium*—I believe honest, genuine mediumship should be recognized, and such mediums be known to all Spiritualists. This is why I pen these lines.

Our sister, and medium, Mrs. S. Cowell, who has just closed her engagement in Los Angeles and has returned to her home in Oakland, Cal., is a fine medium and a good woman; any one may be proud of her friendship, and we need not be ashamed to introduce her to our friends and receive her into our homes. We feel the angels' blessing while so doing for she is a faithful worker, who leaves a clean, wholesome feeling wherever she goes. Any body of Spiritualists needing such a medium can, with confidence, apply to her and feel secure in hiring her. At a circle of over forty persons I heard her give more messages than any other medium I ever listened to. I commenced the investigation of Spiritualism in 1862, and have had great experience with mediums, but I never met one whose works leave a better or more lasting influence than Mrs. Cowell's.

The following is a brief synopsis of an address delivered by Mrs. Cowell during a recent engagement in San Jose, Cal. The subject was, "Spiritualism; What Is It? and What Has It Done?"

As usual, the lecture was so filled with the poetic fire of the spheres of light that it would be impossible to do it justice in a summarized report. However, we will endeavor to give a few of the thoughts conveyed in this lecture, robbing them of their poetic robes and the beautiful pictures surrounding them.

"Spiritualism," her control said, "has opened the flood-gates of wisdom to woman, and made her equal to man in every respect. It has raised the banner of light on the hills of the morning, and sent forth glory-crowned angels of light with glad tidings of great joy to the darkened world.

"It brings out the better part of manhood, and has lifted many a mortal from the mire and placed him upon the rock of truth, justice, and all that is noble in man.

"Thoughts are things—as mortals think, so will be the spirit band they attract to their aid—legions of light or demons of darkness.

"Your Bible is nothing but a record of miracles from cover to cover. But in reference to bringing back the dead, there are no dead to return; they have laid down the garments of life material and passed to the higher spheres of life immortal."

An orthodox death scene was given, and the prayer of the departing one was "O, pray for me, for I go to a land I know not where!" "Alas for his creed-darkened soul! But he *knew* when the morning came."

Then comes the scene of a good old Spiritualist who is about to pass out. He says, "I fear not the sea that rolls between me and my loved ones; I have the chart and compass, and dread not the voyage."

"But you say, 'The old man was in his dotage.' But how do you account for the little child with golden locks who, in passing out, says, 'Good-by, but here comes father from the beautiful country to take me to the crystal streams of life immortal.'

"The chair of science in your colleges will yet bring forth a science that will make yonder church tremble from its foundation."

In reference to frauds and imposters who were duping the public, the control asked: "Did you ever see a truth without a counterfeit?" The injunction was then given, "Be not believers but knowers and doers."

In concluding, the speaker said: "When the voices come back to all through the misty scenes of life material, sorrowing will be no more; knowledge, joy, and peace will 'fill the world as the waters cover the sea.'

"May you all be true Spiritualists, so that you may be able to 'read your titles clear to mansions in the skies '—to homes of light and truth."

J. S. LOVELAND.

Professor J. S. Loveland was born in the Town of Stoddard, State of New Hampshire, on the twenty-first day of March, 1818. He is the seventh generation from Thomas Loveland of Glastonbury, Conn., from whom all the Lovelands in the United States have descended. The family came from England, and landed at Boston, Mass., prior to 1635, as during that year, in company with others, they made their way through the wilderness and settled in what is now Glastonbury, Conn. Some seventy members of the family were soldiers in the Revolutionary War, and Lovelands have been found on nearly, or quite, all the battlefields of all our wars. The Professor's father was in the famous bayonet charge at Lundy's Lane, in the war of 1812; and also under Colonel Miller, who captured a British battery in the same campaign. A Doctor Dickerson, at a family reunion in Brighton, Ills., said of the Loveland family: "No enterprise is too difficult for their energy; no difficulties are insurmountable, and no heights are too lofty for their aspiration. As a family they are equal to any, and surpassed by none."

The father of the Professor was a poor man, and from his early boyhood he was compelled to grapple with hard work. His educational advantages were a few months each year in the common school, where only the rudiments of education were taught. Reading, writing, arithmetic, grammar, and geography, with a little sprinkling of history was the extent of his studies up to his eighteenth year, when he commenced teaching himself, but continued it but for one winter. His family, like most of the prominent people in his native town, were freethinkers, and he grew up without the blight of a religious training; never attended a Sunday School, and for several years never went to any religious meetings whatever. But in his nineteenth year he worked for a farmer in the Town of Gilsum, who was a church member, and as several of the young people went to church, he attended with them. The result was that, at a Methodist meeting, he was converted, and became a member of that organization, when about 19 years of age. And for sixteen years he continued a member of the M. E. Church.

Within a few months after his conversion he had a "call to preach." This was a turning point in his history. Uneducated, poor, and bashful to the last degree, he struggled with the "call," but when, at last, he consulted the older brethren and the preacher who had converted him, he found they had all been expecting such a "call." It is barely possible that their thought and expectation had not a little to do with the "call," though it is not at all improbable that special Spirit influence is largely concerned in giving the "call to preach." At all events, soon after passing his twentieth year, he was on a "circuit" in Vermont as a Methodist preacher. He continued preaching some fourteen years, and when he withdrew could have had the best appointments in New England. During these years he managed to attend several terms in seminaries of learning, and also the first Methodist Theological School, so that, when he withdrew from the church and ministry, he could read the Bible in Hebrew, Greek, Latin, and English, and had been appointed Professor of Mental and Moral Philosophy in an academy in Northern Ohio, but other calls and duties prevented his engaging in that work.

It would readily be inferred that the early modes of thought and active intellectuality of the family would tend to produce serious questionings as to many of the tenets of Orthodox theology. And this inference became, in time, an appalling fact. The very foundations of his theology would crumble to pieces in the crucible of his intellect. Its glaring inconsistencies would stand out in as bold relief in the field of his consciousness as the granite mountains of his native state in the field of outer vision. How could he continue to preach? There was always one complete answer to all the turmoil of an exacting reason. It was his experience. Had he not been arrested like Saul of Tarsus? Had he not been revolutionized in a day from confirmed Atheism into a knowledge of Immortality? Had he not the "Witness of the Spirit"? Did he not realize the overpowering ecstasies of his spiritual union with God? Did not the "Divine Power" attend and seal his preaching? Did not people fall as dead, and, in their entrancement, have wondrous visions of the spiritual world, and this under the preaching of the very doctrines which his reason rejected? Here was the great difficulty: He did not, could not, for a long time, see but what the experiences were naturally and logically the outcome of the theological tenets of the creeds and articles of religion. Hence, he was held in what seemed an inextricable thrall. But during all these years of study, reasoning, and work, he was demonstrating principles, but could not fit them into a unitary system. Indeed, it was not till he had become somewhat familiar with Spiritualism that a unitary system of thought became apparent in his consciousness. Then all the seemingly isolated principles dropped into their proper place—they were all systemized of themselves.

Professor Loveland did not commence his investigations of Modern Spiritualism as do many, who need evidence of the fact that decarnate spirits can manifest themselves to those still in the form. In the Methodist Church he had seen cases of trance, where spirits manifested themselves as clearly as he has ever seen in spiritual circles. The history of Methodism abounded with instances of the return and manifestation of spirits. Indeed, so satisfactory were these instances, that he has never been any more convinced than when a minister of the M. E. Church. He commenced his investigation simply to see whether it was a reality or a fraud. It required but little to show the genuineness of the phenomena; and, hence, to command his assent to the fact. He had, however, little anticipated the bitter hostility with which the manifestations would be assailed by the church; and it was, no doubt, these implacable hostilities which largely tended to still farther open his eyes to the falsities of theology, and lead him to an utter renunciation of the entire system of supernaturalism. But the final step would seem to many extremely hard, and would be thought a great sacrifice. Consider, he had entered the ministry of that powerful church when a boy. He worked up from a country-circuit preacher to the metropolis of New England. The best appointments were before him. He was loved, honored, and desired. He was still poor; not worth a dollar, with a family, and not possessing even furniture for housekeeping, as that was furnished by the societies. He had no trade, no occupation, and no acquaintances outside of that church. Lecturing among Spiritualists had not been thought of. But he could no longer honestly preach the doctrines of Orthodoxy, and calmly walked out of the church by withdrawing from the New England Conference, of which he was a member. It is true, he was giving up the fruits of many toilsome, self-denying years of work and effort—it was abandoning the sure prospect of honor and emolument for the future years, but he never thought he was sacrificing, or doing any very meritorious thing; it fact, it was to him plain, common sense duty, which he performed without regret or the slightest anxiety as to the results. The future was a blank, except that he thought he might leave the city, go out in the country, and rent a piece of land and make a living.

But the Providence of the "Circle of the Higher Harmonies" had other plans for his future. Some months after this event, a Spiritualistic friend by the name of Johnson, said to him, "Brother Loveland I wish you would give us a lecture on Spiritualism." Impressed by the repetition of the request at different times, he consented, thinking he could talk an hour on that topic. A hall was secured, notice given, and on a Sunday afternoon he went to the hall, found it full, also the ante-rooms and hallways. After the lecture the people demanded another and a larger hall. It was secured, and the one lecture lengthened out to some three years, with an audience frequently reaching up to six and seven hundred. This was the first Spiritualistic meeting ever established in this country, and if this lecture was not the first ever given upon Spiritualism, it was the first ever heard of in New England; and one thing is certain, Professor Loveland was the first lecturer to start a regular Sunday meeting and continue it for any length of time; and he believes he was the first person to be entitled a regular lecturer on the Spiritual philosophy, He was the first person to dedicate himself exclusively to that work. He is not anxious for any glory on that account, but simply wishes the real facts of history to be understood.

The first lecture was given in Charlestown, Mass., and for the first season he would lecture in Charlestown in the afternoon, and in Boston in the evening, though the audiences were partly the same, Charlestown being a suburb of Boston. His labors were not confined to the city, but on week-day evenings he lectured in the outlying cities and towns, extending his work into the adjoining States. There is no portion of the country where Spiritualism has obtained so strong and extensive influence as in Boston and the contiguous territory.

The Professor has lectured in all the large cities of the North, except Cincinnati, but only in St. Louis of the former Slave States, and in most of the second-class cities, besides a large number of smaller cities and towns. Unlike most speakers, he has never made a practise of soliciting engagements, but has gone only where he has been called.

In 1883, the Professor was called from California to Clinton, Iowa, to dedicate the grounds of Mt. Pleasant Park for a camp-meeting resort for the "Iowa Conference of Spiritualists." The name of the organization was afterwards changed to the "Mississippi Valley Association of Spiritualists." In 1887 he was elected President of that Association, and presided at each camp-meeting till la grippe assailed him and prevented his attendance in 1894. The first year of his Presidency he found the financial affairs of the Association in a very unsatisfactory condition. There were two legal organizations concerned in the ownership and management of the Park, the Association above-named, and an auxiliary body called the "Mt. Pleasant Park Stock Company." This auxiliary body had assumed almost entire control of grounds and meetings, and apparently part of the directors had determined to close the camp-meetings, sell the grounds, and divide the proceeds. The Professor at once moved to checkmate this effort, and succeeded, with the efficient efforts of faithful members, in paying off the debt on the grounds, purchasing some six hundred dollars worth of tents, securing the transfer of the title to the Park to the Association. One of the Park stockholders brought suit to force the sale of the grounds, but was beaten in the District Court, the decree of which was confirmed by the Supreme Court of the State. So now the Association owns the beautiful Park, worth some fifteen to twenty thousand dollars, has a fine hotel and several other buildings, and the Professor has the satisfaction that he contributed something to that result. Many of his friends feel that but for his efforts the grounds would have been lost, and the Camp broken up.

Professor Loveland has not been a bookmaker to any extent. With the exception of several pamphlets, he has published but one book, consisting of seven lectures on Mediumship. The first edition of one thousand volumes, with the exception of a few copies, was exhausted some three years ago. But la grippe, and a grip on his finances, through the failure of a friend, have prevented printing another edition. He is at present writing another work on Mediumship and also one on Immortality, which he hopes to publish soon. He has one or two more works in contemplation, if time permits.

Of mediumship he has had various phases, from the tipping of tables to what he terms the Higher Mediumship. Though always hospitable to all forms of special or test mediumship, he has never reverenced it as a fetish, or ran after it as a gratification of a blind credulity. On the contrary, it has addressed itself to him as a purely scientific process, on the part of spirit personalities, to prove (1) their identity, and (2) to voice important messages to man on the earth. And, though commiserating the actors, he has a profound contempt and detestation of reading, jack-knives, rings, etc., and telling fortunes, and calling it Spiritualism. Psychometric readings are most interesting and instructive at the proper time and place, but to present them as the manifestations of spirits is a crime against truth. He has sought to discover the philosophy of mediumship, and is satisfied that he has been successful in his researches. He has discovered what he terms the dual unity of man; that he has a dual mentality—a conscious and a subconscious selfhood. The latter is the seat of the mediumistic capacity—it has the great sympathetic nerve system, or in other words, the nerves of organic life for its brain center. It is automatic or controlled in its actions. He holds that a proper understanding of the subconscious self will unlock and explain all the mysteries of mediumship; show the way to perfect health and happiness; furnish the

methods for a more perfect education; as well as opening the way for the evolution of that higher mediumship, which will bring, all attaining it, into a felt and comprehended fellowship with the infinite life of the cosmos. He is hoping to stay on this side of life long enough to write out a full elucidation of the relations, the interworkings of the conscious and subconscious—the volitional and automatic factors of our wonderful life.

He has always been a persistent advocate for the organization of Spiritualists into a strong working body, for the purpose of instituting proper measures for revolutionizing the selfish system of competitive cannibalism, which is miscalled civilization. As Spiritualism is a new evolution of humanitary thought, he cannot see how it can be other than a potential agent in superseding the antagonisms created and fostered by the old religions, and building up in practical conduct the principles of universal brotherhood. He has been amazed, and almost disheartened, by the standstill conservatism and, what is worse, violent opposition on the part of professed Spiritualists to all the progressive movements of the age. To him this new dispensation has been inaugurated, very largely by the fathers of the country, for the express purpose of saving this country from the terrible fate of all past nations, which have disregarded justice, and enthroned selfishness as the law of the land. He claims that Spiritualism should be our religion, morality, politics, and social life; that it includes every principle of personal and civic life, and cannot be laid off anywhere, and the old garment of religious selfism put on.

The literary work of the Professor, in addition to the book and pamphlets before mentioned, has been in the newspaper line, he having been contributor to nearly all the Spiritualist papers, and has performed quite a share of editorial work on several of them. And, in this connection, may be also mentioned the very many discussions which he has held in defense of Spiritualism. In conclusion, it is well to say that he stands to-day the very last of the oldest workers in the Spiritualistic field. But the Professor, though nearly an octogenarian, has still his armor on, and, with intellectual eye undimmed, is hard at work in the Spiritual field, which he does not intend to abandon till translated to the higher fields of eternal life.

DR. W. M. FORSTER.

DR. W. M. FORSTER.

"Lives of great men all remind us
We can make our lives sublime,
And departing leave behind us
Footprints on the sands of time."

The history of Modern Spiritualism is full of the good deeds and actions of those who have sacrificed profit to principle: men and women who were willing to suffer the world's obloquy, that their ideas regarding the happiness of their fellow-mortals should be promulgated.

This volume contains many instances of such like characters; among them we take much pleasure in placing the subject of this sketch.

Born and raised in "blue" Presbyterianism, he nevertheless had the courage of his opinions, and at the early age of fifteen years seceded to the Methodist denomination, of which he was a lay preacher and propagandist at the age of eighteen years. His desires and tendencies being toward the medical course, he was apprenticed to a firm of apothecaries in Ireland, and after graduating in the various schools necessary for the practise of his adopted profession, commenced a tour of the world, which a few years ago ended, for the time being, in San Francisco, Cal. Here his success has been phenomenal.

Dr. Forster, some fifteen years ago (although from an early age aware of his occult powers), became convinced of the reality of "physical phenomena" through the mediumship of his infant son and his own powers; latent powers were developed, and automatic writing, independent slate-writing, levitation of heavy bodies, spirit lights, etherealization, and that much-disputed phase of spiritual phenomena—spirit photography — were developed. Of late years Dr. Forster has confined his mediumship to that phase known as "medical clairvoyance"; the utility of this will be seen when it is remembered that he has been a very extensive traveler, a keen observer of men and things, and an educated gentleman, one whose first thoughts and aspirations were for the benefit of humanity. It is rarely we meet so many good things combined.

Dr. Forster is a descendant of an illustrious English family, whose name is contemporaneous with advanced politics in the middle and later portions of the nineteenth century. We have much pleasure in saying, however, that although his paternal ancestry was derived from the eastern side of St. George's Channel, his maternal ancestry were raised and bred on the green sod of "old Ireland"—a combination which should go to make an ideal American citizen.

Dr. Forster, *in spite* of his early religious training, has a keen sense of the ridiculous, even in such matters as the phenomena of Spiritualism; as an example of this, we cannot do better than quote his own words, published in the *Light of Truth*, March 11, 1893:

"While investigating the phenomena of modern Spiritualism a few years ago, it occurred to me to ask a Spirit friend if such a thing as 'Spirit photography' was possible. The reply being in the affirmative, an appointment was made with my unseen guest for an experimental 'sitting,' with a view of testing our ability— aided by friends on the other side—for producing such phenomena.

"For the first experiment, and a number of subsequent ones, a camera and dry-plates were obtained, and after duly testing the latter and finding them perfect, I focused a lamp on the table, and, extinguishing all the lights in the room, made the exposure (keeping one hand in contact with the camera), our Spirit friend timed the various exposures by raps; the exposures lasted from four seconds to as many minutes. The first experiment revealed nothing, the plate after development being perfectly transparent. On developing the plate taken at our second experiment—a few days later—a very few small spots became visible. At the third and fourth experiments, larger and yet larger spots were developed, and on developing the fifth plate, the pretty form of a child, apparently about seven years of age, appeared. I thought it was about time, then, to let the matter become known—as no one but members of my own family had been present at our sittings—and, accordingly, informed a professional photographer of my experiments. To my chagrin, I was laughed at for my pains, but on my proposition to allow my friend to bring his own camera and plates for an experiment (provided I was allowed to see that his plates were genuine and had not been tampered with) my skeptical friend willingly consented to make a trial. The result tickles my risible faculties to this day. When the plate was developed the headless body of a man became clearly visible, and my friend, with trembling hands, laid down the plate and declared it was the 'devil.'

"Since then, I imagine his religious scruples have led him to eschew such unholy places as Spirit seance-rooms."

One peculiarity of this Medium is that at various times almost every phase of mediumship has been developed through his organism, and though he has never posed as a "professional" physical medium, there are hundreds (particularly in Australia) who have had the privilege and opportunity of witnessing the weird phenomena exhibited through this psychic in the privacy of his home; of late years, as has been said before, he has discontinued these experiments, confining himself to the diagnosis and cure of disease.

> " It is a beautiful belief
>   That ever 'round our head
>   Are hovering on viewless wings
>   The spirits of our dead."

Doctor Forster has added to his faith, Knowledge; that Knowledge which so many millions in past ages have hungered for and were only satisfied when they experienced the change called "death." How many, even now, in the ranks of Spiritualism see only as "through a glass, darkly," hindered by their environments and inherited prejudices, from beholding the glorious sun of Spiritual Truth. We again quote the Doctor in an article written for the *Pacific Coast Spiritualist:*

" What a wondrous thing is the presence of, and desire of our Spirit friends to communicate with those left behind, we have here a discovery more fruitful of results on the lives and conduct of future generations, than anything yet made known to man. We are all spirits clothed in the mortal, and living, each and every one, in spirit-land. How necessary, therefore, to understand the laws essential for communication with those in other spheres of existence! We have here expressed a great truth, viz.: the necessity of a knowledge of the laws governing spiritual intercourse; at present, however, our knowledge in this respect is limited, but the angels are working steadily and persistently for our enlightenment. During the past fifty years, great advancement has been made in this direction, new phases of mediumship are being developed, and multitudes of mediums in private life are convincing their friends that there is in existence, a postal and telegraphic system between this sphere of life and the one peopled by those they have loved, but who "have gone before."

Dr. Forster has been wonderfully successful as a clairvoyant physician. His patients are scattered all over the United States and his daily correspondence is very great. Locally, he holds an enviable position and ranks first in his profession. The good one individual can do whose life is consecrated to humanitarian work is incalculable; and such is the life-work of our friend.

J. J. MORSE.

J. J. MORSE.

Among the many called upon to take part in the great spiritual upheaval of the present century, but few have risen to such eminent notice either in his native land, England, or in the United States, as the justly distinguished gentleman whose name heads this sketch, and who first excited notice in London, England, in the year 1868, and whose subsequent labors as a platform-worker have abundantly justified his selection for that service by the invisible directors of the work in Great Britain.

The early life of this Apostle of spiritual and progressive thought was tinged with some little romance, while, like the lives of so many of the world's most useful workers, it bore the bars sinister of misfortune and reverse upon its field; indeed, it was so distressful and unpromising at one period as to be utterly devoid of all likelihood of that use to the world it ultimately has become.

Of good family, numbering among its members servants of the English Established Church, officers in the nation's civil service, having a branch devoted to the farming interest, located in the beautiful County of Surrey; and singularly enough including in its connections a Captain Denton, though whether a relation of William Denton, the Geologist and Spiritualist, is undetermined,—however, that may be, the family, in itself and its connections, was eminently respectable, and of some social position, thereby ensuring early associations of affluence and social consideration for the subject of this memoir.

The family traces its ancestry back to the time of the Charles', originating in the pastoral County of Berkshire, and it is on record that several of the ancestors of Mr. Morse bore arms in the Cromwellian armies, which may possibly explain, by the laws of descent, the

strain of sturdy independence running through Mr. Morse's character. The family were in possession of a crest and a motto, a raised hand holding a dripping dagger, the motto being *Mors janua vitae*, "Death, the gate of life," which, considering Mr. Morse's life and labors, may almost be considered as having prophetic value.

The subject of our sketch, whose full name is James Johnson Morse, was born on the first day of October, in the year 1848, and at that time the family consisted of the parents and two other children, Charles Edward and Louise Sara and James, the youngest born, all residing in the Parish of St. Clements Danes, the Strand, London, the head of the household following the profession of a wholesale and retail spirit merchant and vintner. From his birth up to some nine years of age, Mr. Morse's health was exceedingly precarious, delicate in body, and a source of great anxiety to his family, who feared he would never reach maturity. In consequence of his weakness, the first few years of his life were passed on the farmstead of the great-grandfather, in the pretty little village of Hook, near Kingston-on-the-Thames, where he greatly benefited by the fresh air which swept across farmer Johnson's lands. When Mr. Morse was five years of age his father retired from active business life, but in the summer of the succeeding year, the large-hearted and loving mother fell a victim to the then prevailing cholera epidemic.

The father, deeply pained and almost disconsolate at the loss of so loving and devoted a companion, found the solitude of a retired life too hard to bear, consequently within a few months of his bereavement he determined to reenter commercial life. Laudable as seemed his intention to him, it was, nevertheless, as after events unfolded, fraught with dire disaster to the entire family. At this length of time, though, it looks as if the misfortunes of those years were stepping-stones placed in the river of life by a wiser providence than ours, stepping-stones over which the youngest member of the family must go to reach his work upon the opposite bank. All that needs be recorded here is the fact that the new ventures proved unsuccessful, and that a final difficulty in which the father became involved, through his over-trustfulness, absorbed his estate, virtually breaking his heart, and, in effect, sending him to the Higher Life some five years after the departure of his life's associate.

Then commenced a trying period for the youngest born, of some nine years' duration, and in the early days of which the three orphans were dependent entire-ly upon the kindness of the paternal uncle. Ultimately a disposition of the children was made, by which Charles, the eldest, was despatched to Ottawa, Canada, in 1859; Louise, the next in age, was placed in suitable circumstances in the old cathedral town of Norwich, in Norfolk; and James Johnson, the youngest, was placed in the care of a boarding-school keeper, in Green-wich, some five miles from London, which was about as injudicious and injurious a disposition of him as could have well been made, for the school-mistress was a victim to dipsomania in its grossest and most aggravated form. During the time James remained in her care, poor and insufficient food, liberal chastisement, and an utter neglect of all educational matters were the current of events, until, out of the desperation born of sheer misery, he fled, and much to the consternation of the servants of the avuncular mansion presented himself thereat, tired, dusty, footsore, and wobe-gone beyond words to express! Subse-quent inquiries verified the correctness of his complaints, and he was then trans-ferred to the care of an amiable lady named Croucher, residing in the before-

mentioned town, and it is a proof of the efficacy of kindly firmness and broad moral teaching, that the trial-tried boy of that period ever remembers, with affectionate gratitude, the loving care bestowed upon him by the above-named valued friend of his boyhood days. A couple of years thus passed pleasantly, when family considerations compelled the uncle to arrange a final disposition of the remaining charge of his departed brother's family, and it was decided that the English mercantile marine would afford the proper opportunity for the future medium-speaker to make a start in life. It was, therefore, decided that he should be entered as a midshipman on board an East Indiaman, but a rascally agent broke his contract, and shipped the youngster on an English coaster, on which he was to be bound as an ap-prentice.

Quite unfit for such a career, one of the roughest and hardest, and meeting a severe accident, the youthful mariner was discharged at the port of South Shields, and with a trifling sum sent adrift to find his way back to London, some three hundred miles away, as best he could. He arrived in the metropolis exhausted, ill, penniless, and but to find himself confronted with a grave family injustice, the nature of which at once put a peaceful solution out of all ques-tion; the indignation aroused in his breast then ended all intercourse with the family, and he has permitted the lapse of years to annul all association therewith.

The ensuing years, from 1863 to 1868, find the self-exiled member of his family making vigorous efforts to sustain him-self in various subordinate positions, until he fancied he saw an opportunity of advancing his fortunes by accepting an offer of employment in an about-to-be formed News and Publishers' office. Alas, further trials awaited him, for the principal of the affair was one of those specious and professing rascals, whose cunning, rather than aught else, keep them from the clutches of the law. The embryo publishing house was never formed, and the to be junior member thereof lost the hard won savings of several years helping to maintain his future principal, which individual ultimately discreetly disappeared from view, leaving his dupe penniless after enduring much privation while waiting for the consummation of his expectations.

It was during the above-described distressful period that the subject of this brief chronicle encountered two matters that have exercised an important influence upon his life, and which proved to be the pivots upon which great changes were to turn. The first of these events was his contact with modern Spiritualism, the second his meeting with the lady who subsequently became his wife.

The first event occurred in the autumn of 1868 when he was introduced to Mrs. Hopps, the mother of the Reverend John Page Hopps, one of, if not the most able and cultured exponent of English Unitarianism, and a confirmed Spiritualist, often writing and speaking upon the subject, and as the subject of Spiritualism was exciting attention in the public mind, it came up in the course of conversation at the above-named meeting.

It may not be out of place here to say a little upon his state of mind at this time upon religious matters in general, for being now twenty years of age he was capable of entertaining some definite opinions. On several occasions he had honestly endeavored to get exercised upon religion, but so far he had utterly failed, either to experience conviction or conversion, and, as a consequence of this failure, had earnestly debated within himself whether or not he was helplessly bad and hopelessly irreclaimable. Reflection showed him the painful truth that the sorrows he had endured had been caused by certain unworthy followers of their professed Master, and, wisely or unwisely, he felt that it was exceedingly difficult to harmonize practise and profession, and, being of a frank and open nature, he was sadly perplexed by a discovery that so many of us are

compelled to make. The result was that religious services became distasteful and religious literature absurd. Alternations of despondency and defiance dominated his mind, until much of its chaos was organized and its gloom dispelled by a friend placing in his hand a copy of Paine's immortal "Age of Reason," in the pages of which he found food he had long hungered for without fully understanding the nature of his wants. Yes, he must be an infidel. This life was hard enough; why ask for another? Miracles were myths, resurrections but rhetoric, while spirits were too silly to think of in any way but as fancies. At this period, it will be seen he was mentally far away from our faith, and a most seeming unlikely recruit for our ranks. Presently this attitude of hostility was to be changed, and in a singularly striking manner; though deep down in his breast, he admits, there was a faint hope that after death there might be some sort of a life where rest and happiness might be, after all.

The result of the meeting with Mrs. Hopps, previously referred to, was that the soon to be neophyte obtained from her the loan of two books, "Six Months' Experience at Home in Spirit-Communion," from the pen of the Reverend J. P. Hopps, the minister already mentioned, embodying that gentleman's own experiences, and another work, "Experiences with the Davenports," by Robert Cooper, the contents of which books astounded their reader, showing him that as honest men said " Yes," knowingly, and in good faith, it was presumption for him to say " No," unknowingly, for evidently there was more in the matter than he first suspected. The mere perusal of literature was, however, insufficient, the mind having become stimulated now asked for proofs, facts, evidence, and with all the anxiety of an ardent nature started on a new inquiry; the eager question was put, " Where can I go to see and know for myself?" Armed with an introduction from the before-mentioned Mrs. Hopps, he at last approached the mystic portals of the séance room, being received by Mr. R. Cogman, who was the host and manager of the assembly, who admitted the half fearful applicant, and welcomed him to the séance.

The house was that of a comfortable middle-class family, a house of some notoriety in its immediate neighborhood by reason of the "Spirit rappings" carried on there. The circle room, a large apartment on the level with the street, and lighted by two large windows. Chairs about the room, the center occupied with a large oblong deal-topped table, the floor carpeted. The room presently lighted by a lamp, the shade curtains being drawn, some fifteen persons present, exclusive of the host, his wife, and daughter. Nothing "uncanny" or out of the ordinary course of things observable. No wires under the table, no electric buttons upon the floor, so far as foot or hand could discover. An air of orderly quiet, sober earnestness, and propriety pervading all.

The séance begins; each is seated at the table. The host, as president, opens a well-worn Bible, reading passages therefrom; he offers a prayer; a simple hymn is sung. The lamp and book are then removed, and all, with hands now resting on the table, resign themselves to a meditative quietness. A tall, pale-faced, black-haired young man sighs heavily, the muscles of his face twitch with nervous spasms, and his eyes close. He arises paler than before, and convulsively at first, then with facility, he talks some ten or fifteen minutes. It is a "control," but the visitor makes a mental note, and says the other name for it is hysteria! A brief pause, then it is a female that is affected. This time the eyes are left wide open with a ghastly and stony stare. Her words are soft and low, the utterances full of love, truth, flowers, angels, earth, children, and so on. The visitor wonders: is she mad? what does it mean? Has he got into a company of lunatics? for others were shaking and gurgling by this time; he began to feel sorry for coming, and was

heartily wishing himself well out of it, when he exclaimed:

"Oh! gracious, what's that?"

The bolt had fallen, the call had gone forth, the portals of future work and destiny were about to be unbarred!

To the neophyte it seemed as if a hand, large, warm, heavy, had suddenly, with force, descended upon his head, a sensation then following as if the brain had been cleft in twain, while into the cavity thus formed, sand, hot and in quantity, had been poured, trickling down over head, face, bust, person, down to finger ends and toe tips. Every sense of motion was paralyzed. Eyes were firmly closed, every limb was helpless Then a swelling of lungs and throat, as though life's tides were battling frantically to keep their accustomed courses, and all the while a fearful dread circling within the mind of the startled subject of these peculiar experiences. Presently an impulse to stand, then up, upon his feet, erect, next an uncontrollable desire to shout with might and main, which overcoming all resistance, resulted in an ear-piercing whoop that almost froze your blood. Then for nearly an hour a series of wild and grotesque gesticulations, a current of exclamations, incoherent, gross, and profane, a general exhibition of noisy disturbance produced by the wretched victim—who, thoroughly conscious of his deeds, but incapable of resisting the influence upon him—continued to manifest the results of the first, and necessarily imperfect control exercised upon him.

Finally the paroxysm ceased, and the now startled inquirer, ashamed of his misbehavior, but unable to account for it, commenced to apologize to his venerable host, whom he had frequently addressed in the most opprobrious terms. Apologies were courteously deemed unnecessary, as the host intimated he fully understood such exhibition was beyond the control of the subject thereof, therefore no offence was taken. After some sympathy, and a little needful rest, the perturbed inquirer wended his way homewards. The remainder of the night was spent in a condition of mental amazement and perplexity, which effectually banished sleep for hours, until the tired body at last succumbed from sheer exhaustion.

With the next day came the reaction from the previous evening's excitement, and the inquirer found himself inclined to slip back again to his previous scepticism, inventing sundry plausible reasons for rejecting his experiences as being in any way attributable to "spirits," formulating the opinion that he was hysterical, and if he pursued the matter would, no doubt, become crazy! What avails our fancies when arrayed against the potencies of the higher life? Truly, but little! So the new medium found, for, presently, indications of the nearness and presence of this power began to manifest themselves. Hot, burning pains, tracing their courses from brain to shoulder, down the arm to hand and fingers—with a sensation like wires, redhot—came over him, and the index finger of the dexter hand traced out words before him leading to the following questions and answers:

" Is this a Spirit?"

"Yes," in a great scrawl by the outstretched finger.

" Is it any one that I know?"

" Your mother," again wrote the finger.

The startled querist not wishing to be thus disturbed, said, " If I get pencil and paper this afternoon, will you then come and write again?"

" Yes," again scrawled the obedient finger. The influence subsided, and the medium was again painfully perplexed—was it a "Spirit," was it his mother, what *did* it all mean?

Provided with the requisite materials later in the same day, the experiment of obtaining writing was undertaken, the following communication being received:

" Yes, my dear son, we are ever watching over you. Fear not, but trust in the Lord, for He is a shield wherein all may trust; He is a bulwark in whom all can rest their hopes; He is a terror to evil-doers, and in time will make all the nations of the earth believe in Him. Those who disbelieve now shall believe by-and-by, and shall welcome spirit-communion as a thing to be sought after, and by encouraging it you will get a foretaste of the joy to be had hereafter. *Oh, my son! follow it, for you will become a great medium: you will yet do great good in the world.* I am glad to see you so earnest in your desire for spirit-communion, for rest assured great good will result from it, not only to you, but for all; and when you leave earth you will be conscious of having employed the gift that is within you profitably. Be not afraid of mockers and scoffers, for those that now mock will soon believe. Your dear father is with you as well as I. He is smiling at your efforts, and tries to help you but finds it very hard. He was with you on Sunday. You must not be afraid, you will not be so tormented again ...... Your ever affectionate parents, Mary and Thomas Morse."

Here was food for thought, indeed! In some lights it looked wild absurdity, for fortune was just then smiling upon the much tried youth, and future prospects were brightening. Also, he queried, how could he "do great good in the world" upon a matter he was not a believer in? He was not at all inclined to embark as an advocate, or a worker in this strange matter. Then it struck him as peculiar, almost degrading, that his parents should leave heaven, or whatever the next life was like, to come back and write such a message. But, argue as he might, there was still a feeling that there was some truth in it all, yet on calming down he did his best to dismiss the matter from his mind, taking refuge in the opinion that the subject was dangerous, and he would have nothing further to do with it under any circumstances. However, it was destined he should not escape the duty before him, so by the time his next opportunity to attend Mr. Cogman's circle came round, he was seized with an uncontrollable desire to attend, to which he yielded, vowing to himself to resist all "influences," observe, note, and sit still.

It needs no prophecy to say that such resolves were likely to prove futile; some twenty minutes terminated their intentions and effects, by the end of which space of time the medium was again under strong control, which, this time, caused him to open the before-mentioned Bible, at Romans xiv. 1, upon which he delivered a sermon, or address, which occupied some forty minutes in its delivery. The manifestation afforded the utmost satisfaction and delight to the members of the circle, but it was the source of the utmost astonishment and mystification to the vehicle, who had never exhibited the slightest talent in such a direction previously, and who had never made the remotest attempt hitherto at the consecutive treatment of any subject whatsoever. More food was thus supplied for wonderment and reflection, and out of it came a determination to persevere in the inquiry to the end, and to obtain certainty, as to whether the entire question of spirit-return and spirit-power was either fact or fraud.

Shortly after the above-narrated events the publisher's scheme, previously noticed, was broached, the effect of which was that the newly developing medium was removed from the sphere of duty he had previously been in, and, through the failure of the enterprise to become a reality, he was unoccupied for nearly eight months, which afforded him the needed leisure in which to attend circles and prosecute his development, which matter was finally accomplished at the house of a Mrs. Main, a person of large sympathies and liberal views, who, with her daughter, a Mrs. Fielden, were very earnest workers at that time in London. By the "tests" obtained through the last named lady, and others through Mrs. Gender, Mr. Frank Herne, Mr. Davis, and other notable mediums of that period, the inquirer was converted into a believer, and the mental quietude resulting was materially valuable in assisting the development of the mediumship which was soon to come into world-wide notice. In the autumn of 1869, the me-

dium, now somewhat widely known among private circles, was brought under the notice of Mr. James Burns, now deceased, but who was then the representative of the central Depot of Spiritual Literature and Information in Great Britain, and on Friday, October 15th, of the above year, a series of weekly meetings was established at the above headquarters of spiritual work, from which fortunate circumstance the medium no doubt was put into that position of publicity which ultimately resulted in that extended popularity which has carried his name around the world.

The distinctly private part of the narrative may be said to close here, as the subject thereof now passes to the front in a public capacity, taking his position as a professional worker, and maintaining his place as such, down to the present period, his entrance to such work dating from October, 1869. In the following year he married Miss Marion Lewis, an event foretold to the lady by the spirits some months prior to her ever having seen Mr. Morse. She is a lady of good Welsh descent, and one child, a daughter, Florence, has been the sole issue of the union.

The purpose of the higher powers was gradually unfolding itself, and the public interest in the weekly séances rapidly increased, so much so, that the spacious reception rooms of the Spiritual Institution were crowded from week to week. Mr. Burns acted as the faithful chairman and considerate friend of the advancing medium, who presently became associated with Mr. Burns in the publishing business conducted at the Institution, and assisting in the issuing of the first number of what was then England's leading spiritual weekly, the *Medium and Daybreak*, but which was discontinued some time since. Undoubtedly the connection was one of mutual advantage, and was only sundered by the claims upon the time and strength of the medium, precluding him from giving that share of his resources to business that was justly due thereto.

Up to the period above referred to, Mr.

Morse had not, it seems, appeared upon the public platform for the purpose of a sustained address being given through him. The spirits were but awaiting the arrival of the suitable occasion, which was afforded them on Thursday evening, April 21, 1870, in the hall of the St. John's Associates, Clerkenwell, London. The first public address, at a regular Sunday Service of Spiritualists, was given at the Cavendish Rooms, London, on Sunday, July 24th of the same year, and the first effort in the provinces was at Northampton, on Sunday, September 9th, also in the above-stated year,—this latter event being in association with our ascended brother and most remarkable healer, Dr. J. R. Newton. The new medium was now fairly at work as an inspired advocate of our cause, and has been in active work ever since. Excepting illness and needful rest, it is computed he has not been absent from the platform more than two Sundays in each year during his term of service which at this time is now in its twenty-seventh year.

As soon as the ability of the controls had made itself known, the now developed instrument was overwhelmed with calls to visit the various societies in England, Wales, and Scotland, and, as a result, he has been a frequent visitant, in his capacity as a speaker, to all the prominent cities and many smaller towns in various sections of Great Britain. In many places his work has materially contributed to the tide of activity and prosperity in our cause that now prevails, and in not a few instances acting as a St. John the Baptist, clearing the ground for others. After some five years of labor the intimation came that he must cross the ocean, leave home, family, and friends, and visit the Birthplace of Modern Spiritualism; consequent thereon in the year 1874 Mr. Morse paid his first visit to this country, landing in the City of New York, on the twenty-sixth day of October. His fame had preceded his coming, and he was immediately overwhelmed with invitations to lecture in various cities; his

first engagement being in Baltimore, Md., which matter had been arranged for him by his old time friend, Dr. J. M. Peebles. During his year's stay he filled engagements in New York City, New Haven, Conn., Greenfield, Mass., Philadelphia, Pa., Bangor, Me., Boston, Mass., and various smaller cities and towns. In many cases so great was the favor with which his labors were received that he had to pay return visits. The numerous reports of his labors, and the abstracts of his lectures, which were published in the *Banner of Light*, disclosed a depth of thought, a beauty of treatment, and a logical arrangement of ideas, which at once placed Mr. Morse in the front rank of our foremost orators. In the delivery of the lectures there was a mingled pathos, irony, imagery, and eloquence, which, combined with the speaker's magnetic personality, compelled the attention and respect of even the most fastidious critic, besides charming and exciting the admiration of the friendly disposed. Mr. Morse left our shores sincerely regretted by all with whom he had come into contact, and upon his arrival in London he was accorded a magnificent reception by the British National Association of Spiritualists, then the leading organization in Great Britain. Some ten years after the above period Mr. Morse made his first appearance on the Pacific Coast. The circumstances that ensured his presence in this State was the holding of the Third Annual Meeting of the "California Spiritualists' Camp-meeting Association," in 1887, the Board of Directors retaining Mr. Morse as the leading speaker of the season. Mr. Morse's arrival on this Coast was warmly welcomed by the Spiritualists of the City of San Francisco and State, the Spiritualist press, *The Carrier Dove* and the *Golden Gate*, the former journal especially, very heartily supporting the new arrival's labors. The City press also accorded him generous notice, and frequently reported him at very considerable length. At the close of his engagement with the Camp-meeting Association he commenced a year's engagement with the then existing "Golden Gate Religious and Philosophical Society," holding its meetings in Metropolitan Temple. Mr. Morse. in accepting the engagement, came to occupy the rostrum that Mrs. E. L. Watson had filled for several years, and whose untiring labors in connection therewith had at that time rendered it necessary that she should take a considerable vacation. It was with a serious sense of responsibility that Mr. Morse entered upon his duties, for following so distinguished a speaker as Mrs. Watson was for the stranger to challenge comparison with one whose talents and abilities have endeared her to the people to whom she had so faithfully ministered. However, Mrs. Watson and her friends accorded the new-comer their loyal support and generous co-operation, and the success already achieved was abundantly continued, and the lectures did an incalculable amount of good. The philosophy of Spiritualism was presented free from crudities and redundancies, and various frank, but always kindly, criticisms were directed against many of the fads and fancies that threatened to attach themselves to the movement. Scarcely any speaker who has visited this Coast has made so deep an impression upon the minds of Spiritualists and the students of spiritual things as has Mr. Morse, and the splendid record he left behind him at the termination of his visit, publicly, personally, and socially is the best evidence of how endeared he became alike to those who attended his ministrations in public, and enjoyed the privilege of his friendship in private. He was accompanied by his wife, and daughter Florence, and their genial presence and kindly tact proved invaluable adjuncts to the labors of our visitor. Since then, Miss Florence, who was the recipient of innumerable kindly attentions during her residence in San Francisco, has become quite an active worker in the Spiritual cause. She has taken a deep interest in the work of the Children's Progressive Lyceum, and has been for several years associated with her father in the editorship of the English *Lyceum Banner*, the only paper in the world devoted exclusively to Lyceum work. She has also used her pen in other directions with credit to herself and usefulness to the cause, and as a sweet singer her voice has lent a charm to innumerable meetings.

During Mr. Morse's stay in California the *Carrier Dove* contained numerous verbatim reports of the lectures delivered by Mr. Morse at the Temple, which were reported by Mr. G. H. Hawes, who is so well known in this direction by the Spiritualists of the Pacific Coast.

Prior to leaving California, Mr. Morse also gave two lectures in Tulare, which were very cordially received, several lectures in San Jose, with equal success, and for two months he conducted a series of independent meetings in San Francisco, part of the time having the co-operation of the well-known test medium, Mrs. Ada Foye. Mr. Morse left the State in November of 1888, proceeding East to take up engagements for the fall and winter, and returned to England in August of the ensuing year.

A period of little over seven years now elapses, which Mr. Morse spent in his own country, little expecting that his feet would ever turn toward the New World again, and least of all toward the State of California, which State, he says, he likes the best in the Union. But so it was to be. In the midsummer of 1895 he received a communication from a former friend, Mr. J. Dalzell Brown, asking if he would be interested in accepting a year's engagement from a new society about to be formed in San Francisco, accompanied by many flattering expressions of the value of his former labors, and assurances that his previous successes would be repeated. So earnest was the request that a response by cable was desired. After due consideration the engagement was accepted, and Mr. Morse's services were retained at the highest fee ever paid to a speaker on Spiritual and Psychic subjects, namely, $3000 for his year's labor, and first-class traveling expenses from London to San Francisco. Mr. Morse arrived in this city at the end of November, 1895, and commenced his labors by a preliminary lecture in Golden Gate Hall, Sutter Street, on Friday evening, December 6th, at which a very large audience assembled, the daily papers giving most favorable reports the following morning. Two days later he commenced his regular Sunday evening meetings at Beethoven Hall, which proved adequate to containing about one-half the people who desired to attend. The lectures were subsequently removed to Odd Fellows' Hall, and again to Armory Hall, where they were conducted with the greatest success.

Apart from his activity upon the platform Mr. Morse has always taken an active part in promoting the cause in private life, as also in various ways affecting the general policy of the public work in his own country. He has been a warm advocate for practical organization, and took an active part in such matters as the formation of the "British National Association of Spiritualists," in Liverpool, in 1872, serving upon its council until it was re-organized as the "Central Association of Spiritualists," and so continuing until that body was reconstituted, and re-named "The London Spiritualists Alliance," in which latter body he is an honored member. He engaged in the sale and importation of American literature, trading as the "Progressive Literature Agency," and which he still continues. He has also been an active correspondent to all the English journals, *The Medium*, *The Spiritualist*, *The Pioneer of Progress*, *The Herald of Progress*, *The Two Worlds*, and *Light*, of which latter named journal he was one of the original promoters and stockholders, and acted as sub-editor thereto under his ever valued friend, its original and present editor, Mr. E. Dawson Rogers, while our own papers have frequently contained contributions from his pen, *The Philosophical Journal*, *The Light of Truth*, and *the Banner of Light* especially, to which last

named paper he has been the accredited English correspondent for many years.

In salient outline, this is substantially the career of this earnest and indefatigable worker, whose life for nearly twenty-seven years past has unreservedly and unstintedly been devoted to the cause of human enlightenment. He has ever been desirous of being guided by the inward light developed within him by the unseen powers he has so faithfully served. A life that has been marvelously illustrative of what the spirit world can accomplish under favorable and orderly conditions and an intelligent co-operation; and all the more noticeable when it is remembered that when this spiritual worker was called to his work he had for years been enduring vicissitudes and trials that quite put the opportunity or possibility of culture, philosophical research, literary excellence, or the development of dialectical ability entirely out of his reach, yet in these respects the character of the work done through him has been excelled in but few instances, and seldom equaled. The secular press has given many reports of lectures through him, which for length, appreciativeness and commendation left nothing to be desired; while our own journals have ever been foremost in printing the choice utterances of his controls, to the edification and pleasure of their readers in various parts of the world.

A writer in the pages of *Light*, the leading English Spiritualist newspaper, recently referred to Mr. Morse in the following commendatory terms, in an "interview" subsequently reported in that journal in August, 1891. He says:

"Mr. Morse is approaching the completion of his twenty-fifth year of service as a public medium, his silver wedding to the cause of Spiritualism. No living man, I should say, has so completely, and for so long a period, given his whole mind and heart and soul to the advance of the cause; no man probably, is owed so much by, and at the same time himself owes so much to, Spiritualism as Mr. Morse. That it has been the making of him—in a different sense, a higher sense, than the meaning usually attached to the phrase—he admits cheerfully and with gratitude; and in the making of the position which Spiritualism occupies in this country to-day Mr. Morse has had a substantial share.

His appearance is an index to the character of the man. Bright, alert, clear-eyed, he gives the impression of en oying excellent health, notwithstanding the harrassing strain that his public work continuously imposes. He is a little below the medium stature and might later on, with less physical activity, develop a tendency to portliness; just now he is sufficiently compact to maintain a pleasing presence.

"The Morses occupy a commodious house about two minutes from Regent's Park. It is a private hotel for Spiritualists, the only establishment of the kind, I believe I am right in saying, in existence—at any rate on this side of the Atlantic. There are Spiritualists who keep hotels, but none of these are necessarily hotels for Spiritualists more than for other people. In addition to the hotel Mr. Morse conducts an Institution for Spiritualists, which is doing excellent work. The visitor, entering the spacious and lofty room devoted to this branch of the effort, is struck first by the excellent library, consisting of some five hundred books connected with all phases of the subject, many of them exceedingly rare and practically unobtainable at the present time. On the reading-table one notices most of the Spiritualist periodicals, America and Australia being both well represented, and prominent among home publications being copies of *Light* and *The Two Worlds*. Mr. Morse possesses a complete file of these journals, from No. 1 to the current issue. A large collection of portraits of mediums, speakers, and writers, whose names are household words in the movement, furnish the walls.

"Quite a number of illuminated addresses, presented from time to time to Mr. Morse, intersperse the portraits, noticeable among them being those from the Glasgow, the Keighley, and the North Shields societies. Over the librarian's desk is a fine enlargement by permanent carbon process, of the portrait of Mr. Morse himself, a present from Mr. Sadler, the well-known physical medium and photographer of Cardiff. Miss Florence Morse, a pleasant and attractive young lady, has charge of this department, and appears to be very popular with the guests, whilst Mrs. Morse superintends the general arrangements of the hotel."

This brief chronicle is but a fragment of the life it refers to, and is but intended as a condensed record of the earlier experiences of one whose name is now a household word wherever Spiritualism is known, or its literature may be found. May he long be spared to labor with us, and continue as an ever faithful advocate and exponent, by voice, pen, and life of the teachings of that Higher Gospel which is destined to establish on the firm foundation of demonstrated facts, that man's conscious soul continues to exist as a rational and personal entity, when his little day on earth is done.

AMANDA D. WIGGIN.

AMANDA D. WIGGIN.

The subject of this sketch was born in the year 1830, in Guilford, N. H., and is one of the early workers in the spiritual vineyard in California, being widely known and beloved as an honest, conscientious medium, to whom truth was above all other considerations and more to be sought after and desired than was riches, place or power. The spirit friends who controlled her spiritual work were of a high order of intelligences and freely imparted to others the angel-lore they had gathered in higher fields of thought and experience. Many were comforted and blest through her gentle ministrations in seasons of affliction and mourning; at the bedside of the dying, and at the graves of loved ones, she has spoken words of cheer and consolation; upon the rostrum, in the seance room, and in the private walks of life she has been sustained and enabled to give the spirit message, impart instruction or lessons of counsel and warning. In whatever place or position her services were required, she cheerfully and willingly obeyed the call giving ever the best that she received. Thus she labored earnestly and faithfully for many years, sowing seeds of righteousness which shall continue to bear fragrant blossoms and beautiful fruitage long after the willing sower shall have passed to the shores of immortal life.

Mrs. Wiggin's early life was one of bereavement and vicissitude, yet cheered and made blessed through the ministrations of an angel mother. Naturally clairvoyant, she saw scenes others did not see, and clairaudiently heard voices others did not hear.

When less than seven years of age she saw and described an accident that was to befall a neighbor, which took place just as described. Later she saw a fire and a boy burning to death, and begged to have him saved, calling the name of the lad. This also occurred as described, although the scene of the fire was two miles distant. When she was twelve years old her mother passed away leaving her alone and friendless. Three months afterwards she was punished severely by an orthodox Christian with whom she was living. That night her mother appeared to her, and standing by the bedside took a corner of the sheet and wiped the tears from her cheeks, bidding her always tell the truth as she had done that day, and promising to take care of her. Then the great sorrow and longing which the loss of her mother had caused was taken away, and sweet sleep came bringing comfort and rest to her aching heart.

On another occasion when about eighteen years of age, her mother gave her a warning concerning a ride she, in company with a number of other young people, were going to take on the Fourth of July. She heeded the warning and declined to go. The young lady who took her place was killed. This made a lasting impression upon her.

Religion took no deep hold upon her mind for she felt intuitively the injustice of the doctrine of eternal punishment, and could never subscribe to any creed or doctrine of the church. In 1852 she was married to Wilson Chase and to them were born two children— a son and daughter. Her deep affectionate nature here found ample scope.

A loving husband, a stepdaughter and her own two children brought out all the sweet maternal tenderness of her soul ; and while the new duties and responsibilities filled her daily life, her heart was filled with hope and happiness.

In 1862, when the dark war cloud enshrouded our fair land, her husband being a loyal man, enlisted in the army and gave his life in defense of the old flag he loved so well.

In the meantime, through the influence of a friend, she had been induced to visit a medium and her spirit friends were there to greet her. She listened to their words of advice and began to sit for her own development. At the third sitting she was entranced and rapidly developed into a mental medium. She could visit battle-fields, find lost friends, tell who was wounded or taken prisoner, and it would prove true. At that time she was suffering with lung trouble and an Indian spirit came and told her he would cure her if she would give herself up to his control. His advice was followed, and a cure effected. Her faithful guide also apprised her of the death of her husband and the very hour of his burial, and she received the news two hours after its occurrence. In a few months the spirit husband came to her and told her to go to California ; the guide also outlined the trip and said it was well to go. The voyage from New York to San Francisco via Cape Horn consumed four months, but at last Golden Gate was reached and the landing made in April, 1866. After residing here about eighteen months she began her mediumistic work which continued for about eight years. On Sept. 6th, 1868, she was married to Mr. Harry Wiggin, the ceremony being performed by Mrs. Laura Cuppy in Maguire's Opera House on Washington St. This was the first marriage service in California at which a woman and a medium was the officiating clergyman ; and it

evoked some newspaper comments. But Mrs. Cuppy was a legally ordained Spiritualist Minister, and therefore entitled to all the rights and privileges accorded clergymen of other religious denominations. Mrs. Wiggin was the next to be ordained and licensed to marry people, officiate at funerals and receive her fee the same as any minister.

The death of her only daughter was followed three years later by the passing away of her only son ; and these bereavements caused her mother heart anguish that years have not obliterated. Her knowledge of an immortal life was the rock to which she clung through these trying ordeals, and the only source of comfort and consolation. Her spirit friends spoke peace to her troubled soul, and she found her sweetest joys in ministering to those afflicted like herself, helping them to see the beauty of the spiritual philosophy and realize the blessedness of angel communion.

In the year 1875 the spirit friends told her husband that they were going to leave her and she was to have a good long rest. Their words were verified. Bitter tears had fallen on the cold, silent faces of her loved ones, but none more bitter or plentiful than flowed when she realized that the spiritual powers were gone. The promise was given, however, that at some time her mediumship would be restored; and she has faith in its fulfillment, as all other promises from the spirit side have been faithfully kept. When that time comes Mrs. Wiggin will gladly take her place once more among the workers in truth's vineyard. During all these twenty-seven years of work her husband has been her faithful helper and co-worker in the spiritual cause, and their lives flow together in the sweetest harmony and perfect accord, exemplifying the happiness that springs from the marriage relation when two souls are perfectly blended as one.

S. J. WOOLLEY.

S. J. WOOLLEY.

The subject of this sketch may justly be called the busy bee philanthropist and author. But few persons may be found with such a combination of temperaments and mental characteristics, having a delicate constitution and highly attuned organism, with more of his mother's nature than his father's.

Mr. Woolley possesses firmness and stability, with persevering qualities seldom found in one man. Born with a love of nature in all her diversified forms, he has written of himself: "My life began in the country, and shall end mid nature's harmonies. In no critical spirit, however, do I say that God made the country and man the town. I freely acknowledge my gratitude for the circumstances and surroundings of my early career, for the innocent and unalloyed freedom of rural life; and rejoice that unsuited as I am to the motley life of the city, my cradle was rocked in the shadow of forests, and my earliest memories go back to the beautiful hills and valleys with their rocks and caves, rippling streams and picturesque landscapes."

The subject of our sketch was born near Zanesville, Muskingum Co., Ohio, on the 12th day of January, 1828. At that time and in that place money was almost a curiosity, and wealth was undreamed of; and yet when speaking of those stringent circumstances he once said, "I was born in the midst of wealth; I count the first radiant gleam of love—the anxious and tender gaze of my mother, of more value than mines of gold, and the remembrance of her love has been a sweet and blessed memory through life."

When but sixteen years of age Mr. Woolley achieved a notable business and industrial success. Through bad management his father's finances became involved, and he was compelled to borrow four hundred dollars at ten per cent. interest, giving a mortgage upon his farm by way of security. A year rolled speedily around and nothing was realized to the extinguishment of the debt. It was considered in the neighborhood inevitable that the mortgagee would get the place by foreclosure. At this crisis Solomon came to the rescue and proposed that while his father should continue at his trade for the support of his family, he would undertake the sole charge of the farm of one hundred and sixty acres, in a vigorous effort to make enough to lift the mortgage. It was agreed to, and within eighteen month the full sum must be raised. Solomon saw that with the best of management it was only possible to effect this by sowing most of the land to wheat, and that then, with a good harvest and fair price, success was certain. He had not only the entire responsibility but almost the entire labor to do, since his adult half-brothers had all gone from home, and his younger brothers were too small to be of much service.

He went fearlessly and bravely to his task. Beginning his days' labor at four o'clock, he worked three hours before breakfast, and then with brief intermissions for dinner and supper, he kept on until dark, and on moonlight nights until far into the evening. His faithful toil, though it brought him many hours of weariness and somewhat impaired his health, met with reward. It turned out to be a good wheat year, and Solomon's good crop of well-filled grain of a superior quality, was the finest in that region. Wheat, too, was higher than usual, and he sold for a good price. Consequently, when the mortgage fell due, he had the proud satisfaction of releasing it in full, and presenting it to his lately burdened and anxious, but now overjoyed and grateful parents.

His mother was of Holland descent, and her ancestors including her father and grandfather had been people of considerable business ability. In Amsterdam they carried on a large manufactory of silk, linens, etc. But his mother, whose name was Elizabeth Askins, was born in this country. Mr. Woolley's ancestors on his father's side were English, but came to this country before the Revolutionary War and were among the first settlers of New Jersey.

With such combined elements as he inherited from his ancestors it is no wonder that he is a lover of liberty. Surrounded as he was in childhood mid the wilds of a new country, his spirit would naturally leap the boundary of common rules, and demand its independece.

He once expressed himself in this manner: "Slavery is intolerable to a man who has once felt the grandeur and sublimity of natural scenery. Let no man own your soul. Let no creed cramp your spirit. Let no doctrine chain your mind. Let no party, church or school become proprietors of your fetterless thoughts. This is the teaching of this magnificent world, with its towering mountains, its extended plains, vast oceans and beautiful starry firmament above."

We next find our subject in a new enterprise; although only a youth of seventeen years, he thought he had discovered that which might make his fortune in the blossom of iron ore on his father's farm, and he set to work manufacturing paint for the entire world. Charmed by its strange and beautiful color, he sought its possibilities as a source of wealth; but all this proved a failure, except to arouse his mechanical skill. He made a mill to grind his paint and when ready to commence grinding, the people for miles around came to laugh at the boy's enterprise; but as Fulton's steamboat moved up the Hudson river, so did the mill go, and the boy's hopes were higher than ever, and we find him next in the great city of Cincinnati trying to find a market for his paints, and taking a few object lessons.

His next dream was of New York City, so he hired to a man who was about to take a drove of horses across the mountains. Here he had many adventures both ludicrous and dangerous. But the trip to New York was enjoyable, and to this young and adventurous spirit was an intense pleasure. The horses were sold and his part of the money was invested in forty brass clocks and a pile of books. And now we find him on the steamer Empire, headed for Albany, N. Y. The steamer met with a terrible accident and many lost their lives. Just as the Empire was about to sink Mr. Woolley leaped for life, like a wild deer, from her deck and landed on the schooner that had sunk her.

After a hard struggle with fate we find the subject of this sketch at home again, his clocks and books all sold, and now he is ready for some new enterprise. This time he undertakes the daguerreotype business, and meets with indifferent results.

We have entered into the details of Mr. Woolley's early life with the hope that his example of perseverence and energy may be of value in its influence for the encouragement of the young. So we will pass on by saying that his whole life of nearly sixty-seven years has been full of marked events. Agriculture and horticulture have been his leading pursuits, and his most successful occupation. One must visit his great tile factory where the best products in that line are made, and one must visit his model farm home called, Apple Dale Devon Stock Farm in order to appreciate his success in that line of business.

Mr. Woolley always sought to bring

himself in rapport with the leading men of his time; prominent among them may be mentioned Horace Greeley, Dr. Chapin, Henry Ward Beecher, Dr. R. T. Trall and many others; by being associated with such minds has enabled him to keep abreast with the advance thought of the age.

But there is another side to S. J. Woolley's life. Like all men who have achieved great success there is a power other than their own assisting them. Mr. Woolley claims that he is concious of some power or inspiration from his earliest experience. Having been a medium, or a sensitive from childhood, few people have really understood him.

At the dawn of modern Spiritualism his impressive nature grasped the hopes of demonstrated immortality, and at his earliest opportunity he sought to give Spiritualism a thorough investigation. In this, as in all of his undertakings, he was determined to know the truth to a certainty that should dispel all doubt. He visited a materializing medium who lived at that time in Terre Haute, Indiana. So eager was he to settle the question of spirit materialization that he engaged the medium for ten consecutive sittings at $5 per seance, and allowed no one present except the members of her own family and her manager; in this way he manifested more wisdom than is usually displayed by investigators. While Dr. King was acting as Chairman at Woolley's Summerland Beach in the season of 1895, Mr. Woolley was called upon to give his experience with the spirits at the time and place mentioned above. His graphic description was so full of interest that the large assembly was held spellbound.

While knowing that the claims of Spiritualism were true, and that only time was needed to give the people an opportunity to investigate, he has contributed largely to assist in the upbuilding of the cause from time to time. After three years of trials and struggles on the part of Dr. King and others to establish the National Spiritual and Religious Camp

Association, Central Ohio department, at Ashley, Ohio, Mr. Woolley came to the rescue. It was necessary to raise money to purchase land, and in order to secure a grove of twenty-eight acres Bro. Woolley contributed one thousand dollars, and the park was named "Woolley Park" in honor of him. Others contributed readily when they had such encouragement, and to-day the society owns its place for holding camps and is out of debt and successful.

But Mr. Woolley's restless and intuitive spirit could not stop here; so he started out to find a place that had all the necessary conveniences, and natural advantages for what he most desired; and after several days of diligent searching he found his ideal—his earthly spirit home. He makes it his own, has planted trees, and is building a large and commodious hotel and sanitarium, cottages and other buildings. One season of camp work has come and gone, and now with all the energy and ambition of youth he is preparing for a large concourse of people next season, commencing on July 1st, and continuing six weeks, with first class instruction from opening until close.

The location of this place is twenty six miles due east from Columbus, O. A network of railroad lines surround it, making it easy of access from all directions. It is a healthy situation being located on the south and west end of Buckeye Lake. This lake is a beautiful sheet of water some ten miles long and is bordered with an immense quantity of Egytian Lotus lillies which form a garland of loveliness that is really enchanting to the beholder.

The great object and purpose of Mr. Woolley in this movement is to establish a spiritual and religious college, also a college of Hygiology and Therapeutics, to build up a brotherhood and sisterhood by bringing together such persons and co-workers as will fraternize, make homes for mediums and speakers and give them proper conditions for culture and protection. Mr. Woolley is aware that this is a large enterprise, and, of

course, cannot hope to see his plans perfected while he remains here; but if it is
like nearly all his other movements success is certain in the end.

There are fifty five acres of choice land
laid out into lots; about twenty acres will
be set aside for the park and pleasure
grounds; the remainder will ready for
sale to those who wish to associate themselves with the movement. Let it be
remembered that Mr. W. has spent
thousands of dollars to promote the
cause of pure Spiritualism, but this is
the crowning work of all, and will be
the greatest achievement of his busy
life. He desires to have established in
connection with the camp a public library
and museum. Any one having old relics,
books or even papers and feel like contributing something toward the cause
can send them to his address and they
will be carefully used and credited.

His Sanitarium will be of far reaching
benefit to humanity. All curable diseases are cured by his corps of mediums.
Magnetic healing and other forces that
exist which are not known to the ordinary practitioner will be used to the fullest extent in this Institution. His Speci-
alist for the cure of cancers eradicates
every vestige of this loathsome disease
without the knife, and without causing
the patient suffering. The Hotel and
sanitarium is located at the south west
side of the Ohio State Park, in a retired
nook, by the beautiful Buckeye Lake.
The atmosphere about this lake is very
invigorating, bracing and health giving.
Persons have been cured of hay fever,
asthma, and other diseases who came
here to spend a few weeks recuperating,
and fishing.

All communications should be addressed to S. J. Woolley, Pres. Milo,
P. O. in the City of Columbus, Ohio.

WALTER HOWELL.

WALTER HOWELL.

The main incidents in this sketch of the early life of Mr. Howell are taken from *The Medium* of London, England; additional notes of the later work of Mr. Howell during the past ten years having been compiled from data at hand, and the author's own personal acquaintance with the subject of the sketch.

The name of Walter Howell is familiar to nearly all English and American Spiritualists, and therefore some particulars concerning his career may be of considerable interest to our readers.

He was of humble parentage, and was born in the city of Bath. Unfortunately for his material prospects he was blind at his birth. During infancy he underwent several surgical operations, under the skillful treatment of Dr. Dolt and Dr. Soden, of Bath; but these operations were only partially successful, and therefore it was impossible for him to obtain an ordinary education; and he had not even the advantage of a blind tutorage. At a very early age Walter was taken from Bath by his parents to the town of Warminster, Wiltshire, where he remained until after the removal of his mother to the higher life. While in Warminster he was sent, as a matter of form, to the British School. In the infant class, where he was allowed to go up close to the alphabet-board, he learned the A. B. C; but he was quite unable to proceed beyond that stage, because his sight did not permit him to read ordinary type. Owing to the affliction of his mother with paralysis, he was presently obliged to leave school, when still under nine years of age, to help to earn his own livelihood. After the lapse of about four years, his mother passed away; then Howell left home and commenced to fight the battle of life alone.

Under such circumstances as these it can easily be understood that Walter Howell's life has not been one of ease and luxury. With the material vicissitudes of his career we have less concern than with those portions of his history which affect his development as a Spiritualist, and which afford convincing proof of the unseen guiding influence which has followed him and remained with him all through his career, and has formed and extended those spiritual powers which distinguish him. In this connection it may not be uninteresting to trace Mr. Howell's Spiritualism to a hereditary source.

Walter Howell's mother was a devout Christian, and from childhood had been a member of the Wesleyan body. In her early life she had no great educational advantages; she was, however, a person of a refined and extremely sensitive nature, and was, no doubt, very intuitional. She was a most sympathetic soul, and always a ministering angel amidst scenes of sorrow. Her earnest prayer ascended to heaven daily that her boys—two in number—might grow up to be good and noble men. When it is stated that her husband was a continual source of anxiety to her on account of his intemperate habits, that she fully realized that her youngest son, Walter, was by virtue of his defect of vision, wholly incapable of doing battle with the world, and that her life was a continual struggle for mere existence, it is not surprising that in early life she broke down, and passed on to a world where angel hands wipe tears from all faces. Truly the world knows not one half of its heroines and heroes. Many a brave heart combats in secret silence difficulties as great as any which are blazoned to the world, and performs actions braver than those for which the battle-field affords opportunity. But though the poets of earth have not sung its praises, heavenly bards proclaim the epic of its heroism. In the sensitiveness, sympathy, conscientiousness and spirituality of Mr. Howell's mother we see the involved mediumship of her son. Mothers, indeed, rock the cradles of the nations, and all men of note in whatever sphere of life, owe their greatness largely, if not entirely, to their mother's teaching, or to the gentle refinement inherited from the maternal parent.

Mr. Howell became connected with the Methodist Church at as early a period of his life as was possible. There are, perhaps, few better places for bringing out latent ability than the class-meeting, the cottage services, and other institutions of that kind in the Methodist Church. Of course we do not mean to say that there is much freedom of thought there. Far from it; but there is an opportunity of expressing such thought as is permissible in that body. Mr. Howell was ten years of age when he first met in class to express his desire to "flee from the wrath to come." This is, as all Methodists know, the simple condition of membership. There never was a time since the beginning of his religious impressibility when it was not Howell's earnest wish to live as far as was pos-

sible, in accordance with his conception of right. And being extremely sensitive, he was during early childhood subjected to the most painful experiences, owing to the manner in which religious thought was expressed. Sometimes in the middle of the night he was thrown into convulsions of fear, as a consequence of his meditation upon some sermon which he had heard. His mother, imagining that the visitation was simply the workings of God's Holy Spirit, felt more gratified than alarmed, and in her pious hope and belief, distinctly encouraged the influence. When we remember what dear little children have had to listen to, in the form of orthodox theology, and knowing as we do the sensitiveness of their natures, ought we not to see that, as far as possible, these influences shall henceforth harm none over whom we are placed in the positions of parents or guardians?

For two years Howell met in class, giving no evidences of a change of heart. The doctrines of the church were by no means understood by him; and his greatest difficulty was to believe that he did believe. In his childish heart he often wished there was no God; for instead of having a desire to know God, his only purpose was not to call down upon himself "the divine wrath." The God of theology was to his mind a monster. For the time the soul seemed imprisoned in a theological dungeon, where the highest hopes and aspirations were fettered. How often, like the winged bird, the aspiring spirit beats itself against the bars of a churchianic cage in utter anguish!

When about twelve years of age—our pilgrim having up to that time made but little progress "in the divine life" —there came a marked change, which has been described by him in the following manner: He was traveling along a country road, suffering as he had done for years, from depression of spirits. The thought occurred to him that he would try Jacob's plan and "wrestle with God." He entered a field, knelt down, and said, "Now, Lord, I will never let Thee go, until Thou dost bless me." Here the child remained for hours "pleading with God." When evening's shadows began to mantle the earth and stars, the sentinels of night, came out to watch over the slumbering orb, a light from realms supernal broke upon the horizon of his soul, and he arose transported with ecstasy. The opaque earth now became transparent, and the air was full of music. Involuntarily the words fell from his lips :

"My God is reconciled ; His pardoning
    voice I hear,
  He owns me for His child; I can no
    longer fear."

All Methodists can well picture the scene at the class-meeting on the following Sunday. He was the first to speak, and his joy filled the class. Even the sleeping echoes in the walls responded in joyful strain. From this time forward he was a missionary spirit.

The experience just spoken of did not destroy his child-likeness. He was by no means a consistent child, in the popular sense of the word. At the same time he was most consistent with his own nature. In illustration of this point it may be mentioned that he would in all sincerity pray with some of his boy companions one hour, and arrange a piece of mischief with them the next. Anything he entered into he did with all his soul. Whilst he was by no means cruel, he was brimful of fun. To some minds, the statement just made will appear paradoxical to an assertion made earlier in this narrative, that Mr. Howell suffered from early childhood from depression of spirits. Those who are familiar with temperaments such as his, however, know that the sensitiveness that occasions keenest sadness, also is subjected to states of hilarity.

It would have been amusing to our readers to have seen the boy walking into some neighbor's house, and informing the inmates "that he had come to preach to them." To satisfy the eccentricity of the lad they used to stand him upon a chair, and on more than one occasion he came to consciousness and found his hearers weeping. It is very easy to trace his mediumship from a very early age.

Although Walter was unable to read, he was recognized as an advanced scholar in the Sunday-school. More than one of the teachers found in him a critic of no mean order. They therefore removed him, before his age warranted it, to the Young Men's Bible Class. Here, too, he was found by the comparatively ignorant teacher, a troublesome element. This fact will explain what follows.

One Sunday afternoon the superintendent came into the Bible Class in search of a teacher for a class of boys. Mr. T——embraced this opportunity of getting rid of his most troublesome scholar, and the position was taken by our friend. After listening to the reading of the lesson by the boys, Walter proceeded to offer some remarks, and became so absorbed that he did not perceive that two other classes with their teachers came and joined the company to listen to his observations. When he came to himself he discovered the enlargement, and asked them why they had united the classes? Whereupon he was informed that his conversation had caused those unruly boys whom no one could control, to bend their heads and listen, and their companions thought there must be something worth listening to, and so they came to see. At the next teachers' meeting our friend was appointed as the teacher of that class. The boys often made mistakes in reading to try if they could cheat Walter, but he always made them go over their verse again; and when he was asked how he knew when they made mistakes, he replied, "Something inside seems to tell me." This evidences remarkable intuition, to say the least. During the time he remained as teacher he was occasionally called upon to address the scholars. This offered him still further opportunity for developing his powers as a speaker. It was his exceptional ability which caused his name to be mentioned at the quarterly meeting, when he was scarcely seventeen years of age.

It was a matter of great surprise to him one evening on entering his lodgings, to find the minister awaiting him. "Walter," said the minister, "your name has been brought before the quarterly meeting, and you are down for three Sundays next plan, on trial, or as an exhorter." "But," protested Walter, "I cannot preach." To this the minister replied, "I am told if you only speak to the people as you do to the children in the Sunday-school it will please any congregation." The minister found considerable difficulty in persuading Howell that he was fit to undertake the task, but quoted well-timed passages of Scripture which were calculated to afford him comfort and strength to take upon himself the new undertaking, and left him in earnest meditation. Howell, having determined that he would attempt the task, was at first in a state of perplexity as to how he should manage about the reading of hymns and appointed chapters of Scripture. He, however, succeeded in obtaining the help of a friend who was greatly desirous of introduction to the service of God, and who undertook to act as reader for him, and take his place as preacher if he should fail and break down.

It can with truth be said that their first ascent into the pulpit was with fear and trembling. Howell's assistant commenced the service by giving out, in thoroughly Methodistical style, the hymn, "Oh, for a thousand tongues to sing." Howell then offered prayer, and the rest of the preliminary service was conducted by his friend. During

the singing of the hymn immediately preceding the sermon, Howell had a strange and indescribable feeling. Everything around him seemed to dance; he felt himself moved to rise, and then he heard himself speak. What he said he never knew, but he went on and on, and could not stop until he finally regained consciousness. When Howell descended the pulpit stairs an old man met him, grasped both his hands, and said, "God bless you, my lad; I never heard such a sermon in my life;" and a member of the congregation assured him that they had had a perfect treat. The *debut* was at the morning service, and at the evening service of the same day the chapel was over-crowded.

After that wherever he went the congregations were large, for country places, and he was regarded as a kind of prodigy. It was often remarked that "the Holy Ghost helped him." Be this as it may, it was not long before some defenders of the faith found in his utterances a heterodox spirit, and at the end of about three-quarters, he was brought before the local preachers' meeting to answer charges of heresy. In some of his sermons the doctrines of eternal punishment, trinity, and plenary inspiration of the Bible had been assailed. Whilst standing before the churchianic judge and jury, he was not the subject of any inspirational influence, and when these charges were made against him, he could answer nothing. At last he burst into tears, and sobbed out, "I did not want to preach, but you compelled me. I said I could not study my sermons and you said God's Holy Spirit would help my infirmities. If it is God's Holy Spirit that has helped me and you could prove that the Holy Ghost was not a Methodist, you would turn him out, wouldn't you." The judge and jury needed no more evidence. They had heard the blasphemy for themselves. His name was taken off the plan, and for fear he should taint the youthful mind, he was not allowed to reoccupy his former position as a teacher of the class of boys.

At this period he had not even so much as heard of Spiritualism. He was now an object of comment everywhere in the circuit. He was preached at from the pulpit, prayed at in the prayer meetings, and exhorted to return to the Lord in the class meeting, and altogether looked upon as something exceedingly dangerous. About this time he took a ticket of removal, and did not deposit it in any other circuit.

Some two years afterwards, Modern Spiritualism came under his notice. At first he did not know what to make of it. There was nothing to attract him in it, for as yet he knew nothing really of it. When in South London he commenced to investigate physical phenomena, and sometime afterwards he was invited to go to Liberty Hall, Church Street, Islington, on a Sunday evening. Mrs. Bullock came on the platform and said, "We've been disappointed of our speaker this evening, but the spirits have told us they are bringing a speaker, and we await the fulfillment of their promise." The audience was then asked to sing. Whilst the singing was going on, Walter was controlled and took the platform. After he had addressed the audience, his inspirers told the audience they had used his organism for years, and had at last found the sphere where their thoughts could find more perfect expression. The influence was the same as that felt in the pulpit, only the control was deeper.

At that time Mr. Howell was engaged in business, at King's Cross. Arrangements were made for sittings at the house of business, and the heads of the firm and employees united in investigating. They were all ere long convinced of the truth of Spiritualism. Friends were also invited, and many of them became Spiritualists; and for more than two years the principals of the firm held

communion with their departed friends through Mr. Howell's mediumship. During this time, it was often observed that the medium would have to take the platform. Mr. Howell, however, seems to have had an objection to so doing, and it was sometime before his scruples could be overcome.

Eventually our friend left London and went traveling in the Provinces. While on a journey he had a misfortune with his glasses, and continued his journey without them. The cold east wind struck his unprotected eyes, and inflammation set in. He was blind for more than six months. When his sight returned to its former state he was obliged to seek a situation. He went to Liverpool in search of employment, but failed to obtain anything to his advantage. Having a kind of agency, he went to Manchester, where he afterwards commenced to speak publicly in behalf of Spiritualism. A gentleman wrote to Mr. Fitton, the chairman of the Manchester Society of Spiritualists, stating that Walter Howell was a medium of promise, and if he could get him on the platform, it might be a boon to the Cause. Mr. Fitton invited Mr. Howell to his house, asked him to accompany him to the hall, and then introduced him to the Manchester audience. The Manchester friends were so much pleased with him that they invited him to occupy their platform often. Mr. Howell's reputation soon spread all over the country, and he was solicited to speak everywhere. The work of this laborer must speak for itself in the hearts and minds of his auditors.

In the year 1882 Mr. Howell crossed the Atlantic. His work in America has attracted the attention of some of the most cultured minds. Those who have listened to the discourses of his guides can bear testimony to their scientific and philosophical character. Audiences have had the opportunity of choosing their own subjects, and have invariably expressed their appreciation of the inspiring intelligence. In September, 1886, he returned to his native land, to visit his old friends.

Mr. Howell acknowledges his entire indebtedness to his spirit friends for his education. Surely, such an instance as this is a striking example of spirit guidance. Mr. Howell's life is consecrated to the work of the spiritual world, and his untiring labors evidence that,

"Life's more than breath, or the quick
　　round of blood;
It's a great spirit and a busy heart.
He lives most who thinks most, feels the
　　noblest,
And acts the best."

Mr. Howell does not pride himself upon having had no educational advantages in his youth, as might possibly be imagined. He deeply regrets not having had the opportunity of being thoroughly cultured, fully realizing that the more cultured the mind of the medium, the more intellectual will be the spiritual surroundings. It is deeply to be deplored that so many Spiritualists glory in the ignorance of the medium, if the controls be only somewhat more advanced. It should be the aim of every medium to cultivate his or her mind so that the influence may find a clearer method of expression.

Mr. Howell is of opinion that those mediums who so desire, can, in a great measure, appropiate the knowledge which passes through them. The brain —being the organ through which thought manifests itself, whether abnormally or normally expressed—retains an impression of that which is transmitted. If, therefore, the medium is in sympathy with the highest thought thus expressed, Mr. Howell says there may be a development therefrom, like developed impressions received upon a sensitized photographer's plate. In this way, he believes, mediums are helped in an educational manner by spirits. Mr. Howell owes much to his guides for their educational influence. Those who know him but imperfectly would not regard him as an uneducated man, but those who know him well do not doubt the accuracy of his statements.

The records found in Bath Eye Infirmary show that Walter Howell was born blind. They also give a full account of the state of the eyes after the operations had been performed. The books containing medical testimony prove that his sight must be, and must always have been, too imperfect to enable him to study. Those who live in the neighborhood where he was brought up, can also testify to the fact that he received no blind education. If, therefore, we find a man who is capable of delivering discourses on any subjects chosen by the audience, and calling forth complimentary criticism from avowed non-Spiritualists, we are surely bound to acknowledge an avenue for acquiring wisdom, other than that of the senses.

During the fall of 1887 Walter Howell labored in Willouby, O., and lectured in Bond's Hall. During the month of December that year he visited Buffalo, N. Y., and from thence went to Cincinnati, where large audiences greeted him for two months. Later on his engagements were in Cleveland, Erie, Titusville, and many other places in Northwestern Pennsylvania, Western New York and Ohio. For two years our speaker lectured every Sunday in Titusville; and, within a radius of two hundred miles he preached the gospel of Spiritualism through the week.

In the summer of 1888, in company with friends, he again visited England, and on this occasion crossed the Channel, making a trip to Paris, Basale, several places in Germany, and through Switzerland, and back to Calais by way of Boulogne, and thence to London once more. For the next two or three years his work was done in Pennsylvania mostly, and in the fall of 1890, he again returned to England, where for about ten months his Sundays and week-evenings were fully engaged in lecturing in all parts of Great Britain.

After returning to America, in 1891, his health was such that it became advisable for him not to travel too much, and to be where his physician could be called at any time: hence he confined his labors to New York City, Brooklyn, and other cities on the New York side of the Hudson near New York.

In the Autumn of 1894 Walter Howell received a call to minister to "The Society of Progressive Spiritualists," of San Francisco, Cal., and here his discourses were appreciated by large audiences in Golden Gate Hall.

During Mr. Howell's sojourn in San Francisco, he endeared himself to a large circle of friends through his genial social qualities, which made him a welcome guest everywhere. He worked for the harmonization of all societies and individuals, feeling that only through unity of purpose and harmony of action could the best results be obtained in the advancement of the interests of Spiritualism. His public services extended over a period of eight months, and when his engagement was ended he left a void in the hearts of his people not easily filled. His return to San Francisco as the settled pastor of a spiritual society is looked forward to as one of the desirable possibilities of the not distant future by many of the devoted friends whose acquaintance with Mr. Howell during his stay amongst them deepened into a warm and lasting friendship.

After leaving San Francisco Mr. Howell returned to New York and soon received a call to Boston. The Spiritual Temple of that city was his next sphere of usefulness in October and November of 1895. He was in New York in December, and the New Year of 1896 finds him in St. Paul, Minnesota, ministering to excellent audiences; and in that city he remains until June, when he contemplates a trip to England again.

EUDORA B. MARCEN.

How much environment, heredity and unseen psychic influence help to mold and develop the character of the individual it is difficult to determine. That they are an important factor, every progressive thinker is ready to admit. So with the subject of this sketch, Eudora B. Marcen: there were many influences, both physical and psychical, connected with the time and place of her birth that wrought themselves into the fabric of her being and made her the sensitive that she is. She is a native of California. Both her father and mother were born in New York; but they represent a cosmopolitan ancestry drawn from the sturdy Anglo Saxon and the more volatile Latin nations. The time of her birth was in those troublesome days just preceding the opening of the late war, when the mental and moral atmosphere of our country was in a state of great agitation; when the very air was pregnant with grand ideas for the advancement and elevation of mankind. The place of her birth was a cottage home among broad fields of waving grain, near what is now the city of San Jose, Cal., at that time just emerging from an old mission town.

Born in this golden land of romance and religion, just after the unhealthy excitement of our early mining days, and just before the grand social upheaval of the rebellion, any one intimately acquainted with Mrs. Marcen can trace the influence of the times in her character. Combined with a somewhat delicate physical organization, she has a highly wrought nervous system and fine mental powers; in short she is a true sensitive.

She is naturally religious in the broadest and best acceptation of the term, with a keen sense of right and justice and a strong desire to aid the oppressed in whatever condition of life. Her natural inclination leads her to mental and moral work, and she is always ready to join hands with those who are striving to advance the welfare of poor humanity. Her childhood was passed in the quiet of rural life, where she early developed a strong love for all animate nature, making pets of all the farm animals, even climbing into the barn-loft to inspect and talk to the pigeons, which, she declared, as well as the other animals, understood and talked with her. Roaming over the fields or lying on the roofs chattering to the birds she much preferred to the usual pastimes of little girls.

She early developed a talent for story telling, conversing with herself for hours, smiling and weeping in turn over the joys and sorrows of her imaginary characters. In the light of present developments, how much of this was imagination and how much unseen influence has often been questioned by her family. As the years of her girlhood passed by she acquired a good education, attending the public schools, the Pacific University, and finally graduating from the State Normal School. She is also a graduate of the C. L. S. C., having read the course after her marriage. She likewise completed a course of Elocution at the California School of Oratory. But being of a quaint and retiring disposition, all her acquired gifts would never have brought her before the public had it not been for the natural gift of inspirational speaking that came to her in October 1883. For the four years previous she had been living a quiet domestic life in San Francisco, with her first husband.

She was an active member of the Howard St. Presbyterian church, and the gift of mediumship came to her unasked and unsought, with a power that was irresistible. First one phase and then another was developed, as if the invisibles were trying to find the gift for which she was best adapted. Finally inspirational speaking seemed to take the precedence.

EUDORA B. MARCEN.

though some of the early gifts still remain with her, and others have since been developed.

Notwithstanding her powerful mediumship, she steadily combatted every effort of the invisibles to place her before the public until thrown upon her own resources. Having tried teaching school and elocution, she was finally induced, through the influence of her seen and unseen friends, to take the platform.

She began her public work at San Jose in Febuary, 1887, where she filled a year's engagement with the Psychic Society of that place, to the pleasure and advancement of all, her controls giving some of the purest and best spiritual truths.

Most of her work has been done as the engaged speaker of various Spiritual societies throughout the State. However, she has done much good work in parlor circles near her native town, where a number of congenial friends have been in the habit of gathering Sunday afternoons from house to house and holding home circles. At these circles all possessing mediumistic powers gave of their best, and from the harmony of the circles, much that was given was superior to public work.

She was also one of the speakers of the State camp meeting held in San Francisco in 1889, and of the Summerland camp meeting of 1891. During the spring of 1890 she was assistant editor of the DOVE, giving the overworked editor of that excellent periodical a much needed rest. The winter of the same year was spent in Massachusetts, where she did some quiet work for the cause of Spiritualism, and formed some lasting friendships with fellow workers at the East.

In December, 1891, she married her present husband, but did not in consequence retire from public life. She has spoken in various parts of the State, though most of her time has been given to labors with her pen, contributing to a number of Spiritual periodicals and also to the secular press.

She occasionally gives some beautiful inspirational poems, and, when in company with her sister, has been able to give a few of them to the public, her sister writing almost as rapidly as the inspired words are uttered.

One of her present gifts is psychometry, she often giving character readings from letters, with advice as to business, health etc. Another gift that renders her public work very interesting is symbol-reading from the platform. After a discourse, some of her guides will give fifteen or twenty symbols and explanations in as many minutes to the entire satisfaction of those receiving them.

Besides her Spiritual work she has spoken for the Grange, the Alliance, the Woman Suffrage movement, and as a speaker for the People's Party, which is aiming at a higher civilization, the intellectual and spiritual advancement of the laboring classes, and the enfranchisement of woman—their motto being, "equal rights to all; special privileges to none."

Mrs. Marcen is a petite blonde, with dark golden hair, and expressive blue eyes sparkling with intelligence. To those unacquainted with this little woman it is a surprise to see her holding an audience with all the logic, force and eloquence of a magnetic masculine orator. It is equally surprising to those acquainted with her quiet retiring disposition, and who know how difficult it is for her to appear in public. To them it is but another proof of the power of the invisibles. Those who are acquainted with her band of guides, guards and teachers, know what powerful force is upholding her as a medium for the unfolding of elevated spiritual truths and the advancement of a refined spiritual life upon the earthly plane.

DR. FRANCES C. TREADWELL.

Dr. Frances C. Treadwell, nee Hinckley, formerly of Philadelphia, now at the Murphy Building on Market street, was born at Walworth, Wayne County, New York.

Her father, who was a captain in the war of 1812, was a farmer near Walworth. Her grandfather was a colonel in the Revolutionary War and fought for the independence of the American Colonies. His granddaughter, a hundred years later, fought for the recognition of ladies in the profession of dentistry.

Her maternal ancestors were French; her paternal ancestors English.

Her mother died when she was eight years old. Her father having married again, she went to her grandparents.

Her grandmother dying she was left alone with her grandfather, but he, too, having married again at the age of seventy, she determined to start out for herself.

The idea struck her at noon one day while she was at school. She had always been inclined toward the practice of medicine, and she now resolved to see what she could do for herself. She left school and procured a situation as a dressmaker. This business she followed for two years in her native country. She then went to Cleveland, Ohio, where she had a brother. Here she secured a position in a large dressmaking establishment as an assistant forelady.

It was her fixed purpose to obtain money enough to enable her to study medicine. While employed here, one of the girls who worked in the house was taken with toothache. Miss Hinckley took her to a dentist who, in extracting the tooth, treated the girl with so much roughness and carelessness that the subject of our sketch forthwith determined to turn her attention from medicine to dentistry. She applied to all the dental schools, such as they were in those days, but was everywhere laughed and sneered at. Finally, however, she secured employment as office girl in one of these dental schools where, it may be said, she learned to fill and extract teeth almost surreptitiously.

After remaining at this school about a year and a half and using up all her money, she was obliged to begin to practice. Here her troubles began in earnest. She had to have a certificate. After much quarreling among the professors of her school, she was awarded one. But a general hue and cry was raised among the dentists of Cleveland against the admission of ladies to the profession. Indeed, their dignity was so much offended, that Miss Hinckley did not dare to commence operations in that city. So she procured an outfit, which was not an easy task for one in her circumstances, especially when we consider that the dealers in dental supplies did not care much about stocking a lady dentist, borrowed a dollar, and started for the interior.

In a week she returned to Cleveland, paid for her outfit which had cost fifteen dollars, and had eight or nine dollars left.

These trips were repeated until she got on a good financial footing. But during this time she was constantly railed at, execrated, called a "she"

DR. FRANCES TREADWELL.

dentist, threatened with arrest, and admonished by ministers of the gospel.

In 1857 she was married to a portrait artist, and in company with her husband, traveled for a year, but her husband's health and business failing, she stopped at Smyrna, Delaware, and again resumed the practice of her profession. She next went to Delaware City, where she remained until 1868; from there she moved to Norristown. Her husband died in 1875. She next removed to Philadelphia, where she built up a large practice. It was owing chiefly to her efforts that female students were admitted to all the dental colleges of that city.

She had one son who received a thorough commercial education, and is now traveling salesman for one of the largest houses on the Coast. One of her brothers came to California in early times. Her son was also in California, and in 1874 she came to San Francisco on a visit. In 1882 she came to California a second time, principally on account of her health, and in two months returned much improved; but her health failing again, she was obliged to go abroad, and so came to San Francisco again. She may well be called the Pioneer Lady Dentist of the United States.

She also took a course in medicine at a medical college in Philadelphia, and is a learned M. D. as well as a skillful dentist. Her career has been one of discovery in a field hitherto unexplored by women.

She has fought her way inch by inch over this ground, and through all she has been as tender, compassionate and charitable as she has been independent and courageous. She has labored earnestly to prove to the world the ability of women, trusting the day will soon dawn when each woman and man can be weighed in the great scale of human justice and not be found wanting. Mrs. Treadwell is an avowed Spiritualist and liberal progressive woman.

JOHN C. BUNDY.

The following sketch of the life and eminent services in behalf of Spiritualism of Mr. Bundy was prepared by Sara A. Underwood and published in the RELIGIO PHIEOSOPHICAL JOURNAL of August 20th, 1892. It was afterward re-produced in the CARRIER DOVE with a portrait, under the date of Jan. 1893.

John Curtis Bundy, late editor and pubisher of *The Religio Philosophical Journal*, was born at St. Charles, Kane Co., Ill., about thirty five miles from the city of which he, a native son of Illinois, was ever loyally proud, and whence on the 6th of August he was born into the higher life.

He was ushered into earth life on the 16th of Feburary, 1841, the eldest son of Asahel and Betsey Bundy. As a youth he, though genial tempered, was quite serious minded and of studious habits. After leaving the common school of St. Charles he was sent at thirteen years of age for better instruction to the Brimmer school in Boston, Mass. Later he attended Phillips Academy at Andover, Mass., to prepare to enter Yale College, but his health gave way, and he returned to his Western home. It was while at Andover that he formed an acquaintance with the eminent writer of psychical stories, Elizabeth Stuart Phelps Ward, for whom he ever cherished an ardent admiration.

Although at the breaking out of the war of the rebellion but a youth barely twenty years of age, yet filled with a patriotic ardor he at once offered his services in behalf of the Union.

Soon after his enlistment he was given the rank of Second Lieutenant in Dodson's Independent Cavalry Company.

Later he was promoted to a Lieutenant Colonelship. His military ardor, however, was greater than his physical strength, and in 1863 he was forced to leave the army in order to recuperate his health.

It was while he was yet in the service, on August 19, 1862, that his marriage to Miss Mary E. Jones of St. Charles occurred. From childhood they had been friends and neighbors, and though both were comparatively young for wedlock, yet the marriage was from first to last a true union of hands, hearts, pursuits and interests. Two bright and lovely children were born to them, a son and daughter, of whom only the latter, Miss Gertrude Bundy, remains in earth life, the son, George a fine and beautiful boy, having been called to the higher life at the age of seven.

Soon after his retirement from army life Mr. Bundy took up the study of law, which he gave up to assist his wife's father, Mr. S. S. Jones, the founder of *The Religio-Philosophical Journal*, in the conduct of his paper.

Mr. Bundy was brought up in the Methodist faith, but desirous always of finding the truth and with mind open to conviction, he began very early that life of investigation and probing for facts for which he was conspicuous, and his search after proof of continued existence was rewarded by evidences which were to his mind indubitable that personality survives the dissolution of the physical form, and that which men name death is but a re-birth into a higher phase of existence. Among the most convincing proofs of this he considered some that were given to him soon after the transition of his only and idolized son, but these were too sacred to be often spoken of.

In 1877, when by the death of his father-in-law, Mr. Bundy, assisted by Mrs. Bundy, was called upon to take charge of *The Journal*, he was well fitted both by conviction and experience to carry on the work of spiritual enlightenment and scientific investigation demonstrative of psychic truths, to which he was thus called, and as Prof. Coues says, to him it is mainly due that here in America, at the World's Columbian Exposition, there will be presented, through the Psychical Congress. of which Mr. Bundy was chairman, a dignified presentation of the scientific proofs for belief in immortal life by cultured and scholarly scientific Spiritualists aided by the investigators of the Societies for Psychical Research. This in itself is something worthy of being born into this life for. Of the good work done for Spiritualism by Mr. Bundy since he took charge of the paper the files of *The Journal* give ample evidence, and we leave these to speak for him in any future history of Spiritualism in this and in all countries, and refer readers of this number to the respect in which he was held by the secular press of this city as evidence of the worth of his honest work.

When Mr. Bundy returned from the National Editorial Convention held in San Francisco in May, where he had been sent as a delegate from the Chicago Press Club, he was far from well, but he kept about until seven weeks before his transition, when he entered his office for the last time Saturday, June 18th, saying he was going to St. Charles with Mrs Bundy for a little visit, but would be back on Monday. A week or two later Mr. and Mrs Bundy were anticipating a trip to Ann Arbor, Mich., to be present at the graduation of their daughter from the Michigan University. After that event it had been arranged that they all should take a brief trip to Europe to give their daughter a taste of the world's pleasure after her years of study. But alas! every bright anticipation was doomed to non-fulfillment. On the same evening that he went to St. Charles, Mr. Bundy was taken suddenly ill with pleurisy. After ten days

of illness at St. Charles, it was deemed best to bring him to his own home in Chicago where he could be attended by his long-time friend and trusted family physician, Dr. J. R. Boynton. Everything that skill and love could suggest was done to save him, but the fiat had gone forth, and seven weeks to a day from the first attack of decided pain he passed away from earthly cares. The daughter, who had hoped to give him pleasure in witnessing her graduation honors, took little comfort in those honors and came home as soon as she could get away to take her place by the side of her beloved father, assisting faithfully in every duty necessary until the last sad hour; and his last conscious thought was of her and her mother, and his last effort was to smile bravely at them both to ease their fears as they bent over him ministering to his needs.

At an early stage of Mr. Bundy's illness which was ordained to be the pathway to his release from earthly cares, a forewarning of that release, it is believed by those nearest to him, was vouchsafed. "O!" he said to his wife at that time, "If I only had strength to tell you of the wonderful psychical experiences I have had since my sickness!—and they are not hallucinations either!" Trusting that he would eventually recover, and fearing that any detailed recital of any thing whatever would unduly excite and further weaken him, he was advised to await recovery before relating his experience, but as he spoke of them in a tone of delighted surprise, it is pleasant now to think that his pathway was brightened by glimpses of the immortal life.

At the time of Mr. Bundy's approach to the other side of life's veil, his eldest sister, Mrs. Frances Bundy Phillipps, was in Colorado, whither she had gone seeking health and strength. Though aware of her brother's protracted illness she did not know how very serious that illness was, but on the night he passed away she had two singular psychical experiences All the evening she felt a remarkable sadness and depression of spirits, so much so that because of it she refused to join a party of her friends at the hotel, who asked her to share in some social pastime going on among them. She went to bed at her usual hour and dreamed that Mr. Bundy had passed away and that she was present at his funeral, many of the particulars of which her dream foretold correctly; for instance, in her dream she heard sung distinctly one of the musical selections rendered by Miss McDonald at the services of St. Charles, viz, "Lead, Kindly Light." When she arose next morning she glanced at the clock in her room for the time, and discovered that it had stopped. She examined it to find the reason for its stopping, but could find none. This fact and her dream so worried her that, though she had promised and intended to accompany a party into the mountains for a pleasure trip that morning, she felt so sure that a telegram with bad news was coming for her that she declined going, and remained at the hotel waiting for the news which came before noon. The telegram gave the hour when her brother departed, and the time at which the clock stopped was the same hour, allowing for the difference between Colorado and Chicago time.

Another interesting incident occurred in *The Journal* office a few days previous to Mr. Bundy's change. Early in the day, when the office boy threw open the windows near the desk which for so long had been occupied by the editor of *The Journal*, a sparrow flew in from out of doors and perched itself calmly on the desk of the sick man and hopped about contentedly, apparently oblivious of the boy's presence. And when, an hour or two later, the acting editor accompanied by a lady came into the room, the sparrow still hopped about the desk, peering into this pigeon hole and that, with a strange disregard for their presence, though eluding their touch whenever they attempted to catch it. To the lady's mind was recalled a superstition of her departed mother that the coming of a bird like that tamely into any room or house was the portent of a death, and she remembered an instance which had fixed

the superstition in her mind when the portent came true, though no one was ill at the time of the bird's coming. Of course it was all nonsense, still she would rather the bird would go out. But though once or twice it flew from the desk to the ledge of the open window, it kept its perch preferably on Mr. Bundy's desk, finally crawling away into the furtherest recess of one of the pigeon holes, where it remained most of the day out of sight, but at intervals startling the visitors, who called to inquire as to Mr. Bundy's condition, by a loud and wholly unexpected chirp. When the office boy closed the rooms in the evening, fearing the bird might come to some harm if left all night, he caught it and attempted to put it outside the window, but twice it flew back, and it was only by quickly closing the window that at last he succeeded in getting rid of it. It never returned.

Another sister, who was in New York at the time her brother passed away, writes that on that night she dreamed that Mrs. Bundy came to her, and told her "John's sufferings are over." His mother, who was at the time ill, also had a strange psychical experience that same night concerning her son.

THE FUNERAL.

The arrangements for the funeral of Mr. Bundy were planned and carried out by Mrs. Bundy in beautiful harmony with the higher spiritual philosophy in which they both fully believed. Death, as popularly thought of, had not occured, but only the natural evolution of a soul in one of the phases of progress toward higher planes of existence. So mourning emblems could not be in place, and instead of the usual "crape at the door," a beautiful spray of white flowers held together by knots of white ribbon spoke of the departure of the soul to spheres of purer life and light.

Mrs. Bundy gratefully declined to accede to the expressed wishes of many friends for some public manifestation of the general sorrow over her husband's departure, and made the funeral as private as possible under the circumstances. But, as was befitting, a few personal friends and representatives of the leading newspapers of Chicago attended the services at his home on the morning of Monday August 8th

Although, in the published notice of Mr. Bundy's departure, Mrs Bundy had requested that no flowers be sent, yet that could not wholly prevent some of their friends from expressing by such gifts a tender tribute of their great regard for him, and in every room, both at his own home in Chicago and at that home in St. Charles whence his body was borne to its last resting place, vases, filled with fragrant, many-hued flowers, everywhere sent forth greetings of cheer and hope to all present. The Loyal Legion, of which Mr. Bundy was an honored member, sent a pillow of flowers with its emblematic rosette in the centre, and at the particular request of that association its mortuary flag was draped about the casket. The Chicago Press club sent a beautiful floral piece—an open book. A spray of fifty-one roses, presented by Mrs. Bundy's sister, Mrs. R. B. Farson, of St. Charles, and arranged by Miss Gertrude Bundy, lay upon the casket representing the years of his earth life. The roses were bedewed with the tears which silently stole from the daughter's eyes as she arranged this tribute to a parent deeply beloved, but they were not tears of hopeless sorrow, for she said, as she looked at the unresponsive passive features from which the light of love had fled, "Oh, indeed, I cannot feel in the least that that is papa! I feel that he is safe and happy in some other form in which he can still communicate with us!" On this assurance she did not clothe herself in garments of mourning, but wore a dress of pure white such as her father would prefer to see her arrayed in. Indeed none of the sorrowing friends, who believed that their dear one had only passed through one of life's portals to gain stronger powers, donned the dismal garments of crepe such as are usually associated with funeral rites, and those who took part in the exercises of the ocassion were relatives and friends whom he would at any time have been glad to welcome to his home. Miss Bessie McDonald the sweet singer, who paid the tributes of song to her friend, was the daughter of an old-time friend and neighbor of Mr. Bundy's boyhood. Before noon, accompanied by relatives and friends, the body was carried to the train and taken to St. Charles, where, in the home in which Mrs. Bundy was born, in which her marriage occured, and where I is last illness came upon him, another service was held in behalf of Mr. Bundy's aged parents and Mrs. Bundy's mother, Mrs. Jones, to whom he was as dear as if he were her own son. Many other relatives were present, among them his sister and brother-in-law, Mr. and Mrs. Phillipps, of Bloomington. Ill.

E. D. BABBITT.

Dr. Babbitt was born in Hamden, New York, February 1, 1828. His father was the Rev. Samuel T. Babbitt; his grand-father, Rev. Abner Smith, graduated at Harvard University in 1770. On his mother's side he was descended from the first Earl of Shaftsbury, the Lord High Chancellor of England. For many years of his earlier life he was engaged as a teacher in private seminaries or in colleges. For a quarter of a century he was an earnest worker in the church and battled against the claims of Spiritualism. Twenty-five years ago he was induced to visit Mrs. Staats of New York, a favorite medium of Judge Edmonds and received an overwhelming array of tests and proofs of communion with loved one gone before. This constituted a new era in his life, a period on the one hand of great joy and realization that the dear ones still lived and loved, and that light from the diviner world could at last be received direct, while on the other hand it was a period of agony to feel that so many precious religious hopes and associations and idols had to be shattered. He soon came out into clear light, however, and felt that he had been spiritually starving all his life for want of a knowledge of the higher world and the sublime truths of immortality. A joy unspeakable came to him as he found his mediumistic nature could be developed so that he was able to see the glories of the interior universe, and learn the mysteries of being from grandly illuminated souls.

In 1874, the doctor published his Health Guide, several editions of which have been sold in this and other countries.

In 1875-6, when General Pleasonton's work on "Blue and White Light" was producing a sensation, the doctor, perceiving its many loose statements and its lack of scientific occuracy, felt that there should be a work on light and color founded on absolute principles; but the whole scientific world was ignorant of basic principles—could not tell what light really is, or heat or electricity or magnetism or chemical force or force of any kind and were in the habit of remarking that these matters were "doubtless beyond human power ever to understand." Then it was, that under the influence of a wonderfully advanced spirit who was able to see actual atoms both large and small, he was made to reason out their very form and working, to see just how the great underlying forces of the world are developed and to open up into clear light a multitude of mysteries. Among other things, the processes of chemical affinity were clearly ascertained, and as this is the great formulating principle of the universe, he deems it the most important of all laws, and declares that by its aid vision, smell, taste, respiration, pulsation and even mental and psychic forces are made possible, while in the whole material world it is the harmonizing and potentizing principle. He discovered also that color is the measure of the style of force in every department of the world and that the chemical and therapeutical character of not only the rays of sunlight but of all other objects may be determined by their color. Not only by a great number of experiments with colored rays of light but by the color potency of drugs as shown by the spectroscope and proved by medical practice has he established this fact. His large work, "Principles of Light and Color," published in 1878, explains the

DR. E. D. BABBITT.

laws of all fine forces, establishes the new science of Chromopathy, and by a series of handsome colored plates shows the terrestrial color forces as seen by the clairvoyant eye, also the invisible radiations from the human head which give the very soul of character, and demonstrate the fact that even mental and psychic forces work on the principle of chemical affinity, another proof that unity of laws rules in both the visible and invisible world. A philosophical journal of France speaks of this work as follows:

"This extraordinary work commends itself to the attention of all who are interested in science and philosophy......... It recalls the celebrated discourse where Clausius has been able to deduce from the relationship of light and electricity, the unity of force in the universe. The *Principles of Light* should, then, be for savants a key which enables them to penetrate to the very secrets of substance. It is indeed that which commends this book, compared with which the bold efforts of the savant, Crookes, seem but as brilliant first steps...........We give all gratitude to Mr. Babbitt, for having consecrated with so much success his high science, who outdoes the genius even of a Pascal, inasmuch as that does not reveal the sublime harmonies taught in this book, and we greatly desire that a French translation may soon spread before us these amazing "*Principles of Light and Color.*"

It may be stated that Mme. Lemaitre of France is now translating this work.

The Rev. Walter W. Mantell, a medical scientist as well as a clergyman, of Melbourne, Australia, speaks as follows: "I have been for some time a careful and enthusiastic student of the system of therapeutics of which you are the discoverer. I have proved its immense value in the cure of disease. I firmly believe your discoveries are the most important ever made."

Dr. Babbitt's "Philosophy of Cure" has been received with equal favor with the "Principles of Light and Color." Another work called "Religion" is, in the

words of Dr. O. O. Stoddard, of Philadelphia, "a most beautiful and glorious gospel. If all could be led to believe in such a gospel, the world would be almost infinitely better than it is now."

His last work called "Health and Power" is a little pocket affair; gives natural methods for the cure of several diseases which have usually been considered incurable.

The doctor has for some time had the manuscript of a work on hand on "Marriage, Stirpiculture, Social Upbuilding," etc., which some philanthropic soul should be glad to help him issue. We learn that it covers some new and wonderful ground including the very philosophy of life itself, the mysteries of sexual development, the ante-natal and post-natal ennoblement of the race, etc. The cost of an edition will be about $800.

Before closing this article we must speak of Dr. Babbitt's Institution for the inculcation of this higher science of life and a more refined system of therapeutics, including chromopathy, or healing by light and color, electricity, vital magnetism, massage, mind cure, the curative use of water, air, earth, etc., the outlines of anatomy, physiology and pathology together with basic principles. For many years the institution has borne the name of the New York College of Magnetics and has had a charter granted under the laws of New York State; but a late law, enacted under the machinations and money of some rich old institutions that have wished to monopolize matters, forbids the confering of degrees excepting by colleges possessing resources to the amount of half a million dollars. On account of this law, one of the State regents visited his institution and although having a favorable impression declared that the charter would have to be revoked unless the degree conferring power was ommitted from the diplomas. Dr. F. G. Welch, a prominent New York physician, who is President of his Board of Trustees, wrote such words as these to the regents of Albany:

"I have known Dr. E. D. Babbitt a lifetime. He has made most important scientific discoveries. As soon as these truths become known every college in the land will gladly claim a department in which these discoveries may be explained."

Another of the trustees, Mr. J. W. Currier, went to Albany, and stirred the regents with his eloquence in behalf of the institution. He showed them that the College of Magnetics was making a new era in curative knowledge and becoming international, having had students in four continents, England, France, Germany, Spain, India, Australia, etc., as well as the United States being enthusiastically represented by them. "If you shall vote against this institution," said he, "and make money rather than science the test of a college, it will be the shame of the State."

The regents spoke well of the college but as the law was absolutely definite in the matter they had no power to vote in its favor.

Dr. Babbitt then got a full charter under the laws of New Jersey officered with a very superior Board of Trustees, changed the name of his institution to College of Fine Forces and removed it and his family to the beautiful suburban city of East Orange, New Jersey, his address being 5 Pulaski Street, East Orange, which is ten miles from New York. He continues to confer the degree of D. M. or Doctor of Magnetics, upon his graduates. By aid of a series of printed questions covering the whole course of study and the proper books, students who cannot leave their homes can take the full course and degree by correspondence.

F. A. DAVIS.

FRANKLIN A. DAVIS.

The subject of this brief sketch was born in the town of Milton, eight miles south of Boston, Mass. When about twenty-one years of age he left his native State to seek his fortune in Australia. At this time wonderful accounts of the marvelous wealth of that country, and the easy road to fortune it offered to the man of enterprise and adventure, had spread over the country, and many were induced to try its realities. After spending two years in Australia, Mr. Davis sailed for San Francisco, where he arrived in 1861. He soon engaged in the business of wool buying, in which he was very successful. As prosperity smiled upon him he shared her smiles with others. No appeal for help was passed by unheeded; and many comforts found their way into homes of poverty and distress, where they had hitherto been strangers. Mr. Davis is not one of those pharisaical specimens of humanity who "give gifts in public that they may be seen of men" or proclaim their charities through the public press in order to obtain the praise and adulation of the people. On the contrary, he is quiet, reticent and retiring, preferring to follow the injunction of Scripture, "Let not thy left hand know what thy right hand doeth." He is a staunch Spiritualist, a great reader and thinker. Mr. Davis has often been heard to remark that he would go much farther to see a sermon *practiced* than he would to hear one preached; that there is too much talking and too little acting among those professing to walk in the light of Truth. How much might be accomplished for humanity could those who have an abundance of this world's goods be induced to follow the noble example of this man whose life is dedicated to such sacred service; refusing thanks, but always thanking his beloved spirit friends for rendering him serviceable, and for sustaining him in his efforts to practically demonstrate the true Christ principle.

We cannot more fitly close this meager sketch than by giving a poem from the pen of "Lupa," the sweet singer whose plaintive notes have many times awakened responsive echoes from the sad hearts she has comforted.

FRIENDSHIP'S OFFERING TO F. A. DAVIS.

Where the waves of the wild Atlantic
  Ever beat against the shore,
On the coast where the Pilgrims landed,
  In a century gone before,
Where the blue hills guard the ocean
  And the men who sail in ships,
While they see their steadfast summits,
  Hold thanksgiving on their lips—

There were subtle forces gathering
  From the powers in air and earth,
There were circling bands angelic,
  And at last a human birth.
It was only the same old story,
  Ever new and wondrous strange,
How the body caught the spirit,
  With the years of earth to change.

All the faith of the Pilgrim Mothers,
  All their hope of a better life,
All the bravery of the Fathers,
  Through those barren years of strife,
All the long-sustained resistance
  That has made this nation free,
All the soul-entrancing beauty
  Of New England flower and tree,

The aspiring, snow-capped mountain
  And mysterious forest wild,
Went to mould the growing nature
  Of this little, laughing child,

While a practical endeavor,
  Joined with love of human kind,
Born of soil and rugged climate,
  Formed and taught the man we find.

In the years of youthful manhood,
  Sailing toward the setting sun,
There to find his El Dorado,
  Where the East and West seem one.
Many years he's lived to bless us,
  With a life that makes no sound,
Never noisy tongue proclaiming
  When or where his gifts are found.

E'en while gazing on these features,
  You know not, you cannot guess,
All the power which his spirit
Holds to stimulate and bless;
All the cheerful, hearty giving,
  All the strong and helpful tones,
All the happy, earnest living
  That have made our friend our own.

Thus we offer friendship's tribute,
  Wishing not for lengthened life—
'Twill be his without my asking ;
  Not for joy --'twill come, I know ;
Not for good—he draws it to him,
  His own nature wills it so—
But that we for long, may linger
  Near the path he walks to bless,
And may share his warmth and sunlight.
  "May his shadow ne'er grow less."

AUTHOR'S ALBUM.

INTRODUCTION.

Acting upon the advice, and in response to the earnest request of highly esteemed friends, and for the purpose of giving greater variety to the contents of this book, some of the biographical sketches originally intended for these pages have been transferred to Volume II, which is now in course of preparation, and the space is given to extracts from my own published and unpublished writings. Since deciding upon this course, I have hurriedly gleaned here and there a few of the thoughts that have been given me by my spirit instructors. Some are from addresses delivered at various times; some are from the editorial pages of the *Carrier Dove*, and others have been given at our private home séances; but whatever of merit any or all of them possess is directly attributable to the intelligences who inspire their expression through my imperfect mediumship. I have not the conceit or egotism to claim for them superior worth or excellence; but such as they are, they have been freely given me—although feebly and imperfectly transcribed. I deeply and consciously realize how impossible it is to depict in material language the beautiful realities of the spiritual world, or portray its exquisite loveliness and magnificence, as revealed to the clairvoyant vision of the spiritual seer, or give voice to its harmonies which sweep in waves of melody through the receptively attuned soul. But, if through these dim pictures, these faint whisperings from the spirit side, one human being, hungering and thirsting for the divine revealments of the heavenly spheres, will be enabled to catch even faint glimpses of the hidden glory, then will the writer feel repaid a thousandfold.

JULIA SCHLESINGER.

MEDIUMSHIP.

During many years of study and observation as an editor, an honest investigator, and searcher for truth, I have come to the conclusion that mediumship is a difficult problem to solve. Some speakers can discourse very learnedly, and some writers explain the entire subject, from the tiny rap up to the most marvelous materializations; and yet when the sum total of their practical knowledge is reached, it can be put in a nutshell. So far as observation and experience (which, as Patrick Henry said, is the only lamp by which my feet are guided), can avail in arriving at correct conclusions touching any subject, the decision reached is that mediumship is universal as mankind. It is inherent in all, and susceptible of cultivation, although possessed by some in more marked degree than by others. Many highly mediumistic individuals cannot determine to what extent they are the agents, instruments, or mouthpieces of the unseen intelligences of the spirit world. They live in the spiritual to such a degree, are so closely allied to angelic life, are so nearly "one with the Father" that the light from the Divine Source illumines them; they are receptive to heavenly harmonies, grand truths are voiced to a listening world; and tender messages from loving angels are wafted to the sad and sorrowing; and yet these same grand, white souls could not "give a test" under any conditions.

It is impossible to "draw the line" and set the stakes where the conscious volition of the medium ends, and the independent, perfect control or manifestation of the spirit begins. The two must of necessity be somewhat blended, and the manifestations partake in a measure of the medium's own individuality.

Public mediums are the open doorways through whom spirits of all degrees of intelligence, good, bad, and indifferent, throng, and pass to communicate with earthly friends. Dying has not transformed these departed ones into angels of wisdom, purity, or goodness, and they return, many times, still holding the erroneous views they held while in earth life, until time and experience in spirit life shall have wrought a change. The more sensitive the medium the more readily is he or she controlled by these various intelligences, who for the time impress their personality upon the psychics to such an extent that they are transformed and transfigured into the semblance of the spirit controlling them. Instances are known where refined and sensitive women have, under such influence, momentarily assumed the manner and characteristics of the ruffian, using profane language, asking for intoxicants and tobacco. Where the laws governing these various phenomena are not understood, the result of yielding to the different spirits who seek access to undeveloped mediums is often disastrous, and ends in obsession or insanity. Although such extreme cases are comparatively few, still such results in modified form are quite common and all manner of idiosyncrasies are manifested and denominated by these deceiving, ignorant spirits as great truths emanating from advanced minds.

Mediums, of all persons, should avoid overtaxation; for in the depleted conditions that follow, the sensitive becomes the easy victim of obsessing influences, who gain control for the purpose of gratifying appetites and desires that have not been outgrown in their brief spirit existence. Many such wrecks are strewn along the shores of Time since the great wave of Modern Spiritualism came sweeping in, that should warn mediums of their danger and guide them in the channels of safety. A number of celebrated mediums are examples of this truth. Brilliant and meteor-like their mediumship began, and ended in the darkness of night through the obsessing influences that doubtless first gained control and ascendency, through the constant subordination of the medium's own mentality and absorption of the vital forces by the many spirits constantly controlling their organisms, until the power of resistance was nullified to such degree as to leave them despoiled of individuality and self-control.

Just here is where the greatest caution should be exercised, and the admonition to try the spirits and see whether they are good or evil should be strictly followed out. "By their fruits ye shall know them"; and if their teachings and influence upon the lives of those whom they control and those they come in contact with is of a refining, elevating nature, inciting to pure and noble lives, then can they be safely trusted as guides and inspirers.

Truth is more desirable than all else, and should be gladly received from whatever source it may come. But no one should stultify reason and intelligence and accept as truth anything that is not susceptible of scientific demonstration. It were as well to go down in the darkness of past ignorance and superstition as to follow a will-o'-the-wisp, darting hither and thither, leading into mire and marshes, over quaking bogs and slippery places, with no steady light or guiding hand.

When a medium will stand before an intelligent audience and discourse for an hour or more, jingling words together like so many pennies in a boy's pocket, and leaving the audience mystified and in doubt as to the subject of the lecture, without a single idea or thought to take home with them, and the whole farce ended with the announcement that Socrates, Plato, or some more modern orator such as Henry Ward Beecher, has been the controlling intelligence, the effect is anything but pleasant and inspiring. Such mediums are the innocent dupes of spirits as ignorant as themselves and need the education and training of a spiritual kindergarten before going out into the world with collegiate honors and credentials.

Had they or their friends "tried the spirits" they would not have accepted high sounding names as the guarantee of wisdom, but rather judged the source by what emanated from it.

The wisest and most observing cannot discriminate, and draw the line with exactitude separating true, genuine spirit impression and influence from the intelligent operation of the individual's own mentality. How is it possible to determine how much or how little of what purports to come from disembodied intelligences really emanates from that source?

On the other hand, how can it be determined to what extent each and all are acted upon by the great invisible forces of the unseen universe? May not all be mediums through whom some spirit or spirits are endeavoring to carry out their own ideas of reforming the world? These and many other questions press upon the attention of the occult student for reply; and until they can be truthfully and scientifically answered and demonstrated it is the part of wisdom to remain an observer and student of Nature's great silent, wonderful forces, as manifested in all the various phenomena of life, and their influence over the lives and actions of men.

The mistaken idea that has prevailed to a large extent among spiritualists that mediumship was a "special gift of God" to a favored few, has been the source of much evil through the medium worship that has been the bane and curse of many possessing these powers in greater degree than others. So common has been the notion that a medium was a superior being, a sort of oracle whose behests were to be obeyed, and whose statements were considered infallible, that many of the best instruments who were selected by the spirit world when innocent and unpretentious, became arrogant, proud, and conceited and looked with contempt upon their fawning flatterers. When the mind becomes disabused of these notions and all individuals are regarded as having attributes and powers in common, although some may be more highly developed than others in certain directions, much of the nonsense attached to the discussion of mediumship will cease.

As there are highly gifted poets, musicians, artists, inventors, orators, authors and so on through all the great variety of talents displayed by different individuals, so, also, are there seers, prophets, and test mediums. But these powers are common to all. Because Patti can sing divinely she should not be designated as a special favorite of the Almighty, but rather as one whose gift of song has been cultivated to a higher state of perfection than others. Some of the most highly gifted mediums the world has ever known have been unconscious instruments in the hands of the angels. Their lives have been so pure, their every thought and aspiration so lofty and ennobling, that they have unconsciously dwelt in the vestibule of the spiritual world and become the recipients of its wisdom, love, and guidance. Its harmonies have been voiced in their songs; its tenderness expressed in their deeds of love; its grandeur and beauty manifested in lives of devotion to truth and humanity. Such grand souls may, never be designated as spiritual mediums, yet the mantle of the angels more surely envelopes them than it does the "wonderful medium" through whose instrumentality tables may be made to dance, or bells rung, or any other of the physical phenomena produced which are considered so desirable. To those, then, who seek the development of mediumship, the first step to be taken is to live lives of such perfect sweetness and love as will attract to you the bright and beautiful, the good and true, wherever in the great universe it may be found; and as surely as the earth draws the refreshing rain unto its bosom and the flowers receive the gentle dew, so will you draw unto yourselves spirits of wisdom and power who will aid and assist you in your earthly labors of love, even though you may never receive a visible sign or outward token of the presence of these heavenly messengers.

A TWILIGHT MESSAGE.

I wandered forth at sunset
  When the weary day was done,
For my soul was tinged with sadness,
  And I longed to be alone;
With the tender skies above me,
  And the quiet earth below,
I could watch the coming darkness,
  And the fading daylight go.

As I mused upon the picture
  That around about me lay,
I could feel a gentle presence
  And I heard a sweet voice say,

"Life, my child, may well be likened
　To the day and night of earth,
Half of darkness, half of daylight,
　From the very hour of birth.

" When the sunshine is the brightest
　Suddenly will storms arise,
And the clouds of inky blackness
　Darken all the summer skies;
Dazzling lightning, heavy thunder,
　And the fiercely beating rain,
Fill the timid heart with wonder
　And the homeless ones with pain.

" But the tempest soon is over,
　And the sweetly smiling sun,
Like a tender, wooing lover,
　Kisses now the timid one,
Bringing faith, and hope and courage
　Where was doubting, grief and fears,
Filling fainting hearts with gladness,
　Giving peace in place of tears.

When this life seems dark, and shadows
　Hide the golden light of day,
Loving spirits linger near you,
　Angel hands wipe tears away;
And their sweet, inspiring presence
　Oft dispels the shade and gloom
Causing buds of hope and promise
　In your weary lives to bloom.

Then, dear one, be hopeful, trusting,
　Always looking toward the light,
For there's just as much of daytime
　As there ever is of night;
Stars shine brightest when 'tis darkest—
　Stars of truth will light the way
To the world of summer sunshine
　Where is never-ending day.

THOMAS PAINE.

[Extracts from address delivered at the Paine Anniversary Celebration in San Francisco, January 29, 1892.]

Those who admire Thomas Paine for his bravery, his courage in the expression of his convictions in a time when to dissent from the old established customs was to call down upon the dissenter the anathemas of the whole religious world, can best express their admiration and appreciation by emulating his example and following where his brave spirit led the way, even though it brings the persecution and ostracism of the bigots of to-day as it did in those trying times, when, with our beloved Washington, he struggled for the Rights of Man, the Age of Reason and Common Sense, which he thought would be evolved from the Great Crisis then pending and upon the result of which depended the success of the American Colonies and the inauguration of a reign of peace and religious liberty the world had never before dreamed of. We, of to-day, who rejoice in the name Liberal will also do well to remember the words of our hero concerning the right of every man to his opinion, however different it might be from our own. He said: "He who denies to another the right makes a slave of himself to his present opinion, because he precludes himself the right of changing it." It is well to avoid the error of becoming illiberal liberals; many good men and women are just as liberal as you upon all subjects—religious, social, and political, who claim they have gone one step ahead—they have dared even to peep into futurity and claim they see something beyond that all can not as yet see; but because they have done this they should not be ridiculed by those who have not looked into the great telescope of clairvoyance that reveals still another world beyond this. One world at a time is sufficient for most of us, and even that may grow wearisome to those who know not rest or comfort, but are compelled from day to day to toil like beasts of burden for the privilege of simply existing, without any of those things that enhance and beautify life or make it worth living.

In writing upon this subject of immortality, Thomas Paine said, "The belief of a future state is a rational belief, founded upon facts visible in the creation; for it is not more difficult to believe that we shall exist hereafter in a better state and form than at present, than that a worm should become a butterfly and quit the dunghill for the atmosphere, if we did not know it as a fact. The most beautiful parts of creation to our eye are the winged insects, and they are not so originally. They acquire that form and that inimitable brilliancy by successive changes. The slow and creeping caterpillar-worm of to-day passes in a few days to a torpid figure and a state resembling death; and in the next change comes forth in all the miniature magnificence of life, a splendid butterfly. No resemblance of the former creature remains; everything is changed; all his powers are new and life is to him a new thing."

If Thos. Paine were living to-day, we would say he was a Progressive Spiritualist.

The time is fast approaching when all who have outgrown the old superstitions of past ages will be called upon to stand unitedly for liberty. The Church of Rome and all her Protestant children are daily drawing the lines closer and closer—daily forcing their old dogmas to the front and compelling at least a tacit submission on the part of American citizens to the domination of religious zealots in matters of State. Sunday laws are being forced upon us, and their violation in some states is even now punished by fines and imprisonment. In a few years—if we do not awake to the danger—we shall see the efforts of the National Reform Association, the W. C. T. U., and other organizations, crowned with success, and have incorporated into the Magna Charta of our liberties—the Constitution of these United States—a clause recognizing Jesus Christ as the ruler of nations and our acknowledged head and leader. How think you will it fare with us then? How many free thinkers will dare assemble as we are assembled here to-night to do honor to the memory of the man who called him "a man only," whom they would have as our "divine head" and "ruler of nations," and who said "I believe in one God and no more," thus emphatically repudiating the divini'y of Jesus. Do you think we would be allowed to so transgress the laws of the land as to openly deny allegiance to our recognized ruler? Many may think that danger afar off, but they who so think must be blind to the progress being made in the direction outlined.

We who so admire Thomas Paine would do well to benefit by the truths he taught by incorporating them into our daily life work. We see on every hand the evils that have grown like noxious weeds from the seeds of ignorance and superstition. We see truth naked and cast out, while error sits clothed and crowned in the high places of earth. We see on every hand wrongs that need to be redressed, customs and laws tyrannical and unjust that should be changed. We see the oppression of the many by the few. We see the poor pittance wrung from the hands of toilers to help build magnificent cathedrals for the worship of an unknown God, and to feast the smooth-tongued priest, who, for a "consideration," will give passports to heaven to the most hardened sinner. It is time liberals were awake and doing something to counteract the tendency to drift with the old theological current and forget the duties of the present life and present time in the preparation for a life to come. We want heaven here and now. We want to see

every poor little waif that drifts into life secured in its rightful inheritance with food, clothes, and the shelter and protection of home. We would have every little cold, hungry, ragged child that to-night is selling papers, matches, or pencils in our streets, warmed, fed, and clothed, and, with the coming of to-morrow, started in a new life and given a taste of that heaven Christians are looking forward to, where all tears shall be wiped away, and there shall be no more sorrow or crying.

Have we not something to do, something to live for, something to work for when the masses of humanity are homeless and clothed in rags? Nature has been so bountiful that even the weakest and meanest of all living things has been provided for. Man alone has permitted himself to be defrauded and enslaved. The earth and the fulness thereof is his to appropriate and enjoy when he shall have grown out of the conditions that have retarded his development and progress, and of these condilious and obstacles the greatest of all has been the incubus called revealed religion. Thomas Paine said: "It is incumbent on every man who wishes to lessen the catalogue of artificial miseries, and remove the cause that has sown persecutions thick among mankind, to expel all idea of revealed religion as a dangerous heresy and fraud. As an engine of power it serves the purpose of despotism; as a means of wealth, the avarice of priests; but so far as respects the good of man in general, it leads to nothing here or hereafter. When opinions are free, truth will finally and powerfully prevail."

Those were brave words that none but a brave man could utter; and even to day their repetition on the public rostrum is certain to excite feelings of hatred in the hearts of many. But for myself I would rather take my chances in the next world beside the great noble soul of Thomas Paine than with that of any crowned and mitred Pope that ever trod the earth or sat upon a Papal throne.

ASPIRATION.

Dear Spirit, thou who dost attend
My daily steps where'er they wend,
Thou whom I call my angel guide—
Who, ever faithful by my side
Through weal or woe, through good or ill,
Art tender, true and loving still;
Thou, who when earthly friends betray
Dost gently wipe my tears away,
And whisper softly, — " Peace, my child,
Cease vain regrets and longings wild;
Lean thou upon my stronger arm,
My love shall shield thee from all harm;
And like a star in darkest night
Shine o'er thy way a beacon light."

Thou whom I love, yea, and adore,
From thy full treasure house and store
Give unto me my heart's desire,
And touch with inspiration's fire
This tongue and pen, until each word
Like a dear, swiftly, speeding bird
Shall find a home and place to rest
In some poor aching troubled breast;
And singing there a sweet, new song
Wake strains of joy and peace among
Discordant strains of human life,
With which the weary world is rife.
Oh, give me words with wisdom fraught,
That shall embody purest thought;
And for the wounds of earth prove balm,
And to the tempest-tossed bring calm;
Words that shall live, and breathe and
    burn,
And cause the wayward ones to turn
And seek the good, eschewing ill,
Until a sweet refrain shall fill
The world with melody and love
Like unto those pure realms above.

THE IMPROVEMENT OF THE RACE.

In considering this subject it is well to have a foundation upon which to base an argument favorable to the feasibility of the proposition that is not incorporated in the theory of the evolution of the race by the slow and almost invisible processes of nature. It has been discovered and demonstrated that growth and development in the animal and vegetable kingdoms can be hastened by scientific methods. This is amply shown in the improvements that have been made in all departments of agriculture and stock-raising during the last half century. Primitive methods and machinery for farming and housework have given place to new and wonderful inventions for expediting and rendering lighter and easier the labor on the farm and in the home.

Great improvement has been made in the various kinds of domestic animals, horses, cattle, sheep, swine, and poultry. The improvement in horses by careful breeding, feeding, and training has been something marvelous. In fact the modern racehorse with a speed of a mile in less than two minutes, seems almost a new creation, as compared with the ungainly, plodding horse of fifty years ago. Cattle have been improved, until the average weight and price of beeves have more than doubled in the last thirty years. The scrub stock that constituted farm herds have given place to fine breeds of Shorthorn, Holstein, Jersey, and others. Butter and butter-making has entirely changed in quality and process. Sheep have been so much improved that the weight of fleece has been more than doubled, while the quality has also been greatly improved. The demand for and use of mutton has correspondingly increased. In swine the improvement has amounted to the creation of entirely new and distinctive breeds, the most popular of which is the Poland-China. The Berkshire, of English importation, originally, is also one of the breeds in greatest demand. Looking at one of these fine fat creatures now, and comparing it with the long-nosed, razor-backed hog of "ye olden time," one would be led to think that man had greatly improved on what was first created and pronounced "good." The barnyard fowls of former times were a motley flock of all sorts. Few distinct breeds existed; now there are at least one hundred. They are bred with such intelligence and care that their characteristics and color are fixed to the shade of a feather. Incubators hatch the chickens, and hens have nothing to do except to lay the eggs. The same improvements and changes made in animals have also extended to agriculture, horticulture, and floriculture. Our grains, fruits, and flowers are wonderfully improved. Our annual fairs in California illustrate the wonders wrought in fruit and flower cultivation. The magnificent chrysanthemums, the wonderful roses, pansies, and pinks seem entirely new creations, so greatly do they differ from those that ornamented the front door yards in our grandmother's days.

As we review all these great changes we can but ask if mankind has correspondingly improved. Has the rearing of boys and girls received the same care and attention that have been given the rearing of colts, calves, and lambs? If so, the results do not appear as satisfactory. Intellectually, as a nation we have made rapid strides; for only through study and experiment have the grand results in almost every department of life been attained. But in proportion as we have advanced intellectually, we have degenerated physically, until the majority of the young men and women of to-day are small of stature, narrow chested, incapable of great physical strain or exertion. Their muscles are soft and flabby; their brains large in proportion to the body; they are given to the use of narcotics and stimulants; they live largely in the sphere of artificial excitement and unnatural lives. They are poor material for the fathers and mothers of the next generation. The people have not given the same care and attention to the improvement of the physical that has been devoted to the mental and intellectual faculties. The average boy and girl of to-day knows more at the age of ten or twelve years than their parents did at eighteen or twenty. But is their knowledge that which is calculated to make them the best and most useful men and women? Will they make wise, loving husbands and wives, fathers and mothers?

Children, like hot-house plants, are being forced into a maturity of manner and expression quite unnatural to childhood. They are miniature men and women. And when one thinks of the years to come, when these little ones shall have attained in reality manhood and womanhood, how dull and commonplace will life have become to them. Those pleasures that should have remained untasted, the amusements and festivities that are designed as rest and recreation for people engaged in the active duties of life—all these are participated in by children who should know only the innocent games and sports of childhood. At school they are overtaxed and crammed with a vast amount of so-called education that will never prove of the slightest avail in after years. Much that is learned in school days is forgotten and useless when the man and woman have life to face in earnest, and the struggle for bread begins. Better that children be taught how to live in harmony with the laws of their being, how to attain physical perfection, how to

regulate their lives so as to avoid sickness, and build up strong, disease-resisting bodies, than to be taught to read Greek and Latin and not know how to avoid taking a cold, or, having taken one, how to cure it. Intelligent men and women know that it is almost useless to talk about generation, and the improvement of human stock while the present social conditions obtain in society. Stock-breeders know that race-horses are not produced from ''scrub'' sires or dames; and what is true of horses is also true of the human animal called man. As long as insane people, criminals, drunkards, idiotic, diseased, and half-made, malformed creatures are allowed to marry and propagate their kind, the human race will continue to degenerate physically and become more and more subject to disease in all its multifarious forms, early decay, and death.

We heard a speaker remark not long ago, that ''enlightened motherhood was the hope of the race.'' This is true to the extent that mothers are responsible for their offspring; but enlightened motherhood without an equally enlightened fatherhood would eventually result in the total destruction of the species, for women would cease to be mothers were they ''enlightened,'' unless fatherhood had attained a standard of enlightenment equal to their own. This seems quite improbable when we realize the fact that tobacco and whisky, twin evils, have their clutches upon the throats of the coming generation, strangling the budding aspirations of early manhood before they have opportunity or time to mature into the perfect ripened fruit of an intelligent comprehension of life's duties and responsibilities, or, that strength of will developed which enables them to rise superior to temptation, and masters of their environments.

BEAUTIFUL GATES OF DAY.

I used to wonder, my darling,
  If, in the days to come,
That death would come like a shadow
  To darken our happy home ;
Or would it come as a blessing
  To open the gates of day,
Through which we would pass with gladness
  To dwell with the loved alway.

But now, since the light which is dawning
  Has gladdened my eager eyes,
I see through the mists of the morning
  The glory of sunnier skies;
And the bright, smiling faces of angels
  Are coming and going each way,
Bringing blessings to those who still tarry
  This side of the gates of day.

If ever you stand by me darling,
  When the last good-bye has been said,
And my eyes have been closed to the sunshine
  And someone has said—"she is dead,"
Oh, drop not a tear on my pillow,
  But look up and joyfully say—
She's done with all suffering and sorrow,
  She has entered the gates of day.

And then I will kiss you, my darling,
  And whisper my unchanging love,
And say—I will wait for your coming
  As constant and true as the dove;
Until you have finished your labors
  And can calmly and joyfully say—
I am ready to go with you, darling,
  Through the beautiful gates of day.

SPIRITUALISM AND ORTHODOXY CONTRASTED.

[An Address delivered before the Society of Progressive Spiritualists of San Francisco, Cal.]

We are often asked the question "What are the superior benefits or blessings conferred by Spiritualism upon its adherents, over those resulting from other and older religious beliefs?"

First, we reply—Spiritualism is not a belief; it is knowledge—the first positive knowledge mankind has received of the continued, conscious existence of the spirit after the dissolution of the body, and its power to communicate intelligently with mortals. This fact has been abundantly demonstrated to the satisfaction of millions of intelligent people within the last thirty-nine years. A great many theories have been advanced and palmed upon an ignorant, credulous world by designing men, as divine revelations from a God who was also a creature of their own imaginations, reflecting only that degree of intelligence and goodness manifested by his creators. These theories have found believers in all ages; and among all people to whom they have been taught, and so great has been their influence over the minds of men that empires, kingdoms, and all forms of government have been swayed and controlled by them.

To judge properly and impartially of the merits of any system of religion we must study and note the effect of its teachings upon humanity.

What does history record of the effects of church dogmatism upon governments and individuals in earlier ages, and what is the result of our own observations at the present time? Its early historical record is one of bloodshed and crime—of the usurpation of the power of governments and the rights of the people. The church was not willing to leave the punishment of those who dared to disobey her edicts to God, but invented all manner of cruel instruments of torture with which to enforce obedience, until, wherever on the green earth the banner of the cross was unfurled, it waved over the graves of murdered heretics and its folds were sprinkled with their blood. Lecky says of that time, "The Church of Rome shed more innocent blood than any other institution that ever existed among mankind. Its cruelties were not perpetrated in the brief paroxysms of a reign of terror, or by the hands of obscure sectaries, but were inflicted by a triumphant church, with every circumstance of solemnity and deliberation. Its victims were usually burnt alive after their constancy had been tried by the most excruciating agonies that minds fertile in torture could devise." So fearful were the scenes enacted, that the wheels of progress were blocked, civilization retarded, and a thick darkness shrouded the world for centuries. The effect of church rule has ever been the enslavement of reason. It has been subjugated to a blind faith in creeds until, like dumb, driven cattle, men have obeyed the dictum of their ecclesiastical masters, who still hold their sway over millions of people by means of their most dangerous, crafty, yet ever potential argument—"thus saith the Lord." Slowly but surely has the light of truth been dawning upon the world. The intellect of man, so long subordinated and imprisoned, began to unfold its divine potentialities, and the time came when, notwithstanding the anathemas of Pope and priests, such men as Voltaire, Hume, Volney, and later on, immortal Thomas Paine, dared to give utterance to the grand truths which, while they rung the death-knell of superstition, were the joy-bells proclaiming mental liberty. Thus was the way prepared for the reception of a new and later truth in the world, which, in its magnitude and beneficence, eclipses anything the mind of man has ever conceived of, bringing hope, comfort, and joy to humanity, through this, the crowning gift of the ages—Modern Spiritualism.

Since the advent of this grand truth, there has been a rapid and wholesome growth of liberal thought. Men and women have received higher and broader conceptions of the duties and responsibilities of life, and are beginning to shake off the dust—sweep down the cobwebs of many centuries' growth, and open the windows of their souls that the light may stream in, and in that light they discern the dark forms of ignorance and bigotry, born of priestly rule and teaching, fading and melting away. We have seen the direful effects of the subjugation of reason to a blind, intolerant faith in creeds, in the religious wars of the past, whereby Europe became one vast battlefield, and all manner of crimes were committed in the name of God and the Holy Church. To-day we do not see the smoke of battle, or hear the cries of anguish from tortured victims, but we see still brooding over us the clouds of superstition, and hear, from every pulpit in the land, thunderbolts of wrath hurled at the man or woman who dares to think, and through thinking aright become free. Among the free-thinkers thus denounced, hated and despised by the Christian churches, are those calling themselves Spiritualists; and as the time was not many years ago when the word abolitionist was especially abhorred by these same churches and is now claimed as a title of honor by those who fought for universal freedom, so shall the time come when Spiritualist shall be spoken with reverent tongue as the grand liberator of the human race from Spiritual bondage.

It is only by observing the contrast between day and night that we are enabled fully to appreciate the glorious sunshine, the sweet songs of birds, the beautiful flowers, the glowing landscape, the picture of loveliness that everywhere greets the eye when earth is bathed in all the golden glory of a perfect day, as compared with the shadows of night, when darkness has spread her sable pall over land and sea, and hidden from our admiring gaze the beautiful vision of the day. So with the physical, intellectual, moral, and spiritual conditions of mankind. It is by contrasting vice and virtue, ignorance and education, truth and falsehood, disease and health, that we are enabled to decide what is best calculated to advance and secure the attainment of the greatest good possible to be realized by all. Every thoughtful person knows that the theological teachings of the past and present have failed to bring into our lives the actualization of benefits which should accrue from any system to which has been, and still is, devoted so great an outlay of time and means wrung from the needy and oppressed for its support, as is devoted to the maintenance of Christian churches. Look at the thousands of magnificent churches, costing millions of dollars, exempt from taxation, closed six days out of seven, built for the purpose of gratifying the vanity of priests and awing their followers into obedience through an ostentatious display of wealth and power. God's houses—sacred temples—they are called. What a travesty upon Omnipotence. God's houses—in which are luxurious carpets, soft-cushioned pews, warmth and beauty — closed — locked while His little ones are freezing in attics and cellars and dying outside.

And, when within these temples are heard the grand anthems of praise from the worshipers, without are heard the plaintive moans of distress, from hungry, naked little children, the appeals for succor from the aged and helpless, the curses and imprecations of the depraved and vicious, the bacchanalian shouts and revelry of the desperate and abandoned, all mingling and ascending in one mournful chorus to the listening ears of angels who sadly behold in all this wo and degradation the triumph of ignorance and superstition over the reason and intelligence of man. We would like to see the temples converted into educational homes where the children of the government could be properly clothed, fed, and educated to lives of usefulness and honor, instead of allowing them to grow up in wretched homes of poverty, where they become skilled in vice, and finally go out to prey on society, filling asylums, almshouses, and prisons with paupers and criminals, thus becoming a tax and burden upon the government far greater than would be required to adopt them as its wards at first and educate them accordingly.

Is it not time for intelligent people to investigate candidly the teachings of Spiritualism and see if it does not offer them something better to live and labor for—something that will right some of the monstrous wrongs now existing in the world, and give them more rational views of life here and hereafter, than any other religion has yet offered them? Let us contrast its teachings with those of orthodoxy and see which holds the greater promise for humanity.

Spiritualism teaches progression and universal salvation for all mankind, not through a "vicarious atonement" but through individual effort and the divinity within which will ultimately lift every human being from the depths of ignorance and sin, and place their feet firmly upon the mountain heights of wisdom, where the sweet inspirations of angel souls will ever help them to "come up higher" through all the ages of eternity.

Orthodoxy teaches that mankind must accept a tradition two thousand years old, written we know not where, when, nor by whom, of a man called Jesus, and claimed to be the Son of God, who had sent him into this world to suffer and die as a sacrifice for the sins of the people, that all who believed in him should have everlasting life, and those who did not believe should be doomed to suffer excruciating torture in a lake of fire and brimstone for ever and ever. This tradition does not state what is to be the future condition of the many, many thousands who had lived, loved, and died ages before the Bible was written.

Spiritualism teaches that there is no forgiveness of sin; that we must abide the consequences of our acts be they good or evil, and if evil make restitution to those we have wronged before we can hope to find peace or happiness. Orthodoxy teaches that "though your sins be as scarlet they shall be made white as wool" through the atoning blood of Jesus. No matter to what depths of infamy a man may have descended—though his hands be stained with the blood of his fellow-man, if, as the time approaches when he is to suffer the penalty of the law, a terrible fear and dread of future punishment in that place "where the worm dieth not, and the fire is not quenched," takes possession of him, he calls in the services of a priest who performs the ceremonies required by the church—the sinner is baptized, partakes of the Holy Sacrament, receives absolution, then swings from the gallows into glory, there to enjoy the companionship of God and His angels, play upon a golden harp, arrayed in shining garments of righteousness, walk the golden streets of the New Jerusalem, singing praises to the Lamb forever and ever; while the poor victim he sent into eternity without time for this preparation must suffer the torments of the damned throughout the vast cycles of unending time. Oh! Consistency thou art a jewel, but thou dost not adorn the crown of Orthodoxy.

Spiritualism advocates the perfect freedom and equality of all, irrespective of race, color, or sex.

Orthodoxy says: Servants, obey your masters; wives, obey your husbands in all things, for the husband is head of the wife even as Christ is head of the Church; and this infamous command is being reiterated from the pulpits of orthodox churches to-day, thereby helping to rivet the chains which have so long bound and fettered womankind making her the victim of man's caprice and passion, instead of his equal and true helpmate.

It has been stated that Spiritualism has built no orphan asylums, supported no charitable institutions, etc., while Christianity has done all these things. But we must remember Spiritualism is not quite half a century old yet, it is but an infant just beginning to stand alone. Wait until it has been preached to the world nearly two thousand years as Christianity has been, then, methinks, as now, it will foster no charitable institutions, for its exalted teachings will have leveled all distinctions of caste—and there will be no more poor.

Jails, asylums and prisons will cast no dark shadows upon the beautiful earth, for long ere that time arrives, enlightened, spiritualized men and women will have ceased to beget criminals. There will be no need of orphan asylums, for love shall have become a vital, living principal in the life of every human being, and our neighbor's child will be as tenderly cared for as our own. No little tender hearts will go starving and famished for love, for it will be everywhere manifested, even unto the lowest of all created things.

Unto thee, O Spiritualism, the faces of humanity are longingly and expectantly turned to-day! In the light which thou bringest, they are beginning to discern the errors of the past, and, quickened with thy loving inspirations, they are turning their steps toward the mountain heights of wisdom and truth. Through the teachings of these dear ones whose feet have trod the immortal shores and return with their garnered sheaves of knowledge to scatter the seeds of truth broadcast upon the earth, many have broken the shackles which ignorance had bound upon them, and are now laboring in harmony with the great invisible hosts to bring to all of earth's children some glimpse of that better way, that higher and diviner life, when injustice shall no longer triumph over justice, when the strong shall no longer oppress the weak, when the nations of the earth shall learn war no more, when each sovereign human being shall become obedient unto the higher law of the spirit, instead of the law of brute force which now rules the world. Then there shall be no more master and slave, for all shall be free. Then shall the rights of little children be respected as being equal to those of larger growth. At present there are none so much abused, none so little understood, none whose rights are so thoughtlessly trampled upon, as those little helpless ones whose very helplessness should be a constant appeal to all the tenderness and love the human heart is capable of feeling. Then shall men and women understand the true meaning of parenthood, and not ignorantly and thoughtlessly project upon the rough sea of life a frail little craft without the compass and chart of a sound mind in a sound body, to enable it successfully to battle with the winds and waves which must sweep over it. Then shall a free and enlightened womanhood throw off the fetters of unjust, man-made laws, and those other fetters which fashion has imposed upon her, whereby the feet which should ever be free to speed upon errands of mercy and love are now shackled and bound, and the beautiful form which nature models so exquisitely is dwarfed and compressed into ungainly deformity, ultimately resulting in disease and premature death. When motherhood shall be considered a divine prerogative and the choicest blessing nature confers, instead of a curse to be dreaded and avoided if possible. When woman shall stand up, free and unshackled, a peerless queen, the perfect equal and true helpmate of her kingly brother. When man —grand, brave, true man—shall deal justly with the weak and helpless, carrying them in his strong arms, tenderly, lovingly.

Then shall our dear departed ones no longer feel the shadow of death resting upon them, veiling their faces from those they love, but recognized and remembered as still belonging to the household, of which they are a part, they will walk joyfully beside us, counseling and advising in times of perplexity, soothing and comforting when the waves of adversity break over us; and when we stand upon the borders of that unseen land, they will be there to greet us with words of welcome and songs of rejoicing.

Oh, Angels, haste to usher in that golden
   morning,
Toward which we turn to-day, expectant,
   longing,
When superstition from the world shall
   vanish,
And Truth's bright rays the darkness
   banish,
When free and equal man and woman
Grow more divine and less of human ;
When from each heart spontaneous
   springing
Shall joyous songs come sweetly ring-
   ing,
Saying to each, thou art my brother,
Come, let us live to bless each other.
On that blest morn, methinks the Angels
Will sing anew their glad evangels,
And "peace on Earth, good-will to
   men,"
Will echo through the Heavens again.
For lo ! the Christ of love and wisdom
Is born in every human bosom.

"SOUL COMMUNION."

We have been repeatedly asked what we thought of the "Whole World Soul Communion," of which so much is being said and written among our spiritual brethren. We think it is well to have "soul communion" often; in fact, every day and hour of our lives. The truly spiritual man or woman needs not an hour set apart *once a month* for this communion with the soul-world. It is a daily experience to those who live the proper spiritual life. This spiritual life is the condition described as being "one with the Father," where the person has attained that degree of soul-growth and unfoldment that the divine influx of light, love, and wisdom from the highest spheres is a daily and hourly experience. Such need no special day or hour; the light of truth continually streams in through the open windows of the soul, and its warm, life-giving beams are reflected upon all who come within its radius. They live the life of the spirit here and now; and manifest by their daily lives and conversation, their oneness with the Divine Soul of Being. For those, however, who are enwrapped with the materialities of their surroundings, and catch only stray gleams of the infinite soul-world pulsating and throbbing with divine potentialities all around them, who are tethered to their idols of flesh, for them it may be well to have an appointed time in which to lay aside their material engrossments, and seek the angelic aid and upliftment which comes from supernal realms; for it is better to come once a month, even, into the vestibule of the "holy of holies," and breathe in the invigorating atmosphere of realms supernal, than to remain forever enveloped in the fogs of earth. It is better occasionally to feel the grandeur and beauty of the higher life than to never have a pulse-beat in accord with the rhythmical harmonies of the celestial universe. If, by a general observance of a certain hour set apart for "soul communion," any new light can be received, and spiritual aid and guidance invoked that will meet with a response from the angelic hosts who are supposed to be in general attendance upon mortals on that day, then, by all means, observe the hour. If even one benighted fellow-creature is blest and enlightened by this observance, then has the hour been well spent; and those to whom has come such light should ever bless and revere the day which gave them *one hour* of "soul communion."

SPIRIT-MESSAGE.

'Twas far away on distant shore
My spirit-bark was wafted o'er
The sea called death, which quickly passed,
I found my spirit-home at last.
It seemed so hard, at first, to die,
When those I loved stood weeping by,
And little children kissed the face
So soon to find a resting-place
Beyond the reach of lips that press
The seal of love and tenderness!
Another, too, bent o'er my bed—
A husband, dear as wife e'er wed,
He in whose arms I found repose
When life seemed full of pain and woes;
Full oft I sank to sweetest rest
Upon that loving, manly breast,
Now throbbing with the keenest pain
That it could never hold again
The loved one there, or soothe to sleep
The eyes that could not help but weep
Fond tears of thankfulness and bliss,
That so much love I found in this,
Your cruel world, where thousands pine
For want of that which e'er was mine.
I knew a chilling void would come
In that sweet bower, my earthly home,
When one, the mother, was not there
In her accustomed place and chair,
And little ones would call in vain,
By every fond, endearing name,
The one for whom all else beside
Seemed nothing since their mamma died.
But oh, the joy, the bliss indeed!
When all was o'er, the spirit, freed,
Found not its home in far-off heaven,
Where all the ties of earth are riven,
But close beside my loved and dear.
Although I could not make them hear
Assurances that "all is well,"

I did not, could not say farewell,
But longed to stay the tide of grief,
And give their sorrowing hearts relief,
To whisper, "'T was *not* dying, dear,
For I am with you, and can hear,
And see, and love you, just the same
As ever, ere the living flame
That lit those eyes and that pale cheek,
And caused that silent tongue to speak,
Was taken far from mortal sight,
Your daytime changing into night,
And yet that flame beyond the gloom
And darkness of the earthly tomb,
Still glows a living spirit, free
As breezes fresh from o'er the sea."
But ah, I could not make them know
That all their pain and grief and woe
Mistaken were, and that ere long
We'll meet again, and sing the song
Of gladness, in the happy land
Where *those who love* go hand-in-hand
Together through the circling years,
Set free from earthly cares and fears,
Unfolding every day and hour
Some fresh and beauteous spirit-flower
Of truth and love, whose fragrance rare,
Like incense rising on the air,
Seeks that supreme and central Good
That we call Truth and you call God!
They had not learned the glorious truth
Which then to man was in its youth,
Unknown, save to a favored few
Who angels testing found were true.
Those few defied a sneering world,
And to the breeze Truth's flag unfurled.
To every land, from sea to sea,
Came proofs of immortality:
"Eureka!" through the heavens rung;
"Eureka!" thankful mortals sung;
"Away with all our doubts and fears!
Away with all our bitter tears!
No longer mourn in grief and pain,
For angels come to earth again!"

They come with love and blessings sweet
Their mourning friends below to greet,
And bid them sing, in joyful strain,
Although man dies he lives again—
He lives a glorious being, fraught
With all the wondrous powers of thought
And research now intensified,
While fields of science yet untried
Lure him their fastness to explore,
His fervor kindling more and more
As Nature's secrets he lays bare,
Revealing beauty everywhere;
Till now, with aid from heavenly shore,
The tree of knowledge blossoms o'er
With grander truths, diviner thought,
Than ever ancient sages taught.

ENCOURAGEMENT.

The mistakes of the 'past are but stepping stones upon which the progressive individual climbs to higher ground. Growth comes only through the varied experiences of life; and the broadest, grandest souls are they whose windows are open to catch every ray of light that may stream in, and who can receive and appropriate to their unfoldment all the joys or sorrows that are strewn along life's pathway. From this standpoint, glancing backward, the past, viewed in the light of the present, seems but a rough and slippery steep o'er which we have toiled, sometimes almost fainting by the way, and anon rested, comforted, and refreshed, as some cool shade was reached, when Love reached down her snowy hands and led us into repose and peace, where happier conditions are enjoyed, and from which standpoint brighter scenes and more signal victories await us. The future may hold for us much of joy or sorrow, much of defeat or success, much of pain or of pleasure, much of usefulness or of apparent idleness. We cannot tell which way our lines may be cast, whether in pleasant places, or in the valley of sorrow; but, whatever may come, whatever of joy or of grief, of success or defeat may await us further on, we shall go bravely forward, trusting and knowing that wisdom rules the destinies of individuals as well as nations. We do not anticipate ill; there is a bright, rosy glow in the east that betokens the dawn; the night has been long, but it is almost past; and we hear, even as we write these lines, the whispered words of encouragement. Faint not, brave workers, for the seed sown in sorrow, ye shall reap in joy; for every sacrifice shall bring reward, and every noble effort shall return an hundredfold of satisfaction and pleasure. Since the beginning, the world has crucified its Saviors, the earth has been red with the blood of its heroes, and the very winds have scattered broadcast the ashes of its martyrs; but a new cycle has begun, and, hence, true worth shall be appreciated, great truths shall be accepted, and the world shall erect not only monuments to the martyrs and saviors of the past, but to those of the living present.

THE PROGRESS OF SPIRITUALISM.

[Extracts from an address given at Scottish Hall, San Francisco, March 31, 1887, before the Society of Progressive Spiritualists.]

It is a time-honored custom among the civilized nations of the earth to celebrate the natal day of noted personages.

Dates of important events of national or general import, political, religious, or otherwise, are also marked as holidays, and their annual return observed with appropriate services and ceremonies, thus perpetuating their remembrance and securing for them the respect and veneration their merits demand. As the Christian era dates from the supposed birth of Christ, the whole Christian world celebrates the twenty-fifth of December with festivities and rejoicing. Even so, in time, will the multitudes of grateful people celebrate the thirty-first day of March as the day upon which was born a new savior and the ushering in of a new dispensation, the dawning of a new day of promise, the discovery of a more brilliant star of hope and peace than the famous star of Bethlehem.

Where to-day a few are gathered to commemorate this golden dawn, in the near future thousands will congregate; and while to day we are grateful for the faintest whisper of the angel loved ones, and cherish every test and token from the other side as a most blessed boon, in the near future will come far more astounding revelations than have yet been dreamed of. There will come such mighty waves of spiritual light and truth breaking upon the shores of the mortal, that the tides of ignorance and error will be beaten back and the glory of the new day fill the whole earth with rejoicing.

Glancing backward over the years that have passed since the first system of intelligent communication between spirits and mortals was established, what changes do we discover! Previous to that time darkness, indeed, brooded over the face of the whole earth. A portion of humanity was endeavoring to feed its famished heart upon the teachings of Christianity which, at best, could offer but faith and hope as a foundation upon which to build a belief in the future life; and when the belief was established it offered no comfort to the believer, for, in the cold, cheerless glitter of the golden-paved New Jerusalem, where all the inhabitants were arrayed in regulation garments of white, and the only occupation was that of singing psalms and waving palms throughout all the cycles of eternity, there was almost as little that was comforting to a wide-awake, active, progressive individual as the contemplation of that other place—the lake of fire and brimstone into which thousands of human beings were irretrievably plunged for eternal torture.

The raps at Hydesville were the death blows to this fallacious doctrine. A new gospel of love, justice, and mercy supplanted the old dogma of a wrathful God and eternal punishment. The voices from the spirit side echoed only songs of gratitude and happiness that there was still another chance for earth's unfortunate children to retrieve their mistakes and commence a new and higher life.

These angel messages spread with lightning rapidity over the whole civilized globe. They were the leaven of truth which shall eventually permeate all systems of religious thought, all forms of government, shaping and molding them so as to give highest expression to all that is noble, godlike, and divine in man. Already has this fact been demonstrated in many ways in our own country within the last thirty-nine years. Since the advent of modern Spiritualism, four millions of human beings have had the shackles of slavery broken, who were being bought and sold as the beasts of the field, and many times treated far more cruelly, and this result was finally brought about by liberty-loving spirits on the other side, who, through a medium, counseled that grand, great-hearted man, Abraham Lincoln, to issue the Emancipation Proclamation. The Czar of Russia, Alexander Second, also freed twenty millions of serfs by request of his spirit father, Nicholas, the First.

Since the first testimony from the spirit world was recorded against the absurd and horrible doctrine of an endless hell, the Christian pulpits, with few exceptions, have caught the glad echoes and are modifying their teachings in harmony therewith. The press also is becoming more liberal, and through all the current literature of to-day there runs a vein of spiritual thought, which, forty years ago, was unheard of. Even the drama has caught the spirit of the times, and upon the stage of the most popular theaters are rehearsed representations of spiritual manifestations. A humanitarian feeling which is the direct result of spirit teaching, has become so largely developed among the thinking classes that it has many times been found almost impossible to secure twelve honest, intelligent men to serve as jurors when crimes have been committed which would seem to justify the death sentence in accordance with the laws of the land. Men are beginning to realize that when a murderer is hanged, his prison doors have been opened and the criminal set free. He is none the less a criminal after death than before, and carries with him into the other life all the feelings of hatred, malice and revenge which were burning in his bosom when he was forced through the gateway of an ignominious death into the spirit world. Spiritualism advocates the reformation of criminals instead of their legalized murder.

In all the departments of life, in every issue involving the highest interests of mankind, the leaven of Spiritualism has entered with its benign and elevating influence. Beginning at the fireside of a humble home, with innocent, guileless children for its evangels, it has spread over the whole world, to peasant's cot and palaces of kings. It has entered halls of learning—courts of justice, orthodox pulpits, legislative assemblies, and left a glimmer of its glistening garments amid the darkness of ignorance, the rubbish of old-time creeds and laws. Spiritualism is universal in its application. It is no respecter of persons, high or low, rich or poor, all come within its encircling arms of love.

God of Wisdom has not opened here and there a few small windows, through which the radiance of celestial spheres may shine upon a favored few, leaving the greater portion of humanity sitting in darkness and doubt, but the golden glory shines alike for all, the only obstruction being the small degree to which the spiritual perceptives have been developed in the masses of mankind. The manifestations of its presence are many and varied. The number of its mediums or channels of expression are countless; all animate and inanimate things are outward embodiments of the spiritual forces of the universe.

To the spiritually awakened consciousness of man, every bursting bud, blooming flower, or blade of grass is a message of love from the great Over-Soul. In every murmur of the breeze, every sobbing wave as it breaks upon the shore, the thunder of the cataract, the roar of the storm, the gentle patter of the rain, is heard the voice of truth—of divinity speaking in no uncertain tones the needed message to the receptive soul.

The guardian angel of each human life knows best when and how to impart the special word of truth when conditions favor and require it. To one who is carefully observant in the realm of cause and effect many wonderful spiritual phenomena will be discovered which would be relegated to the world of chance by the thoughtless and unobserving.

To such an one there is a deeper, a more profound meaning to the most trivial affairs of life, than outward appearances would warrant or indicate. It is not necessary to be a seer—so called, in order to perceive spiritual forces working and shaping the destinies of men and nations in many silent, unseen, yet potential ways. It was but the lifting of the lid of a tea-kettle by the force eliminated from the boiling water within, that revealed to the prepared and receptive mind of Watts something of the powers and possibilities of steam. Some persons would say this was the merest accident—that it just happened so, but looking back of the effect we trace the cause to the guiding, directing intelligence of spiritual beings who had so shaped events that when the opportune moment arrived a new truth could be given to humanity. It was not by chance that Franklin caught the lightning from the clouds, and through that first discovery revealed something of the uses of one of the most mighty forces in nature, of which but little has yet been made available in comparison to the revelations of the future, awaiting the development of some conditions whereby it can be demonstrated to the world. It was no idle dream of Columbus, of a great continent beyond the vast expanse of waters lying before him, but the reflected impression from some mighty angel, who had in charge the destinies of nations under whose guidance he was as a bit of clay in the hands of the potter.

Men are not always conscious of being guided by unseen powers. Many would scout at the very suggestion, yet conscious or not, humanity at large represents only the outward effects of the great invisible world of cause operating upon and through it. That there always have been people who recognized spiritual guidance and direction, history clearly proves. Through all the ages of the past of which mankind has any record, be it either the written testimony of reliable witnesses, or the legendary fragments transmitted verbally from parents to children, through successive generations, history has revealed the fact of spiritual communications having been received by all nations and people on the planet.

In the days of Moses when, it is said, God revealed himself to the Children of Israel, going before them as a cloud by day, and a pillar of fire by night, or when speaking to Moses through the burning bush, or amid the thunders and lightnings of Mount Sinai, the manifestations were suited to the requirements of the people.

A race who had been slaves in Egypt, ignorant and brutalized under the lash of their Egyptian task-masters, were not prepared to receive the beautiful teachings of the Golden Rule. They could comprehend a communication commanding them to exact "an eye for an eye, and a tooth for a tooth," while the sermon upon the Mount would have been wholly unintelligible and practically impossible to such crude natures as theirs. Wherever and whenever an attempt has been made to impart spiritual or scientific truths to mankind in advance of the enlightenment of the people sufficient to comprehend such truths, the instruments through whom they have been given have been made the objects of scorn, ridicule, persecution, and, in many instances, they have been put to death by the most cruel tortures. We who live in an age and country where freedom of speech is accorded unto all can scarcely conceive of the amount of moral courage required in the man or woman who, in defiance of established opinions and laws, would face the consequences and give to the world some message of truth before the world was prepared to receive it. Yet, notwithstanding all this apparent lack of receptivity on the part of mortals, there have always been some souls to whom new truths were acceptable, who have waited and longed for their coming, and were the chosen evangels to proclaim them to the world.

These have been the illuminated ones —the messiahs of every new dispensation—the great teachers, who have been as watch-towers along the shores of time shedding light across the dark waste of waters, where many poor, shipwrecked mortals have found the harbor of safety —the shores of the promised land. At the present time, not a few but many are receiving spiritual illumination. The whole civilized world is bathed in the radiance reflected from immortal spheres. True, there are those still, who, having eyes see not the grandeur and beauty, and having ears hear not the immortal symphonies of the spiritual universe around and about them, awaiting only the quickened perceptions to feast the souls of humanity with its divine realities. The voice of the spirit speaks to all, varying only in outward methods of demonstration. To the devotee at the shrine of St. Peter's it speaks through the outward symbols of the Holy Virgin, the Madonna and Child, the crucifix with its murdered Christ, the apostles, saints, and martyrs. The Buddhist hears its whispers in his sacred groves and temples—in the seclusion of caves and convents, where endurance rather than action is the highest morality whereby Sansara is to be outgrown and the beatific franchisement of Nirvana attained. It speaks in audible voice to

"The poor Indian whose untutored mind,
 Sees God in clouds and hears him in
    the wind,"

and although his conception of the Great Spirit may not harmonize with the prevailing idea of an orthodox God or Jewish Jehovah yet, may it not be possible as much of truth has been revealed concerning one as the other.

It has been reserved for the spiritual man and woman of the present to obtain clearer views, more perfect knowledge, loftier ideals and conceptions of life, physical and spiritual, than those of any preceding age. The invisible world is daily becoming more visible and real, and its divine harmonies are vibrating through every sympathetic heart-throb of those whose souls are attuned to its receptivity.

In the daily experience of every individual come little things, unimportant in themselves, but freighted, many times,

with much of weal or wo to one or many. The spirits voice their messages in various and often peculiar ways. It may be a careless word spoken without thought or meaning by some friend and yet prove a message to you sufficient to change the whole current of your life. It may be a song or a strain of music from some grand organ that spoke to you more then anthem or sermon because it voiced the guardian angel's message in a language you could understand and interpret. The Christian does not go to church every time he wishes to pray, but lifts his voice in prayer at his own fireside, or in the solitude of field or grove, when silent or alone his thoughts go out in supplication to the God whom he believes is everywhere present. So the true Spiritualist need not always enter the séance-room in order to commune with the angel loved ones. To those who are investigating, who stand upon the threshold of the open door of knowledge, the séance-room is the school-room where the alphabet is mastered. It is the iniatory chamber where the facts of spiritual existence and communion are demonstrated, and the first positive evidence gained of the great unknown lying out and beyond, where the earnest seeker after truth finds unlimited fields of observation and research ever broadening and expanding before him as his eager feet traverse their devious paths. To remain lingering in the school-room forever would be as unbecoming the progressive Spiritualist as for the student who wished to master the higher mathematics to confine his studies to the first pages of addition and subtraction.

Spiritualism teaches continuous progressive unfoldment. It does not say to the aspiring mind—"be content,—remain where you are"; but it says, onward and upward forever.

Let it suffice for the earth-worm to grovel in the dust; but man—immortal man, may build his home among the stars.

To-day you behold the harvest of the last thirty-nine years; and as you gather in the golden sheaves you are also sowing seed for future harvests.

To-day holds the fulfilment of the promise of yesterday, and is the prophecy of to-morrow; and judging from its manifold victories, its blessings and triumphs, its achievement in the fields of spiritual and scientific research, its greater light and knowledge of the heretofore mysterious and incomprehensible country to which our loved ones departed when the awful silence of death fell upon them— what may we not hope and expect of to-morrow? Already do we feel the ecstasies of the coming day throbbing and beating in the bosom of the present. As the mother feels the quickening of the embryo life that is to become the god-like man of the future, so is the present hour pregnant with the unrevealed and hidden glory awaiting the fulness of time to gladden the hearts of all humanity, and fill the whole earth with its ineffable splendor.

The gates which were just ajar thirty-nine years ago, are now wide open, and coming and going upon the golden stairway, are the whitely shining feet of angels bearing their messages of love to men. Listening, we can hear the sweet songs of gladness,—looking, we can behold their radiant faces beaming with love and tenderness upon us, and recognize among the happy throng, the darlings of our hearts and homes; who have only gone before us, leaving the door unclosed behind them, through which our longing eyes can follow them until they rest upon the flower-decked borders, the evergreen mountains, the silver seas, beautiful islands, glowing, love-lit skies of the glorious summer land.

SPIRIT MINISTRATION.

In our hours of deepest wo, when the sunlight seems to have faded, and the stars of hope forever set; when darkness without and heaviness of spirit within fold their mantles of gloom about us, then comes the blessedness of spirit ministration and spirit communion. Then, although we may be treading the wine-press of sorrow alone, though human love and sympathy seem afar off, the bright, the beautiful, the loved ones draw near unto us and pour into our wounded hearts the balm of their tender and devoted love, then come the faithful and true, the noble, unselfish ones, who, knowing our griefs, our trials, and temptations, gently fold us in their arms of love and whisper words of hope and trust, of encouragement and sympathy. After such baptisms of angelic ministry, we emerge from our Garden of Gethsemane strengthened, uplifted, purified, and blest. The sun again shines, the stars beam on us lovingly; friends once estranged seem nearer and dearer than before; our own hallowed experiences having drawn us nearer to them and they to us, until we wonder that a thought of coldness or unkindness could have crept in and opened a gulf between ourselves and our friends.

Let us ever welcome these angelic visitors who came to us with blessings manifold; without them life's burdens were too grievous to be borne; its paths too rough for our untried feet; its friendships too false and fickle; its joys evanescent; its gloom impenetrable, and its climax—death—an unsolved mystery, a grim and horrible specter ever haunting our dreams, and blighting the fairest hope buds on the tree of human life.

THE WORLD'S NEED.

The world needs men and women
　Willing to do and dare;
True souls who never falter,
　Or shrink at pain or care.
It needs the wise and loving
　To lead the faint and weak;
To help uplift the fallen,
　And words of comfort speak.

Willing for truth to suffer
　And patiently endure,
In every thought and action
　Be just and true and pure;
Whose lives of perfect sweetness,
　Like melody of song,
Shall charm the world to goodness,
　And change to right the wrong.

Lo! the glad time is coming,
　By prophets long foretold,
When men for love shall labor,
　And not, as now, for gold;
When all with one grand effort
　Shall work for human good,
And nations be united
　In one great brotherhood.

Then darkness, which now hovers
　All over the fair land,
Shall scatter as the sunshine
　Of Truth's bright beams expand.
Oh, workers, be brave-hearted,
　And struggle for the right;
At last you'll be victorious
　And right shall conquer might.

OUR BRAVE WORKERS.

If there is one virtue to be cherished above another—one sentiment most worthy of cultivation and expression, it is that of grateful appreciation and recognition of noble, unselfish work for others' good. In times of peril and war, when heroes are wanted—brave, noble souls who will sacrifice home, friends, yea, even life itself, for the protection and safety of others, then does this feeling of gratitude find largest expression. Then the multitudes crown, the heroes with laurel wreaths, while titles of honor and positions of trust are awarded them. The victorious general who has led armies to battle and conquest receives the nation's gratitude; wherever he goes cities are decorated in his honor, and his journey from State to State witnesses one grand ovation, the tribute of the grateful multitudes to whom he has been a benefactor; and for the heroes who fall, a nation's tears are shed. She erects monuments to their memory, and immortalizes them in the pages of history. Each year when the springtime brings its wealth of fragrant blossoms, she sends her sons and daughters laden with tributes of love and remembrance to strew their graves with flowers, and recalls to mind their valorous deeds in glowing words, in poetry and song.

This is well; but we say unto you, there are other wars waged than those of national conflict; there are other battles fought than those with sword and gun; there are other heroes deserving the full meed of praise than the victorious generals; there are other martyrs who perish for the sacred cause of human liberty than those who fall amid the roar of cannon, the rattle of musketry, and the shouts of frenzied men upon fields of carnage and death. This other conflict now being waged is between the opposing forces of Truth and Error. The weapons used are not those of carnal warfare. The soldiers fighting under Truth's banner use the "sword of the spirit," which is kind, loving, helpful words, noble deeds, and pure, unselfish lives. These are far more effectual in demolishing the old walls of superstitious strongholds than all the armaments of the world combined.

Their battle cry is also Freedom! but it is set to the sweet music of peace on earth, good-will to men. Their enemies are the mighty hosts of Error, whose weapons are pride, lust, intemperance, greed of gain, tyranny, and injustice, old-time creeds, dogmas, and superstitions from which have sprung the multitudinous wrongs we are called upon to combat on every hand.

In this warfare are also struggles with self, for the overcoming of inherited or acquired passions and propensities, which, if left unrestrained, would run riot like swine in a beautiful garden, destroying individual usefulness, and with it all the sweet hopes and promises of a grand and noble manhood and womanhood, blighting the lives of dearly loved ones as surely as the hot breath of the simoon would poison and blight the tender buds and flowers; and the heroes are they that overcome; they who, alone and single-handed, have battled and conquered, when no eyes but those of the ever-present angels have witnessed the conflict; when no ears have heard their prayers for aid and strength save the ever-listening ones of faithful spirit guardians, who are always ready to reach out snowy hands of helpfulness, and whisper words of hope and encouragement in such hours of struggle with the forces of evil. Though no laurel chaplets crown the brows of these victors, though the adulation of the multitude should never be their reward, yet there is an inner peace which passeth understanding, a consciousness of affiliation and companionship with angels, which surpasses all outward demonstrations of appreciation by men, as the full effulgence of the noonday sun surpasses the first faint gleams of morning. They stand upon heights the multitude can not perceive, victorious, self-crowned, royal men and women, who, knowing their own struggles, have great, compassionate hearts, full of tender pity and sympathy for their weaker brothers and sisters, who, when beset with like temptations, have fallen in the conflict, weak, helpless victims of their appetites and lusts. There are generals who are bravely striving to marshal their forces and aid those on the spirit side in their efforts to bless and elevate the denizens of earth. They are to be found wherever work for humanity is to be done. They are the leaders in all reforms—the pioneers in the cause of universal liberty; they are the heralds on the mountain-tops proclaiming the birth of a new day; they are the organizers, directors and administrators of all public efforts for the advancement and spiritualization of mankind; they are the torch-bearers whose light is scientific truth, which reveals to mankind his right relations to material and spiritual things.

IMMORAL PLAYS.

A great deal is said about immoral books and their baneful influence upon the youth of the land; but, disastrous as is the reading of pernicious literature, it is no more evil in its effects than is the witnessing, upon the boards of a theater, of an immoral play. By immoral we do not mean lewd or vulgar, as such plays are never seen in a respectable theater; but we mean those plays wherein the vicious, cruel, and devilish aspects of human nature are presented in all their hideousness; where theft, murder, and other crimes are portrayed with life-like fidelity. Not long since the writer witnessed a play of this sort, the blood-curdling scenes of which were truly horrible. In one act an old man—a miser—commits a murder; his victim is choked to death with a handkerchief, and the terrible death-struggle — the death-rattle in the victim's throat—the old man gloating over the corpse—all presented a scene so ghastly and sickening as to cause a thrill of horror in the beholder. In the same play other terrible crimes are portrayed; the finale being the death by suicide of one of the villains.

The result was depressing in the extreme; and the thought came what must be the effects of witnessing such plays upon a delicate, sensitive, pregnant woman? Surely the mental picture engraved upon the impressible mother's mind must result disastrously upon the embryo child. It is well known that a momentary fright or sight of some repulsive object will leave an indelible impression upon the unborn babe, thus sometimes disfigured for life. Is it not probable that the impress of some horrible crime thus stamped upon the unborn, may, in years to come, yield the fruit of murder? How can a prospective mother, cognizant of the laws governing pre-natal life, dare to witness such a play? We do not understand the public sentiment that approves of such representations upon the stage and furnishes crowded houses nightly to witness the shocking spectacle. Much more good and much less evil would result if our theaters would present the better side of human nature—portraying noble deeds, and thus stimulating the people to imitate the good, the pure, and the beautiful.

DEDICATED TO J. V. M.

I see a man with silvery hair,
  A noble, thoughtful brow!
A face well marked by time and care,
  A worker even now
When age should bring repose and peace,
And from life's busy cares release.

Thou hast a form from Nature's mold,
  Perfect and full of grace,
Wherein the spirit ne'er grows old
  And time can leave no trace
Upon that inner self of thine,
  Approximating the divine.

For thou hast passed through many a change
  And many a life hast lived,
To give the soul that broad, free range,
  Which only is achieved
Through various phases of earth-life—
  Love, hatred, envy, peace and strife.

And though I may not trace them all,
  This much now comes to me;
The Spririt's growth through rise and fall,
  Repeated oft in thee;
By peasant's garb and kingly crown,
Progression of the soul is shown.

I see thee first robed as a priest,
  Lighting the altar fires;
Then joining in the solemn feast,
  With holy, pure desires
To rise above the rabble rude,
Whose lives and thoughts are low and crude.

A slave thou toilest with the meek,
  Beneath the Master's lash,
Content no higher good to seek
  Than to perform thy task;
Feeling thy greatest earthly gain
Was food and shelter to obtain.

A warrior brave thou goest forth,
  Unmindful of the cost;
Regarding life as little worth
  When liberty is lost;
Preferring death upon thy sword
Than such a life thy soul abhorred.

Again a nobleman art thou,
  Of station, wealth and rank,
To whom the multitude doth bow,
  Whose health is often drank
By those who emulate thy fame,
Thy noble qualities and name.

A teacher, thou, of ancient lore
  In Egypt's palmiest days,
When nations gave her of their store
  And poets sung her praise;
When the proud Ptolemies ruled the land
With selfish and unsparing hand.

Upon the low banks of the Nile,
  Where the sand waves stretched away,
Thou often didst the hours beguile
  Of the warm, slumbrous day,
With softly sweet, enchanting lays
In Isis and Osiris' praise.

From out those lives of joy and pain,
  Thy soul of priceless worth
Reincarnated once again
  Hast come to bless the earth,
To teach mankind of angel lore,
From thy full treasure-house and store.

The faith that raises man above
  This world of petty cares,
And fills all human hearts with love,
  And heeds the humblest prayer,
Of those who plead with streaming eyes
For one faint gleam from Paradise.—

This thou wert sent to prove and teach,
  That all may surely know
That arms of loving angels reach
  And shelter all below—
That none are lost to heaven's call,
For God's great love is over all.

PRACTICAL SPIRITUALISM.

[Address given before the Spiritualists of San Jose.]

The world needs men and women willing
to do and dare—
Brave souls who never falter or shrink at
pain or care.
It needs the wise and loving, to lead the
faint and weak,
To help uplift the fallen and words of
comfort speak.
Willing for Truth to suffer and patiently
endure;
In every thought and action to be just,
and true, and pure;
Whose lives of perfect sweetness, like the
melody of song
Shall charm the world to goodness and
change to right the wrong.

It is the mission of Spiritualism to revolutionize the world; to sweep away the
accumulated rubbish of centuries of ignorance and superstition. It has come into
the world as a light-bearer to those who
sit in the midst of darkness and desolation,
revealing unto them "a new heaven and
a new earth wherein dwelleth righteousness." It has come in answer to the
earnest, intense longing of human hearts
everywhere, and has shown that there is a
higher and diviner life within the reach
of all; that none are so unfortunately cir-
cumstanced—not even the lowest and
most degraded of all humanity—but that
there is within each a spark of divinity
which shall ultimately triumph over all
untoward environments, and bring forth
from the crude and chrysalis condition
the perfect man, the aspiring and ascending angel. It has come as a messenger
of light and gladness to the bereaved and
desolate, who, like Rachel of old, are
mourning for their loved ones and refuse
to be comforted because they are not. It
has rolled away the stone from the sepul-
chers, and has said unto the mourning,
"Behold! your beloved ones have
arisen." With the light of eternal truth
it has demonstrated the existence of the
spiritual world of life and beauty lying
all around you, awaiting the coming of
this angel to give you spiritual sight and
hearing, that you may perceive its divine
harmonies. It has made plain the way
which has been shrouded in darkness and
beset with demons of theological inven-
tion apparently ready at every juncture
to pounce upon the unwary and hurl them
into the pit of perdition. It has removed
these terrors and opened to your enraptured vision a flower-strewn highway
leading through verdant fields, shady
groves and pleasant meadows, beside
murmuring fountains and still waters,
where singing birds and laughing, happy
children make melodious the air, and
love's eternal sunshine brightens and
beautifies the enchanting way.

Spiritualism has done all this for humanity, and still there are those who
grope along blindly, in darkness and
sorrow, while all around them lies this
world of surpassing beauty and ineffable
splendor. Why is this? Is Spiritualism
at fault? Are the ministering spirits who
are sent to carry "glad tidings of great
joy" remiss in deeds of tenderness and
love? Or do you, through lack of earnest
endeavor, fail to attain to this state of
blessedness and peace? You see, in your
daily life, no shining highways, but in
their stead your feet press thorny paths.
You see no sparkling fountains, but are
fainting by the wayside with the toil and
heat of the day. You hear no sweet
music, but sighs and moans from an
overburdened people everywhere greet
your ear. Error is sitting in high places,
clothed in the royal vestments of power,
while truth—sweet, loving, beautiful
truth—goes naked through the world.
Greed and avarice are piling up their
shining millions, while honor and virtue
are starving in cellars and attics. Vice
and idleness are arrayed in fine linen and
purple, faring sumptuously every day,
while honest labor is clothed in rags, and

goes begging for its just dues. The debauchee, who glories in the spoilation of innocence and virtue, is pampered and petted, feasted and praised, while his helpless and hapless victim is doomed to a life of shame and digrace. But why enumerate the woes and miseries—the wrongs and abuses of mankind—unless, by so doing, the masses can be aroused to a realization of their condition, and incited to adopt methods of reform? No reformation can ever come except by persistent, untiring, individual effort. Each should feel the importance of individual responsibility. Endeavor to feel that upon you alone depends this work of reformation; and begin at once to labor in that direction. Do not commence with your neighbors, but with yourselves. See to it that your own life is pure, that your motives are unselfish, that your souls are full of love and charity for all humanity. Never lose an opportunity of saying a kind word, or reaching out a helping hand to any unfortunate struggling in the depths of despair, even though his own wrong doing may have been the cause of his desolation and distress. If you aspire to reach a condition of angelhood by and by, strive now to imitate those messengers of love and mercy whose arms are ever extended unto the helpless and abandoned in tenderest sympathy—the whiteness of whose celestial raiment is never dimmed, but shines with radiant glory in the hovel of the wretched and dying, where the feet of human charity do not tread, and where human sympathy does not reach.

Spiritualists, like many of their orthodox brethren, are too much inclined to expatiate upon the glories and beauties of a far-away Summer Land, and refer lovingly to the dear angel friends who are waiting "over there" to greet them when the labors of this life are ended. They do not seem to realize that the Summer Land is here and now, and that the dear spirits who most need their tender love and care, are those who are still dwelling in physical forms with little of human sympathy, and in want of

homes, food, clothing, and such earthly environments as will best develop angelic attributes. While we would not detract from the tenderness which clusters around the memories of the dear departed, yet we would have you remember that they are beyond the need of material assistance, and while you love and remember them none the less tenderly, we would have you pay tribute to their memory, not by erecting costly monuments of granite and marble, but through your ministry of love to the living. Here is a great field of labor for the earnest worker who desires to put into practise the lessons of love and wisdom it has been the mission of Spiritualism to teach; for only so far as the teachings of any system can be made of practical use in the amelioration of the distress and woes of life are they of value to humanity. In this direction Spiritualism offers incentives to noble effort far surpassing those of any other system or religion yet presented to the world. It offers no vicarious atonement for sin through the death of an innocent person. It teaches that good works are the only sure passport to a life of peace and happiness beyond the gates of death; that the only sure way of becoming an angel in the future is by beginning to be one now, by cultivating in yourself all those attributes you have been accustomed to call divine. Be honest and true with one another, avoiding all hypocrisy and deceit, remembering the time is not far distant when you shall be known by all as you are now known by the ever-present angels who encompass you as a cloud of witnesses. You may be able to deceive one another now—to cover up your misdeeds with a mantle of hypocrisy, to live a lie daily, and to all outward appearances remain undiscovered; but remember there comes a time when you will stand in your true light, the masks will drop off and concealment be no longer possible, and you shall be known for just what you are, not, as here, for what you seem to be. That hour of humiliation is well depicted in the Scripture account of the Day of

Judgment, when evil-doers shall cry unto the rocks and mountains to fall upon them and hide them from the face of the great Judge of the Universe. Your judge will be a quickened and illuminated conscience—a vivid memory of past misdeeds, with all their painful consequences. From this judge there will be no escape—no commutation of sentence. Then will you have to begin doing the things which should be done now. The great work of reformation and purification of self will then be entered upon and consummated through your labors to help and bless others. By lifting up the fallen yourself shall rise; by comforting others you shall be comforted; by blessing others you shall be blest; and by laboring in every available channel to elevate and spiritualize your fellow-men shall you be elevated and spiritualized. There is no royal road to happiness over flowery beds of ease, but work, earnest, helpful, noble work for other's good.

"But," says one, "what can I do? There is no use of one struggling alone to reform the world?" Divine Omnipotence does not place this responsibility upon any one individual; but each and all are called by the Voice of Truth to do their part wisely and well. Meet together and discuss ways and means of usefulness. There is work enough for all, and if entered upon in a thorough, systematic manner, you will be astonished at the results. Let a handful of earnest, devoted persons decide upon some special work, and enter into it with all the zeal and earnestness that comes from a lofty inspiration—a divine purpose—and there is no possibility of failure. Like casting a pebble into the brook, the circle upon the surface grows wider and wider. You cannot estimate the extent of your usefulness by the apparent temporary results. The good seeds sown may not at once germinate and bloom, but by and by, when the gentle rain of sorrow shall have watered, and the sunshine of love warmed and revivified them, they will spring into beauteous life, the blossom and fruitage

of which shall be as manna from heaven unto the starving souls of men. Many capable, willing persons need only to have the work mapped out for them, and gladly will they enter into it. All are not capable of taking the initiatory steps in enterprises involving grave responsibilities, but there are those who are born leaders, who can successfully plan gigantic reforms, and, with the assistance of their fellows, inaugurate and execute them, while single-handed and alone they would prove as useless and inefficient as the weakest one among you. Therefore, harmonious cooperation is the only way of meeting and combating the existing wrongs of society with any assurance of success.

The churches expend vast sums of money sending missionaries to heathen countries to preach that which, in the light of Spiritualism, is in great part error. Cannot Spiritualists make an effort to send out missionaries also, not to heathen countries, but to people in their midst who are starving for the bread of life, which they alone can give? Let a few, who are thoroughly imbued with the importance of such a movement, form a nucleus, and around this will soon be gathered a powerful band of both seen and unseen workers who will systematize a plan of operation, whereby speakers and mediums can be sent in all directions, under the auspices of the parent society, for the purpose of teaching the philosophy and demonstrating through the phenomena this beautiful truth, so dear to every true Spiritualist, and organizing minor societies in every section of the Pacific Coast.

Let this Pacific Coast Missionary Society be independent of any local associations or interests. Let it be general in its ministrations, and let it continue its work until, from its northern to its southern extremity, this beautiful Coast shall be alive with spiritual truth, leavening the whole social, political, and religious body with its divine humanitarian inspirations. Let your missionaries be selected according to their fitness for the duties assigned them. Lay aside all individual preferences, and let true merit be the highest credential required. Send them out under the auspices and pay of the parent association, that they may labor wholly and unreservedly for the general good, and not for the selfish purpose of gain. Let your commendations and preferences be for those who are most untiringly and unselfishly devoted to the promotion of the cause whose chosen representatives they are. Should this suggestion be acted upon, it would give a great impetus to the cause, which, in many places, now languishes for the assistance which could thus be rendered. Every person having even one talent could be made available, and many of your needy mediums could be usefully and remuneratively employed in a work, the grandeur of which time alone can reveal. The greatest obstacle to the rapid advancement of Spiritualism is the lack of thorough, systematic organization. United you will stand, divided you will fall, or, at least, fall short of the accomplishment of the greater good a combination of forces would effect.

Some objectors claim that organization would have a retrograde tendency—that Spiritualists would fossilize and their associations degenerate into creed-bound bodies. This supposition, from a spiritual standpoint, is fallacious. True Spiritualism can have but one creed, and that is unrestricted liberty of opinion for all. There is no fossilization possible in that—on the contrary, it assumes a steady onward and upward march toward the perfection of Spiritual growth and attainment. Not only have all religious bodies recognized organization as a vital step, but in all the various departments of life it is a recognized necessity for the accomplishment of any desirable end. The working men and women of this country have discovered this effective weapon of power, and are forming leagues and unions for the purpose of self-defense against the encroachments and tyrannies of capitalists. The

future will reveal the wisdom of this course, for thereby will the differences between capital and labor be adjusted by peaceful arbitration, and the lava-tide of rapine, murder, and war, which for a time threatened the life of the republic, will be averted. Every throne in Europe stands upon a foundation of straw, and ultimately the tempests that are agitating the great sea of humanity will sweep over them, and wash into the ocean of oblivion the last vestige of human tyranny and oppression. Then will the new republic arise from the ruins of old monarchies, clothed with majesty and power, representing the rights and interests of every human being alike, black and white, red and yellow, male and female. Then will the goddess of liberty no longer be a hollow mockery to one-half the human family, and that the half she now so unjustly symbolizes, but with universal liberty for her watchword, the new republic shall welcome to her counsels the fathers and mothers of the nation, and together they will legislate wisely and well, bringing into requisition woman's love and tenderness, her deep spirituality and clear intuition, combined with man's larger experience, his courage, skill, and intellectual greatness. The machinery of government will be adjusted to meet the requirements of all the great variety of peoples and conditions, and administer justice to all.

Spiritualism does not ask its votaries to build magnificent temples wherein to worship, for the spirit of truth is everywhere present, and can come to you in the humblest home, or in the open fields, with only the canopy of heaven above you and the green earth beneath your feet. It only asks you to build the temples of love and charity in your own hearts, that the spirit of peace which passeth understanding, may come in and abide with you. Open wide the windows of these temples that the angels may come and go, bringing and leaving their beneficent gifts, which you in turn shall dispense to others, for in the giving of truth shall you be abundantly blessed. We would impress upon you the importance of earnestness of purpose. Do not undertake anything until you are fully and deeply imbued with its importance, then bring into the work all the energies of soul of which you are possessed. Have faith in yourselves and in the ultimate success of your labors, and rest assured the word failure will never be written on your brow. If men and women could only be made to believe in themselves, to realize the grand, god-like powers lying dormant within them—realize that all things are possible to the truly awakened and illuminated soul—they would rise above all the lower elements of their material surroundings and become as gods and goddesses in strength and wisdom. They would hold the elements of the material universe in their grasp, and all would be subject to their will. They have been told they were but poor weak worms of the dust, totally depraved, until it is a wonder there is even as much true nobility in the world as there is. Strive to outgrow and forget the errors of the past; strive to have more faith in the saving power of truth, honor and goodness, than in any personal savior.

Spiritualism teaches that eternal progression is the destiny of all, and those who can realize the full meaning of this will find it a great assistance in every relation of life to be just and charitable to every one. Remember, that person who has spoken unkindly of you, who has tried in various ways to injure you, and for whom you feel such an aversion, is destined sometime to become a bright and shining angel. Can you then afford to hate that beautiful one so full of love, tenderness, and purity, the angel that is to be? Would you not rather through your kindness and gentleness, through your forgiving helpfulness, assist that person to begin the divine life now—to begin now to retrace false steps and eradicate erroneous opinions?

If all men could become imbued with this fundamental principle of Spiritualism—universal brotherhood—a great advance step would be taken in the reformation of the world, for then no one would wish to meet his brother on the field of battle. Human life would then be held in greater reverence, and the millions of treasure now expended in human butchery would be used to make more beautiful and attractive this world in which you live. There would be but one army, and that would indeed be the grand army of the great, universal Republic, whose watchwords would be freedom, equality, fraternity. Reunions of that grand army would bring no sad memories of dark days of carnage, no heart-rending partings with loved ones, when the clinging grasp of little darlings, the agonized farewells of wife, sister, mother, daughter, filled the air with pain, as they kissed perhaps for the last time, the dear ones departing to slay or be slain. There would come no tearful memories of far-off graves beneath sunny, Southern skies, no recollections of horrible prisons, where starvation with all its untold agonies was the warden that opened at last the prison doors to many a brave boy in blue, and revealed to him the glories and beauties of the immortal Kingdom, where the nations of the earth learn war no more. Instead of a dark picture of sorrow would come a bright vision of gladness, wherein would be preserved the memory of noble deeds of love, tenderness, and mercy, whose radiance makes life bright and beautiful.

When universal brotherhood is recognized in your political world what a revolution will have been wrought. Instead of the poverty, crime, and inequality, the gross injustice and corruption of laws and law makers, justice will sit enthroned the empress of the world. The schemer, who now by tricks of trade called legitimate business, defrauds the laborer of the product of his toil, will then find it impossible to amass millions of dollars, while an honest man may toil a lifetime for a bare subsistence. Jefferson said: "Taxation without representation is tyranny." When justice rules, you will not see this vital principle, upon which the foundation of your government rests, ignored by your legislators. This principle is now applied only to the male portion of the common-wealth, while the females, who, in many instances, own property, the direct fruit of their own labor, are taxed and allowed no voice in the matter whatever.

Woman should ever love and bless Spiritualism, for it has done more toward breaking down the barriers of sex and opening wider fields of usefulness and freedom for her, than any other "ism" the world has ever known. The wheels of progress will never cease turning until equality shall exist, not in name only, but in all the outward manifestations, social, religious, and political. If Spiritualism cannot inaugurate this reform for humanity—if it cannot set free the captives—if it cannot uplift the downtrodden, and revolutionize and Spiritualize all stratas of society—then are all the ministrations of the angel world useless, and all the beautiful sermons delivered from spiritual platforms but vain and empty words. If you cannot bring it into your daily lives as a divine, living reality, and practise its beautiful teachings, then are you, indeed, no better than those who for eighteen hundred years have preached "peace on earth, good will to men," and have practised with the sword. Now the time has come when the sword of the spirit, which is love, mercy, gentleness, charity, long-suffering, patience, and forbearance with one another, must prevail; now must the old yet new commandment "that ye love one another," be practised. If the Millenial day, so long foretold by the prophets, poets, and seers, ever dawns upon the earth, it will come as a result of obedience to this command, and by the daily application of the golden rule. In the light of this elevating philosophy we find a remedy for all the inharmonious and discordant elements of life.

Spiritual light and truth work from within outward; and for every manifestation of inharmony we must seek the cause in the realm of causation, not in the world of effects. We must look into the spiritual condition of the individual for the seat of the outward demonstration; and, rest assured, if the world seems to you a dark and dreary wilderness, with no sunny, peaceful glades and still waters, it is because the unrest is within—the darkness is of your own spiritual state and does not in reality exist in the world of loveliness around you. If you are disconsolate and unhappy; if you miss the brightness of love and the tenderness of affection; if you fail to find truth and goodness, virtue and happiness, then look within for the cause. Go down deep into the recesses of your own soul, and there you will find the discordant note—there you will find the instrument which is out of tune, producing all these inharmonies which so mar your peace and enjoyment. Harmonize yourself and you will be astonished at the divine melodies of life, at the goodness and virtue of your fellow-men. When you have done this—when you place yourself in a state of passive receptivity to beneficent influences—you will feel a divine afflatus lifting you into a state of mental ecstasy you never before dreamed of. You will find yourselves living in two worlds at a time, the world of spiritual love, light, and beauty, and the material world of work and duty, which is made sacred and holy by being blended and united with the higher sphere enveloping it. That it is possible to attain to this state of blessedness and peace is well known, for there are those in your midst who have realized it. There are those who, while living in the flesh, are not of it, in the sense you are accustomed to regard life physical. They live and move in the vestibule of celestial habitations; they consort with angels, and when their earthly vestments fall away, and their earthly tabernacles are dismantled—when the Grand Master confers the next degree—they will be prepared to go up higher, and still higher, through the great grand lodge of heaven, until the height of perfection is attained.

HOW THE ANGELS COME.

Softly, silently, tenderly, lovingly,
  Glide they in heart and in home;
Bearing sweet messages whispered so gently—
  'Tis thus, that the dear angels come.

Guiding and guarding, entreating and saving
  Loved ones who in danger might roam;
With beautiful blossoms each weary path
    paving—
  'Tis thus, that the dear angels come.

Comforting mourners, healing heart-broken,
  Forgetting or slighting not one;
Bringing to each some fond treasured token—
  'Tis thus, that the dear angels come.

Whispering of hope unto souls that are griev-
    ing
  For dearly loved ones they deem gone;
Telling of joys beyond mortal conceiving—
  'Tis thus, that the dear angels come.

Hovering over the sufferer's pillow,
  Into the death-shadowed home;
Bearing your darlings safe o'er the dark
    billow—
  'Tis thus, that the dear angels come.

Joyfully greeting the newly-born Spirit,
  Bidding it sweet " welcome home "
Into the mansions that all will inherit—
  'Tis thus, that the dear angels come.

COOPERATION.

How little mortals understand the value or meaning of cooperation in its broad humanitarian significance. Some spiritually illuminated minds have come into the sphere of intelligence where they could receive impressions from the master minds in spirit life, who are working through every available channel to introduce this system among mortals. They have witnessed the struggles and defeats, the want, wo, and misery attending the competitive system in vogue at this time, and have seen with pain and sorrow its disastrous effects upon the human race. Instead of the universal brotherhood of man, they behold the universal spirit of greed and avarice prevailing, which stimulates the stronger to overreach and destroy the weaker. They see giant monopolies of wealth and power filling the coffers of the rich to overflowing, enabling them to build palace homes, where, surrounded with luxury, and surfeited with the sensuous pleasures of life, the idle inmates riot in extravagances, while those who have been defeated in this struggle for wealth—the toilers, by whose sweat and very life blood these gigantic fortunes have been amassed, are living in poverty and degradation, their meager pittance from day to day being scarcely sufficient to keep gaunt hunger from the door, or to protect the weak and helpless from the fury of the storm.

Every day the lines are being closer drawn, and the gulf between the rich and poor is growing deeper and broader. Aristocracy founded upon wealth is rearing its hydra-head in the bosom of our great Republic. Striving to ape the titled aristocrats of Europe, who have inherited colossal fortunes from their robber ancestors, whose motto "might makes right" still prevails, the people of America are rapidly drifting into the errors of their European forefathers, and may not discover their mistake until, fired with the love of liberty, and burning with indignation under the wrongs inflicted by their money-masters, the spirit of revolution will become aroused, and what has been denied by peaceful asking will be taken by force of arms.

In order to avert the impending crisis, which is slowly but surely approaching, there is one remedy—cooperation. Let the rich put in their capital — gold — against the laborer's capital—muscle— and each endeavor to aid the other; in fact, let a spirit of humanity and brotherhood prevail, and soon the dangers which now threaten will be avoided, and peace and plenty smile upon our land.

Then will the wail of the widows and orphans cease; the cry of hunger and distress no longer be heard; our cities will contain no squalid pestilence-breeding quarters where sin, shame, and crime riot in their own degradation. Instead of vast tracts of land being kept waste and idle in the hands of crafty speculators, there will be thousands of homes, cultivated farms, orchards, and vineyards, whose golden grains and luscious fruits will feast and gladden those long used to meager fare of coarsest food.

Going through our cities, the painful sights of the decrepit old beggar, the pinched, pale features of ragged, destitute children, the brazen, dissolute faces of wantons peering from their dingy casements, and inviting to their iniquitous dens the innocent youth as well as the grey-haired man, the discordant revels of besotted, drunken creatures, from whose bleared eyes and bloated faces almost every trace of manhood has departed, all these unpleasant sights and sounds will be seen and heard no more, for the causes which produce such deplorable conditions will have been done away with under the new orderly system of true fraternity, based upon cooperation and mutual helpfulness, instead of the soul and body destroying system of competition.

TREASURES IN HEAVEN.

"Naked came man into the world and naked goeth he forth." Gold bags, bonds, stocks, and palace homes—all have to be left behind when the rich man launches his lonely barque upon the unknown sea of death. He enters the other life as the pauper's babe enters this. His treasures were all laid up on earth and he is a penniless tramp over there. The few good deeds, the few charities bestowed, weigh but little in the scales against what might have been done.

Charity that takes nothing needed from the giver is not charity but selfishness. It is parting with something that cannot be used and getting in return the undeserved title of a public benefactor and great philanthropist. It is little credit to a man who has lived in luxury and ease and accumulated millions from the toil of others, when he finds himself nearing the grave to give back a small portion of what he cannot take along, to some public charity. Such giving does not count much as " treasures in heaven." It is as worthless as counterfeit coin, and will not pass in the business circles of the New Jerusalem.

NONA.

A happy, joyous little sprite,
With rosy cheeks and eyes so bright,
Coming with love's own blessed light,
 Is precious Nona.

So full of mirthfulness and glee
Like singing bird, bright, glad and free,
As busy as the honey bee
 Is darling Nona.

She comes with gentle loving power
To soothe us when the storm-clouds lower;
She changes storm to springtime shower
 Dear spirit Nona.

Her mission is to cheer and bless,
And comfort those in deep distress
With words of love and tenderness;
 Sweet angel Nona.

THE INFLUENCE OF CHEERFULNESS.

Dear readers, do you ever stop to consider what shall be the result, the outcome of good that shall follow your labors in whatever way they may be directed? Did you ever think that every word and deed, no matter how insignificant and unimportant they might seem, were shaping the lives and destinies in some degree of those around you? Did you ever realize that you were in a measure responsible for the good or bad conduct of those with whom you daily associate, and that your responsibility was in the proportion of your personal influence upon those with whom you came in contact? If you have never thought of these things may you now resolve to do so; for in no other manner can you learn so successfully the lesson of prudence and the value of example as a teacher. The finest sermons, the most eloquent, spiritual, and inspiring discourses are lost upon the hearers when they come from one whose life is a denial of the truths uttered. In the home, in society, business, and all the affairs of life, the potential influence of an unselfish upright person is felt and manifested in the lives and conduct of those with whom such individuals daily associate. How often has it been remarked in the home that one cross, ill-tempered person could bring a "reign of terror" through the entire household. A harsh word, a sour look from one member of the family is quite sufficient to induce an element of discord and inharmony that will be felt throughout the entire day, and carry its baneful influence into the business office of the father, the schoolroom where the children are sent, and hang like a pall of darkness over the mother who remains at her tasks in the home. Is it not, then, a duty of first importance to cultivate cheerfulness, to put away the sour visage, the long face, and in its stead cultivate a smile where the frown once habitually rested? Smile mechanically if you must at first, but smile anyhow; and when you get into the habit of it, the spirit of mirthfulness and happiness will prompt the smiling, and it will no longer require an effort on your part to do so. As you grow cheerful and pleasant the cares and crosses of life that once weighed so heavily upon you, crushing out the joys and hopes that blossomed in the springtime of youth, will all disappear, and your load of care grow lighter each day as the effort to appear cheerful is successful. There is nothing like a sunny face to brighten the darkness of the way so many are obliged to travel. It is strength, it is hope, it is courage, and *it is success.*

> " To the sunny soul that is full of hope,
>   And whose beautiful trust never fadeth,
>   The sky is clear, and the flowers abloom,
>   Though the wintry storm prevaileth."

PRESS ONWARD.

Amid all the trials and tribulations of life, its clouds and darkness, there shines forever one star brighter than all the rest; it is the Star of Hope. Its clear, pure rays illumine the deepest night-time of our lives, and inspires and encourages us to press onward over rough places and almost insurmountable obstacles until the highway is gained, and the sunshine floods the vales of life with glory, and success crowns all our efforts. It is the Star of Hope gleaming over the mad billows that gives courage to the storm-tossed mariner in his hour of deadly peril. Its tender beams penetrate the smoke of battle-fields, and as the soldier catches faint glimpses of their radiance, in them he beholds his far-off home, where wife and babes await his return; and the sweet vision nerves his arm to nobler deeds of daring, and courageously he presses on to vanquish the foe.

In the gloomy prison-cell where brood dark shadows of unforgiven crime, the blood-stained convict sits and dreams of by-gone days when a free and innocent child he roamed the fields at will. A light streams in upon him. It is the Star of Hope, and it in he sees the dawn of a new and brighter future in which he is once more a man, redeeming past errors and sins by a life of labor for others' good. And as the vision fades, it leaves the hardened criminal penitent and self-accusing, ready to retrieve his lost manhood at any cost of physical suffering to himself; and to many such the dawn comes not before, but follows the night of death.

Angel visitors bear to stricken mortals the beautiful star-beams of a deathless hope, of an abiding trust, which to many becomes absolute knowledge of a brighter world than this, where the broken cords of affection shall be united, and the sweet, beautiful dreams which faded so suddenly will become the living verities of existence.

They sing to us of " the beautiful home over there," until the cares and annoyances of life seem infinitisimally small and inconsequential in comparison with the eternity which lies before us wherein we can attain the mountain heights of aspiration and noble endeavor.

Let us all press onward more resolutely than ever to the attainment of our highest, purest desires, and most worthy ambitions, hoping and trusting that—

Sometime, somewhere, good will fall
Like a bright mantle over all.

TO AN AGED FRIEND.

You may not know the hand
  Which guides your fragile bark;
You may not see the land
  Through clouds so thick and dark;
Yet know, dear one, you're near the
    shore;
  This tumult is the breakers' roar.

Fear not, though clouds of mist and
    spray
  Obscure the green-clad hills,
Where golden sunbeams dance and
    play,
  Where murmur sparkling rills;
There loved ones wait with outstretched
    hands
  To greet you on the shining sands.

THE VALUE OF THE PHENOMENA OF SPIRITUALISM.

A. Wilford Hall, author of "The Problem of Human Life," says: "The much derided, much doubted, and much believed in physical phenomena of Spiritualism—the tipping of tables and chairs—would come in and prove useful, and even invaluable, in demonstrably crushing out materialism, could these physical manifestations be absolutely established without the possibility of collusion or trickery. Such visible and sensible manifestations would be demonstrative of the substantial nature of man's vital and mental being, and would utterly wipe out materialism by physical tests, the one thing so much courted by advanced scientists." This admission is made by a man of letters—a man who attempts in the above-mentioned work to review Darwin, Huxley, Tyndall, Haeckel, Helmholtz, and Mayer, and overthrow the theory of man's evolution from the lower orders of life, and answer affirmatively the question, "Are we destined to live after this earthly pilgrimage is ended?" It shows how very ignorant a learned man may be—ignorant of the existence of the very facts which he admits would demonstrate the immortality of the soul and "utterly wipe out materialism." We, who have investigated, know that these facts abound; that the spirits of the so-called dead do communicate with those in the material form; we know they can move ponderous bodies—tables, chairs, pianos, and even persons have been carried about in séance rooms above the heads of the company present. The writer was at one time, in the presence of Henry Slade, lifted in her chair several feet from the floor, with no visible force applied. This was done in a bright, sunny room, in the presence of four witnesses. It was done in response to the request of Mr. Slade, showing an intelligence present that could see and hear, and had the power to comply. If *inert matter cannot move itself*, what force in nature is it that moves these bodies? It cannot be *electricity* or *magnetism*, as some are ready to affirm, for there is no *intelligence* in these forces. The body of a dead man possesses no more intelligence than the block of marble above him; it is a mass of *inert matter*; whence then has the intelligence which once guided its movements flown? Is there any process in Nature by which it could have been destroyed or annihilated? How much more reasonable and natural to suppose that this power is just what it claims to be—our dear departed kindred and friends, who are seeking to unveil the mysteries which have so long shrouded in gloom and uncertainty the future of humanity.

IS SPIRITUALISM A SCIENCE?

Herbert Spencer asks: "What is science? To see the absurdity of the prejudice against it, we need only remark that science is simply a higher development of common *knowledge*, and if science is repudiated, all knowledge must be repudiated along with it."

Huxley says: "Knowledge upon many subjects grows to be more and more perfect, and when it becomes to be so accurate and sure that it is capable of being proved to persons of suitable intelligence, it is called *science*. The *science* of any subject is the highest and most exact knowledge upon that subject." If the definition here given be a correct one, then we need no argument to prove the scientific basis upon which rests the Spiritual philosophy, for Spiritualism "*is capable of being proved to persons of suitable intelligence*," as thousands of earnest, thoughtful investigators can testify, who have demonstrated its facts under the most crucial test conditions; hence, it must be admitted that *Spiritualism is a Science*, and Herbert Spencer says that "if Science is repudiated, all knowledge must be repudiated along with it." Now what can our opponents do about it? These statements are made by men who are recognized authority, learned scientists. Let us then, as Spiritualists, take comfort in the thought that if *the scientific demonstration of Spiritualism is repudiated, all knowledge must be repudiated along with it*. There is the whole thing in a nutshell.

SOMETIME.

Sometime, my child, when all is o'er,
    And memory backward turns
From some grand height, on fairer shore
    Where lovelight ever burns

With no uncertain, flickering ray,
    As earthly loves oft do,
But shining like eternal day,
    Soft, gentle, tender, true—

You'll see how well the guiding hand
    Has led your faltering feet,
O'er thorny roads to that fair land,
    To rest in places sweet.

You'll see divinest love in all
    These trials so severe;
And through them hear the angel's call,
    "Come nearer, child, come near."

Draw closer to the Heart of Love,
    Whose arms are open wide;
Seek shelter there; no storms can move
    The soul where love abides.

There, only, is perpetual spring,
    There, only, peace is found;
There, fairest buds are blossoming,
    There, angels hover 'round.

OPEN DOORS FOR CLERGYMEN.

Not long since we heard a clergyman say that whenever Spiritualists could open doors for ministers to enter into spiritual work and be assured of a living support, there would be a stampede from Orthodox pulpits to the liberal platforms of Spiritualism. Many clergymen, he said, were only waiting to see Spiritualists united and organized in strong societies, to step down and out of the pulpit forever and enter into the broader field of usefulness offered by Spiritualism. Men who have devoted their lives to pulpit work are unfitted by education and training to enter any field of labor not in the line of their acquired tendencies. They cannot successfully till the soil, use the ax, saw, or hammer; neither can they enter other professions with hope of successfully competing with those who have been trained to fill them. The lecture platform offers splendid inducements to those who have something to say and know how to say it; but where one man can command public attention and support by his powerful oratory and brilliant intellectual efforts, a thousand men would fail utterly unless backed by some society organization.

The platforms of spiritual societies are, in many instances, occupied by speakers of indifferent attainments, who depend entirely upon the inspiration of the occasion for what they have to say. Where such persons are highly mediumistic, and susceptible to the impression given them from intelligent spirits, they succeed in giving instructive lectures; but in the greater number of instances the result is unsatisfactory to listeners who have been accustomed to forming words into sentences that express something. Such people cannot be satisfied with words that merely "jingle" together like pennies in a boy's pocket.

We have heard "inspirational" speakers talk glibly for an hour or more, flinging words together in all sorts of fantastic groups, and, when they had finished, the bewildered listeners could not tell what had been said. Not one new thought had been advanced, and even old ones had been so distorted and twisted as to be rendered meaningless. When Spiritualists are thoroughly organized and systematized in their methods of imparting instruction, we shall have schools for the training of speakers. Then mediums may be educated in the philosophy of Spiritualism, and learn to present it in a clear and comprehensive manner. When this shall have been accomplished, the talented men and women now in Orthodox pulpits will make our most apt and ready pupils and most successful teachers.

OUR AIM.

The paramount aim of the *Carrier Dove* is to present a practical, every-day Spiritualism that will assist the people into higher physical, mental, and spiritual conditions; a Spiritualism that takes hold of the live issues of the day, and from its higher, purer plane reflects light upon the darkness, and imparts wisdom to the ignorant; that will bring order out of chaos, and plant the white banners of peace upon the field of strife and discord. We do not wish to expatiate so much upon the beatitudes of a life to come—of a beautiful "summer land" in the "sweet bye-and-bye," as we wish to learn how to start a "summer land" *here and now*, where the sweet, rare plants of human love, true friendship, and that much-talked-of "charity" may find congenial soil in which to take root and send forth their fragrant blossoms. We want a "summer land" right here, where every child of humanity shall have a home, food, and raiment, and where the unfortunate and erring who are waiting, hoping and praying that they may have another chance, when they get over there, can have that chance here instead. We look about us, and on every hand see the lavish bounties of Nature. We see broad, fruitful valleys and plains, where shining harvests yield their golden grain. We see orchards, vineyards, and "cattle upon a thousand hills," flocks of fowl, herds of sheep and swine—in fact, everything that the mind of man can conceive of that would contribute to his comfort and happiness. We see vast mountain ranges, great oceans, extensive continents covered with grand forests, crystal lakes and shining rivers. There is room enough for every living creature, man or beast, upon the broad surface of this beautiful world, the natural resources of which belong to them—its offspring.

Who is to blame that the children of the planet are defrauded of their birthright? Who is to blame that thousands live and die in the most abject poverty, yea, even starve for the pitiful amount necessary to support life, when surrounded with plenty; die like dogs for a crust of bread within a stone's throw of overflowing granaries, and piles heaped up of shining gold and silver? Who is the arbiter of human destiny that has hedged us in with such monstrous laws and unjust conditions? Who but man himself; and man alone can save himself from this degradation. The great creative power of the universe has not been parsimonious of His bounties. The material is at hand for a first-class heaven, "without money and without price," if humanity would but pre-empt its claim. It is the mission of Spiritualism to teach the ignorant their rights and duties here and now. For ages millions of self-disinherited human beings have yielded their natural rights to a share of the physical comforts necessary to material life, and passed into the spiritual world defrauded and beggared. These spirits, more wiser grown, are now endeavoring to impress upon humanity the importance of right physical conditions for the perfect unfoldment of the higher and spiritual nature of the race. It is to bring about such improved conditions here that all true Spiritualists should labor in harmony with those of larger experience from spiritual spheres, until at last the kingdom of heaven will, indeed, have come upon the earth.

THE SPIRITUAL OUTLOOK.

"Watchman, what of the night? What of the night?" The night has passed. It is dawn now. Do you not see the golden tinge of the Eastern sky? It is the herald of a new day. What of the new day? Shall we tell you? It is a day pregnant with new joys, new hopes, and new blessedness. It is the day which poets have sung of, prophets have prophesied, seers have described, and the hearts of all humanity have longingly waited for. A day of promise; a day of peace; a day when justice shall triumph —when great wrongs shall be redressed, when right, not might, shall rule. It is a day when the new light from the upper heavens shall flood the world with its glory. Then Error, the child of Ignorance and Superstition, will die, and Truth, angel-eyed Truth, daughter of Love and Wisdom, will walk your earth, clad in her shining robes, unsullied by contact with evil, for evil shall have perished. It is a day when the superstitions of the past, which have hung like a dark pall over the world, shall roll away, and the light of heavenly truth shed its illuminating rays where heretofore darkness brooded over all. It is a day when the gods born of the perverted imaginations of ignorant men, and endowed with the attributes of revengeful, merciless, unforgiving fiends, shall give place to the living realities of angelic ministrants who bear only love, peace, forgiveness, and blessings unto the suffering children of earth—coming among them on errands of mercy, comforting the sorrowing, and healing the afflicted, until, under the influence of their loving ministrations, their lessons of wisdom, their pure and holy examples, mankind will turn from evil and seek only that which is good, true, and beautiful, obeying the higher laws of life, the consequence of which will be that disease will vanish, and all its attendant train of evils. Death will then come to the perfected man as comes the autumn winds to the yellow leaf, causing it to drop noiselessly and peacefully among its fallen kindred, while the spirit goes out into a new form of beauty and perfection. It will come only to the fully ripened grain, leaving the tender young buds and blossoms to fill the earth with their beauty and fragrance. Such is the new day which is dawning. Prepare yourselves, O mortals, for the divine quickening which shall follow its full dawn. Spiritual forces are being developed and concentrated, and very soon their mighty power will be felt among the children of earth as never before. Make yourselves ready temples in which the spirit of Truth can enter and abide forever.

RECOMPENSE.

Patience, dear heart, thine own shall come
　　Sure as the waves break on the shore;
Sure as the stars and placid moon
　　Shall come with night, forevermore.

Thy spirit long has sought its mate,
　　And grieved that death was everywhere;
Patience, a little longer wait,
　　Love holds for thee a bounteous share

Of all the joys thy soul doth seek,
　　Of all thy fondest dreams of bliss,
And sweeter than the words we speak,
　　Shall be love's token and love's kiss.

This precious heritage hath all
　　Earth's children; though for some
No voice respondeth to their call;
　　The lips of love seem cold and dumb.

Yet sometime, somewhere, love meets love,
　　Soul unto soul its greetings send,
And hearts attuned, in sweet accord,
　　In heavenly unison shall blend.

"BEHOLD, THE DAWN COMETH."

These words seem especially prophetic to Spiritualists just at the present time. The night, with its gloom, its blackness and horror, is upon us; and in our anxiety and almost despair for the safety of the cause we love a voice whispers softly and sweet, "Behold, the Dawn Cometh." Reassured and hopeful for the best, we are again receptive to angelic aid and inspiration, and through the mists of doubt and skepticism which surround us on all sides, we behold with spiritual vision the green fields of waving grain, the flower-decked hills and sparkling, crystal streams. We behold beauty, harmony, and peace, succeeding the destruction and overthrow of the idols of the past, and following in the wake of the tempest. What has been uprooted and destroyed has been the useless and worthless; error has been smitten, and Truth still lives.

'Twas but the wasting of the bad,
  The ruin of the wrong and ill:
What e'er of good the old-time had,
  Is living still.

Nothing true and good can ever perish; and if the seeming evil has caused any to lose faith in the truth, let them renew their faith, for the truth is immutable and cannot die. A sifting process, which was absolutely necessary to the life of the cause, has been inaugurated and the chaff has been severed, in part, from the wheat, and much that has been regarded as golden grain has been found to be worthless chaff. No one should grieve or murmur at this work; it is the work of the angel world just as much as the first little raps at Hydesville were their work. They have witnessed the unholy desecration of their gifts on the part of some of their instruments, who, for love of gain, have sold their birthrights for messes of pottage; they have witnessed the most sacred feeling of the human heart made the butt of ridicule and devilish mockery by the human vampires who trade upon grief, and grow fat upon the mourner's tears. They have witnessed the young and innocent made the tools of wicked, designing, unscrupulous men and women, to carry on their nefarious traffic, and play upon the affections and loves of their deluded victims. No wonder that they have caused the tempest to burst upon us, and arouse us from the stupor, apathy, and indifference into which the whole body of Spiritualists had fallen.

The spirit world saw how the true and genuine mediums were crowded to the wall, while the false and spurious were eulogized and exalted; they saw discouragement and despair in the hearts of the workers, and determined that the idols of iniquity should be overthrown, the masks removed from the faces, that all might be known for their worth alone. That has been done, and the cruel ulcers that were destroying the life of the cause were laid bare to the gaze of the world. No wonder that horror and disgust have followed the revelation, and that some have turned away, thinking the whole body rotten also; but not so, friends; beneath all outward seeming of ill, the beautiful truth lies fair and lovely still, waiting for brave, true hands to pluck away the rubbish with which it has been covered, and it will stand before the world spotless and undefiled in all its native purity and loveliness. Let us take new courage, friends, and patiently wait and trust. Let us bring forth our facts in refutation of false charges, and demonstrate to the world that our foundation rests not upon the shifting sands, but upon the eternal rock of truth, and cannot be shaken or overthrown. Be faithful, vigilant, and watchful, for the dawn cometh on apace.

THE VOICE OF ANGELS.

Listen! 'tis the Voice of Angels
  Ringing through the crystal sky;
Hear you not their sweet evangels,
  As to earth they now draw nigh?

Oh, ye sorrow-stricken mortals,
  Listen to the news we bring:
Love has opened death's dark portals—
  Let the joyful tidings ring.

Lonely mourner, cease your weeping—
  Death is but the door to life,
And your loved ones are not sleeping,
  But set free from pain and strife

They now live where fields are vernal
  With a never-fading bloom;
Crowned with Love and Life Eternal,
  Far from shade or taint of tomb.

Let your voices join with gladness
  With the Voice of Angels dear,
Till each soul now bowed with sadness
  Shall the heavenly music hear.

ONE DAY.

Oh blessed day so fair and sweet!
  Memory will fondly hold thee fast
When all the days of earth are past,
  And heaven's joys be more complete

For that one day of perfect bliss—
  When angel presence, angel love
Breathed benedictions from above
  And sanctified thee with love's kiss.

THE SUMMER IS COMING.

The years may pass with footsteps fleet
  Our broken lives be severed wide;
Yet that sweet dream will still abide,
  Until beyond the stars we meet.

'Mid earthly pains and sorrows deep,
  When joy lies pulseless, hope has fled,
And all we love are cold and dead—
  That star will still its vigil keep

And send its rays athwart the night,
  Until within the weary breast
Shall creep a blessed sense of rest,
  And darkness fade in Heaven's light.

THE SUMMER IS COMING.

The summer is coming for you, darling,
  The Summer is coming for you;
The Summer with blossoms of sweetness,
  Red roses and violets blue.

The Summer with sunshine and brightness,
  And cloudlet with silvery hue:—
Soft breezes with balm odors freighted,
  Is coming most surely to you.

Already the sweet buds are bursting,
  Disclosing bright colors to view;
The song-birds again are returning
  To warble their old songs anew.

And over the hillside and valley
  Nature decks all her children anew
With beautiful garments of gladness
  For the Summer that's coming to you.

You have borne the keen blasts of Winter
  And ever to duty been true;
Now the clouds and the shadows are drifting,
  And the Summer is coming for you.

NEW YEAR GREETING.

To the friends and patrons of the *Carrier Dove*, to the earnest searchers into the treasures of the Spiritual kingdom, to the aspiring, soaring minds who are seeking "light, more light," to the purified ones, who having lingered long in the "Valley," and, become refined in the crucible of affliction, are now standing on the mountain tops, to those who still stand with hands outstretched and faces upturned toward the sublime heights they have not yet attained, to the lowly and sad ones, to the outcast and abandoned ones, to all of earth's children, everywhere, do we send our New Year greeting. We have not heretofore spoken to you of our personality; we have been content—yea, indeed, blest—to labor silently and unseen among you seeking only the higher good that might result from our ministrations. We have sought each month to send you some star-gleams from the infinite shores, some hope-buds from the immortals gardens, some crystal draughts from the living fountains, some rays of light to illuminate your darkness, some words of comfort for your sorrow some joy for your mourning, and in your hours of trial and temptation, in your seasons of despair and doubting, when faith, hope, and courage all have failed you, when utter darkness within and without encompassed you, then have we sought to impart that sublime faith which faileth not, that beautiful hope which anchors the soul to the everlasting rocks of truth, that courage which lays hold upon Spiritual potentialities, saying "ye are mine, and all things are possible unto me, even to the banishment of pain, disease, and death." Though but few of you have grasped the great soul-truths we have sought through many channels to impart unto you, yet some glimmerings of the great light shining steadfastly far out into soul realms have reached you, and you have been quickened and renewed thereby. Some of you, in moments of exaltation, have caught the radiance of the far-off glory, have laved in the billows of light from the other shore. Some of you have beheld the faces of your beloved ones dwelling in the light of the eternal worlds. You have heard the murmur of voices long silent, and clasped the hands long since folded upon peaceful, quiet breasts. The gates have swung wide open, and noiselessly as the falling dew have the shining ones descended with their gentle ministrations soothing the wounds of the stricken souls of earth, And as we have ministered unto you, so shall you, in return, minister unto one another; as the angels have loved you, so love ye one another; as we have comforted you, so comfort ye one another. This is our New Year message unto you: *Love* more; cherish more; be more gentle, patient, and forgiving; if you have been blest in "basket and store" of the material things of earth, so also should you dispense your blessing among those less favored. Strengthen and uphold the hands of those who are striving to become the worthy ambassadors of the angels; give them encouragement when they are weary; give them your love, sympathy and hearty cooperation in their good work, and thus make smooth the way and open wide the doors, that nearer and still nearer we may draw unto the hearts of men, turning them ever from darkness unto the everlasting light.

TRIBUTE TO OUR ARISEN ONES.

[Delivered by the author at the Spiritualists' Memorial Services, held at the Camp-meeting in Oakland, Sunday, June 17th, 1888.]

We twine the fragrant blooms to-day,
 In garlands sweet;
And from the fullness of our hearts we say,
 'Tis very meet
That our dear dead and fondly loved ones still
With tender memories our bosoms thrill.

We bring to mind their noble lives and generous deeds
 With glad recall;
And love's sweet offerings bring as the best mead
 Of praise to all;
And here 'neath Stars and Stripes, 'mid fragrant flowers,
We crown with fondest love these friends of ours.

We cannot name them all; for, lo, they stand
 Beside us now;
We see their angel forms; they press our hand
 And touch our brow
With the same tender fondness that they did before
They passed within death's flower-wreathed door.

And as they gather round us here to-day,
 A shining host—
They calm our fears, they wipe all tears away;
 They are not lost.
We know their helpful love and watchful care
Enfolds us here, and now, and everywhere.

Among the friends we dearly loved comes one –
 A matron grand,
Whose tender ministrations here are not yet done,
 Whose healing hand
Brought ease and rest to weary heart and brain,
And caused the roses on pale cheeks to bloom again.

Eliza F. McKinley—true and noble soul—
    We all revere,
And know that, though she now has reached life's goal,
    She's with us here,
The same devoted mother, sister, wife, and friend,
. Faithful to all in life, in death, unto the end.

These angels, full of tenderness and grace,
    Gather around,
And with their presence consecrate this place,
    As holy ground;
While over all the seen and unseen throng,
In rhythmic waves floats their angelic song.

They sing of "peace on earth, good will to men,"
    As long ago
Throughout the peaceful vales of Bethlehem
    'Twas chanted low;
They sing of true fraternity; and, lo, the sweet refrain
Is caught by distant bands and echoed back again.

And our dull ears may catch each heavenly note
    Of joyous song
That downward from the choirs celestial float,
    And borne along
Reach many fainting, sad, and weary hearts,
And to despondent ones new hope imparts.

O friends, brothers, and sisters dear,
    They plead to-day,
Wait not until ye strew pale flowers upon the bier
    Kind words to say;
But say them now; bring love's pure oil and wine,
And pour into bruised hearts the balm divine.

Cheer up the mourner; strengthen ye the weak,
    And freely give
The helpful word each one of you may speak.
    Oh, strive to live
And work in love and peace and harmony
On earth, in heaven, through all eternity.

SPIRITUALISM DENOUNCED.

Reverend Thos. Chalmers Easton delivered a sermon at Calvary Church, in this city, in which he denounced Spiritualism in a manner that showed conclusively he had never investigated the subject and consequently knew nothing of the matter he was discoursing upon. His ignorance was not confined to what is known as Modern Spiritualism alone, but extended to the historical records of the Bible from which he quoted various texts and interpreted them according to his own ideas and not according to the written testimony. He called the woman of Endor a "witch" and said she had doubtless gathered information from the servants of Saul that enabled her to recognize him, and that the voice of Samuel was simulated by the witch who was a ventriloquist. If ministers can stand in their pulpits and deliberately misrepresent and distort plain Scripture statements until the original meaning is entirely lost sight of and still retain the support and countenance of their congregations it will be but a short time until every truth-loving, self-respecting member withdraws from such churches, and leaves the ministers and their unreasoning dupes severely alone. About the only truth uttered by the said divine in the said sermon was that he "did not know of a single individual who had ever gone into Spiritualism who had ever changed from it."

No; people do not change from their faith when they once become satisfied of the truth of Spiritualism. They are not like some members of orthodox churches who "get religion" every winter and lose it during haying and harvesting in summer. It sticks to them and they to it. It is an ever-abiding presence that is real and tangible; something that remaineth forever and ever.

The advertisements the speaker referred to do not represent Spiritualists by any manner; but bear on their face the "signet and superscription" of the trade they represent. When you read of "Miss So-and-So, young healer, assisted by Maudie and Belle," or of the greatest living clairvoyant, seventh daughter, born with a double veil, etc., you are not reading the advertisements of reliable or recognized mediums; and Spiritualism is no more responsible for such quackery than is the medical profession, as fraudulent imitators of both are represented by these advertisements. When a crank springs up and declares that he is Jesus Christ, who has come the second time, and goes about preaching and has a considerable following of fanatical believers, no one pretends to claim that he represents the large body of Christians of any denomination, or holds Christianity responsible for such nonsense. Spiritualism is not to be judged by the eccentricities of any individual, but courts the candid, earnest investigation of thinking, reasoning people. Millions of such have embraced its truths after having applied the test of scientific research to its phenomena. Let our ministerial friends come out from the bondage of ignorance and superstition, and bravely and honestly investigate before they denounce and ridicule the greatest discovery of the centuries the discovery of that land toward which we are all hastening, and from whose bourne it has been said "no traveler returns," but which Spiritualism demonstrates to be false, as travelers are returning daily and hourly with messages of love and consolation, and the "good tidings of great joy," that if a man die he shall live again,

ANGEL MINISTRY.

From the infinite sources of being—
    From the great Over-Soul—the Divine,
I came at the call of thy spirit,
    My soul it responded to thine.

Away mid the star-begemmed spaces,
    Afar from the borders of time,
Where the beauty, the rapture, the graces
    Of life is a poem sublime—

In a realm of most wondrous beauty—
    Beyond flights of the fancy to tell,
Where free and untarnished—unsullied
    By contact with evil there dwell

The bright and the sinless—the pure ones,
    Who have passed through the chastening fire,
'Till all dross and all weakness have vanished,
    And quenched is all human desire.

They dwell on the summits so holy,
    They bathe in the infinite fount
Of love and of wisdom, whose glory
    Enwraps and envelops the mount.

There transfigured, transformed, and uplifted,
    With faces that shine like the sun,
They turn toward the earth and its children,
    Whose journey has only begun.

And with hearts of compassion and mercy,
    Leave soul-land—their heavenly estate,
And go to the rescue of mortals,
    Who in darkness and bondage await

The touch of the breath that shall quicken—
    The voice of the Spirit of Love—
The hand that shall beckon and lead them
    From lowlands to highlands above;

From sin, and the darkness and sadness
    Of wrong and its withering blight,
Into sunshine and freedom and gladness,
    Into purity, beauty, and right;

From all that enthralls and enchains them—
    From bondage of centuries past,
To the glory-crowned summits of freedom,
    Untrammeled, unfettered at last.

Oh, mortals! we fain would enfold you
    In arms of the tenderest love;
We would bear you the symbol of safety,
    Like the olive branch borne by the dove.

When the waters surround and submerge you
    And dark seems the night and the way,
On the bosom of Love you shall slumber,
    To wake in eternity's day.

ANGEL GUIDANCE.

How many of us have heard that inner voice and counseled with it in times of mental distress, doubt, and fear. How many times we, who are not conscious of having a personal guide whose individuality is pronounced and distinct from our own, and to whom we can always turn for advice, counsel, or encouragement have, nevertheless, turned imploringly to the nameless inward monitor for that friendly aid we so sorely needed. Years ago we believed this inner voice was conscience, and that it was always safe and wise to heed it. Now we know that conscience is always the result of early training and education, and will always advise us in accordance with preconceived opinions of the settled convictions that came as a result of the teachings of our youth. The conscience of the cannibal does not warn him against devouring missionaries, but would rather reprove him if he should let slip the opportuniy of having such a feast. While we cannot, then, rely upon conscience as a guide, from what source come these grand inspirations and intense longings for higher and better things? We are satisfied they come from the spiritual spheres of life, and are the promptings of wise and beneficent intelligences who are ever on the alert to sow the seeds of love and wisdom in every receptive soul. Though we may not be aware of an individual presence counseling with us, and our dull ears and blind eyes may not perceive the spiritual beings who would lead us into paths of peace and pleasantness, yet are they ever present, whispering words of hope, encouragement, or counsel, and if we heed the angel voices we cannot go far astray. All who have come into a knowledge of spiritual truth have realized this angel guidance and presence, and so closely does it seem blended with our daily life experiences that it almost seems to be our inner self, and yet something distinct and apart from us. The writer has realized this presence daily for many years, and at one time expressed this nearness and sympathy in a poem which was addressed to her spirit guide from which the following lines are an extract:

Beloved Angel Guide thou nearest and
    dearest,
      Who knowest my thoughts and readest
        my soul,
Whose love is the strongest, whose sight
    is the clearest,
      Who is true unto me as the needle, the
        pole, —
Thou who guards, guides, and leads me,
    as day after day
      My feet wander on through the byways of life,
Thou, who seest the motives that silently
    play
      The keys that evoke peace, discord, or
        strife;
Thou knowest the longings, the prayers,
    and the tears,
      The striving and struggles, the battles
        I've fought,
To live and to do whatever appears
    As purest and best, in word, deed, and
      thought;
Thou knowest my failures, how oft I
    have erred,
      And slipped when my pathway was
        rugged and steep,
Then again how I've soared light and
    free as a bird,
      Far away toward the heavens so boundless and deep.
I ask thee to tell me as a true, trusted
    friend
Who has walked by my side through the
    long, weary years,
All my faults and my failings, and help
    me to mend,
      Though I wash them away in an ocean
      of tears.

ANGEL WHISPERS.

We come to the faint and weary
    Who toil through the heat of the day;
Whose lives seem so hopeless and dreary
    Without even one cheering ray
To brighten the cloud of the present,
    Or tinge with a faint streak of gold
The shadowy ways of the future,
    As they dimly before you unfold.

We sing of a brighter to-morrow,
    But our songs fall on ears that are dead
To their sweet soothing strains; for to sorrow
    And toil you are hopelessly wed.
We would open the sources of knowledge,
    And pour its clear waters on all;
But you cling to your idols in blindness,
    Your souls respond not to our call.

So we hope on, and wait for the dawning
    Of a brighter and holier day,
When the mist and the clouds of the morning
    Shall be swept from your visions away;
And you see all the grandeur and beauty,
    That everywhere lovingly lies,
Like a mantle of glory the angels
    Have tenderly dropped from the skies,
When the songs that we sing shall awaken
    An echo in every sad breast
When sorrow and care shall be taken
    As coming from one who knows best.

REVIVAL INSANITY.

During the recent Mills' revival meetings in this city, a young woman went violently insane and commenced tearing off her clothing and screaming that she wanted a robe of white, she wanted to be an angel. It required the combined efforts of seven men to overpower her and get her out of the vast throng (it occurred at the Mechanics' Pavilion) and conveyed to the Receiving Hospital. Her husband was sent for, and in sorrow he declared that it was what he had feared would come, as his young wife had attended the revival meetings every day and he had noticed signs of mental derangement resulting therefrom.

The trouble with this lady was the fact that she believed what she heard preached, and, as a natural sequence, lost her reason. All that saves the majority of religious fanatics from a similar fate is the lack of belief in the infamous doctrines taught. No sensible, right-minded person could absolutely believe in a lake of fire and brimstone where the vast majority of the human family were to be eternally tortured and never consumed, and still retain their reason. The contemplation of such a terrible, horrible doom would unseat reason from its throne, and leave a set of gibbering idiots to run the religious business of the world and conduct its "revivals."

From the newspaper reports of the sermons of Revivalist Mills, we learn that his stock in trade is a choice selection of sensational stories of deathbed scenes, most of which are of lost, unsaved, unrepentant, irreligious people, who had never "given their hearts to Jesus," and consequently were doomed to hell eternally.

And that is the kind of stuff that thousands of people flock to hear, and think they are listening to a divinely inspired teacher. Why, such preaching is absolutely wicked and should not be allowed in the nineteenth century of civilization. It is a lie, and blasphemy against Divine Love and Wisdom. If there be a God, as our orthodox friends teach, he will not hold them guiltless who so defame and malign his goodness and tender mercy. God, means Love; and Love "worketh no ill," but is long-suffering, patient, gentle, meek; in fact, is anything, everything but the demon of implacable fury and wrath so graphically pictured by the religious revivalists as the God who would condemn to eternal torture countless numbers of poor, suffering, ignorant human beings, whose struggles through this life should entitle them to happiness hereafter, even if they never heard the name of Jesus, or dreamed there was a God.

Friends, Spiritualists, Freethinkers, what can we do to dispel the clouds of superstition and ignorance which have settled so darkly over us? How can we break the good news of the beautiful, immortal life the angel friends come back and tell us of, to these poor, deluded, mentally shipwrecked souls? "Oh, for a thousand tongues to sing," the glad tidings of great joy that come like healing balm to bruised and bleeding hearts, telling them of life, beautiful life, amid the fairer scenes of the eternal world, where every hope, every aspiration, shall find sweet fulfilment; and feet that now stumble and grow weary shall joyfully climb the everlasting mountains of progression and unfoldment.

Oh, what a contrast between the disheartening, crushing, debasing doctrine of eternal punishment, and the inspiring, ennobling and elevating teachings of the angels, of a future full of promise, of sweet fruition, of endless growth and unfoldment!

BIRTH OF MODERN SPIRITUALISM.

[An anniversary poem delivered March 31, 1883, at the celebration in Oakland, Cal., under the auspices of the Oakland Spiritual Association.]

Thirty-five times the softly flitting, ever-changing years
Have placed to human lips the cup of happiness and tears,
Since the bending heavens were opened, and lo! upon the earth
An angel band descend to celebrate the birth
Of a lovely child of promise within an humble home,
Where no breath of foul suspicion would ever dare to come,
For the guileless, trusting inmates, with no motive to deceive,
Those who came to see the infant they kindly would receive.
' Twas a quaint, strange, wondrous being they could scarce make out,
And its origin and mission was a question of much doubt.
Wise men, scholars, theologians came from *very* far and near
To investigate the matter and to hear what they could hear—
For although the child was speechless, it was rumored all about
 t could hear and solve their questions, and would *rap* the answers out.
And they went away confounded at the wise replies it gave
In regard to earthly matters and to those beyond the grave—
Showing that it was familiar with another life than this,
Whether it was life in Hades, or a life of Heavenly bliss.
Many thought it was the former, although why they could not tell,
For it taught them much of Heaven, but denied there was a Hell—
Which of course upset old notions, therefore must not be allowed,
Or their churches, creeds, and dogmas all would vanish like a cloud.
So they wrapped their robes about them and most solemnly withdrew,
Leaving the fair child of promise to a wise and noble few
O'er whose minds old superstition could not hold its iron sway;
For when reason's lamp is lighted, superstition fades away.
So with love and care they watched it, as it daily did unfold
In symmetrical proportions that were pleasing to behold;
And it quickly mastered language—then the precious golden words
That came from lips of angels none before had ever heard,
Telling of a life immortal, and a destiny sublime,
That awaits earth's lowliest children far beyond the shores of time,
That our loved and lost are with us, and the change that we call death
Is the putting off old garments—but a gently, fleeting breath—
Setting free the prisoned spirit from its worn out house of clay;
Bidding it to soar in gladness to its native skies away.
Thus the balm of consolation that their loving words impart,

Heals the wounds of those afflicted, and binds up the broken heart,
Bringing faith and hope and courage, where was doubting, grief, and fears.
Filling weary lives with gladness, giving peace in place of tears.
So this child of Heaven prospered, and attained a wondrous fame,
Till the islands of the ocean speak with joyfulness her name.
Now, prophetically, we see her budding into woman's prime,
With the fruits and flowers about her of the glorious summer time—
Winning with her heavenly graces and her real intrinsic worth,
Suitors from all climes and nations of the noble ones of earth.
And among them, grand and gracious, with a proud, imperial mien
That would stamp him prince of wisdom, first among the great ones seen,
Science comes to woo and win her, lays his laurels at her feet;
She accepts the true heart-offering, making thus her life complete.
Hand in hand united truly, with their banners now unfurled,
Marching over Superstition, Spiritual Science rules the world;
And its birthplace teach your children—it is something they should know—
Was the little town of Hydesville, thirty-five brief years ago.

INDEX.

BIOGRAPHIES.

AUTHOR'S ALBUM.

PROSE.

PROSE—CONTINUED.

POETRY.

MISCELLANEOUS.